By Richard Kadrey

KILL THE DEAD
SANDMAN SLIM

KILL THE DEAD

RICHARD KADREY

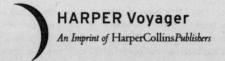

HARPER Voyager
An Imprint of HarperCollins*Publishers*

HARPER Voyager
An Imprint of HarperCollins*Publishers*
10 East 53rd Street
New York, New York 10022-5299

Copyright © 2010 by Richard Kadrey
Excerpt from *Aloha from Hell* copyright © 2011 by Richard Kadrey
Cover art: Bird © by Colin Underhill/Alamy; Building © by Guy Jean Genevier/Archangel Images
ISBN 978-0-06-201736-9
www.harpervoyagerbooks.com

First Harper Voyager mass market printing: August 2011
First Eos hardcover printing: October 2010

Harper Voyager and) is a trademark of HCP LLC.

Printed in the U.S.A.

10 9 8 7 6 5 4 3 2 1

For G and K

Where all life dies, death lives, and nature breeds
Perverse, all monstrous, all prodigious things
Abominable, unutterable, and worse . . .

—PARADISE LOST, BOOK 2

I don't want to achieve immortality through my
work. I want to achieve it through not dying.

—WOODY ALLEN

ACKNOWLEDGMENTS

Many thanks to Ginger Clark, Diana Gill, Holly Frederick, Sarah LaPolla, Nicola Ginzler, Suzanne Stefanac, Paul Goat Allen, and Pat Murphy.

Thanks to Lustmord, Controlled Bleeding, The Germs, Tool, and Les Baxter who provided most of the soundtrack for this book. Also Zamfir for "The Lonely Shepherd," the best spaghetti western theme that's never been used in a spaghetti western.

Thanks also to the folks at Borderlands Books and Mysterious Galaxy for their support.

KILL THE DEAD

IMAGINE SHOVING A cattle prod up a rhino's ass, shouting "April fool!", and hoping the rhino thinks it's funny. That's about how much fun it is hunting a vampire.

Personally, I don't have anything against shroud eaters. They're just another kind of addict in a city of addicts. Since most of them started out as civilians, the percentage of decent vampires to complete bastards is about the same as regular people. Right now, though, I'm hunting one that's trying for a Nobel Prize in getting completely up my ass. It isn't fun work, but it pays the bills.

The vampire's name is Eleanor Vance. In the Xeroxed passport photo Marshal Wells gave me, she looks like she's about seventeen. Probably because she is. A pretty blond cheerleader type with big eyes and the kind of smile that got Troy burned to the ground. Bad news for me. Young vampires are all assholes. It's part of their job description.

I love older vampires. A hundred and fifty, two hundred years old, they're beautiful. The smart ones mostly stick to the El Hombre Invisible tricks that urban monsters have worked out over centuries. They only feed when they have to. When they're not hunting, they're boring, at least to outsiders. They come off like corporate middle management or the guy who runs the corner bodega. What I like best about old bloodsuckers is that when you've got one cornered and it knows it's coffin fodder, they're like noble cancer patients in TV movies. All they want is to die quietly and with a little dignity. Young vampires, not so much.

The young ones have all grown up watching Slayer videos, *Scarface*, *Halloween*, and about a million hours of Japanese anime. They all think they're Tony Montana with a lightsaber in one hand and a chain saw in the other. Eleanor, tonight's undead dream date, is a good example. She's got a homemade flamethrower. I know because when she blasted me back at the parking garage, she fried one of my eyebrows and the left sleeve of my new leather jacket. Ten to one she found the plans on the Web. Why can't vampires just download porn like normal jailbait?

It's Sunday, about a quarter to six in the evening. We're downtown. I follow her along South Hill Street toward Pershing Square. I'm about half a block behind her. Eleanor is wearing long sleeves and carrying an umbrella to keep the sun off. She strolls along happy, like she owns the air and everyone has to pay her royalties whenever they breathe. Only she's not really relaxed. I can't read a juicer's heartbeat or breathing changes because they don't have them. And she's too far away to see if her eyes are dilated, but she keeps moving her head. Microscopic twitches left and right. She's trying to look around without looking around. Hoping to catch my shadow or reflection. Eleanor knows she didn't kill me back at the garage. Eleanor's a smart girl. I hate smart dead girls.

At the corner of Third Street, Eleanor shoulder-butts an old lady and what's probably her grandkid into the street, in front of a flatbed truck carrying a backhoe. The driver slams on the brakes. The old lady is on the ground. Cue the screaming and squealing tires. Cue the sheep who stand around pointing and the Captain Americas who run to help. They pull the old lady and the kid back onto the sidewalk, which is great for them, but it doesn't do anything for me. Eleanor is gone.

But it's not hard to find her. Fifty people must have seen her pull the stunt and half of them point as she sprints down Third before cutting right onto Broadway. I take off after her. I'm fast, a hell of a lot faster than the flat-footed civilians trying to chase her down, but I'm not quite as fast as a vampire. Especially one who's lost her umbrella and wants to get out of the sun before she turns into chicken-fried steak.

She's gone when I hit Broadway. This part of town isn't that crowded on Sundays. I have a clear view in both directions. No perky blondes running down the street in flames. It's mostly stores and office buildings down here, but all the offices and most of the stores are closed. There are a few open doors in the small shops, but Eleanor is too smart to get cornered in one of those little cracker boxes. There's only one place a smart girl would go.

God said, "Let there be Light, and cheap take-out Chinese," and the Grand Central Market appeared. The place has been on South Broadway since before the continents divided. Some of the meat they use in the burritos and Szechuan beef is even older. I think I once saw Fred Flintstone's teeth marks on some barbecued ribs.

Inside, I'm facing down tacos and pizza. There's a liquor store to my left and ice cream against the far wall. Every spice known to man is mixed with the smell of sweat and cooking meat. Not too much of a crowd at this time of day. Some of the shops and kiosks are already counting up receipts. I don't see Eleanor down the central walkway or either of the side ones. I start down the middle of the place, cut to the right, and walk by a fish stand. I'm reaching out. Listening, smelling, feeling the movement of the air, trying to pick up any tiny vibrations in the aether. I'm getting better at this kind of hunting. Ambush predator stuff as opposed to my old Tyrannosaurus-with-a-hard-on moves that don't go down quite as well in the streets of L.A. as they did in the arena.

Subtle hunting, acting like a grown-up, I really miss Hell sometimes.

A tourist dad asks me how they can get back on the free-way to Hollywood from here. I ignore him and he mumbles something about his taxes and how come we don't have more cops to clear out these drug addicts.

Six months after the New Year's bash at Avila and I'm still not used to this place, these people. In a lot of ways civilians are worse than Hellions because at least Hellions know they're miserable sacks of slaughterhouse shit. More and more, I want one of these mortal types to have to face down a vampire, a Jade, or a bat-shit demon elemental. Not a ghost glimpse in the dark, but having to stare straight into a beast's red meat-grinder eyes hungry for the souls of the terminally clueless.

Be careful what you wish for.

A long orange jet of fire rains from overhead and there's Eleanor, standing on top of the glass-and-chrome cases at a spice kiosk. The business end of the flamethrower is a little thing, no bigger than a .45 semiauto. A tube runs from the pistol to an Astro Boy backpack, where the gas and propellant are stored.

Eleanor moves her arm in a wide arc, torching produce, signs, and the backs of a few slack-jawed market workers. She's smiling down at us. Annie Oakley and Charlie Manson's demon baby, jacked up on that sweet and special prekill adrenaline.

Then she's down and running with a small bubbling laugh like a naughty six-year-old. I take off after her, running deeper into the market. She's small and fast and a second later she cuts left, down the far aisle, and doubles back toward Broadway.

I can't catch her or cut her off, but there's an empty utility cart by a produce stand. I give it a kick and send it through the empty dining area. Tables and chairs go flying. The cart slams into her legs at the end of the aisle, knocking her through the counter of Grand Central Liquor. Suddenly it's raining glass and Patrón Silver. Right on cue, people start screaming.

Eleanor is back on her feet a second before I can grab her. She's not smiling anymore. Her left arm is bent at a funny angle and a chunk of bone the size of a turkey drumstick is sticking out just below her elbow. She has the flamethrower up, but I'm moving flat out. No way I can stop. Instead, I go faster. She pulls the trigger and I'm drowning in fire.

I hit her a millisecond later. I can't see anything, but I know it's her because she's the only thing in the store light enough to fly like that. My vision clears, but even I don't want to see this. When she pulled the trigger to hose me down, all the liquor on her clothes and the floor went up. Eleanor is an epileptic shadow puppet pirouetting around in a lake of whiskey fire.

Vampires don't scream like regular humans. I don't know how they scream at all without lungs, but when they let loose, it's like a runaway train meets the screech of a million fighting cats. You feel it in your kidneys and bones. Tourists pee and puke at the sound. Fuck 'em. Eleanor still isn't going down. And the fire is starting to spread. Grease on the grills of nearby food stalls starts going up. A propane tank blows, setting off the sprinkler system. When I look back, Eleanor is sprinting out of the market back onto Broadway, still covered in flames.

Chasing a burning girl down a city street is a lot harder than it sounds. Civilians tend to stop and stare and this turns them into human bowling pins. Slow, whiny bowling pins. You'd think that on some basic animal level they'd want to get the hell out of the way of a burning schoolgirl screaming loud enough to crack store windows and the stupid son of a bitch chasing her. Not that I'm doing this for them. I'm doing it for the money, but they still stand to benefit from it.

When Eleanor runs across Fifth Street she isn't burning anymore. She's a black beef-jerky Barbie doll running on charred stick insect legs.

Up ahead, there's an abandoned wreck of a movie theater called the Roxie. The lobby and marquee areas have been converted into an open-air market. Eleanor blows past the racks of knockoff T-shirts and toxic rubber sandals. Slams straight through the inch-thick plywood screwed over the theater doors where the glass used to be. I follow her inside, but hang back by the smashed door, letting my eyes adjust to the dark.

The na'at would be a smart weapon in a place like this, but I feel like shooting something. Besides, Eleanor won't know what a na'at is, so it won't scare her the way I want. I retired Wild Bill's Navy Colt pistol a while back and replaced it with a Smith & Wesson .460 hunting pistol. The thing is so big and mean it doesn't even need bullets. I could beat Godzilla to death with it if I stood on a chair. The gun is loaded alternately with massive .460 rounds and shortened .410 shotgun shells, all coated in my special Spiritus Dei, silver, garlic, holy water, and red mercury dipping sauce. It only holds five shots, but it does its job well enough that I've never had to reload.

When you're going in someplace blind, don't know the layout or what's waiting inside, a place you know a Lurker likes to hang out, a smart guy will hang back, circle the perimeter, and look for traps and weak points. I'm hot, annoyed, and in a rush, so that's exactly what I don't do. Besides, I'm just chasing one dumb little Kentucky fried blonde. She can't be much trouble now that she's cornered. Yeah. That's probably what all those G-men said about Bonnie Parker before they saw the tommy gun.

Inside the theater, it's a sauna. Burst water pipes in a sealed-up building. I haven't moved and I'm sweating like a lawyer at the pearly gates. It smells like they invented mildew in here. How the hell did suburban Valley girl Eleanor end up day-squatting here? She didn't run into the theater by accident. She knew where she was going. By the sound of all the broken beer and wine bottles under my feet, so do a lot of other people. Make that "did," past tense. The winos are probably what attracted her to the place. Who doesn't love a free lunch? I have a feeling that there aren't too many random squatters in here anymore.

Turns out I'm half right.

The squatters aren't random. They're vampires. Friends of hers. A guy and a girl.

They jump from the balcony and the guy slams a piece of two-by-four between my shoulders. I go down on my knees in the crunchy glass, but I roll with the blow and come up with the .460 cocked. That's when Eleanor's other friends hit me. Two more guys from beneath the seats on either side of the aisle. I grab the smaller one by the throat and toss him into the second. The girl vampire pair hits me from behind and jams a broken bottle into my arm. I drop the gun and it's too dark to see where it went. I throw an elbow back and feel the side of the girl's skull crack. She jumps up like a gazelle and stumbles over two rows of seats, screaming. That gives me a second to sprint down the aisle toward the screen and put some distance between Eleanor's dead friends and me.

That's where Eleanor has been waiting. Not only is she smart, but she has titanium balls. Even when she was on fire and running through the boarded-up front doors, she never let go of the flamethrower. The other bloodsuckers fall back as she opens up.

The shot back at the market was her just introducing herself. This one is a "fuck you very much and good night" just for me. Eleanor pulls the trigger and doesn't let up until the gun is empty.

Stabbed and cold-cocked, I'm still not dumb enough to just stand there. I dive to the right, behind a row of seats. Fire wraps around them like it's reaching for me. I'm getting burned from above and below, steaming like a pork bun in my leather jacket. Even when the flamethrower is empty, the burning seats keep right on cooking me, and the two-by-four shot left me too dizzy to move very fast. I stagger over to the wall and try to run up the aisle, but I'm tripping on the garbage snowdrifts and land face-first in candy wrappers, needles, and malt liquor bottles.

I've turned into Buster Keaton and Eleanor and her friends are getting a real kick out of me gimping along on all fours. She's burned beyond any human recognition, but she's a juicer and they get over pain pretty quick. I do, too, but I'm not there yet. Not even in the same time zone. I give up and lie down on the sticky-sweet carpet to do what I should have done in the first place.

I press my right hand down into the broken glass and put my weight on it. The jagged bottle shards slice deep into my palm and I keep pushing until I feel glass hit bone. Most hexes don't need blood to work, but a little of the red stuff is like a nitrous afterburner when you want a hex to come on hard and fast.

Eleanor takes the two-by-four from the boy bloodsucker and thumps it on each seat as she strolls over to me.

"Hey, Speedy Gonzales. You like chasing things? Why

don't I knock your head across the street and you can chase that?"

"Get him, Nellie. Look at that scarred piece of shit. He's too ugly to drink. Waste that faggot."

It's one of the boys talking. The one who got me with the chunk of wood. He has a southern accent. Somewhere deep, old, and hot. You can almost hear the kudzu wrapped around his words.

Eleanor says, "Shut up, Jed Clampett. Jethro is waiting for you to blow him in the parking lot."

Everyone laughs but Jed.

While Eleanor does an "Evening at the Improv" thing for her dead friends, I do a Hellion chant over and over, keeping my hand in the glass and letting the blood flow. For once, Hellion's guttural grunts work in my favor. The Lost Boys think I'm moaning.

"Why were you following me, asshole? Did Mutti send you? Mom, I mean? Does Daddy know? All she has to do is put on her knee pads and she can get him to do anything."

The wind starts as a breeze from the back of the theater, sweeping from the balcony and ripping down the rotten curtains that flank the dead movie screen. Eleanor drops the comedy act and the others go silent as the wind picks up force. Now they're the ones unsteady on their feet.

Even though I can't read the dead like the living, vampires still have minds and I feel around for Eleanor's. I can't tell you her lottery numbers or her kitten's name, but I can pick up images and impressions. She's gone from pissed to nervous and is steering into the skid, heading for scared. She hasn't been a Lurker long enough to run into anybody with real hoodoo power and she can't figure out what's happening.

Mommy is in her head, too, a black hole of anger and fear. Eleanor might even have gotten herself bit just to spite her. She has a secret, too. She thought it would save her in the end, but now she's having her doubts.

A gust blasts down the aisle like an invisible fist, knocking all five of them ass over horseshoes into the air. Eleanor loses the two-by-four and lands on top of me. I can smell the fear through her burned skin. The wind keeps going, moving up from Hurricane Katrina to space shuttle exhaust.

With all her strength, Eleanor pushes herself off of me.

"It's him! He's doing it!" she yells. "What do we do?"

Jed Clampett hauls his ass up off the floor and pulls himself to me using seat backs like crutches. I've changed the chant, but he hasn't noticed yet.

The wind shifts from a wind tunnel to a swirling twister. I haul myself to my knees and shrug off my leather jacket. The twister rips the carpet from the floor, throwing a junkyardful of broken glass into the air. The shards circle us like a million glittering razor blades, which doesn't do much more than annoy Eleanor and her friends. They bat the glass away like flies. Each of their hundred cuts heals before the second hundred happen. But I'm getting cut, too. In a few seconds I'm the fountain in front of the Bellagio Hotel and all that broken glass is doing a water ballet in my blood.

The swirling air turns pink as I bleed out, which Jed and his girlfriend think is goddamn hysterical. They stick out their tongues and catch drops of my blood like kids catching snowflakes. About ten seconds later they're both screaming and tearing open their throats with their fingernails. Then the other three start to feel it. They try to run, but the wind and glass are everywhere. It's one big Veg-O-Matic in here, spraying my tainted blood down their throats and onto their million wounds.

Eleanor already looks like a Chicken McNugget, so it's hard to tell what's going on with her, but the others are starting to sizzle and glow from the inside like they swallowed road flares on a bet and lost. That's what happens to vampires dumb enough to drink angel blood.

It doesn't take long for them to go catatonic, then flare fast and hot. Human flash paper. They sizzle for a few seconds and cook down to a fine gray ash. I growl the end of the hex and the air grows still. The vampires are all dead, except for Eleanor. She hunkered down and held on to me during the twister. My body blocked enough of the wind for her to survive, but just barely. She moves her cracked lips like she's trying to talk. I lean my ear close to her.

"When you see Mutti, tell her I'm sorry. I only did what I did to scare her like she scares me and Daddy sometimes."

When you're hired to kill someone, the last thing you want is to have to give them absolution. You want them dead fast, not lying there asking you to be their therapist. Worse, you don't want to hear anything that might make you feel sorry for them. I don't want Eleanor's mommy trauma in my head. She's a monster just like me, but I want her to be a dead monster like her friends. She lets go of my leg and gives me a Say Good Night, Gracie sigh. A couple of minutes ago, I wanted to stick her on a spit and toast marshmallows on her while she burned. Now I cover her eyes with my hand and get out the black knife.

"Don't move."

I jam the blade between her ribs. One clean, surgical, pain-free thrust up into her heart. Eleanor stiffens, flares, and ashes out. The dead girl is finally dead.

I look around, making a quick mental map of the bodies and checking that we're still alone. I can hear voices outside. Now that the wind has died down, some curious civilian is going to stick a nose in here soon. I have to work fast.

Eleanor's clothes are pretty much gone, but I give her a quick pat-down. She's wearing a gold locket that's half-melted into her blackened chest. A couple of rhinestone rings have fallen off her fingers, so I grab those. No money in her pockets, but there's a flat metal thing, about the size of a rodeo belt buckle. One side is blank. There's a snarling demon encircled by a spooky monster alphabet on the other. Junk. Goth bling. That's the other problem with baby Lugosis. Eleanor's friends were brainless street kids and she wasn't a vampire long enough for any educated bloodsuckers to clue her in to what she really was. Death in go-go boots. A V-8 devil doll who could explode like a cruise missile and bite like an armor-piercing shark. Silly, stupid kid. Maybe if she hadn't pissed off whoever it was that got the Golden Vigil to call in the hit, she would have had enough time to figure that out.

Good night, Eleanor. I'm sure Mutti forgives you and maybe even misses you. As long as she never finds what you've been up to these last few weeks. She sure won't find it out from me.

I give the ghoul belt buckle one more look. It's heavy like metal, but the edges are chipped like an old china saucer. The dumbest fence in L.A. wouldn't give me a dime for it. I toss it into the dark with the other trash and get to work on Eleanor's friends, going through their pockets, bags, and backpacks. These aren't Beverly Hills Lurkers, just a bunch of downtown scroungers, so I'm not exactly coming up with the crown jewels. Still, it's tourist season, so there's about three hundred in cash that didn't burn up when they ashed out. Some joints, movie ticket stubs, car keys, condoms, and Eleanor's play jewels. I toss everything but the jewelry and the cash. Looting the dead might seem harsh, but they don't need the stuff anymore and the Vigil doesn't pay overtime. Besides, killing monsters is my day job. The way I look at it, me stealing from the dead is like regular people pocketing Post-its on their way out of the office.

I go out into the sun and take a breath to clear the greasy flesh smoke and ashed bodies out of my lungs. I sit on my haunches, head down, my back against the broken theater door, just breathing. My face and chest are covered in darkening bruises and enough blood that it looks like I've been sumo wrestling in a barbwire kimono. My burned arm, the one Eleanor got back at the garage, is starting to flake black skin. When I look up, a dozen faces are locked on me, mostly old Mexican women holding T-shirts and pink-and-orange flip-flops.

I stand and the women take a step back like maybe they're doing *Swan Lake*. There's a knockoff *Evil Dead* T-shirt on a hanger at the end of the nearest rack. I take it. The woman by the market cash register is holding an unopened bottle of water. I take that, too, and give her twenty dollars from the cash I took off the shroud eaters.

"*Gracias*," I say.

"*De nada.*"

She nods at me nervously, a big "please get the hell out of here before my brain explodes" smile plastered on her face. I take off my bloody shirt, drop it into the trash can by her register, and slip on the new shirt. I kill the water in three big gulps before walking back into the theater.

In the dark, Mason's lighter sparks on the first try and I hear sirens just as the cigarette begins to glow.

The woman from behind the counter leans her head in the door.

"Hey, mister."

She points out at the street.

"Thanks. I heard."

She shoos me away with her hands.

"Just go. No trouble here."

"Plenty of trouble here," I tell her, pointing into the theater, where I left the bodies.

"*Los vampiros?* No trouble. Only bother turistas and *pendejos.*"

So, they knew about the pod. L.A. is a get-along kind of town. The ladies work the day shift and *los vampiros* work the night. As long as they don't shoplift flip-flops, the undead are probably pretty decent neighbors. The muggers and dealers will learn to stay away. Hell, as long as you wear a muffler 24/7, this might be one of the safer streets in L.A.

The woman standing in the door turns to someone outside. I can hear them talking, but I don't really listen. The cop's voice is loud and clear and I know what he's asking. I take my phone out of my pocket, go to Eleanor's body, and snap a proof-of-death shot. When I get back to the lobby the cop is coming in, his hand on his Glock. He goes for it when he sees me. He's pretty smooth, but his body is all wrong for this game. He's been exercising for bulk at the gym, all showy slow twitch muscles, going for a Terminator look. He can probably throw a mean choke hold, but I bet even the old ladies outside could outdraw him. I flick my cigarette and it bounces off his chest before he has the gun belly-button-high.

He screams "Freeze!", but I'm already slipping into a shadow.

GETTING IN TO see Wells is always a merry little dance. At the gate, the guys in suits go through an elaborate security and ID check. They scan my photo and fingerprints. Scrape cells off the back of my hand for quickie DNA profiling and species confirmation. Then they have to call inside for verification because maybe there's another guy who shows up at their gate from out of a shadow.

There are two agents on the gate today. One is the usual fresh-faced new guy that always pulls door duty and the other is a Shut Eye. A salaryman psychic. This one is young, almost as young as the guard. He's ambitious, too. I can feel him sizing me up. Most people don't like having their minds read. It doesn't bother me.

When I was a kid, I once took a sharp piece of wood from the backyard and smacked one of our neighbors'

Dobermans with it. The dog chased me all the way to the end of the block, and when he was done, I had bruises and bloody teeth marks all down my left calf. My father was in the driveway, working on my mom's old Impala, and saw the whole thing. When I asked why he didn't stop the dog from biting me, he said, " 'Cause you deserved it."

"What's that line from *The Maltese Falcon*?"

"Excuse me?" asks the guard. His name tag reads *Huston*.

"Bogart says it. 'The cheaper the crook, the gaudier the patter.' You ever think about that when you're patting people down?"

"We're just doing our jobs, sir."

"Trust me, I know. I've been coming here about every week for six months. You're doing a really thorough job of looking at my fingerprints for the four-hundredth time and talking to the same guy inside you always talk to, the one who always gives you the same answer. I mean, I always get invited in, right?"

"We have to establish your identity, sir. It's procedure."

"You know who I am. Or do a lot people show up here covered in blood and goofer dust?"

That last bit sets off the Shut Eye. An unsubstantiated claim of identity. Catnip to psychic snoops. I can feel it when they're slipping their ghost fingers into my skull. It tickles behind my eyes.

There are two basic ways to deal with a peeper. You can back off and go blank. Name all the presidents or run through multiplication tables.

The other way to deal with psychics is to welcome them in. Throw open all the doors and windows and invite them deep inside your mind. Then grab them by the throat and drag them straight down to Hell. Well, that's what I do. It's not mandatory. The point is that once you've led them deep enough into your psyche, you're the one behind the wheel and they're strapped in the kiddy seat in back.

I give them the grand tour of Downtown, starting out with a quick jolt of the early days in Hell when it was all nausea and panic. Give them a quick taste of psychic rape. Experiments and Elephant Man exhibitions. Being the fox in a mounted hunt through forests of flayed, burning souls. Then some highlights from the arena. Killing, eleven years of killing. I let them see exactly what being Sandman Slim is all about. Most of them don't get that far.

This Shut Eye doesn't make it past my first week Downtown, when a drunk Hellion guard slit me open and tried to pull out my intestines because he'd heard that's where humans hid their souls. But I don't let the Shut Eye off that easy. I hold him inside long enough to feel me running away from the neighbor's dog and getting my leg chewed up.

When I let go, Criswell flies out of my head like a goose through a jet engine. He gasps and is on the verge of tears when the connection finally breaks.

Huston grabs him by the shoulder.

"Ray, you okay?" Ray doesn't hear him. He's looking at me.

"Why?" he asks.

"'Cause you deserved it."

Ray takes a key card from his jacket, waves it over a magnetic reader, and the gate swings open.

When I go through I turn back to them.

"I don't have to do this, you know. I could come out of a shadow on this side of the fence and not deal with you assholes. But I'm trying to fit in a little better around here, so I'm polite and I try to play by your rules. You might consider cutting me the tiniest piece of slack."

I head for the warehouse. Huston keeps asking Ray what happened and Ray keeps telling him to fuck off. I wonder if Ray is just a psychic reader or a projector, too, and what parts of the tour he'll show Huston to shut him up.

WELLS YELLS AT me halfway across the warehouse floor so that everyone turns to see me looking like an executioner's practice dummy.

"Damn, son. Did you stop to gut a deer on the way over or did that little girl do all that?"

I hold up my burned jacket with my blackened arm.

"Your little girl did this. Her four friends did the rest."

"There's a pod?"

"Was. Five of them."

"That doesn't jibe with our intelligence."

I take four wallets from a jacket pocket and drop them on a table.

"Here's your goddamn intelligence."

Wells snaps, "Watch your language."

"I took those off Eleanor's pals. Their ash is still on them. Probably prints, too."

"What about Eleanor?"

I take my cell out of my back pocket, thumb on the photo album, and hold it up so Wells can see the screen.

He frowns.

"What did you do to her?"

"Silly girl had a flamethrower. She fucked—I mean, messed up and set herself on fire. Then she ran out into direct sunlight. I would have been happy to quietly take her heart, but she had to turn it into D-day."

"Are the remains still at the scene?"

"Yeah."

"We'll secure the site for now. Clean up isn't a priority if the pod has been cleared out."

"I didn't see anyone else there and they didn't seem to be looking, so that was probably all of them, but I can't be a hundred percent. Like I said, I went in thinking it was one girl."

"I'll need a copy of that photo. E-mail a copy to my account."

"Just did."

Wells isn't looking at me. He's put on Nitrile gloves and is examining the wallets.

He says, "They're empty."

"Are they?"

"Was there anything inside when you found them?"

"How do I know? I was killing vampires, not checking their IDs. I've seen plenty of Lurkers that don't use money. They steal what they want."

"Then why carry a wallet?"

Shit. Good point.

"Ask a shrink. I get paid to kill things."

"Right."

He turns to a female agent standing on his right.

"Bag these and take them downstairs for identification."

"Yes, sir."

Wells motions for me to follow him. We head out across the warehouse floor.

I kind of like the organized chaos of the Golden Vigil's headquarters. There's always something fun to scope out and think about stealing. A group of agents in Tyvek suits and respirators forklifting a massive stone idol onto the back of a flatbed truck. The idol is on its back, and from where I'm standing, it's all tentacles and breasts, but I swear some of the tentacles move a little as they tether the idol down. Across the floor, welders are modifying vehicles. Agents are examining new guns as they're uncrated. A guy as skinny, leathery, and looking as old as King Tut's mummy wanders the floor sprinkling holy water on everything.

"What kind of a bonus am I getting for taking out those four extra bloodsuckers?"

"From the look of those wallets, seems to me that you already got your bonus."

"Is that what it seems to you? If I happened to find anything at the crime scene, trust me, it's barely enough to cover the cost of a replacement jacket. Besides, with intelligence as bad as that, I deserve extra money just on principle."

"Do you?"

"Unless you knew what was inside that building."

Wells stops and looks at me.

"Come again?"

"Unless you knew there was a pod in there, but sent me in looking for one inexperienced girl. Isn't that exactly the kind of thing you'd tell someone if you were setting them up?"

"Are you asking me or telling me?"

"How's your lady friend downstairs?"

"Don't talk about her like that."

Wells gets a little defensive whenever I mention Aelita. He's got a thing for her but an angel is just a little out of his league.

"Okay. How is Miss Aelita? Healthy? Happy? I haven't seen her since right after Avila."

Aelita is a kind of drill sergeant angel. She runs the Golden Vigil, Heaven's Pinkertons. She knows I'm a nephilim and has a cute nickname for me: "The Abomination." I'm pretty sure she'd like to see me dead.

"Did you send candy and flowers on Valentine's Day, Wells? It's okay, you know. He was a saint."

His phone goes off. He walks away and speaks quietly into the receiver. I think an angel's ears are burning.

Wells nods and pockets the phone.

"You get a twenty percent bonus added on to your next check."

"Twenty percent? What am I, your waiter? I got you five vampires, not a BLT."

"Twenty percent is what I've been authorized. Take it or leave it."

"I'll take it."

He takes a white business envelope from his jacket and hands it to me. The check for my last Vigil hit. A bunch of suburban Druids in Pomona were trying to resurrect the Invidia, a gaggle of transdimensional chaos deities. The Druids were hilarious. They looked like extras from *The Andy Griffith Show* trying to call up the devil in matching white housedresses. What's even funnier was that their plan almost worked. Their scrawny Barney Fife leader was one murdered infant away from annihilating Southern California.

I wonder if I'd just held back a little and Barney did get to unleash the Invidia, would we really be able to tell the difference?

I look at the check and then at Wells.

"Why do you always pull this shit?"

"Do what? Obey the law?"

"I'm a freelancer and you're deducting things like taxes and Social Security."

"You don't strike me as the type who files his taxes on time. I'm doing you a favor."

"I don't pay taxes because I don't exist. You think I'm going to apply for Social Security when I'm sixty-five?"

"You're going to want to wait until you're seventy. The extra benefits are worth it."

"I'm not waiting for anything. I'm legally dead. Why am I paying any of this bullshit?"

"I told you to watch your language."

"Fuck you, Miss Manners. You get me to kill for you and then you screw me out of my money."

"That money belongs to the government. It funds what we do here. You don't like it, run for office."

I don't want to run for anything. I want to shove this miserable cheap-ass check so far up Wells's ass he can read the routing number out the back of his eyes.

But Max Overdrive is just limping along these days and I don't want to have to find someplace else to live. Landlords in L.A. don't want you to have pets. What am I going to do with a chain-smoking severed head? Dignity is nice but it's money makes the lights and shower work.

I watch the welders working across the warehouse so I don't have to look at Wells while I fold the check and slip it into my pocket.

"At the end of time, when your side loses, I want you to remember this moment."

Wells narrows his eyes.

"Why?"

" 'Cause Lucifer doesn't expect you to thank him when he fucks you over. That's why he's going to win."

Wells looks down at the floor for a minute. Puts his hands behind his back.

"You know, my mother watched a lot of Christian TV when I was growing up. Hellfire-and-brimstone hucksters telling Bible stories and yelling about damnation to get fools and old people to send them their welfare checks. I never paid much attention to 'em, but one day out of nowhere this one wrinkled old preacher starts telling what he says is a Persian parable. Now, that's weird for a Baptist Bible-thumper.

"You see, there was once a troubled man in a little village near Qom in ancient Persia."

"This is the story, right? 'Cause I don't want to hear about you and your dad going off-roading."

"Shut up. One day the troubled man got out of bed to work his fields and maybe he was killed or maybe he just kept walking, but he was never heard from again. The sun was shining through the door as the man left and threw his shadow on the wall by the hearth or whatever it is you call it over there. When the man's wife and children came home and found the house empty, the wife sees her husband's shadow and asks who he is. The shadow says, 'The man is gone and become a shadow to this house. I am the shadow of the man who did not go, but will remain here.' The shadow stayed and over time became a man and he and the woman and her children lived there happily together for many years."

Wells puts his hands together almost like he's praying. It creeps me out seeing this side of him.

"Later, when I heard that the Golden Vigil was founded in Persia, I knew it was God speaking to me through the TV that day. He was telling me that here is where I'm supposed to be."

"That story doesn't even make sense, and what exactly does it have to do with anything we're talking about?"

"It means we've done our job for more than a thousand years, so you can shove your disapproval."

"That sounds like the sin of pride, Marshal. Better run downstairs and let Miss December flog it out of you. Webcam it and charge by the minute. You won't ever have to take government money again."

Wells looks at me. His phone goes off. He ignores it.

I want to tell him to go fuck himself.

"You done whining? You ready to work? I have something else for you."

But I need this.

"What do you want me to do?"

"I want you to walk through a murder scene with me. The victim was Sub Rosa. No rough stuff. Just observation."

"You have forensics people. Why do you need me?"

"I don't want them getting too deep into this one yet. I want you."

"Why?"

"Because you've been to Hell."

"So?"

"I want you to take a look at a body and tell me what you think it means."

"Are you sure it's just one body and not five?"

"Funny."

"I want my full fee."

"Half. No one is asking you to kill anything."

"You're using up my valuable drinking and smoking time. I need compensation."

"As you just pointed out, we're government funded, which means that we work within a simple and predetermined pay structure. In other words, looking and pointing doesn't pay the same as hunting and killing."

"Tell you what, go down to Chinatown, find a club called the Owl's Shadow, and hire yourself a Deadhead. Those gloomy necromancers are a bunch of low-self-esteem Siouxsie and the Banshees bitches. They'll fall all over themselves to help a fed do a murder-scene magic show."

Wells takes the phone from his pocket, looks at the caller ID, and frowns.

"Look, you can sprinkle some pixie dust around while you're at the scene. Do some damn magic that won't break anything and I can get you two-thirds of your normal fee. But that's it."

"Done."

I put out my hand. He puts the phone to his ear so he doesn't have to shake on it.

"We'll meet at three A.M., when things are quiet and the bars are closed. I'll call you with the address."

"Nice doing business with you, Marshal. Give the missus my best."

"Get out."

I DECIDE TO skip the Ray and Huston show on the way out, so I slip through a dark patch on a wall outside the warehouse. Come out in the alley across the street from the Bamboo House of Dolls.

What I thought was a one-night blowout right after I saved the world on New Year's has turned into a six-month running party. After I tossed Mason to the mob Downtown, it seemed like half the Sub Rosa in L.A. showed up at Bamboo House to kiss his ass good-bye. And they never left. Carlos is happy enough. Sub Rosa tip big at civilian places where they can hang out without ending up part of the floor show.

Most Sub Rosa, you'd never notice. They look boringly human, are human, and go out of their way to fit in with other humans, even if they sometimes dress like nineteenth-century dandies or Mayan priests. Others in the bar look like they stepped off a steam-powered zeppelin from Neptune. They're the Lurkers, and good, upstanding Sub Rosa don't like them soiling the furniture at their clubs so they come here. There are succubi and transgendered Lamia. Shaggy Nahual wolf and tiger beast men laughing like frat boys and stacking their beer cans in a pyramid until they knock it over. Again. A group of blue-skinned schoolgirls with pale blond hair and horns peeking out through their pigtails are playing some kind of betting game with ivory cups and scorpions.

Carlos is a big part of the reason Bamboo House of Dolls is still standing. He didn't even blink when the crusty half of L.A.'s magic underground dropped in to get shit-faced. If Jesus was a bartender, He would still only be half as cool as Carlos. With all his newfound lucre, all the man has done to the place is get some new bar stools, a better sound system, and cleaned up the bathrooms so they're a little less like a Calcutta bus station. It's good to have one thing that hasn't changed much. We need a few anchors in our lives to keep us from floating away into the void. Like Mr. Muninn said the one time he came in, *"Quid salvum est si Roma perit?"* What is safe if Rome perishes?

"Swamp Fire" by Martin Denny is playing on the jukebox. Carlos comes over with a cup of black coffee.

"You didn't have to get dressed up just for me," he says.

"Like the look? It's from the Calvin Klein Book of Revelations line."

"The crispy black arm is nice even if it is shedding dead skin all over my floor, but that burned-up jacket is *un pedazo de basura*."

"Time to let it go?"

"One of you needs to be buried and my Dumpster has a lovely lakeside view of the alley. Give it to me and I'll get rid of it."

I push the charred pile of leather across the bar.

"Do me a favor and pour some salt and bleach on it when you put it out."

"Is that a magic thing or a cop thing?"

"Both. Bleach for DNA. Salt for any leftover hoodoo someone can use in a hex."

He nods and puts the jacket under the bar.

"I'm guessing since you haven't even looked at that coffee that you want a drink."

"Some of the red stuff."

"You sure?"

"Does the pope live in a nice house?"

"At least have some food, too. I just pulled some pork tamales out of the steamer."

"Maybe that and some rice?"

"You got it."

"City of Veils" by Les Baxter comes on. Crazy trumpets and drums at the beginning, then it slides into old-fashioned strings and Hollywood exotica. I half expect to see Errol Flynn dressed like a pirate in a corner booth trying to get a hand job from Lana Turner. After some of the red stuff, maybe I will.

I haven't heard that Alice song again since the night it came blaring out of the jukebox, like nails being hammered into my ears. I had Carlos check and the song wasn't even on the machine. He had the company bring him a new box, just so I wouldn't sit at the bar getting twitchy, waiting for it to come up again.

Later I knew that the song had never been on the machine. It was one of Mason's hexes. He wanted to watch me go crazy. If he'd pumped me full of LSD and locked me in a spinning mirrored room full of rats, he couldn't have done any better.

That was six months ago. Half a year since I sent Mason to be poached in Hell and waved bye-bye to his Kissi pals as they burned up and blew away on the solar winds. A hundred and eighty days since I watched Alice's ashes drift away like fog into the Pacific. I'm doing fine, thanks. Maybe a little bruised around the edges, but I have all the medicine I need right here in this glass.

Carlos sets down the plate of tamales and pours a double shot of the red stuff into a heavy square tumbler, the way we used to drink it in Hell. Aqua Regia is so red it's almost black, like blood under moonlight. It goes down smooth, like gasoline and pepper spray. It probably saved my life Downtown. When I discovered I could swallow Aqua Regia and keep it down, Hellions starting looking at me differently. I think that's when one of them got the idea of putting me in the arena instead of killing me. Just when my novelty was wearing off, I was interesting again.

"I should have killed him when I had the chance."

Carlos shakes his head.

"You weren't strong enough to kill him."

"How would you know that?"

"Because you told me. We've had this conversation about fifty times before."

"Really?"

"Maybe you should stick with coffee or maybe a beer. You don't need the red stuff."

He reaches for my glass and I slide it away from him.

"Yeah, I really do."

"You couldn't have beaten him. He was too strong. You knew it, so you did what you could."

"Yeah, but sometimes it's not about winning and losing. It's about doing the right thing. I didn't do the right thing. I shouldn't have walked away. Lucifer was right. By leaving Mason in Hell I gave the prick exactly what he wanted."

"You're alive and you're walking around. Long as you can say that, doing the right thing remains an option. Just keep your head down until you figure out the right time and place."

"Thanks, Carlos. You're the best dad a boy could ask for. Will you adopt me?"

"I thought I already did."

Carlos looks past my shoulder and shakes his head. I don't have to look. I can feel them. Behind me are college girls with pens and paper. They want to stand too close and ask for my autograph in breathy voices. If I'm dumb enough to sign, as dumb as I used to be, I'll be able to buy my autograph off eBay in an hour. I sip my drink and dig into the tamales with my fork. Pretend I don't notice as Carlos waves them off.

The real problem with college girls is that they usually have college boys with them.

A second later someone is leaning on the bar to my right.

"You're the superhero who can do the portaling trick, aren't you? Let's see it."

He looks like Ziggy Stardust on a *GQ* cover. NASA engineers built his three-piece pinstripe suit. It's a work of art.

"Are you talking to me?"

"They say you can shadow-walk. I want to see."

He looks at me with a combination of arrogance and boredom. You never know what a guy like this is going to do. He has one hand in his pocket. What he's holding could be anything from a joint to a water pistol to a box cutter.

"Sorry. I don't speak French. Or is it Chinese? I can't understand a word you're saying."

"You think you're hot shit because you have a cartoon nickname and the Golden Vigil watching your back? Do you even know who I am? Do you know who my father is?"

"Maybe what you need is an asshole-to-English phrase book. I hear they have some fine bookstores in Kansas. You should start walking."

"My family owns this place. This city. L.A. to the Valley and out to the desert."

Carlos gives me a look and I give him one right back. He stays put, but starts cutting up limes so he has an excuse to hold a knife.

"People listen to me when I talk."

"I guess the rich really are different. Most of us come from monkeys, but you're giving off a whiff of rattlesnake."

Ziggy has a friend with him. Not quite as handsome. His suit isn't quite as nice. He's trying to maintain his cool in front of the girls, but he's about sixty seconds from running.

The friend says, "Please just do the trick, man, and we'll get out of your hair."

"I just killed five people. I'll show you that trick if you like."

I go back to my drink and the tamales. Ziggy is about to make another strafing run, not knowing that when he opens his mouth, I'm going to stick my fork into his eye and make him dance like a marionette. But the girls get on either side of him and pull him to the door.

As they go out, I hear one of the girls say, "Daddy would say that man looks like a sheep-killing dog."

When they're gone, Carlos curses quietly, so fast I can't tell if it's English, Spanish, or Urdu.

"I hate that shit."

He wipes off the spot where Ziggy was leaning.

"No, you don't. You encourage it. Look at you. You walk in here with that burned-up arm and dried blood all over a monster movie T-shirt and you don't want to be noticed? Normal people bet on football or collect stamps to pass the time. Your hobby is telling people to fuck off, but you can't do that unless they notice you in the first place."

"You understand how being a bartender works, right? I complain and you bring me drinks and sympathy. Don't start trying to get reasonable with me."

"You like these little fights because you don't have any real ones right now, is all I'm saying."

"I'll keep my fingers crossed for Armageddon."

"Don't sweat it. I think your star is beginning to fade. New people keep coming in, but a lot of old ones have disappeared."

"If I take up knitting, think the rest will go away?"

"Louie Toadvine is one of them, which is funny because I owe him money."

Carlos pours himself a glass of seltzer and drops in some of the lime wedges he was cutting.

"Your friend Candy was in here last night."

I dig into the tamales.

"Good for her."

I haven't seen or spoken to Candy more than three times since we saved a bunch of about-to-be-sacrificed angels on New Year's. We killed a lot of people that night, but none who didn't deserve it.

"She's a pretty girl."

"Is she? I don't entirely remember."

Since then I'd only seen her a couple of times with Vidocq and once when I got Doc Kinski to drain the venom from my arm after a Naga purse snatcher went king cobra on me. Kinski is the medical man for a lot of Sub Rosa and Lurkers. Most people think being a doctor is a big deal, but Kinski used to be an archangel, so for him, being a doctor is sort of like flipping burgers at McDonald's after you were president.

"Candy's nice. Asked about business. How is it dealing with the Sub Rosa? When am I ever going to get some new tunes on the jukebox?"

"What do I care about any of this?"

He shrugs.

"I thought you two were friends. More than friends maybe."

"Where'd you hear that?"

Carlos holds up his hands.

"Sorry, man. I didn't mean nothing. It's just something I heard. Anyway, she said she and Kinski had been moving around a lot. That's why she hasn't been around. She's heading back out to wherever he is."

"Did she mention where?"

"Nope."

"She was sick for a while after Avila. It isn't good for her to be around all that blood. It affects her funny."

Candy's a Jade, which is kind of like a vampire only worse. She's trying to lay off the people eating, but dragging her up to a massacre pushed her over the edge and she fell off the wagon for a while.

"I didn't get the feeling she was in here to talk to me. She asked when you usually came in. I had to tell her you come and go and don't keep regular hours."

Was Candy looking for me? It's funny she'd come to Bamboo House. I'd thought about waiting out in the strip mall by Kinski's clinic, but that felt more stalkerish than friendly.

"I'm glad she's feeling better."

"Is she why you're hitting the red stuff?"

"I'm drinking it because you have it. Do you know how rare Aqua Regia is? Rare isn't even the word. It doesn't exist anywhere outside of Hell. I'm going to have to thank Muninn the next time I see him."

"I don't know that it comes from Muninn."

"Who sends it?"

"I don't know. A bottle just shows up every now and then. First time I found one by the door, I tasted it. It's disgusting and you're one sick little *pinche* for drinking it. And you drink too much of it."

"Sometimes it's nice to know I'm not crazy. You know when you wake up and for a minute you don't know where you are and aren't sure if you're awake or still dreaming? This reminds me what's real. Who I am. Where I've been.

How I got these scars. Living up here, sometimes I need that."

"It also gets you hammered fast."

"And it reminds me of . . . Never mind."

Carlos stabs a finger at me.

"Say it. I've been waiting to hear you say something like that. Go ahead. Say it out loud so everyone can hear you. This poison that comes from Hell reminds you of home. That's what was about to come out of your mouth, wasn't it? Think about that for a minute. How fucked up that is."

"Excuse me. I'm sorry to interrupt. One of those men over there said that you were the gentleman they call Sandman Slim."

Carlos doesn't miss a beat.

"Now, why would a nice lady like you be looking for a bad man like that?"

It's so obvious even Carlos, the most unmagic über-civilian of all time, can see it. The woman isn't Sub Rosa. She's around fifty-five, but picked up a beauty allurement potion so she can tell people she's thirty. She dressed up to come here. She's wearing an expensive Hillary Clinton pantsuit, but it's a little off. The symmetry isn't quite right, but not in a way most civilians could see. It's probably from an outlet mall and it's brand-new.

"He's not Sandman Slim?"

"I didn't say that."

Carlos points to one of the bar stools. The woman sits.

"Would you like some coffee?"

She has dark, pretty gray eyes. Her pupils are pinpoints. This bar isn't where she wants to be.

I push the tamales and rice away. After Ziggy's anger, being jolted by her fear has ruined my appetite. I half turn and do a quick scan of the faces in the room. It's ninety-nine percent Sub Rosa, with a few civilian hangers-on and groupies. If she found me here, she must have asked questions in places she wouldn't normally go. And when she finally heard about Bamboo House of Dolls, people would have told her what happens to strangers who come here to bug me. But she did it anyway.

Good for her.

"Call me Stark. No one calls me that other name."

"I'm sorry. It's the only one I knew."

"No problem. Why are you looking for me?"

She takes a picture from her purse and sets it in front of me. It's a young man, about my age when I went Downtown. He's broad across the shoulders, like a football player. He has her eyes.

"This is my son. His name is Aki. It's Finnish, like his father."

"He's a nice-looking kid. But I don't know him, if that's why you're here."

"You don't know him, but he knows you. Your kind, I mean. He's Sub Rosa, just like my husband's family. Eighteen years ago we lived here, but we moved to my mother's property in Lawrence, Kansas, when Aki was born. We weren't sure we wanted him growing up here . . ."

She trails off and looks around the room. A bald man in a white silk suit takes what looks like a whiskey flask from his pocket and snaps it open. Inside is damp soil and pale, gray worms. He picks a worm up by its head and blows on it. The bug straightens, and when it's rigid, the man lights one end with a cigarette lighter and smokes it.

"Aki just had his eighteenth birthday and wanted to come back to where he was born. Alone, of course. A young man wants to feel independent. How could we say no?"

A corn-fed Kansas farm boy full of bumpkin magic loose in L.A., what could possibly go wrong with that?

"My husband still knows people, Sub Rosa, in the area. He asked them to keep an eye on Aki, but it's a big city. We haven't heard from him in weeks. I know he knew people out here. He was corresponding with a Sub Rosa girl. I forget her name."

"Do you have the letters with you?"

"No. They're gone. He must have taken them with him."

"Have you talked to your husband's friends?"

"None of them knows anything."

"Why are you coming to me about this?"

"I have a feeling something has happened to my son. I heard that you do things other people can't or don't want to do. There was a crime in the city earlier this year. I believe a cult was planning on sacrificing a group of kidnapped women. You stopped it."

Is that what the tabloids are saying happened now? It's annoyingly close to the truth. Couldn't they have worked in some ETs?

"Listen, Evelyn."

"How did you know my name was Evelyn?"

"Listen, Evelyn, I know you need help, but not from me. I'm not what you think I am."

"What are you?"

"I'm a monster."

I let that sink in for a second. She's a nice woman, but Ziggy really fouled my mood. I kill off the tumbler of Aqua Regia.

"Don't take this the wrong way, but if your husband really is Sub Rosa, why isn't he out here with you doing locator spells? Or echo tracing? Sloppy teenybopper magic usually leaves a fat shiny trail of residue all over the aether. Easy to follow."

"My husband is dead. It was very recent and sudden. That's why I was trying to get in touch with Aki. Now I might have lost both of them."

She looks down at the coffee cup. Her heart is slowing, but not because she's any more relaxed. My blackened arm is starting to heal. It burns and itches. I can't help this woman. I don't want to be here.

Carlos says, "I think you're getting a little ahead of yourself. Why don't you go to the cops or hire yourself a private investigator? You don't need magic for this kind of thing. And from what I've seen around here, magic doesn't really help anything. It just makes everything more confusing."

She puts her hand on my arm.

"You saved all those people. Why won't you help me?"

"Carlos is right. You need to go to the cops or hire yourself a detective. I'm not Sam Spade. That's not what I do."

"But you saved all those people."

"I didn't save anyone. I just killed the bastards who needed killing. Get it? I don't save good people. I murder bad ones." I wish I was saying this quietly and reasonably, but really, I'm way too loud.

Evelyn straightens and turns to ice. She puts her kid's photo back in her bag and gets up.

"I'm sorry to have taken up your valuable time."

"Wait a minute."

This time I grab her arm. I look around for someone who was here a minute ago.

"Titus. Come on over here."

A whippet-thin black guy in a purple velvet suit and glasses with round, yellow-tinted lenses walks cautiously to the bar. I hold a hand out at Evelyn.

"Titus, this is Evelyn. Evelyn, this is Titus Eshu. Titus is a Fiddler. Do you know what that is?"

"He reads objects by handling them."

"Right. He plays around with things, then tells you all about the owner. He can even use them like a divining rod. Do you have any of your son's things?"

"I have his high school class ring."

I look at Titus.

"That good enough?"

Titus nods.

"It's a good start," he says to Evelyn. To me he says, "And after I do this, you're going to owe me a favor, right?"

"Right."

He smiles, takes Evelyn by the elbow, and leads her to his table.

"This way, ma'am. Let's see if we can track down your wayward child."

Carlos says, "You were a real world-class prick there for a minute. Then you turned it around right at the last second and came out sort of looking like a person."

"I've gotta get out of here."

"I'm kidding, man. You did fine with the old lady."

"No, I didn't. This is my punishment for not killing Mason. I don't know what I'm doing anymore. There's no reason for me to exist. I kill things I don't care about for people I hate. I yell at old ladies. And now I'm going to owe goddamn Titus a favor."

"I'm going to wrap up this food so you can take it home with you."

I turn in my seat and look at Evelyn and Titus. He has Aki's ring in one hand and the photo in the other. His eyes are half closed and he's whispering an incantation. Evelyn hangs on his every word. She doesn't look happy, but maybe a little more hopeful.

I'm suddenly aware that while I'm watching Titus, pretty much everyone else in the bar is watching me. I'd like to think they're staring because of my white-hot animal magnetism, but I know I'm not Elvis. I'm Lobster Boy, hear me roar.

Carlos gives me the tamales in a Styrofoam carrier.

Thanks and good night. Be sure to tip your waitresses.

I leave through a shadow near the fire exit in back.

You know how they put out oil well fires by setting off an explosion that's so big it snuffs out the first fireball with a bigger one? Sometimes the only way to get past something impassable is to smash it with itself. Like kills like. When you live with a dead man's head that won't shut up and smokes all your cigarettes, the only way to deal with the awfulness is to make it so unbelievably awful that it becomes kind of weirdly beautiful. Like an exploding giraffe full of fireworks. (Hellions really know how to throw a birthday party.)

Kasabian calls it his "pussy wagon," but I can't go there, so I call it the "magic carpet." Really it's a polished mahogany deck about the size of a dinner plate, supported by a dozen articulated brass legs. When I brought it home from Muninn's—partial payment for a quick smash-and-grab job—one end of the deck was loaded down with prisms, mirrors, and gears that must have meshed with another long-lost machine. The top is covered in what looked like teeth marks and stained with something black. I don't want to know what used to drive the thing or what happened to it.

After I unscrewed and sawed off all the extra hardware, I let Kasabian take it out for a test drive. What do you know? His low-rent, third-rate hoodoo was just powerful enough to keep the brass legs in sync, so he can move around on his own now. It's nice not to have to carry Kasabian everywhere anymore, but it means that every day I come home to a chain-smoking Victorian centipede.

He's standing on what used to be the video bootlegging table and using his brass legs to tap numbers into a PC. Ever since he got mobile, Kasabian has been doing Max Overdrive's books again. He and Allegra set up a little in-store wireless network so he can do the banking and buy new inventory online. *Race with the Devil*, a decent piece of mid-seventies trash with Warren Oates and Peter Fonda trying to outrun a bunch of rural devil worshippers, plays on a monitor next to the PC. Ever since his visit Downtown, Kasabian has been on a devil movie kick. He doesn't look up when he hears me come in.

"So, how did it go?" He turns and looks at me. "Oh, that bad."

"Just about that bad, Alfredo Garcia."

"I told you not to call me that."

"I had to go *Wild Bunch* in the theater. Left me in a Peckinpah state of mind."

"Did you get paid, at least?"

"Yeah, here's the big money. Plus the usual deductions."

I drop the check next to the keyboard. Kasabian pinches the ends of the check between two of his brass legs and holds it up to read it.

"That prick. He just does this to humiliate you. It makes him feel better about not being able to do the stuff you can do and needing you for his dirty work. It's pure envy. "

"Yeah, it's a glamorous life here in Graceland."

I pick up the bottle of Jack Daniel's from the bedside table and pour some into the same glass I've been using for three days.

"And he's trying to keep us on the hook by starving us. You know that, right? You ought to let me hex his ass."

I sip the Jack. It's good, but after the Aqua Regia, it's about as potent as cherry Kool-Aid.

"Save your hoodoo for real work. And, technically, he's only starving me. If he knew about you, he'd shit his heart out."

"Great, get him up here. I'll video it and put it up on YouTube."

"Aelita would be the fun one to get on tape. I'm an Abomination, but I don't even know if angels have a word for you."

"One does. 'Hey, shithead.'"

"Lucifer always had a way with words. He's just like Bob Dylan, but without all the annoying talent."

"That's hilarious. He loves it when you say stuff like that. Every time you do, he turns up the temperature Downtown ten degrees."

"Then he should be able to cook biscuits on his tits by now."

"I'll ask him for you."

"No, you won't. When you download your brain or play video highlights or whatever it is you do for the old man, you'll only show him what you want him to see. You hold back crumbs 'cause when you know something he doesn't it gives you power. Just like you hold back things from me. And I hold back things from you and he holds back things from both of us. We're a little clusterfuck of liars."

Kasabian nods to the Styrofoam container I set on the bed when I ditched my weapons.

"Do I smell tamales?"

"Yeah, you want them? I lost my appetite."

Kasabian kneels down on six of his legs and hangs over the edge of the table. He uses four of his free legs to open the door of the minifridge I installed and uses two more legs to grab a bottle of Corona. He pops the top off the beer while pulling himself back onto the table and waggles a bunch of his other legs at me like a horny lobster.

"Slip me some crimson, Jimson."

I hand him the container.

"Don't forget your bucket."

"Have I ever?"

"I just don't want a first time."

He doesn't answer. He's already diving into Carlos's spicy tamales, working a plastic fork with two of his front legs. After each bite of food, a glob that looks like white-orange putty oozes from the bottom of his neck, through the hole I drilled in the magic carpet and into a blue kid-size plastic beach bucket. There's a pop-top trash can at the end of that table. Kasabian is good about dumping his scat when he's done, but he's short, so he needs me to step on the pedal to open the top. It's nice to be needed.

I'm not in the mood for Cirque de Puke right now, so I find a pad and pencil and try to remember what Eleanor's monster belt buckle looked like. Alice was the artist in my family. Even my handwriting made my teachers weep. When I'm done, I have a sketch that's pretty good if I was a half-blind mental patient in the last stages of tertiary syphilis. I hold it up so Kasabian can see it.

"You recognize this?"

"I'm on my lunch hour, man."

"Just look at the goddamn paper."

He doesn't move his head from the food, just swivels his eyes and squints at the image.

"Nope. Never seen it before. What is it, some monster you're supposed to kill or have you started dating again?"

"It's something I saw today. Like a belt buckle or an icon or something. I didn't think much about it at the time, but it's been bugging me."

"I don't recognize it."

Plop goes the tamale putty.

"Can you check it out in the Codex?"

Now he turns to look at me. He hates it when I ask him to look things up. I'm not even supposed to know about the Daimonion Codex.

"I don't think so. Someone's using it. *Occupado*, you know?"

"Bullshit. I saw this kind of thing when I was Downtown. It might be a book, but you don't read it like one. It's conceptual, mental. Like a mystical database."

"If you know so much about it, why don't you look it up yourself?"

The Daimonion Codex is Lucifer's private notebook, reference book, strategy, spell and wisdom book, and anything-else-you-can-think-of book.

"The Codex is for official Hellion business and I only use it when the big man asks me because he's too busy to find something himself."

Satan's Big Little Book of Badass. A kind of Bizarro World Boy Scout manual. High-grade Gnostic porn. The Codex is the second most important document in the universe, right after the Scroll of Creation in you-know-who's personal library.

"Bullshit. Every time I leave the room, you're in there trying to find some angle that'll get your body back."

"No, I'm not."

"You always were a terrible liar, Kas. A career crook should be able to bull better than that."

"Leave me alone. When I get a spare minute, I'll look for your monster. Now let me eat these while they're warm."

I sit back on the bed and sip the glass of Jack. On the

monitor, Peter Fonda is shooting at carloads of backwoods demon fanciers from the roof of a speeding camper.

"You been watching this all day?"

Kasabian talks between mouthfuls of food.

"No. Before that it was *Shout at the Devil*, only there wasn't any devil in it."

"No. That's a war movie."

"Why doesn't it say that on the box? 'Warning: Lee Marvin might look pissed off, but he's not the devil. There's not one fucking devil in this thing.'"

"Watch what you want, but promise me that I'm never going to ever come in here and find you spanking yourself to *The Devil in Miss Jones*."

"You're a scream, Milton Berle. Now I'm not going to tell you the good news."

"What good news?"

Kasabian takes a last bite of tamale and lets it fall into the bucket. Then he takes it and the Styrofoam container to the end of the table and waits. I haul my ass up off the bed and step on the trash-can pedal. When it opens, he tosses in the Styrofoam and upends the bucket into the can.

"What good news?"

Kasabian goes back to where he'd been working, leans over the table, and sets the bucket underneath, next to the minifridge. Then he finally looks at me.

"You have an actual job. Starting tonight. Something a lot better than stepping on bugs for the Wells."

"I've already got a job tonight. Straight consulting for the Vigil. No killing."

"When are you supposed to do it?"

"Around three? Why?"

"Good. You'll probably be done by then."

"Done doing what?"

He smiles at me exactly the way you don't want a dead man to smile at you.

"The big man is in town. He wants to see you tonight at the Chateau Marmont."

Damn. I finish my drink.

"What's Lucifer doing in L.A.?"

"What do I know? I'm just the answering machine."

"And snitch."

"That, too. He knows every time you jerk off. Unfortunately, so do I. You really need to get a girlfriend."

"What time am I supposed to be there?"

"Eleven. And be on time. He hates late. It's a real thing with him."

"Christ. I don't even have a jacket anymore. I need to get cleaned up."

"Don't freak out, man. You've got hours. This is a good thing. We need the money. Doing the deed for the Vigil tonight and picking up some new work from Mr. D might just let us keep the lights on for another month."

I go into the bathroom, close and lock the door. I've never been a shy boy until recently.

I peel the *Evil Dead* shirt off over my black shoulder. The pink flesh under the peeling black skin looks like the worst sunburn since Hiroshima. I kick off my boots and jeans, and check myself in the mirror.

A pretty sight, I am not. I turn the light on over the sink and lean close to the mirror, turn my head from side to side. The thousand tiny cuts from the flying glass at the theater are mostly gone. I tilt my head forward and back. Run my hands over my face and neck, looking at the shadows of the lines and creases from my neck to my forehead, feeling familiar contours.

Maybe not so familiar.

I felt the changes before, but over the last month they're undeniable.

I'm pretty sure my scars are healing.

The one thing I brought back from Hell that I wanted. The one thing I counted on. I spent eleven years and shed a thousand pounds of blood, flesh, and bone to grow my armor, and after six months of living in the light, I'm losing it.

I hate this place.

Hell is simple. There are no friends, just an ever-shifting series of allies and enemies. There's no pity, loyalty, or rest. Hell is twenty-four-hour party people, and the buddy you shared a foxhole with yesterday is a head on the end of a stick today, letting everyone in shouting distance know, "Abandon all hope ye who piss me off."

Back here in the world it's all soft, fish-belly white, "normal" people with jelly for backbones and not even the basic kill-or-be-killed honor of the arena. The L.A. sky doesn't turn brown because of smog. It's the metric tons of shit coming out of people's mouths every time they open them to talk. Know the old joke, "How do you know when a lawyer is lying?" "He's moving his lips." Up here, everyone is Perry Mason.

Little by little, I've been preparing for this moment, when I couldn't lie to myself anymore.

I upgraded my guns. Easy.

Before I got my ass kicked by malt-liquor-swilling teeny-boppers this afternoon, my new working policy has been to duck when I see bullets, knives, and/or two-by-fours coming at me.

I've been shifting back more to hoodoo and hexes and relying less on muscle. It isn't as fun, but so far, the change has helped me keep my internal organs internal, where they fit better and don't attract flies.

A scalding shower helps to scrub off Eleanor and Ziggy Stardust. With an old hand towel, I scrape off as much of the burned skin as I can.

I even shave. It's a good, mindless activity and I'm sure the boss will appreciate me looking like I live indoors when I go to his hotel.

I wish I hadn't given Wells that body armor back after the shoot-out at Avila. The next time I'm at the Vigil's playhouse, I'm going to have to steal some.

Of course, to wear armor in the street, I'm going to need a new jacket. But not now. Not this second.

I go back into the bedroom with a towel around my waist, leaving my clothes on the bathroom floor. The dead girl's ash sifts onto the tiles. Except for the boots, I doubt that I'll ever wear those clothes again.

The bedroom reeks of cigarettes, whiskey, and tamales. I crack open a window.

Kasabian is back working at the computer.

"Careful, you're going to make L.A. smell funny."

Walking back to the bed I feel dizzy. All of a sudden I'm very tired. I shove the weapons to one side of the mattress, lie down, and pour a little bit of Jack.

"Do me a favor and watch that with headphones. I need to lie down for an hour."

"No problem."

Kasabian takes a set of earbuds, plugs them in, and the movie sound cuts out. He takes another beer from the mini-fridge and pops off the top.

"Before you zone out, have you heard anything about Mason?"

Ever since he became Lucifer's conduit to Hell, Kasabian has learned to overhear and "accidentally" stumble on a lot of information he's not supposed to have. He's Lucifer's personal ghost, so he doesn't really exist Downtown. Even Hellions can tell the truth when they think no one is listening.

He says, "Not much. He's in deep with some of the boss's old generals. Lucifer's original bunch. Abaddon. Baphomet. Mammon. They're trying to recruit the younger officers for a full-on revolution. But I haven't heard anything from Mason himself. He's pretty well insulated. He's the man with the plan, so they're keeping him out of harm's way."

"Is that the truth?"

Kasabian sets down his beer and looks at me.

"I wouldn't lie to you about Mason. I want him as dead as spats."

"Okay."

"Get some sleep. You want to look good for the cotillion."

"I'll save you a slow dance."

"Just keep your hands off my ass."

"What ass?"

THERE'S THIS GUILTY dream I have. Been having it on and off for six months, since right after I dropped Alice's ashes in the ocean.

We're in the apartment smoking and talking. *The Third Man* is playing on TV, but the sound is off. A desperate Harry Lime runs through the sewers under Vienna. What I hate about the dream is that I can't tell if I'm remembering something that happened or inventing something. A confession or apology to the ghost that lives in my head.

"I blew up at a junkie on the street today. He just bumped into me. He smelled like piss and I wanted to strangle him and I almost did."

"Your father beat the shit out of you. Everyone who's been abused has those thoughts."

Alice is pretty forgiving when I get like this. She's a better human than me in almost every way possible. I don't know if I could be with someone whose main topics of conversations were movies and who I wanted to kill today.

"You need to get away from Mason and those others. They're no good for you," she says.

"You're right. But I've already blown off the Sub Rosa world. If I walk from the Circle, what am I? Should I pretend I don't have power? That was my whole childhood. Hiding so people wouldn't know I was what my granddad called an 'odd case.'"

"You're not an odd case."

"What am I?"

"You're my odd case."

"I'll tell you a secret. Mason's an odd case, too, but he doesn't care. I admire the hell out of him for that."

Alice rolls her eyes like she's a silent-movie star.

"Put a dress on, drama queen. Admiring anything about him is kind of fucked up."

"It's most definitely fucked up. But it's true. He's relentless. He's a force of nature. And he's always going to be just a little better than me. You should see the old books he's collected. Half of them are in Latin and Greek. He knows magic I've never even heard of."

"I thought you didn't need those things, all the books and objects he uses. You can pull magic out of the air."

"Maybe. Maybe that's not enough."

"From what I've seen and heard he's jealous of what you can do, which means you're doing fine."

"He says he can invoke an angel."

"Why would he want to do that?"

"To gain secret knowledge. Learn how the universe runs behind the scenes. And to prove he can. He says he's talked to demons, too."

"Now, that's just bullshit."

"Probably."

"Is that where all this is coming from? Demon and angel envy?"

"I can't help it. The sheer balls to say it is something. And if he can do it, I don't know. He'll be my hero and I'll have to put up a poster of him, like Bruce Lee over my bed back home."

"I hope you like this couch 'cause you're talking yourself into sleeping here tonight."

"Mason says he's making a deal with some kind of demons to get even more power."

"I don't believe in angels and devils."

"Why not?"

"I was raised Catholic."

She stubs out her cigarette and lights another. She was in a Robert Smith mood before I pissed her off, so she's smoking cloves. The apartment smells like a junior high girls' bathroom.

"He's Beverly Hills hoodoo. Going to be big in the Sub Rosa. He plans ahead. I skate by."

"So? If Mason's your big guy crush, be more like him and make some plans."

I smoke for a minute and watch Joseph Cotton following Harry Lime's girlfriend on the road from his grave.

"You're right. I can't just wing it for the rest of my life. Time to turn over a new leaf. I'll start planning ahead tomorrow. Or the day after."

"Or the day after that."

"Maybe next week."

"You're better than Mason and you can read people really well. If he starts waving his dick around and wants a Dodge City gris-gris shoot-out, you'll see it coming a mile away and kick his ass."

"Maybe I ought to get some of my own demons."

"Next week. Or the week after."

"Yeah. There's always time, right?"

IT TOOK ME months to start thinking of the apartment as Vidocq's and not mine and Alice's. François-Eugène Vidocq is my oldest friend. He's two hundred years old and French, but don't hold that against him. I'm glad he took the place after Alice died. Six months in, the apartment is so transformed that I can't find a shred of my or Alice's life there. It was strange the first time I saw it that way. Allegra told me that in ancient Egypt, when the new pharaoh smashed the statues and hieroglyphs of the old one, it wasn't just good old-fashioned hooligan fun. The new pharaoh was trying to wipe the old one out of existence, erase him from the universe. To the Egyptians, no images meant no person. That's how it was when I first walked in. I felt erased. Now it's a relief not to be reminded of my old life every time I go over.

Vidocq, with Allegra's help, has turned the place into the Library of Alexandria, only French, with a schmear of L.A. art school punk. On a floor-to-ceiling bookshelf sits the foot-high three-thousand-year-old statue of Bast that Vidocq stole from an aristocratic bastard back in France. Next to Bast, Allegra has propped a pink Hello Kitty doll with tentacles. Hello Cthulhu.

The rest of the place is stacks of old manuscripts, crystals, weird scientific instruments, potions, herbs, and the gear to cut, cook, and mix them. Merlin's workshop with a big flat-screen TV and stacks of movies Allegra brings home from the Max Overdrive. There's porn stashed under the sofa, but they don't know I know about that. I think they watch it together.

"Where did Vidocq say he was going?"

"Out for mazarine ice."

"Sounds like wine cooler. What is it?"

"When he gets back, he can tell us both."

When I met Allegra her head was shaved smooth. Now she's letting it grow out short and shaggy. It suits her. It's pretty.

My shirt is off as she smears green jasmine-smelling paste on my burned shoulder with her hand. Somewhere in L.A. there's some poor guy who dreams about having a pretty girl rub paste on him, but none of the girls he knows will do it. Here I am taking his turn at bat and not even appreciating it.

"Does this hurt?"

"It's fine."

"That's not what I asked."

"Nurse, some psycho is making mud pies on my blisters with her hairy meat hooks and it hurts."

"That's more like it, baby boy. Knowing when I'm hurting you and not hurting is how I get better at this."

"You're doing fine. I'm a happy guinea pig."

Allegra sets down the jar and uses the lid to rub the excess paste from her hand.

"Why is it you come to me these days instead of Kinski? I'm not complaining. Patching you up is a great crash course in the whole healing thing."

"You're good at it, too. When people find out, you'll steal all of the doc's business."

She puts a couple of wide red leaves on top of the paste and wraps my arm in gauze, then uses white medical tape to hold the gauze in place.

I put my shirt back on. The arm still hurts, but it's definitely better.

"As for Kinski, I don't need any more neurotic angels

in my life. Aelita wants to mount my head on a wall like a stuffed trout and Kinski is in his own remake of *Earth Girls Are Easy*."

"Avoiding Kinski doesn't have anything to do with Candy?"

"You're the second person who's asked me about her today."

"You should call her."

"Candy doesn't factor into anything. And I have called. She doesn't answer the phone anymore. It was only Kinski for a while. Now it's no one. I haven't talked to either of them in weeks."

"You only come over here anymore when you're bleeding. You don't talk to Eugène. Kinski is gone. You've been avoiding everyone who cares about you. All you do is lock yourself up with Kasabian, drink, and drive each other crazy. Speaking as your doctor, you've got serious issues. You're like those old guys you see at diners, staring at the same cup of coffee all afternoon, just sitting around waiting to die."

"Sitting around? Tell that to my burns."

"That's not what I mean. You came back to get the people who hurt you and Alice and you did it. Great. Now you need to find the next thing you're going to do with your life."

"Like learn the flute or maybe save the whales?"

"You should grow up, clean up, and treat yourself like a decent person."

"I'm pretty sure I'm not either of those things."

"Says who?"

"God. At least everyone who works for Him."

Allegra looks past me into space, thinking.

"If I gave you some Saint-John's-wort, would you take it? It might help your mood."

"Give it to Kasabian. He's the shut-in."

Allegra pulls me over to the window and examines me under the light.

"Do you think your face is getting worse?"

"Define 'worse.'"

"Are the changes becoming more noticeable?"

"I know what I think. Tell me what you think."

She nods.

"It's worse. Your old scars are healing and your new cuts aren't disappearing like they used to. You still heal fast, just not ridiculously fast."

"Can you stop it?"

"Leave it to you to ask for the opposite of everything I've been learning for the last six months."

"I need my scars. Come on, if you can fix something you should be able to break it, too, right?"

"I can beat the shit out of you with a claw hammer. That'd be easier than working up a scar potion."

"What about something that'll just stop the healing where it is?"

"I don't know about that."

The door opens as Allegra is talking.

"But I do," says Vidocq.

He comes in with a paper bag full of what looks like weeds, bugs, and most of the animal parts the dog food company rejected. He holds up a jar full of turquoise liquid.

"Blue amber."

He hands the jar to Allegra, who gets up and gives him a peck on the cheek.

"That's mazarine ice?"

"*Oui*. If you look in *The Enochocian Treatise*, the large gray book by the old alembic, you'll find notes on the Cup-bearer's elixir. Take the amber and start gathering the other ingredients."

"That will bring my scars back?"

"No, but we might be able to halt the healing. The Cup-bearer brewed and served the gods the elixir that gave them eternal life, keeping them as they were forever. Her elixir doesn't cure; it holds illness and infection in place. Teutonic knights brought it back from the Holy Lands during the Crusades for comrades who had contracted leprosy. I suspect that if it will stop the spread of a disease, I can make it hold your scars where they are."

"But you don't know."

"How could I? Only *un homme fou* asks for a way to stop healing."

"*Fou* me up, man. Give me skin like rhino hide. Make me look like the Elephant Man."

"It might take some time to get it right, but we'll see what we can do."

Vidocq and Allegra gather plants and potions, cutters and crushers, on the worktable. They don't have to talk much. Just whisper a word or two to let the other one know what they need. They're a nice team. Batman and Robin, but without the rough-trade undertones. For a second, I really hate their guts. I could have been like that with the right partner, but I'm stuck with the Beast That Wouldn't

Shut Up. I wonder how smooth these two would be after a week of Kasabian screaming for porn and cigarettes. I should bring him over for a family dinner. Vidocq must have a ball gag around here somewhere.

Damn. What a childish little prick I am. There they are, working to save my ass, and all I can do is whine about poor, poor pitiful me. I need to go kill something real, not snuff dead cheerleaders, but something alive and nasty, something that deserves it.

"It's ironic, isn't it?"

I look up into Vidocq's eyes.

"You spent all those years in Hell fighting to stay alive, becoming injured and earning your scars. Then you come back home in hopes of destroying both your enemies and yourself, but instead you find yourself healing and becoming your old self again."

I get up and glance at my phone. There's still time to make a couple of stops before I have to be at the Chateau.

"Fuck my old self. My old self got his life stolen by morons and the person he cared about most killed. If I start turning into that asshole again, I'll peel these scars off myself and put a shotgun to my forehead."

"But how do you really feel?" asks Allegra.

"Thanks for fixing me up. I'll see you later."

"Where are you going?"

"I've got to buy a prom dress."

I MAKE A quick stop at the Bamboo House of Dolls. You don't want to play into the "do me a favor, I'm a rock star" thing too often, but when you're being followed around because you're the celebrity killer of the month, why not use it occasionally, like when you need a human in the paranormal biz and you don't have time to screw around?

Mediums, exorcists, and sin eaters at Bamboo House aren't the big-money kind, so most of them have to do odd jobs to stay afloat. When you've been career-counseling ghosts all night, it's hard to answer phones or sling lattes for yuppies all day. Most human paranormals tend to dabble in things like gambling, sex work, and cream-puff crime. I only have to ask a couple of people to find a well-stocked thief. He sells me a new leather sport jacket and a rifle frock coat for a hundred, which even by booster standards is cheap. Of course, now he can tell his clients that he sells to Sandman Slim and jack up his prices. Let the circle of celebrity be unbroken. Amen.

There's still time to kill before I have to head over to Chateau Marmont and I'm restless. I haven't stolen a car in a month. All death and no play makes Stark a dull boy.

Hollywood Boulevard is long and the side streets aren't always well lit. You'd be surprised how cheap rich people can be when it comes to parking. They'd rather leave a half-million-dollar Lamborghini in a drugstore parking lot after hours than pay a valet fifteen bucks. Their car insurance payments are what most people put out for a mortgage, and they pay them for the privilege of being stupid, so they can leave their car on the street alone and unprotected, like a four-wheel Red Riding Hood waiting for a wolf like me. I'm doing people like that a favor when I take their cars. Every time stupid rich people get ripped off, it makes them feel better about hating poor people. All they did was leave the equivalent of a big pile of cash by a parking meter, and when they came back, they were horrified to find it was gone. Leaving their stuff out for people to steal proves to them that people want to steal their stuff. Fear is like curling up under a warm blanket for some people, especially the rich.

Something evil and full of testosterone must be smiling down on me tonight. About half a block from Sunset on Cahuenga Boulevard, parked right out in the street like Grandma's Camry, is a silver Bugatti Veyron 16.4. An easy two million dollars in precision engineering and eyeball kicks. If Hugh Hefner designed the Space Shuttle, it would look like the Veyron. Luke Skywalker would be conceived in the backseat of this car, if it had a backseat.

The Veyron is stuffed with more tech than a particle accelerator, so the black blade won't get me through the electronic lock without alerting every screaming bit of it. Fortunately, this isn't the first time the genius who owns the car has left it out in the open. A thin layer of dust covers the top. Just enough for me to draw in. I face west and move my finger slowly over the swept-back plastic roof, trying not to trip the alarm. I finish with a counterclockwise twist on Murmur's sigil. Murmur is a big-mouth Hellion prick with a voice like a 747 engine, but when you reverse his name, you can hear a pin drop from a mile away. When I'm done, I give the car a good shove. It rocks for a second, the lights flutter as the alarm tries to activate, but it gives up and dies. I slip inside through a shadow, jam the black blade into the ignition, and start it up. There's something very satisfying about stabbing two million dollars in the heart.

Murmur's silence fills the car inside and out. My brain starts to untangle after a long, weird day.

Which is good and bad. It leaves me asking the big question I need answered: Why is Lucifer in L.A.? There's nothing I've picked up from Kasabian that gives me a clue, and he can't lie as well as a five-year-old. Have I done anything to piss Lucifer off or make him especially happy lately? Not that I know of. I haven't done anything for him at all except take his cash. His retainer checks are a decent amount of money, and if I didn't piss it all away on the big black money pit that is Max Overdrive, I'd be doing all right. If I was a regular desk monkey with a regular apartment and a used Honda Civic, I'd be living pretty well. But I like my little tree fort. Any more room and I'd get lost. Vidocq would find me a week later, starving and hallucinating in the breakfast nook. Max Overdrive is all I need or want. There's a bed, a closet, a bathroom, and a million movies downstairs. I didn't crawl out of Hell to hit the pillow sales at Bed, Bath & Beyond. I have a hard enough time keeping clothes for more than a week.

So, what the hell does Lucifer want? I don't have my gun or the na'at with me, which is probably just as well. I have the black knife and the stone Lucifer gave me the last time we saw each other. I tested it. I've thrown every kind of magic I can think of at it and it seems to just be a rock. I don't know why I carry the damned thing around. Superstition, maybe. When the devil tells you you might need something someday, I figure it pays to listen. Between the rock, Azazel's knife, the na'at, Mason's lighter, and Kasabian's head, I'm starting to feel like a Gnostic junkyard.

As I cruise the streets, my mind wanders. Never a good idea. An image of Alice tries to form in my brain, but I concentrate on the lights, the billboards, and the other cars and it goes away. I spend a fair amount of time and energy not thinking about Alice these days. On the other hand, I think about Mason all the time. I know Kasabian knows more about Mason than he's telling me. I'd love to get some alone time with the Daimonion Codex, but I'm not willing to get my head cut off for the privilege.

THE KISSI I don't think about much, but I dream about them. Their vinegar reek chokes me while their fingers dig around inside my chest like bony worms.

I PUSH A recessed sci-fi button on the armrest and one of the Veyron's windows slides down silently, like a tinted ghost. I turn off Hollywood Boulevard onto Sunset, go about half a block, and flip a James Bond U-turn in the middle of the street. Kick the Veyron back into gear and burn rubber to the little strip mall where Doc Kinski's clinic is located. The Veyron bottoms out as I turn into the parking lot. A couple of local geniuses have broken into the doc's office and are carrying out armloads of junk. Nice timing. I'm just in the mood to hit someone.

I throw open the door and come around the car looking for which one to smack first and all the fun goes out of it. It isn't thieves after all. It's Kinski and Candy. They're loading boxes of scrolls and the doc's strange medicines and elixirs. They're as surprised to see me as I am seeing them. We all just stand there looking at each other for a minute like kids caught with their hands in the cookie jar. I threw a perfectly good cigarette out the window for this. The doc hands a box to Candy. She keeps loading while he comes over to talk to me.

"Nice to see you, doc. I don't suppose you got any of the like fifty messages I left you? With most people I'd stop calling, but I used to think we were friends. Then after a while I kept calling because I was plain pissed off and thought I'd spread the joy."

"Things have been a little crazy. Sorry. We're doing a lot of work away from the clinic."

"So I noticed."

Candy is carrying smaller and smaller boxes one at a time to the car so she doesn't have to come over. I give her a big talk-show smile.

"Hi. How are you?"

She stops loading for a second, but stays by the rear of the car.

"Okay. How have you been?"

"Getting my arm about burned off and the rest of me beat to shit by vampires. I was hoping maybe one of you would return my call and help me out with that since that's what I thought you did for a living. Don't worry, though. I got some Bactine."

"Problem solved, then," says Kinski.

"I hope you're doing some superfine doctoring wherever it is you've been going. You better have figured out how to cure cancer with ice cream or something 'cause your reputation is going to shit around here."

Kinski takes a step closer, speaking quietly.

"There's a lot going on in the world that doesn't have anything to do with you."

"What does that mean?"

"It means you're always going to get burned up. Or your ass kicked by vampires. Sinatra sings 'My Way' and you crack your ribs. You're a walking disaster area and I can't fix that for you."

"Thanks all to hell, doc. You're a real chip off the Hippocratic oath. I'd ask you for a referral to another doctor but L.A. is full of assholes, so it shouldn't be hard to find one."

"You want some advice? Start stealing ambulances instead of flashy cars. Allegra can take care of you until we get back. That's all I can do for you right now."

"Where is it you need to be so fast? Are you two okay?"

"Candy and I need to be elsewhere. We need to be there soon, and standing here talking to you isn't getting us any closer."

Kinski goes to his car and Candy gets inside. I walk around to the passenger side and look in the window at her. She looks at me, away, and then back. There's something in her eyes that I can't quite figure out. It's more than being uncomfortable about when we kissed at Avila, but I can't tell what. Did she fall off the wagon again and kill someone?

Kinski starts the car and guns the engine. He takes the brake off, and I step out of the way so he can line up the car for the street. I'm getting back in the Veyron when I hear a car door open and slam shut. A second later Candy is next to me. She grabs me around the neck.

"I miss you, but we have to go. Things will be okay soon. You'll see."

She pecks me on the lips, turns, and gets back in the car. The doc steers them out onto Sunset, where they disappear into traffic.

THE CHATEAU MARMOT is a giant white castle on a green hill and it looms over Sunset like it fell out of a passing UFO. It fits in with the surrounding city with all the subtlety of a rat on a birthday cake. Make that a French rat. The place is a château, after all.

When the parking attendant sees the Bugatti, he mistakes me for someone he should care about and rushes over. His interest lasts for maybe a second, the exact amount of time it takes me to step out of the car. People have cash registers for eyes at places like this. By the time my feet are on the ground, he's totaled up exactly how much my clothes and haircut are worth and I've come up short. Still, I'm driving a two-million-dollar car, so I might be an eccentric foreign director who's just flown in for some meetings and sodomy, which means he can't quite work up the nerve to shoo me away like a stray dog that just crapped in the pope's big hat.

"Good evening, sir."

"What time do you have?"

He checks his watch.

"Ten to eleven."

"Thanks."

He tears a numbered parking tag in half, hands me half, and sets the other half on the Bugatti's dashboard.

"Are you staying at the hotel?"

"No. Meeting a friend."

"That will be twenty dollars, sir."

I tear up the parking tag and drop the pieces on the ground.

"I've got a better idea. Keep the car."

"Sir?"

He wants to come after me, but other cars are arriving, so he drives the Bugatti into the garage.

Inside, I go the front desk and it hits me that I don't have a room number or any idea who to ask for. Point for Kasabian.

"Good evening, sir. How can I help you?"

The desk clerk looks like Montgomery Clift and is better dressed than the president. He's smiling at me, but his pupils are dilating like he thinks I'm going to start stealing furniture from the lobby. I stashed the leather jacket in the Room of Thirteen Doors before coming over and am wearing the rifle coat. I thought it looked classier and more formal, but maybe I was wrong.

"A friend of mine is staying here, but I don't have his room number."

"Of course. What's your friend's name?"

"I don't know."

"Excuse me?"

"He's not going to give his real name and I don't know what name he's using. He has a lot of them."

The clerk raises his eyebrows a little. Now he has an excuse to release his inner snotty creep.

"Well, I'm not sure what I can do about that. You and your friend should probably have dealt with that in advance. Are you even sure he's here? We specialize in a fairly exclusive clientele."

"He'll be in your penthouse. The biggest one you have."

The clerk smiles like I'm a bug and he's deciding whether to step on me or hose me down with Raid.

"Unless your friend is a Saudi prince with an entourage of thirty-five, I'm afraid you're mistaken."

"Check your register again. I know he's here, Maybe the prince checked out."

"The prince's rooms are booked through the summer, so, no, there's no mistake."

I get out my phone and dial the direct line to my room above Max Overdrive. I know Kasabian is there, but he doesn't answer. He knows what time it is and he's probably dancing a centipede jig and laughing at me as the phone rings and rings. I put the phone back in my pocket. The clerk is looking at me. His expression hasn't changed. What I want to do is punch a hole in the front of the desk, reach through, grab his balls, and make him sing *The Mickey Mouse Club* song. But these days, I'm working on the theory that killing everyone I don't like might be counterproductive. I'm learning to use my indoor voice like a big boy, so I smile back at the clerk.

"Are you sure you don't have another penthouse lying around here somewhere? Some off-the-books place you keep for special guests?"

"No, I'm sure we don't have anything like that. And without a name or a room number, I need to ask you to leave the hotel."

"Is needing to ask me to leave the same as telling me to leave? That's a really confusing sentence."

"Please, sir. I don't want to have to call security."

No, you don't want to call them because then I'd have to make you into a sock puppet.

"Would you like me to tell your fortune?"

"Excuse me?"

I pick up a pen from the counter.

"Give me your hand a minute."

He tries to pull both of his hands away, but I'm faster by a mile and get a death grip on his right wrist. His heart is pumping as fast as the Bugatti's engine. He wants to yell for security, but he can't even open his mouth. I don't want the poor guy to stroke out, so I draw a single Hellion character on the palm of his hand, and then ball it closed. It's a mind trick I saw Azazel use a few times on his dumber enemies. It's like sticking the magic word in a golem's mouth. The clerk's eyes glaze over and he stares past me at nothing in particular.

"Can you hear me, hotshot?"

He smiles at me. It's nice this time. Like he's a human talking to another human.

"Yes, of course. How can I help you?"

"I need you to tell me the names of your extra-special guests. Not princes or movie stars. Your really special guests."

He looks away and taps something into the computer terminal behind the desk.

"We only have one guest who sounds like the kind of person you're looking for. A Mr. Macheath."

Another point for Kasabian. Alice loved *The Threepenny Opera* and I played the 1930s German version at the store a few times when I was extra drunk and maudlin. Kasabian must have told Lucifer. I wonder what else I let slip that he could pass on to his boss.

"Yeah, that'll be him. Where's his room?"

"That particular room isn't a where. It's a when."

"Say that again, but use smaller words."

The clerk laughs a little. I might have to leave him like this.

"You take the elevator to the top floor. On the east wall you'll see a very beautiful old grandfather clock. Open the cabinet where the pendulum swings and hold it to one side. Count to three and step into the cabinet."

"Inside the grandfather clock?"

"Of course, you're not actually stepping into the clock, but through it. A kind of time membrane that opens into the room. I don't know if the room is forward or backward in time, but I'm sure it's one of those."

"I'll try it. Thanks."

"Thank you. And Mr. Macheath."

"How are you feeling right now?"

"Wonderful, sir. Thank you for asking."

"Yeah, that's going to wear off in a while, so enjoy it while it lasts."

"Thank you. I will."

I go to the elevator and get out on the top floor. The grandfather clock is where he said it would be. I don't pick up any hoodoo from it, so I open the front and grab the pendulum.

One. Two. Three.

I push the pendulum to the side and step through.

And come out in a room so big, so stuffed with golden

statues, marble, and antiques, that Caligula would think it's tacky.

"You're late."

Lucifer stands by a marble pillar as big around as a redwood. A tailor is marking his suit with chalk, doing a final fitting.

"I would have been here early if you and Kasabian weren't playing name games with me."

"You should have noticed that little detail before or factored in more time to work it out when you arrived."

"Kas said you hated it when people were late."

"I hate when people I pay aren't doing their best work. You're a smarter boy than you act, Jimmy. You need to start taking things more seriously."

"I'm taking this room seriously. This is what Liberace's nightmares must have looked like."

Lucifer turns around and looks at me. He's an angel, so I can't read him at all.

He tilts his head slightly and says, "Love the coat. Are you on your way to the O.K. Corral?"

I nod.

"Yeah, it's a little Doc Holliday, but it's called a rifle coat for a reason. I can hide a double-barreled shotgun under here. Or do you want me in slippers and a sweater vest, fighting off your enemies with a hot cocoa?"

"Not now, but when you come back down below, I hope you'll fight that way in the arena."

"Is that why you're here? To take me back?"

He frowns.

"No, no. That was just a terrible joke. Forgive me."

He turns to the tailor.

"We're done for tonight."

The tailor gives him a small bow and helps Lucifer take off the half-finished jacket and pants. Suddenly I'm alone in a room with the Prince of Darkness in his underwear. I wouldn't have pegged him for a boxers guy.

Actually, he's still wearing a silk maroon shirt and he slips on a pair of pressed black slacks folded over the back of a chair. I can't get into Lucifer's mood or mind the way I can with humans, but I can see him move. As he pulls on pants, he makes the tiniest imaginable move with his shoulders. He flinches, almost like he's in pain. I look over at a statue of a headless woman with wings before he turns around.

"Would you like a drink?"

I don't turn right away.

"That sounds great."

"I have some Aqua Regia, but I hear that's not such a rare thing for you these days."

"No. Are you the one sending it up?"

"Don't be stupid. I pay you enough to take care of your own vices. I'd like to know who is importing the stuff."

"You don't know?"

"I have a fairly full plate at the moment what with your friend Mason trying to turn my armies against me. Or hadn't you heard?"

"Tell the truth, the revolution was already going when he got there. He just jumped on the crazy train."

"And I have you to thank for that."

"I didn't plan it, if that's what you're thinking."

"I would never accuse you of planning things. Come over and sit down."

I follow him to an area where chairs and sofas are grouped together, facing one another. I sit on a leather easy chair. It's the most comfortable piece of furniture in the universe. My ass wants to divorce me and marry it.

"So, Jimmy, killed anyone interesting lately?"

"No. The ones I killed today were already dead and just needed reminding."

"I'm sure they appreciated that."

"No one complained."

"What flavor of undead were they?"

"Vampires."

"Young ones? God, I hate them."

Lucifer lights up a Malediction. I know he wants me to ask for one, so I don't.

"Why are you up here? Shouldn't you be Downtown spanking the guilty and slaughtering your generals? Or are you taking early retirement so you can spend more time with the grandkids?"

"Nothing so dramatic. I'm in town doing some consulting work."

"What kind?"

"Why does anyone come to L.A.?"

"To kill people."

"No, that's just you. Normal people come here to get into the movies."

"You're in a movie?"

"Of course not. I'm here as a technical adviser. A producer friend is in preproduction for a big-budget film of my life story."

"Please tell me you're bringing Ed Wood back from the dead to direct it."

"This is strictly an A-list project. I'm disappointed, Jimmy. I thought you'd be more excited. You love movies."

"Why do you need a biopic? About half the movies ever made are horror flicks and aren't all horror flicks really about you? So, you already have about ten thousand movies."

"But those are metaphorical. Even the ones where I'm depicted, it's never really me. This will be the real thing. The true story. My side of the story."

"Don't take this the wrong way, but who fucking cares? Are there really enough Satanists and girls in striped stockings to pay for a flick like that?"

"It's a prestige picture, Jimmy. Sometimes a studio makes a movie it knows won't show a near-term profit because they know that it's the right thing to do artistically."

"You own the head of the studio, don't you? Someone sold you their soul for fame and power and hot and cold running starlets and this is them paying you off."

"It's only a partial payoff. I still own the soul."

Lucifer goes to a desk and comes back with a framed piece of black velvet, like something a jeweler would have. It's covered with small shiny objects. A pocketknife. A pair of wire-rimmed glasses missing one lens. A pair of Shriner cuff links. A sleeping netsuke cat. He picks up a small gold necklace.

"I take something from everyone whose soul I hold. Not

take. They choose what they want to give me. It's a symbolic act. A physical reminder of our deal. These are trinkets from Hollywood friends."

He holds the gold necklace higher so I can get a good look.

"This is Simon's. Simon Ritchie. The head of the studio. Simon imagines that he's very clever. Very ironic. The necklace belonged to his first wife. It was her First Communion gift. A rosary necklace with a pretty little cross. Of course, she was just a girl when she received it, so at some point she added a gold unicorn charm. A darling thing, though I'm not sure the Church would approve."

"What does he or she get for all this?"

"Simon? He gets a little more time."

Lucifer takes a long drag on the Malediction and puts the necklace back with the other soul souvenirs.

"That's all you people ever want. A little more time in a world that all of you, in your heart of hearts, secretly despise."

"I don't keep it a secret."

"And that's why I like you, Jimmy. We're alike in so many ways. Plus, you're so very good at making things dead. That's what you're going to do for me while I'm here. Not kill so much as prevent a killing, namely mine. You're going to be my bodyguard whenever I'm out in public."

"You're the devil. You gave God a rusty trombone and lived to talk about it. Why would you need a bodyguard?"

"Of course, no one can kill me permanently, but this physical body I inhabit on earth can be injured, even destroyed. Wouldn't it be embarrassing if it turned up riddled with bullets? We don't want that kind of negative buzz just as the production is getting off the ground."

"You need a new PR guy, not a bodyguard."

"All the most famous people travel with private security these days, don't they? You're mine. Sandman Slim by my side, ready to snap necks at a moment's notice. That will be quite a photo op. For both of us."

"That's exactly what I want. More people knowing who I am."

Lucifer laughs.

"Don't worry. The civilian media won't see either of us. This is purely for the benefit of our sort of people."

"The Sub Rosa."

"Exactly."

"Is that who owns the studio?"

"No. It's a civilian gentleman, but most of his staff is Sub Rosa. The studio even has an outreach program, providing unskilled jobs to Lurkers that want to crawl out of the sewers and into the real world."

"Sub Rosas get the corner office and Lurkers get to clean the toilets. Same as it ever was."

"That sounds like class warfare, Jimmy. You're not a socialist, are you?"

"Considering who and what I am . . ."

"An abomination?"

"Right. Considering that most Sub Rosa probably consider me a Lurker, do you really want me around so one of them can say something cute at a party and I have to pry his head off with a shrimp fork?"

Lucifer seems to think for a moment, sets down his drink, and leans forward in his seat. He speaks very quietly.

"Do you think for one second that I would allow any of the walking excrement that infests this world to insult me or anyone in my employ? You might be a natural-born killer, but I specialize in torment that lasts a million years. You think you've seen horrors because you were in the arena. Trust me, you have no idea what real horror looks like or the terrible things I've done to keep my throne. You'll be by my side while I'm in Los Angeles because in this task and in all others, I'm as much your bodyguard as you are mine."

It's moments like this, when Lucifer gets rolling and the words and the intensity start flowing, that I understand how one lone angel convinced a third of Heaven's worker bees to turn the dump over. And that was just the third with the cojones to follow him. I have a feeling that a lot of other angels listened, but were too scared to join the party. If I was some lower-class grease-monkey angel caught in the cross fire of an argument between Lucifer and Aelita—oh wait, I am—I'd probably think twice about giving God the finger and running off to never-never land with Satan and the Lost Boys. But I'd still go.

I want to ask what that part about us being each other's bodyguard means, but when he gets like this, it's scary to ask direct questions, so I go another way.

"What do I have to do as your bodyguard?"

He picks up his drink and relaxes like nothing ever happened.

"Not much. I don't expect any trouble, but all the major celebrities travel with their own security these days. Who better for me to have by my side than Sandman Slim? All you have to do is remember to wear pants and occasionally look menacing. Really, you'll be less my bodyguard and more of a branding opportunity, like Ronald McDonald."

"It sounds better and better all the time."

"You've already taken a lot of my money and you're not in a position to pay it back, so let's not argue the point. You know you're going to take the job. You knew it before you walked in here."

"When do I start?"

"Tomorrow night. Mr. Ritchie, the head of the studio, is throwing me a little welcome party. We'll make our debut then."

"I have something I have to do later tonight."

"I'm not going anywhere tonight, so feel free."

"Does Kasabian know about all this?"

"Why would I tell him my business? His job is to send me information."

"What's he been telling you about me?"

"That you're at loose ends. That you're depressed. That you're drunk much of the time. That ever since you locked up Mason, all you've done is kill things, smoke, and drink. You need to get out more, Jimmy. This will be the perfect job for you. You'll meet lots of exciting new people to hate."

"I hope you're a better salesman when you're buying suckers' souls."

He pours us both more Aqua Regia. When he holds out the pack of Maledictions, I take one and he lights it for me.

"I'm not a salesman. I don't have to be. People offer me

their souls every second of every day. They bring them to my door ready to eat. It's like having pizza delivered."

"You're making me hungry. There any food around here?"

"You want to eat with me? You don't know much mythology, do you? Persephone's story?"

"Who's she?"

"She was abducted by Hades and taken to the Underworld, where she ate a single pomegranate seed. She was able to return home, but for the rest of her life she had to spend half of the year with her husband on earth and half of the year with Hades in the Underworld."

"Was she hungry when she ate the seed?"

"I expect so."

"Then what's the problem? I once ate some greasy scrambled eggs at a truck stop near Fresno and puked and shit myself for two days. That was six months in Hell right there."

Lucifer picks up a phone next to his chair.

"I'll call room service."

LATER, MY PHONE goes off. It's Wells texting me the address of where I'm supposed to meet him. I go out the *Alice in Wonderland* clock and down to the garage, where top-of-the-line cars are laid out like Christmas morning on repo-man island. There's a white '57 T-bird with a white top. I pop the knife into the ignition, fire it up, and head outside. On my way out of the lot, I nod to the valet I gave the Bugatti to. He raises one arm and gives me an unsure little half wave. He won't be able to keep the Veyron, of course, the cops and insurance company will make sure of that, but I hope he gets to have some fun before he has to ditch it.

I DRIVE EAST along Sunset. Cut south into what the chamber of commerce calls Central City East, but the rest of the universe calls skid row. The corner of Alameda and East Sixth is so boring and anonymous it's amazing it's allowed on maps. Warehouses, metal fences, dusty trucks, and a handful of beat-up trees that look like they're on parole from tree jail. I turn right on Sixth and drive until I find a vacant lot. It's not hard. A half dozen of the Vigil's stealth supervans are parked by the curb, looking just a little out of place. Flying saucers at a rodeo.

The lot isn't one hundred percent vacant. There's a small house in the middle, an overgrown wood-frame shit box that's so swallowed up by weeds, vines, and mold that I can't even tell the original color. It's not much more than a shack. A leftover from the days when L.A. was open enough to have orchards, oil wells, and sheep farms. Not that this place was ever any of those.

Rich Sub Rosas aren't like rich civilians. Civilians wear their wealth on their sleeve. They get flash cars, like the Bugatti. Twenty-thousand-dollar watches that can tell you how long it takes an electron to fart. And big beautiful mansions in the hills, like Avila, far away from God's abandoned children, the flatlanders.

Sub Rosa wealth works on sort of the opposite idea. How secret and invisible can you make yourself, your wealth, and your power? Big-time Sub Rosa families don't live in Westwood, Benedict Canyon, or the hills. They prefer abandoned housing projects and ugly anonymous commercial areas with strip malls or warehouses. If they're lucky or been around long enough, they might have scored themselves an overgrown wood-frame shit box in a vacant lot on skid row. Chances are this house has looked exactly this feral and miserable for the last hundred years. Before that, it was probably a broken-down log cabin.

I park the T-bird across the street and jog over to the house. Just a few streetlights and warehouse security lights. There's nothing else alive. Not a headlight in sight.

There's a tarnished knocker on the door. I use it. A woman opens the door. Another marshal. She's in the female equivalent of Wells's men-in-black chic.

"Evening, ma'am, I'm collecting for UNICEF."

"Stark, right? Get in here. Marshal Wells is waiting."

"And you are?"

"No one you need to know."

She lets me inside. The interior of the place is as rotten and decayed as the outside. She leads me into the kitchen.

"Nice. Defensiveness and moral superiority in two-point-four seconds. A new land speed record."

"Marshal Wells said you liked to talk."

"I'm a people person."

"Is that before or after you cut people's heads off?"

"I only cut off my enemies' heads. I break my friends' hearts."

"So, that's, what, zero hearts broken?"

"The night's still young."

She stops by the door. Where the back porch would be, if it hadn't collapsed back when Columbus took his big cruise.

"Wells is in the study."

"Thanks, Julie."

"How did you know my name is Julie?"

Her heartbeat just spiked. I'm here in the middle of the night and being underpaid because of Wells. I don't need to take it out on her. I smile, trying to look pleasant and reassuring.

"It's nothing. Just a silly trick."

"Don't do it again."

"It'd be a little stupid guessing someone's name twice."

Marshal Julie listens to something coming through her earpiece.

She says "Got it" into her cuff and looks at me.

"Is that your Thunderbird across the street?"

"No."

"But you drove it here."

"Yes."

"You came here in a stolen vehicle?"

"Define 'stolen.' It's not like I'm keeping it."

"I don't suppose you have the keys?"

"You're kidding, right?"

She walks back to the front door, talking to whoever is in her earpiece.

"I need someone to evacuate a red and white Thunderbird coupe from the 6th Street inquiry."

I head out back, pretty sure that Marshal Julie will not be my secret Santa at the Homeland Security Christmas party.

I'VE ALREADY GONE down one rabbit hole tonight at the Chateau, so it's no surprise that the house beyond the porch door has nothing to do with the wreck I entered. The house through the door is a sprawling old-fashioned California mansion. Very western. Almost cowboy. Lots of wood. Two-story-high ceilings. Leather and animal-print furniture right out of an old Rat Pack movie. Massive picture windows look out over the desert and San Gabriel Mountains.

This, the Sub Rosa house hidden inside the other, is crowded with Wells's people. There are at least a dozen forensic agents in the living room alone. They're using a lot of strange gear I've never seen before, more of the Vigil's weird angelic technology. The room is full of agents lost behind flashing lights, on their knees shoving beeping probes under furniture or lost behind transparent floating screens showing weird images of supermagnified carpet fibers.

"Down here, dead man."

It's Wells, yelling to me from the far end of the house. He never gets tired of reminding me that I'm officially dead and off the radar of the cops and most of the government. But only as long as I make nice with the Vigil. It's a good threat. Without them, my life would be a lot more complicated.

I pass another ten agents in the hall on the way to the study and six more in the study. Between agents chattering, vacuums sucking up evidence, and probes flying around checking for aether residue, I can hardly hear my own voice.

"Why the hell do you need so many people, Wells?"

The marshal doesn't look at me. He's staring off at something across the room.

"You do your job and let my people do theirs."

What Wells is looking at is worthy of some top-drawer staring. There's an altar and above it, a six-foot-tall statue of Santa Muerte, a kind of grim reaper parody of the Virgin of Guadalupe. Despite her bony looks, she's someone her believers pray to for protection. I guess whoever owned the statue wasn't very good at it. It looks like half of his blood is sprayed across Saint Death, the altar, and the walls. The rest is in a nice congealed pool of rust-colored Jell-O around what's left of his body. You can't even call what's on the floor a corpse. There isn't enough of it. It looks like he tried to crawl into a jet engine, changed his mind, and tried to crawl out again.

I say, "I think he's dead."

Wells nods, still staring at the slaughter.

"I'll be sure to write that down. Anything else?"

"This was no boating accident."

Wells looks at me like he's a trash compactor and I'm week-old bacon.

"Damn you, boy. A man is dead here and he was one of yours. Sub Rosa. And he died badly. Do you have anything to contribute to our finding out what the hell happened here?"

I want to get closer to the death scene and I have to walk around several agents to do it. Glad I'm not claustrophobic.

The body is lying in pieces scattered inside a strangely modified calling circle. The edges are sharp. It's not a circle. It's a hexagon, a shape only used in dark magic. It looks like at least part of the circle was painted with blood, though it's hard to be sure with pieces of the guy laid out across the floor like a buffet. There are a lot of bones scattered around. Too many to all be his. He probably used them to reinforce the hexagon.

I have to walk all the way around the room to get back to Wells.

"He doesn't stink. How long has he been lying there?"

"At least two days. There's been very little tissue breakdown. No blowfly eggs. Not even rigor mortis in the one elbow joint we found."

"Did you find anything in aether tracings?"

"There's definitely dark magic residue. We're not sure what kind yet."

I go back to the body and stand as close as I can without touching it. Even without trying, I can feel something radiating off the mangled flesh and bones. But I can't tell what. It's ancient and cold. For a minute I wonder if the Kissi could have done it, but there's no vinegar reek. If Wells's crew would quiet down for a goddamn second, it probably wouldn't be hard to figure out. Some of the angel devices are pumping out celestial energy fields, stinking up the aether.

"Can you get these people to quiet the hell down for a minute?"

"This is a priority job. It's a big crew and everybody works. Do some magic, Sandman Slim. You've worked loud rooms before."

I can't get hold of whatever it is that's coming off the body. I touch part of what I think is an arm with the toe of my boot. Turn it over. One of the forensic techs says something.

"Get that machine out of my way so I can work," I say.

I'm not sure exactly how I sounded, but half of Wells's crew suddenly find other parts of the room to work.

Kneeling down, I take a close look at the not-rotting

skin. There are funny marks there. Old ones. He'd tattooed over them, like he was trying to camouflage them. There are marks on the bones, too. New ones.

The altar is a jumble of magic objects. Saints and rosaries. A sephirot stitched together from separate pieces of parchment and linen. Pentagrams and swastikas drawn on Post-its. An old bottle of no-name whiskey. Animal bones. Bowls full of meth, joints, and poppers. Yojimbe bark. *Gray's Anatomy*. And a very nice selection of dildos, gags, butt plugs, nipple clamps, and antique handcuffs.

I drag a chair over to where Wells is standing. The forensic crew is falling in love with me.

"Who is this guy? *Was* this guy?" I ask.

"Enoch Springheel."

"Springheel, like the Springheels?"

"Yep. Supposedly, the first Sub Rosa family in L.A. I guess a couple of hundred years back, when this was mostly Indians and coyotes, they were the cock of the walk. But other families settled here and things sort of fell apart for the Springheels. Lost most of their land. Lost their status. Homeland Security doesn't know why. Neither does the Vigil. I was hoping maybe you knew something."

"When I was a kid, I spent most of my time trying to get away from the Sub Rosa. I know the names, but not much of the family histories."

"What a blessing it is to have you around."

While Wells complains I climb on the chair to get a better view of the room. Whenever I reach out with my mind, the combination of whatever is coming off the body and the Vigil's goddamn machines start making me dizzy. But from up on high something clicks in my brain and the scene falls together like a series of snapshots of things I've seen over the last eleven years.

Who needs nephilim superpowers when you've got the devil's slide projector in your head?

I go back to the body and cut some skin and bone with the black blade. Then I spit on the incisions. That gets their attention.

"Give me some salt."

One of the forensic drones pulls a vial from a potion case and tosses it to me. I sprinkle the salt over where I just spit. Nothing happens. Then there are bubbles. Steam. The saliva begins to boil.

"You know much about demons, Marshal Wells? What they are? How they work?"

"They're elementals. Not like you pixies or Lurkers. Demons are primitives. Like insects. They're pretty much programmed to do a single thing. Killing. Inciting lust. Planting lies."

"They're so dumb because they're fragments of the Angra Om Ya. The old gods. They're powerful but brain-dead crumbs of whatever god they fell from."

"That's blasphemy, boy. There were no gods before God."

"Okay, forget that. Did your team take a look at these marks on the skin? They're teeth marks. Señor Chew Toy could have healed himself, but he didn't. He liked the scars. He just covered them with tattoos to hide his dirty little secret from the other Sub Rosa."

Wells is looking at me now.

"Keep going."

"If you find Enoch Shitheel's head, check his teeth. I bet you'll find he gave himself some of those scars."

"Demon possession?"

"Think simpler. Ever heard of autophagia?"

"No."

"I bet you've never seen any Sub Rosa porn either. You're out of your depth, choirboy. In the books, autophagia is a mental disorder, but Springheel made it into a fetish. He got off on eating himself."

Wells is giving me his disapproving squint, but he's listening. His team edges in closer, not even pretending to work anymore.

"Santa Muerte is death and protection all rolled into one. A gangster Kali. She'd tighten Springheel's jeans."

"Watch your language."

"Fuck you. You brought me in. I'll do this my way."

Pause.

"Keep going."

"The altar is a dark-magic sex shop. All you need is Lucifer's cock ring to have the party of the century. I only mention that because that's what Springheel wanted to do. Party very hard."

I walk over and stand in the hexagon, trying to step around the sticky bits.

"The hexagon with blood and bone calls dark power. Yojimbe mixes in sexual energy, but that's not a big surprise considering all the speed and poppers on the altar. Well, maybe for you. Look at this one side of the hexagon. There's maybe a half-inch gap where the edges don't touch. If this is a protection configuration, it won't work. Whatever Enoch calls will be able to slip in through that hole. That's stupid and it's sloppy. Unless it's deliberate."

"What did Springheel invoke and why did he let it in?"

I step forward to the broken edge of the hexagon.

"He would have been here, near the opening. He's thrown yojimbe around. He's probably been snorting meth and doing his poppers. He starts his spell and he calls up a demon."

"What kind of demon?"

I hold up one of the still-smoking bones with my finger-tips and point to the broken edge.

"An eater. Five hundred years ago, an eater was what you called when you wanted it to look like locusts chewed up on your neighbor's crops or wolves killed their cattle. Enoch wanted something more up close and personal. That's why there's a break in the hexagon. Springheel built himself a cosmic glory hole. He was a Bone Daddy."

Wells is frowning. He really wants me to shut up. I keep going.

"He's got a hard-on for demons. For eaters. Springheel wanted to stick as much of himself as he could get through that glory hole and get it nibbled on by a primordial retard with ten rows of shark teeth. Only something went wrong."

"What?"

"Damned if I know. Let your techs figure it out. Springheel called an eater because that's how he got off. But he fucked up. Broke the circle too wide or made some stupid stoner mistake to completely break the hexagon's protection and got himself eaten."

"You're sure about this sick shit?"

"Who else lived here?"

"No one. He was the last of the Springheels."

"All alone with no one to look over his shoulder. That's a nice setting to work out really elaborate fantasies. There's one other thing you probably ought to check out."

"What's that?"

"If end-of-the-line Enoch was the last member of a house that went from number one to less than zero, getting eaten might not have been a mistake. It could have been a nasty, lonely little suicide. A hard-core player partying one last time as he pisses off this mortal coil."

Wells turns and walks away.

"Enough. How do you live inside your head? I'm not saying you're wrong or that I disagree with your conclusions or that disgusting scenario that you obviously know a lot about. All I'm saying is stop. I don't want to hear any more. You've done your job. My team will finish up. Thank you for your valuable contribution to the investigation. Now please, get the hell out of here. I don't want to look at you for a while."

I've seen Wells screaming crazy, but I don't think I've ever seen him upset. I guess when you're in love with an angel, the idea of someone spending his alone time shoving his cock down demons' throats might be disturbing. Welcome to my world, G-man. I'll show you Hellion hobbies that make Enoch Springheel look like Jiminy Cricket.

I go back to the porch and into the kitchen. Marshal Julie is still alone up front.

When she sees me she asks, "Did you do your job?"

"I just got thrown out. That usually means I did."

"Good for you. I'm sure the marshal is grateful that you came through for him."

"Not really."

"Your car is gone."

"It wasn't my car."

"That's why it's gone. Do you need a ride?"

"Are you offering?"

She gets quiet for a minute. Stares past me over my shoulder.

"What's going on back there? I know it's a murder scene, but I'm supposed to stay up here and guard the doorknobs."

"You're the new kid, right? They give you the worst hours, shit duty, and they short-sheet your halo?"

She almost smiles.

"Something like that."

"Yeah, it's a murder scene. A rotten one, too. Dark magic gone bad. It even got your boss upset."

"Damn. I wish I could see that. You don't know how much I want to be back there."

"Cool your jets, Honey West. Don't be in such a rush to get what's back there stuck in your head. It doesn't come out again."

"I don't care. I need to know what's in rooms like that. I've prepared for it my whole life. Now I'm here, but I'm still missing out."

Scratch a cop, find a pervert.

"Don't worry," I tell her. "L.A.'s not going to run out of psychos anytime soon."

I go outside. The steps crack and crunch beneath my feet. Good special effects.

Marshal Julie says, "You never told me if you wanted a ride."

"Mind if I steal one of your vans?"

This time she does smile.

"Yeah. I kind of do."

"Then I think I'll walk awhile. I can use the air."

I get half a block down Sixth Street before I'm sure that someone is following me. Whoever it is isn't very good at it. The heavy footfalls say it's a he. And he's dragging one of his feet. He kicks and steps on things. For a second I wonder if it's Marshal Julie, but no one from the Vigil would be that amateur hour. I turn around twice, but the street is always empty.

At the corner of South Broadway, I look again. A man stands half lit under a streetlight. His posture is funny, like he needs a back brace but forgot his on the bus. He just stands there. When he tries to turn around, he stumbles on the foot he's been dragging. For a split second, his face is in the light. I swear it's Mason. His face is dead white and gaunt, the skin torn. But then it isn't him. It never was. I don't recognize him. By the time I run over to where the stranger is standing, he's moved back into the dark and disappeared.

Hissing sounds of car tires rolling by on Broadway. Gurgle of water from the sewer at my feet. There's nothing else. I'm the only thing alive on the street. Serves me right for turning down a ride home from a cannibal play party, even if it was with a cop.

I step through a shadow into the Room and stay there

long enough to smoke a cigarette. I'm nowhere in here. I'm outside space and time. The universe crashes around me like cosmic bumper cars. Somewhere out there stars are being born while others flare out, frying planets and whole populations. A few billion here. A few billion there. Lucifer promises some pimply kid ten years at the top of the music charts for his soul. Of course, the kid is too dumb to specify which charts and is about to find himself with number one singles in Mongolia and Uzbekistan. God watches while a bus full of his worshippers spins out on a patch of black ice, flips, and catches fire, burning everyone inside alive.

The universe is a meat grinder and we're just pork in de-signer shoes, keeping busy so we can pretend we're not all headed for the sausage factory. Maybe I've been hallucinat-ing this whole time and there is no Heaven and Hell. Instead of having to choose between God and the devil, maybe our only real choice comes down to link or patty?

When I got back to my room above Max Overdrive, I put Kasabian in the closet where I used to lock him up. I built him a bachelor pad in there. Padded the shelves with cabi-nets where he can keep beer and snacks, along with a bucket where he can slop the remains. There's a computer inside, so he can surf the Web and watch any movies he wants. It's soundproof so I can sleep and not hear if he's watching *Behind the Green Door*. I know I'm going to dream about Springheel's chewed-up carcass tonight and I don't need Kasabian and Marilyn Chambers joining the party.

I DON'T WAKE up until almost two the next day. It took a fair amount of drinking to fall asleep last night. All the pillows are on the floor and the blankets are in a knot by my feet, so I know I dreamed, but I can't remember what about. Kasabian probably knows. He's back over on the table at the PC going through online video catalogs, pretending he doesn't know I'm awake. I think Lucifer gave him a touch of clairvoyance so he can get snapshots of my mind. That's okay. I've been playing a lot more with hexes lately so I don't always have to go for the knife or gun. I have some tricks I've worked up that he doesn't know about yet.

Losing the Bugatti has punched a car-size hole in my heart, so I steal a Corvette from in front of Donut Universe and drive to Vidocq's. Maybe I should start thinking of it as Vidocq and Allegra's. She's always there when I go. I don't think she goes back to her apartment to do anything but change clothes.

I hate Corvettes, so I leave it in front of the most obvious crack house in Vidocq's neighborhood and walk the last few blocks to his place.

Inside, I take the elevator to the third floor and head down the hallway. I can't find my cigarettes, so I stop in the hall to pat myself down. A gray-haired guy in a green windbreaker and worn chinos stops beside me.

"Didn't you used to live here?"

I nod, still patting myself down. If I left the cigarettes in the car, the crackheads have them by now, dammit.

"A long time ago."

"With a girl, right? Pretty. And she kept the place after you left."

Why do I do this to myself? This is what happens every time I try to be a person. I do something normal, like walk in the front door of a building, and the Neighborhood Watch is on me.

"Yeah, she was very pretty."

He gives me a just-between-us-guys half smile.

"What happened, man? She throw you out for doing her sister?"

Sometimes there's nothing worse than the truth. It can be harder and sharper and hurt more than a knife. The truth can clear a room faster than tear gas. The problem with telling the truth is that someone then has something on you that they can use against you. The good part is that you don't have to remember which lie you told who.

"I got dragged to Hell by demons from the dawn of time. While I was down there, I killed monsters and became a hit man for the devil's friends. How have you been?"

The guy's smile curdles. He takes a step back.

"Don't let me catch you hanging around the halls anymore, okay? I'll have to call the manager."

"No problem, Brenda. You have an extra cigarette?"

"My name's Phil."

"You have an extra cigarette, Chet?"

He walks away and gets a good twenty feet before he mumbles "Fuck you," sure I can't hear him.

I knock on Vidocq's door to let him know I'm there and go inside.

"Hi," says Allegra from behind the big cutting table where she and Vidocq prepare their potions. Vidocq is in the kitchen making coffee. He holds up the pot when he sees me.

"Good afternoon. You look like you're still asleep."

"I'm fine, just don't wake my brain. I think it's been drinking."

Allegra walks over with a shit-eating grin on her face.

"No thank you, little girl. I don't want to buy any of your cookies."

Her smile doesn't waver.

"Is it true? Is Lucifer really here in L.A.?"

I look at Vidocq.

"Word travels fast around these parts."

He shrugs.

"We have no secrets."

I turn back to Allegra.

"I spent the evening with a guy in a magic hotel room the size of Texas and decorated like the Vatican, if the Vatican was a whorehouse. I think there's a pretty good chance it was Lucifer."

"You knew him down in Hell, right? What's he like?"

Vidocq brings me a cup of black coffee, holds up his cup in a little toast.

"Girls are obsessed with bad boys, man. How can we compete with the Prince of Darkness?" I ask.

He sits on the worn sofa and shrugs.

"We've already lost the battle. We accept defeat and move along, sadder but wiser."

"Well?" says Allegra.

"What do I know that isn't in the Bible or *Paradise Lost*?"

"Are those right? Are they accurate?"

"Maybe. I don't know. I never read 'em, but they're popular."

She takes away my coffee cup and sets it on the table behind her.

"I want to hear it from you. Tell me what he's like."

"He's exactly what you think he is. He's good-looking, smart, and the scariest son of a bitch you can possibly imagine. He purrs like a cat one minute, and the next, he's Lex Luthor with a migraine. He's David Bowie, Charlie Manson, and Einstein all rolled into one."

"That sounds pretty hot."

"Of course he's hot. That's his job. He's the guy you meet at a party that you take home and fuck even though every sensible part of your brain is screaming at you not to."

"What's so scary about him?"

"He's the devil."

"I mean have you ever seen him do any devil stuff. Anything really evil?"

"I live with a dead man's talking head. I'd say that's pretty fucked up."

She hands me back my coffee, but is clearly not satisfied.

"That's not what I mean."

"I've never seen him turn a city into salt or make it rain blood. He doesn't do that kind of thing. Why should he? We do most of the shitty stuff in this world. He can just sit back and watch us like HBO."

I take a long swig of my coffee. It burns my tongue and throat all the way down. It feels good and tastes better. Allegra walks to the window and crooks her head at me.

"Come over here."

I set down the coffee and go to her.

She holds my face in her hands, moving my head back and forth, looking me over in the sunlight.

"Your cuts have all healed, which is pretty normal for you."

"Why's this happening to me?"

Vidocq says, "It could be a curse or some residual effect from being stabbed by Aelita's sword. I just don't know. I'm sorry. Your case is pretty unique. I'm still looking through my books."

"Your scars haven't changed much since the last time I checked," Allegra says. "Whatever's happening, I think it's happening at a steady rate and not getting any faster. Once we stop the healing where it is, we can figure out what to do next."

"How do we do that?"

"I'm making you a magic cocktail. It'll take just a few more minutes."

"And my scars will stay?"

"For now."

"What can I do to help?"

"Relax."

She pats me on the cheek, goes back to the worktable, and grinds up ingredients with a mortar and pestle. I stay by the window.

Vidocq says, "What does the Golden Vigil have to say about socializing with *le diable*?"

"Nothing. Why would they? I sure haven't told them anything about it."

"Do you really believe that Lucifer can come to Los Angeles and the Golden Vigil be utterly unaware of his arrival?"

"Who cares? I owe him. I'm supposed to go to a party with him so he can show off Sandman Slim."

"I'm sure Aelita will see it that way when you explain it so simply."

I turn to the old man. He looks more concerned than I've seen him since the day Aelita stabbed me with her flaming sword. The day he quit working for the Vigil.

"You think she knows? Wells told me about their magic radar. Supposed to track the Sub Rosa and any big hoodoo going on in town, but I've never seen a bunch with less of a clue."

"The Vigil's technology is, at best, inconsistent, but they have psychics and Lurkers who can smell and taste changes in the aether. I have to think that the arrival of an angel as powerful as Lucifer will cause quite a ripple."

"He's not here for anything they'd care about. He's here for his ego. He thinks he's Marlon Brando."

"Is that all?"

"And he wants out of Hell. Whatever fight's going on down there, I think he's losing. Maybe it's Mason or maybe it's just his time. I get the feeling he's looking for any excuse not to be home right now."

"Or he has another agenda altogether."

"What?"

Vidocq shakes his head, sets down his coffee.

"I have no idea, but this is Lucifer we're talking about. Next to God, the brightest light in the universe. He might not lie to you, but don't assume just because he tells you the truth you know what's going on."

"Don't start talking that way. My head already hurts."

Allegra is still grinding ingredients, concentrating. Ignoring us. It's nice to have a job and know exactly what you're doing, what's expected of you, and that you can do it all yourself.

"Sometimes I miss the arena. I miss being pointed at some monster and told, 'It's you or him, little drytt,' and just going for it. No decisions. No motives. No guessing games. Just blood and dust, and afterward, I have a gallon of Aqua Regia and go to sleep."

Allegra asks, "What's a 'little drytt'?"

I guess she is listening after all.

"A drytt is a bug that lives in the desert outside Pandemonium, Lucifer's capital. Drytts are like sand fleas. They're everywhere and get into everything. They live in the dirt and they eat and shit their body weight every day for two days. Then they die. They lay eggs in their shit and that's where their young are born."

"You miss being called a shit bug?"

"It's what they call all mortals," Vidocq says. "Angels, even fallen ones, are eternal. We, the story goes, are made from dust. We eat. We shit. We grow old and die. We are born in filth, decay, and return to filth. We're all little drytt to them."

Allegra shakes her head.

"I bet you were one morbid little kid, Stark. Your poor mother."

"You have no idea."

Vidocq asks, "How is the potion coming?"

"I have all the ingredients together. It just needs to be digested."

"Show him what you've learned."

Allegra turns and raises her eyebrows at me. I go to where she's working at the table.

"In alchemy, digesting something just means cooking it. You need the Friosan nostrum to stop your scars from healing, right? The storax, the liquid amber, is the base for the other ingredients. There's also white cedar, salamander bones, ground sea horse. All things that grow slowly."

"What's that other powder?"

She glances at Vidocq.

"I don't know. Mysterious things in old jars with Latin names. Eugène helped with that part."

"Good. I was worried about the Latin part."

Vidocq leans forward on the sofa.

"Don't be shy. Show him the rest."

Allegra dumps all the ingredients in a silver bowl and sets it on a tabletop brazier.

"Remember that fire trick you showed me?"

"The one you used on Parker? You saved my life, so, yeah, I remember."

Allegra smiles like a girl with a secret.

"Watch this."

She blows across her fingers the way I showed her back when she was just another civilian. Flames flicker to life on her fingertips, but she keeps blowing, moving her hand in a slow circle in front of her lips. In a few seconds, the flames have moved from the tips of her fingers to burn all the way down to her palm. She puts her hand under the silver bowl with the ingredients. As she blows, the flames rise and the storax begins to boil. Steam comes off the amber, filling the room with the smell of burned pine. The powder and other ingredients quickly dissolve. She holds her hand near her lips again, blows lightly, and the flames shrink and disappear.

"Damn. I showed you a party trick and you took it and turned pro. You're practically Evel Knievel."

"I'm McGyver, baby. Stick around. I'll make you a philosopher's stone from Barbie dolls and spark plugs."

Vidocq says, "She's a brilliant girl. She's learning much faster than I did."

"What do I do with the snake oil, doc?"

She pours the thick liquid from the silver bowl into a beer stein and hands it to me. The liquid has darkened from amber gold to something more like maple syrup.

"Slam it back. Every bit of it."

"You sure? I think I still see some of the salamander moving around in there."

"Drink."

It tastes every bit as good as you'd guess lizard and tree bark would. It's thick enough that I have to upend the glass to get the last dregs.

"Is that it? Am I cured?"

"Not even close. But it should keep you where you are for a while. Eugène and I'll keep looking for a long-term fix."

"Thanks. Both of you. I mean it."

"If you're really that pathetically grateful, take me as your date to the party tonight."

Vidocq is up getting more coffee.

"Did you put her up to this?"

He fills his glass and leans on the kitchen counter.

"Allegra is one of us now. She should see everything."

"I want to see everything," she says

"A while ago, Vidocq could have taken you to the soiree. You know why he won't now? 'Cause the Sub Rosa don't like me, but they don't like him even more."

She looks at him.

"Because you're not Sub Rosa?"

"Because I'm a thief."

"Because you steal their shit."

"Only because they want what each other has, but are afraid to do it themselves. They need me to take it and Muninn to sell it back to them because the wealthy and powerful have always preferred to pay their lessers to commit their crimes for them."

Allegra looks back at me.

"Take me with you tonight. I want to see the crazy people you two are always talking about. I'll brush my teeth and wear underwear and everything."

"Trust me, neither of those things are mandatory with this crowd. But you can't be my date. I'm Lucifer's date."

"Bull. He wants you there to intimidate people. I'll be Lucifer's date. You can loom behind us like a teddy bear with a Gatling gun."

"I'll introduce you to Lucifer when Hell freezes over and Jesus opens a sex shop on Melrose."

"Don't be such a grandma. Vidocq would introduce me if he could."

"No, he wouldn't."

"It does no good to hide the world from those determined to see it for themselves," Vidocq says.

"We're talking about Lucifer, not taking little Susie down to Planned Parenthood for birth control."

"When you introduce yourself to the devil willingly, you take away his power to surprise you."

"And an apple a day keeps the doctor away, except for all those people who got cancer."

Allegra yells, "This is what I'm talking about. You two are arguing like I'm not here about things I've never seen. I want to know about these secret people and places and I will, with or without your help."

"You're not coming with me tonight. Maybe I can get you into something else later. Lucifer is in town for this movie thing and those can drag on forever, so there'll be lots of other parties with plenty of magical douche bags for you to meet. But you're not coming tonight. And I'm not introducing you to Lucifer. Not now. Not ever. That's it. You want to do alchemy, you're in Vidocq's world, and you two can work that out however you want. You get near the Sub Rosa or anything to do with Hellions, you're in my world and I make the rules. Understand?"

Allegra turns away, nods.

"I understand. Okay."

I take my cup to Vidocq for some coffee to wash the taste of the nostrum out of my mouth.

Allegra says, "I'm sorry. I just don't want to be left out of the big things. I get frustrated because you and Eugène have done and seen so much. I don't think you want me to see anything. You want me to go back and be the cute little ignorant girl who runs the cash register at Max Overdrive."

"I wouldn't mind seeing you over there sometimes, but I

don't want to nail your feet to the floor. Try to understand, if Vidocq or I seem like we don't want to show you something, maybe it's because we're not the best role models. We're basically a couple of huge fuckups who ought to be dead. Eugène screwed up his chemistry set so bad he made himself immortal by mistake. He could have ended up a worm or slime on a wall in a Paris sewer, but he got lucky. Me, I'm so good at what I do that I've spent more than a third of my life in Hell. Sometimes, if you ask a question and we don't jump in right away with the secrets of the universe, it's not because we think you can't handle it, but because we don't have all the answers either."

Allegra takes something out of her pocket and holds it behind her back.

"Put out your hand," she says.

I do it and she drops something heavy. It looks like a cigarette box, but it's dense enough to be full of buck shot.

"What is this?"

"It's an electronic cigarette. All the cool kids have 'em. They look just like normal cigarettes. You charge the cigarette part off the computer and there's a nicotine cartridge in the filter end. Basically, you're just sucking in nicotine and steam. It's just like smoking a real cigarette, but these won't kill you as quick."

"Doesn't that kind of defeat the point?"

She takes the pack from my hand and slips it into my jacket pocket.

"Sometimes being smart is more important than magic."

I say, "Thanks for looking out for me."

She smiles and shrugs.

"What choice do I have if I want to get into one of those parties?"

Vidocq gets up and puts his arm around Allegra's shoulders.

"I think the real reason he doesn't want to introduce you to Lucifer is that he's afraid you'll be running Hell within the week, which would make you his boss."

Allegra brightens at that, saying, "Make me a sandwich, beeyotch!"

I head for a nice shadow on the side of a bookcase.

"I'll call you tomorrow and let you know what the beautiful people are wearing this year. Thanks for the smokes."

A COURIER DELIVERS a package from the Chateau Marmont. It's addressed to "Wild Bill Hickok," which is annoying, but better than if it was addressed to Sandman Slim.

Inside the box is a brand-new tuxedo, a white shirt, socks, and shoes. A small box covered in dark green snakeskin holds miniature silver Colt .45 cuff links. Throw in a hat and spurs and I could be one of Roy Rogers's pallbearers.

Kasabian says, "Someone wants you pretty tonight."

"Let's trade. You go to the party and I'll stay here and drink beer and watch *The Wizard of Oz*. We can both spend the night with witches and monkeys."

"I'll pass. But you have fun with the beautiful people. I bet they've missed you."

"Every bit as much as I missed them."

"Try not to do anything too stupid, okay? If you piss off Lucifer and get sent back to Hell, I'm going to be on a coal cart right behind you and I don't want to go back again for a good long time."

"The next time I go back to Hell it'll be because I mean to."

"Gee wow, that's a comfort."

I put on the butler suit and the new shoes. Everything is a perfect fit. Lucifer must have had his tailor run the thing off for me. He would have to do it after eyeballing me for just a couple of minutes. That's impressive, even for a Sub Rosa rag sewer, but then having the lord of the abyss looking over your shoulder is probably even more motivational than an employee-of-the-month fruit basket.

My only problem with the suit is that the jacket is too tight for me to wear a gun without looking like I have a conjoined twin. Allegra took me to a local fetish shop and I had them make me a kind of leather shoulder holster for the na'at. It fits under my left arm pretty well, and unless I get the urge to do jumping jacks at the party, it should stay hidden. If I was designing the suit myself, I would have run a twelve-inch Velcro strip from the pants cuff up the leg so I could strap the black knife under it. For now, I just slide it into my waistband behind my back. I check the bedside table for anything else I might want to take with me.

"What's that?" Kasabian asks.

"It's an electronic cigarette. Supposed to be better for you than regular ones. You want it?"

"I might not have balls anymore, but I still have a little pride, so no."

At ten, my phone rings. The limo's arrived to take me to pick up Lucifer. I go downstairs and out the back of the store, trying to get out without anyone seeing me. I know it's stupid to use the door when I can just as easily go out through a shadow, but I like using the door at Max Overdrive. I think I'm the only person I know who still has a normal door.

The limo is just like the kind you see in the movies. Long, shiny, and black. The driver opens the rear passenger door for me, and then gets back in the driver's seat. He doesn't say a word for the whole drive, probably because his throat has been cut from ear to ear and looks like it was sewn up by a blind man with bailing wire. This is going to be an interesting night.

When we're down the block from the hotel, I dial the number Lucifer gave me last night. Yeah, I have the devil on speed dial.

The phone rings once and a voice I don't recognize says, "He'll be right down. Wait for him in the lobby," then hangs up.

I tell the limo driver to wait in the parking lot outside the lobby. The staff seems to know that someone important is on his way down because none of them tell me to move the car. None of them even look at me. Does everyone at the hotel owe Lucifer a favor?

There are thirteen well-dressed people in the lobby when I go in. I'm pretty sure I know what this means. They confirm it a few seconds later when Lucifer steps out of the elevator and all thirteen jump up like kids on the last day of school. A woman in an expensive Jackie Kennedy black dress and pillbox hat leads the pack. Her face is young and her skin is perfect, but when she takes off a glove, her hands are like buzzard claws. Old as King Tut and dry as a Death Valley rattlesnake's eyeteeth.

"Master," she says, breathy and excited. The million-dollar coven behind her mumbles the word in stage whispers like stuttering ghosts.

"Amanda, lovely to see you," Lucifer says, all diabolical charm. "I have someplace to be, so I'm afraid I can't stay and chat."

The old woman with the Lolita face smiles like a maniac when he says her name.

"We don't want to keep you, Master. Will you be in L.A. long?"

"I'm not sure."

"We'd like to hold a special Mass for your arrival."

"No need. But thank you all the same."

Amanda is disappointed, but keeps smiling. Her heart is going like the drum solo in "In-A-Gadda-Da-Vida." Lucifer hasn't touched the woman's buzzard hand, and while he's probably technically smiling, you'd need a microscope to be sure. His contempt for these people is so obvious, it's even giving me the creeps. I don't know if I'm on bodyguard duty yet, so I stay put.

Amanda pulls back her hand and reaches into the huge damned purse that all old ladies seem to carry. I take a couple of steps toward her, just to make sure she's not taking anything too sharp or explosive out of her bag. Lucifer couldn't look more bored. She pulls out a carved whitish-yellow box and hands it to Lucifer. As he takes it he gives her a tiny nod. The *Rosemary's Baby* Mouseketeers behind her start mumbling "Master" again. Lucifer shifts his eyes toward me for a second. Now I'm on the clock.

I move in as Lucifer raises his left hand and touches the top of Amanda's head, like he's blessing her. She's thrilled and, to tell the truth, I like the move, too. A priest would have blessed her with his right hand, but Lucifer put his devil horns on and went lefty. If we had some pea soup we could do a scene from *The Exorcist*.

I put an arm up, and when Lucifer takes his hand off Amanda's head, I get between him and the crowd and stay there while I walk him to the front door. Amanda yells, "Praise thee, Master! Praise thee!" Lucifer ignores her. As he gets in the car, the limo driver opens and closes the passenger door behind him and gets in the front. Guess now that the big man is here, I don't rate door opening. A good thing to remember. I'm back with the ruling class, where everyone knows their place. Except for me, but I don't think Lucifer is going to be shy about telling me whose ass to kiss and whose to punch. I open my own door and slide in the back of the limo.

"You're like all the Beatles rolled into one. Getting you out of there is like them trying to get out of Shea Stadium after the concert in '65."

"I was there that night. The sound was terrible."

"You knew them? They didn't make a deal with you, did they?"

He gives me a look.

"Don't be ridiculous. Pete Best wanted to make a deal back in Hamburg, but he was already out of the band, so who cared?"

I nod at the box Amanda gave him. "What's the deal with the pyx?"

"You know what it is. I'm impressed."

"I'm trying to take the hoodoo thing more seriously.

Been reading some of Vidocq's books and thinking about getting my magic, I don't know, more organized."

"Have you had any results yet?"

"Not much. But I've been thinking that killing everyone is maybe counterproductive. Been playing around with some stunning hexes. I wasn't big on stunning back in the arena, so it's all new to me."

"I'm impressed again. I know that thinking goes entirely against your ethos, so the fact you're considering a new approach to things is a good sign."

"A sign of what?"

"That you might actually live. That you'll become a new and improved monster. Not killing everyone means that if something happens there will be survivors to question."

"Of course, none of it means shit. Wells hires me to kill things and so do you. Thinking is like playing in a band when you're fifty. It only happens on weekends and holidays."

"Why don't we agree on a new policy starting tonight? I don't expect any problems, but if something does happen, try using magic instead of violence. I want to support the idea of a newer, better you."

"We're still talking about killing, right? Not potty training."

Lucifer turns the pyx over in his hands.

"Who was that bunch back at the hotel?"

"The most important human-only coven in the city. They had a lot of power back in the day, when Los Angeles was changing from orange groves into a city, but now they're mostly a nuisance."

"The Sub Rosa took over."

"The Sub Rosa have always been in charge here, but it helped to have civilians as go-betweens with politicians and business. These days everyone has moved beyond that kind of Checkpoint Charlie thinking. The Sub Rosa are powerful and there isn't a politician or businessman alive who doesn't like to rub shoulders with that."

"So, what's in the box?"

He hands me the pyx.

"Take it. Consider it your first bonus."

I wonder how much buzzard-claw Amanda liked being blown off back at the hotel? Is she the type to throw some disrespect back at Lucifer? Slip him some bad juju or an underwear bomb? I hold the pyx at arm's length and open the top. Nothing happens. I look inside.

"Are those fingernails?"

"Yes. A few toenails, too, probably. No, you don't want to know where they came from."

"I was just telling Kasabian I hoped I'd get to see a pile of ripped-out fingernails tonight. I guess dreams really do come true."

Lucifer lights a Malediction.

"The box is Grecian ivory and very old. Take it to a good auction house. You'll be able to open a dozen video stores."

"How much do you think I can get for the nails?"

THE DRIVER TAKES us south on the Hollywood Freeway, gets off at Silver Lake, and steers us up the hills to the old reservoir. There's a concrete path all around and a steep descent down to the water. The driver stops on the street

bordering the reservoir, gets out, and opens Lucifer's door.
Neither of them says anything as the driver closes his door,
gets back in the front, and drives away.

Lucifer says, "He'll be back when we need him," and
leads us through a typical L.A. excuse for a park—parched
grass and a line of half-dead trees—to a walkway sticking
out over the water.

At the end of the walkway is a burned-out three-story
concrete utility building. Technically, it's only two stories
now. It looks like the top one collapsed and caved into the
second during the fire. The city bolted wire shutters over
all the ground-floor windows to keep kiddies from playing
in the death trap. Naturally, most of them are torn down
or bent back enough for someone skinny to squeeze inside.
The double metal doors in front are shut with a padlock
and chain heavy enough to hitch the Loch Ness monster to
a parking meter.

Why am I not surprised when Lucifer pulls a key from
his pocket, pops the lock, and throws open the doors? A
blast of cold, wet air hits us from inside. The place smells
like Neptune's outhouse. There's a set of stone steps inside,
winding down to the waterline. A few high school kids are
hunkered on the stairs below the first turn, drinking forties
and passing around a joint. They lurch to their feet, a little
shaky in that panicked stoner kind of way where cops and
pigeons are equally terrifying. I guess they don't see a lot
of tuxedos down here. Lucifer nods to them and one of the
boys nods back.

"You cops?" he asks

As we pass the group, Lucifer turns to the boy.

"Sometimes. But not tonight."

I don't know if it's the dark, the narrows walls, or just being in a strange place for the first time, but the stairs seem to go down a long damn way. Feels like well below the waterline. When we hit the bottom, there's another door. Instead of rusted metal, this one is covered in red leather and has brass hinges. There's a doorman next to it in a gold silk coat and short breeches dripping with enough gold filigree to make Little Lord Fauntleroy look like he shops from the discount bin at Walmart. He opens the door when he hears us. I guess standing in the dark doesn't bother him. His eyes look black and blind and his lips are sewn shut.

I start to say something, but Lucifer cuts me off with a dismissive wave.

"Golem. Salvage from some Parisian potter's field. French revenants are all the rage among the Sub Rosa gentry this year. I wouldn't waste my money. Golems aren't much more than windup toys. You could train a dog to open that door and it could still fetch and bark on cue. This dead thing will open the door from now until doomsday, but that's all it'll ever do. Ridiculous."

"At least you don't have to tip him. Are they all sewn up like that?"

"Of course. Golems are lobotomized so they don't bite, but they're not so easy to recall if something goes wrong."

Past the door is another golem, this one with stapled lips, but that's not the hilarious part. There's a gondola floating in an underwater canal lit by phosphorescent globes hovering near the walls. The golem is dressed in a gondolier's striped shirt, black pants, and flat-brimmed hat like the ticket taker at a Disneyland ride, if the ride was hidden under an L.A. reservoir and full of animated corpses. It's a small dead world, after all.

Lucifer steps down into the gondola and I follow him. The golem poles us along the narrow canal until we hit a T-intersection where he steers us right into a wider channel.

"The limo driver, he was cut and stitched up, too. Is he a golem?"

"No, he's alive. He's just annoying."

"You cut his throat?"

"Of course not. When he apologized for what he did, he cut his own throat to prove his sincerity."

"I guess it's better than ending up in a box of fingernails."

"That's what I said."

"Where the hell are we? How far are we under the reservoir?"

"We're not under the reservoir anymore. Our brain-dead friend has taken us out into an old tributary of the L.A. River."

"Huh. It never crossed my mind that the L.A. River was ever anything more than scummy concrete runoff."

"Everyone here thinks that way. It's only the ones who remember when the river was wild who appreciate it."

"Muninn would remember."

"I'm sure he does. If I remember right, his cavern isn't far from another of the underground channels."

"Will he be here tonight?"

"I doubt it. He's worse than you when it comes to socializing with the Sub Rosa."

"Where are we going? Who's going to be there?"

"The party is being thrown by the head of the studio,

Simon Ritchie. I think I mentioned that he's a civilian, so the party is being thrown in the home of one of the truly outstanding Sub Rosa families, Jan and Koralin Geistwald. Lovely people. They came here all the way from the northernmost part of Germany when this river roared along the surface."

"So, that makes them a couple of hundred years old?"

"I'm sure they're considerably older than that, but they came to America two-hundred-ish years ago."

"Why?"

"They were ambitious and they had the guts to do something about it. Europe was lousy with ancient Sub Rosa families who'd consolidated power centuries before. If you wanted to advance, the only way to do it was create your own dynasty and the only way to do that was to go very far away and start from nothing."

"Like the Springheels."

"Exactly. They were the first. They came a very long way and gave up virtually everything to get here."

"I guess we won't be seeing any of them tonight."

"Why not?"

"Damn. I know something you don't. Do I get a prize?"

"Be happy with your box."

"The reason why you won't see any Springheels is that the last of them, little Enoch, died a couple of days back."

"How?"

"There was a severe chewing accident. The guy was playing around with eaters."

Lucifer shakes his head and tosses his Malediction into the water.

"That family fell apart and just kept on falling. What a perfect way for the last of them to go."

"That's where I was going when I left you at the hotel. I met Wells at the Springheel place to help suss out what happened there."

"Do you do a lot of magical forensics for the Vigil? Or was it a Homeland Security matter?"

"I don't know if there's any difference to Wells. And it was the first time."

"And you're sure it was eaters?"

"All the signs were there."

"Good for you. Congratulations on your new job. I didn't know you were such an expert on demons."

"I'm not, but once I started looking, it seemed pretty obvious."

"Did Wells agree?"

"I think so. It's hard to tell with him. And his crew were everywhere. It was goddamn Woodstock at five hundred decibels in there. I could hardly think."

"Sounds like a hard way to work."

"It was a pain in the ass."

"Interesting that he'd call you in just to have you working in such terrible circumstances."

"That's Wells. It was probably a test. Like he was hazing me."

"Or distracting you."

"What?"

"It's what I'd do if I didn't want someone to find something. I'd call in someone new and then make it impossible for them to do their job. They'd be flattered I'd asked them and too embarrassed to say anything when they didn't perform well."

"Why would Wells do that?"

"I have no idea. I didn't say he did it. I said it's what I'd do."

"You have a lot more to cover up than Wells or the Vigil."

"Fair enough."

We come around a bend and up ahead the cavern place opens up into a huge marble room lit with hundreds of torches and candles. A dozen other canals cut through the place and there's a golem-powered gondola in each one, steering guests under arched stone bridges.

There are two Venices I know about and one of them is a hotel in Vegas. The other is an L.A. beach where pretty girls walk their dogs while wearing as little as possible and mutant slabs of tanned, posthuman beef sip iced steroid lattes and pump iron until their pecs are the size of Volkswagens. This Venice is pretty damned far from those. This is the old fairy-tale Venice with Casanova, plague, and Saint Mark's stolen bones, meaning it's a high-quality hoodoo copy. Hopefully without the plague. It's not as big as a real city and there's a vaulted roof over our heads, so we're probably still in part of the old L.A. River system.

Every few yards, there's a dock with a couple of steps leading up from the water. The golem stops at one and Lucifer and I get out. There must be a couple of hundred people down here. People and other things. Big-shot Lurkers and civilians laugh and chat with heavyweight Sub Rosas. They can talk shit about each other behind the others' backs, but when it comes right down to it, money is the one true race and everyone down here is the color of greenbacks and as tall as mountains.

Lucifer checks his tie and gives me a quick once-over like maybe I'd changed into clown shoes during the boat ride. He nods and says, "Let's get a drink."

I'm a little surprised that the total fucking ruler, grand vizier, and night manager of Hell can just walk into the place without us getting mobbed like he was back at the hotel. But of course, people like this don't do that kind of thing, do they? If Jesus, Jesse James, and a herd of pink robot unicorns strolled in walking on water, this bunch wouldn't even look up. I wonder if Lucifer had his tailor make my jacket too tight to wear a gun on purpose because I'm genuinely inspired to start shooting things just to see if anyone jumps.

A golem in a white waiter's jacket comes by with a tray of champagne. Lucifer takes one glass and hands me one.

"No guzzling tonight. You're on duty, so you get to sip politely."

"Don't worry. These golems all need a good moisturizer. I'm not drinking anything that might have dead-guy skin flakes in it."

"Don't worry. They're all certified as hypoallergenic."

"It's coming back to me why I fucking hate the fucking Sub Rosa."

When the costumed corpse that brought our drinks turns away, he bumps my shoulder, and his tray and the rest of the drinks crash to the ground. A few dozen heads turn in our direction. So, that's what it takes to get their attention. Wasted booze. A tall, heavyset guy pushes through the crowd. He's big, but not fat. Like maybe he was a cop or a boxer in some former life. He sticks out one hand to shake and the other goes to Lucifer's shoulder.

"Mr. Macheath, it's good to see you. Please forgive me for the mess. It's so hard to get really good subnaturals now that they're so popular."

Lucifer shakes the guy's hand warmly.

"It's no problem, Simon. You should see the kind of help I have to put up with at home."

The big man laughs. Not a big L.A. suck-up laugh, but a small relaxed one. His heartbeat isn't even going up that much. He's got some juice, being this relaxed around Lucifer.

"Simon, I'd like you to meet an associate of mine." Lucifer half turns to me while keeping an eye on Simple Simon. "This is James. You probably know him as—"

"Sandman Slim," says Simon. He puts out his hand to me. I shake it, but don't say anything. I'm not exactly sure what kind of performance Lucifer wants from me tonight, but I'm guessing it isn't bright and cheery.

Lucifer smiles.

"Be nice and say hello, James."

"Hello."

"I'm really happy you could make it tonight. I've heard so much about you, James. Or do you prefer Sandman Slim?"

"Stark. Just Stark."

Lucifer says, "James, this is Simon Ritchie, the head of the studio doing my little movie."

"Have you cast him yet?"

"Cast who?" asks Ritchie.

I nod at Lucifer.

"Him. Your star. Do you have a Lucifer yet?"

"Not yet. You can probably imagine he's a hard part to cast."

"No shit."

I look at Lucifer.

"You must have a lot of actors Downtown, Mr. Macheath. How about Fatty Arbuckle? Maybe you can put him on work release for a few weeks."

"What an interesting idea. I'm going to give it no thought whatsoever."

Ritchie laughs and shoots me a glance, measuring me up, probably wondering if I'm really the monster he's heard about. Ten to one he was LAPD before burrowing his way into the movie biz. He has those eyes that see everyone as guilty until proven otherwise. He wants to know if I'm for real or more Hollywood window dressing. Great. That ups the chances of something stupid happening while Lucifer is in town.

"Would you like something to eat? I can assure you that unlike the waiters, our chefs are very much alive and the best in town."

"We're fine, thanks," says Lucifer. "I think we're just going to stroll around and say hello to a few people. Care to join us?"

"I need to put out a small fire first. Our new imported starlet has gone rogue. You can't let Czechs wander around without a minder. They'll organize the workers and start a revolution."

"Do you know where Jan and Koralin are?"

"In the big ballroom straight through there," says Ritchie, pointing a couple of bridges away. "Why don't you go in and I'll catch up?"

"Excellent," says Lucifer. "We'll see you there."

Ritchie puts his hand out to me.

"Nice meeting you, too. I'd love to pick your brain sometime about your experiences in the underworld. There might be a story in it."

"Uh. Okay."

After he's gone I say, "If he calls, I don't really have to talk to him, do I?"

Lucifer shrugs and starts walking.

"You might as well. If you don't, someone else will and they'll get it all wrong. Trust me. I know about these things."

"Think they'd make me into a toy? I'd like to be a toy."

"Only if it talks a lot and doesn't have an off switch."

As we go over one of the stone bridges, I see something funny.

"Damn, I'd forgotten about that."

"What?"

"Elvis and Marilyn Monroe are talking to some drunk blonde over there. I hate that stuff."

"Don't be so judgmental just because it's not your kind of fun."

"People shouldn't rent ghosts for their parties. Ghosts shouldn't have better agents than live people."

"I never pegged you for a Puritan, Jimmy."

Errol Flynn is standing on the bridge railing, pissing into the canal. It's just ghost piss, so it doesn't make a sound, but he still gets a round of applause when he's done.

"Man, these rich assholes really love dead people."

"Do the math. Most celebrities are more valuable dead than they ever were when they were alive. Why shouldn't they get a cut? Almost everyone important has a wild-blue-yonder contract these days. They get to keep working and it puts off the damnation that most know is waiting for them."

I want a smoke, but I'm tired of bumming Maledictions off Lucifer. I check my pocket and find the electronic cigarette. I take a tentative puff. It isn't nearly as horrible as I thought it would be.

"That's the first time I ever heard you crack a joke about Hell."

"Hell is hilarious if you're the one in charge."

The ballroom is like Rat Pack Las Vegas in a *Hellraiser* theme park. The Sub Rosas, civilians, and Lurkers are all sporting tuxes and evening gowns, but even here there are a few holdouts. Cabal Ash looks like he slept under a leaking Dumpster and he smells worse. Being repulsive is an Ash family tradition. A sign of their big-league status. And they're not the worst clan. At least they wear clothes.

There's a band onstage, but no one's dancing. Dead people are okay, but I guess metal bands are too harsh for this crowd. It takes me a minute to recognize them over the noise.

"That's Skull Valley Sheep Kill."

Lucifer sets his empty glass on a wandering golem's tray.

"Is it?"

"Not the kind of band I'd expect at a party like this."

"That's because they were my daughter's favorite music, not mine."

It's a woman's voice, deep, melodious, and with an aristocratic German accent. Her skin is as white as a full moon and the irises of her eyes are gold.

Lucifer says, "Koralin, so lovely to see you."

He takes her hand and she kisses both of his cheeks.

"It's been too long, my dear," she says.

"You're one of the things that make coming to this silly world worthwhile."

She laughs and means it.

"How interesting that your daughter chose tonight's band. I think James here knew her."

"Is this true? You knew Eleanor?"

"I don't believe that she was using the family name at the time. What was she calling herself? Eleanor Vance?"

"Yes. It was some foolish thing from an old book."

She looks at me.

"Did you know Eleanor?"

"No, ma'am. Mr. Macheath made a mistake. I didn't."

It's true enough. I didn't know her at all. I just put her down. Sorry, Eleanor. I'm ignoring your last request. No way I'm telling your mommy you stole whatever it was 'cause you wanted to make her mad. Not this woman. Not here.

"Is Jan around?"

"He's helping Simon find his Prague whore."

"They make some awfully good ones," Lucifer says.

"Better than the French make their damned golems, I hope."

Koralin accepts the cigarette Lucifer hands her.

"You must be the little monster I've heard so much about. The one who tried to burn Beverly Hills to the ground."

"Just Rodeo Drive. And it wasn't my fault. The other guy shot first. Sorry if I messed up any of your friends' thousand-dollar jeans."

"Fuck those hausfraus and their witless rent boys. I'm sorry I missed the fun. The next time you're feeling genocidal, you must call me before acting on it."

"It's a date."

I look at her gold eyes, but I can't read them. Can't hear her heart or get a feel for her thoughts either. Some Sub Rosa keep a kind of antihoodoo cloak over their homes. It keeps hexes and general magic mishaps to a minimum. I bet the Geistwalds have it cranked to eleven tonight. The most excitement we can hope for is Cabal getting drunk enough to pick a fight with Bruce Lee's ghost.

"Here come the boys," says Koralin. "And they found the little slut. I wonder how many dicks she's sucked tonight?"

I look at Lucifer, but he's ignoring me and the remark.

Jan Geistwald is as dark as Koralin is light. He has a dark olive complexion and a deeply lined face like someone who's spent too much time in the desert squinting at the sun.

Ritchie has his arm around a woman's shoulder and he's smiling like he just won the lottery.

The woman is brunette and her dark pupils, within the bright whites of her eyes, look like bullet holes in the snow. She has the perfect bird-bone cheeks you see on French girls, but her non-plastic-surgery nose and full lips look more Italian or Greek.

Hollywood beauty can make your IQ drop, but there's that other kind that's like the end of the world. Armageddon gorgeosity. She walks in the room like the Angel of

Death in a miniskirt and all you can think is, *If I got shot in the head right now, I'd die smiling.*

The brunette gives me a crooked smile. I was staring and she caught me. Outdrawn already.

"You found your way home," says Koralin.

"She gave us a good chase, but we tracked her down," says Jan. "Poor Simon was almost in tears."

"That was sweat, not tears. I usually make other people hunt-and-gather for me these days," says Simon.

The brunette holds out her hand to me.

"Hello. I'm Brigitte."

"Stark. Nice to meet you."

"And you."

Ritchie wakes up.

"Sorry, darling."

He takes her shoulders and points her at Lucifer like she's artillery.

"This is Brigitte Bardo. Brigitte, this is Mr. Macheath. *Light Bringer*, his film, is the one you're going to be in."

"Nice to meet you, Mack the Knife. Did you bring your dagger?"

Lucifer nods toward me.

"I brought him. He carries the knife."

"Only because I couldn't fit a gun under this damned jacket."

Brigitte and Koralin smile.

"I'm glad you're here taking care of our special guest," says Ritchie. He claps his arm around Lucifer's shoulders.

"Did you hear? Spencer Church is gone," says Jan.

"Missing?" asks Ritchie.

"No one knows."

"Spencer Church is a drug addict, a gambler, and a pusher," says Koralin. "He's either sleeping in a ditch or buried in the desert. But this isn't the time or place to be talking about these things. This is a party."

Jan says, "Why don't we make a circle around the room? I know there are a lot of people who'd like to pay their respects."

Lucifer nods.

"I always enjoy a little genuflecting. Shall we walk?"

Lucifer, Jan, Koralin, and Ritchie stroll on ahead looking impressive and important. Brigitte and I follow a few steps behind. Close enough to keep an eye on things, but far enough back that we look like a couple of sixteen-year-olds pretending we're not with our parents.

"So, you're the famous Sandman Slim. I supposed we both have to have funny names to do our jobs. Do you get that my name is a little joke?"

"You mean how there's Brigitte Bardot, a jet-propelled French succubus from the sixties? Got famous in *And God Created Woman*. Got respected in *Contempt*. Kind of a nut job, but she liked dogs. Then there's Bardo, like the Buddhist states of being. Life, death, enlightenment, and a side of fries. Yeah, I think I got it."

"Very nice. Most Americans don't understand."

"Don't be too impressed. Everyone in California is a Buddhist for fifteen minutes. Then they realize they're not allowed to eat chili dogs and enlightenment starts sounding like a real drag."

"You know, I thought you would be uglier."

"Huh. Thanks?"

"I heard that you were covered in scars. You don't look so bad, really."

"You sound disappointed."

"You were looking at me before. Have you seen my work?"

"Ritchie said you were an actress in France. You coming to work in Hollywood?"

"Simon is going to help me do different sorts of movies than what I was doing back home."

"Were you stuck in those rotten American action-movie rip-offs they do over there?"

"No, pornography. I'm very famous for it in Europe. In Japan, too."

Hey, at least she didn't tell me she's dead.

"I've met a couple of local porn girls in clubs over the years. I'm never sure what's worse for them—not recognizing them or recognizing them too quickly."

She smiles.

"It's fine either way. All that matters is that the person isn't too mean or too happy to meet you."

"Good way to put it. I've been trying to work through something like that myself."

"I know. You may not know me, but I recognized you and your funny nom de plume."

"Don't blame me. Hellions gave me that behind my back. I didn't even know about it until a cop told me."

"It's better than 'whore.' That's usually what's said behind my back."

"Most people are idiots. There's nothing worse than idiots who tell you their opinions."

I puff my fake cigarette. It really doesn't taste that bad, but the plastic texture is hard, like sucking nicotine through a spackle gun.

"So you're in *Light Bringer*. You an angel or what?"

"Don't be silly. I'm Eve, the destroyer of men and, so, the whole world."

"And here I am without a drink to toast you with."

"See? I'm much worse than you could ever be, Sandman Slim."

"People call you names behind your back, but trust me, they'd call me worse if they weren't afraid I'd skin them and wear them like oven mitts."

"Being friends with Lucifer must help."

"I'm not stupid enough to think we're friends, but we're not enemies. We have some common interests."

"Then you are what people say you are?"

"What's this week's theory?"

"That you're a bit of a vampire, but without the blood. You're strong like a vampire. You're fast. You heal and you can see inside people. Some believe that you were a vampire, but that Lucifer cured you and now you are his property."

Out of habit, I tap my finger on the cigarette to knock off the ashes. Moron. There's no ash on a piece of plastic.

"I'm no one's property. I get paid for my services," I say. "I also freelance for the Golden Vigil. They're not exactly on Mr. Macheath's side."

Up ahead, Lucifer is getting glad-handed by Cabal Ash. I think the guy took out his spinal fluid and replaced it with tequila. He's epically, gorgeously drunk. If his drunkenness had legs, it would be Alexander the Great and conquer the known world. Then it would puke for a week into a solid gold toilet it stole from Zeus's guest room.

Right now, Cabal is stinking up the party with the death grip he's got on Lucifer's hand. He's pumping it like he thinks he'll strike oil. A woman dressed in the same kind of dirty rags as Cabal is trying to coax him away with more booze. Maybe I'm supposed to step in and pull the guy off, but it's not my party and it's too damned fun standing right where I am.

Cabal's ragged lady friend finally gets his meat hooks off Lucifer and quickly steers the drunk into the crowd and out of sight.

"It's nice to hear that no one owns you. Men, especially Americans, have quite a desire to buy and sell each other. For me, they're attracted to me because I model and do sexy things in magazines and in movies, then when they have me—or think they have me—they want me to transform overnight into a mousy little housewife."

"I can see how what you do could intimidate a guy."

"But it doesn't feel as if you are judging."

"I'm pretty out of judgment for this lifetime."

"What is that you're smoking?"

"I'm not sure. I think it's low-tar crack for underage robots."

"May I try?"

She puffs away and gets a nice red glow going on the LED at what's supposed to be the lit end of the thing. Opens her mouth in an O and blows a series of perfect smoke rings. She gives the cigarette back to me, smiling.

"Is this what you smoke in Los Angeles these days? I'm

not sure I approve. Vices shouldn't be safe. They're what remind us we're alive and mortal."

I toss the thing, sending it skipping across the floor into one of the canal tributaries that run along one wall.

"There. Thanks for saving me from a too-long life."

"So, you don't like to be called Sandman Slim. Your Wikipedia page says that sometimes you are called Wild Bill."

"I'm on goddamn Wikipedia?"

"It's a tiny entry full of notes saying that no one knows if any of what's there is real. It's very funny. You'd like it."

"Read it to me sometime. I have a feeling it'll sound better in Czech."

"But none of this answers my question. What should I call you?"

Up ahead, Lucifer turns away from his admirers with his phone to his ear. From the look on his face, someone is going to get a Cadillac-size pitchfork up the ass.

"Call me James. Not Jimmy or Jim. Just James. What do I call you?"

"Brigitte is fine."

"Ah. I thought we were confessing true names."

"No. I just asked what to call you."

Now that he's not getting the royal treatment for a couple of seconds, Ritchie's realized that Brigitte isn't next to him. He looks around like a *Titanic* survivor hunting for a life vest.

"I think you're about to be called back to the stage."

Brigitte gives a little sigh.

"You're lucky. Your patron doesn't spend all his waking hours worrying that you might fuck someone else."

"Not that he's mentioned."

She smiles and waves to get Ritchie's attention.

"I have to go. It's been lovely talking with you, Sandman. Pardon. James."

"You too, Ms. Bardo."

As she goes, she runs a finger lightly over the back of my hand.

I don't usually think of porn girls as actresses, but Brigitte might be an exception. When she goes to Ritchie, she gives him a *Pretty Woman* smile like she thinks he's the center of the world.

It looks like the center of Lucifer's world has gone sour. He crooks his finger at me and we start out of the ballroom. No good-byes. No handshakes. Nothing. It must be nice to just start walking and know that everybody else will follow. Which is exactly what happens. Jan, Koralin, and Ritchie practically sprint after him. Ritchie is pulling Brigitte like a puppy on a leash. She laughs as they go. I push through the crowd, cut around a hairy Nahual beast man and a couple of Jades eating raw meat off a golem's tray. Wolf Boy has hold of the golem's arm so it can't wander away.

I catch up with them just as everyone is saying good night. Lucifer shakes a last few hands, blows some air kisses, and we're moving again.

"What's going on?"

He looks at his phone one more time and stuffs it into his pocket.

"We're going back to the hotel. Apparently Amanda and her coven never left and they're not playing nice with the hotel staff who are too afraid to throw her out."

"Whose followers are dumber, yours or God's?"

"Mine are simpletons and his are self-righteous prigs. Take your pick."

"I should have known that little shit would be here."

Lucifer looks at me. I nod at a pretty young guy drinking and scowling at the edge of a group of other pretty young things. It's Ziggy Stardust, the bad-mannered kid from Bamboo House of Dolls who thought I was a dolphin who'd do a trick for a fish.

"That's Jan and Koralin's son. Rainier I think is his name. An angry little bore and a ne'er-do-well."

"Sounds like a typical Sub Rosa to me."

Lucifer heads for the first gondola he sees, cutting off an angry Sub Rosa woman who was stepping into it. She starts to say something, sees me, and shakes her head.

It's Medea Bava, head of the Sub Rosa Inquisition.

I step down into the boat and she says, "Judge a man by the company he keeps."

"Admit it. You live alone with thirty cats, all named Mr. Whiskers."

She stands there scowling at me as the golem gondolier poles us away.

"Friend of yours?" Lucifer asks.

"She either wants to burn me at the stake or shut off my cable. I forget which."

"Why don't you kill her?"

I look at him. I can't tell if he's serious or not.

" 'Cause she hasn't done anything yet."

"Don't be an idiot. If you always wait for your enemies to move first, you'll be dead before breakfast."

"But it's your fans, not your enemies, that ruined your night. You just can't win."

"We might have put your no-killing policy on hold. Amanda and her people can be unruly, but they have to be dealt with one way or another."

"You want me to slaughter thirteen people in the hotel lobby?"

He shrugs.

"Do it in the parking lot if you're worried about the rugs."

"These aren't sulfur-sucking Hellions. I'm not promising to kill anyone."

He lights a cigarette and doesn't say anything. He doesn't offer me one this time.

"If you need to play at being the humanitarian, deal with Amanda first. Put her down and the others will most likely slink away home. I'll deal with them later."

"While we're dealing with annoying situations, fuck you very much for that Eleanor thing back there with the old lady."

"Don't be so serious. You hate the Sub Rosa because you don't know how to have fun with them."

"*Light Bringer* sounds fun. Great title, by the way. It makes you sound like Luke Skywalker's harelip cousin. Maybe they can get Ewoks to play the other fallen angels."

When the golem docks us by the reservoir stairs, Lucifer dials the chauffeur and tells him to wait back where he dropped us.

When we get back to the street, he isn't there. Does this moron want his throat slit all the way around back, too, so it matches the front?

I say, "Go back inside. I'll wait."

"Calm down. Here he is."

The limo pulls up to the curb and Lucifer heads straight for it. I grab his arm and hold him until the driver gets out. When he does, I do something I'm pretty sure no one but God has ever done before. I knock Lucifer down. The guy getting out of the limo doesn't have the heartbeat or the nervous breathing of someone who's just kept the lord of the flies waiting. He sounds more like me when I'm hunting.

Five more men follow him out of the car. They're dressed in black jumpsuits, boots, and balaclavas, typical tactical drag, but they don't have insignias on their suits. For all I know, they could be LAPD, Dr. No, or the SPCA.

Next time, no matter how tight the damn jacket is, I'm bringing a gun.

The six men split into two groups. The four with what look like nonlethals go for Lucifer. Two with guns come at me.

The taller one has an AA-12 auto shotgun. Looks like his pal has a G3 assault rifle. This is only interesting because it means that they work for people who can afford the best toys on the shelf, which means they're probably pros. Damn. I was hoping to buy them off with free movie rentals. Microwave popcorn included.

Shotgun Guy starts blasting the moment he hits the curb, pushing me back toward the reservoir, trying to cut me off so I can't help Lucifer. It's a good plan. I'm not running in front of the double-ought shot and I'm not charging him while he has that hand cannon. I do exactly what he wants me to do. I fall down.

In gunspeak, it's called a fall-away shot. You fall over backward while raising your gun and firing. If you're good at it, a fall-away is a great way to shoot at an armed assailant without getting shot. Unfortunately, I'm not great at it. Fortunately, hitting something in the dark with a na'at is a lot easier than with a bullet.

I snap the na'at up and out, tagging him on the side of the throat. Judging by the red fountain that erupts there, I must have nicked his carotid. Lucky shot. Double lucky because his buddy with the G3 turns to check him out and gets hit in the face with some of the blood spray. Blinded, he snaps up his rifle, but he's too afraid he'll hit Lucifer or one of his own men to shoot. He tries to wipe his eyes with his sleeve. It takes him all of about ten seconds to get one eye clear. Long enough for me to collapse the na'at's shaft and spin it like a whip so that it slams him in the center of his chest. His body armor stops the spear point from going all the way in, but the way he's gritting his teeth tells me I've made contact.

I sprint forward and pull my knife. Still half blind and hurt, he starts popping off panic shots. It's more dignified than just standing there. My jacket is open and the material snaps back when a couple of his shots get way too close to me. He finally clears both eyes, but I'm right on him, so it's not going to help. I drive my shoulder into his chest right where the na'at hit him and he thuds down onto his back. Before he can react or smack me with the gun butt, I drive the black blade straight down into his throat until I feel it snap through his spinal column.

I look over at Lucifer. The other four guys have him surrounded.

Two of the tactical team have Tasers as big as RPG launchers. The other two are carrying what look like industrial-strength tangle web guns. Those two are in a ready position waiting for the electric boys to drive Lucifer into their loving arms. That means they're standing there like a couple of macho ducks that got high and had targets tattooed on the sides of their heads right before hunting season. But I can't be sure their weapons don't have rifle fail-safes built in in case the nonlethals don't work.

I grab the G3 and put two rounds through the closest duck's head to see if anyone shoots back. Everyone looks at me, but no one fires. I give the second duck two in the chest and one in the head to make sure he stays down. The other two aren't so lucky.

There are lots of theories about fighting and warfare, from Sun Tzu's *Art of War* to Der Führer's Total War to when you're a Jet you're a Jet all the way. The one thing all these theories have in common is this: Know your enemy. His tactics, strengths, and weaknesses. When you do, ninety-nine percent of the time you're going to make him squeak like a church mouse and run away like the Road Runner. Of course, if you get it wrong, you're going to be a ten-foot banana and the guy you're fighting will be King Kong with the munchies. That sort of describes the glimmer twins with the oversize Tasers.

Seeing the rest of their team dead, they do the only thing they can. They fire at Lucifer and keep pumping the juice into him, hoping to knock him down by themselves.

This whole time, all I've seen Lucifer do is watch what's happening like he's at the zoo and wondering what funny thing the monkeys are going to do next. When the Taser darts hit and the electricity starts to flow, though, he flinches. Then he stands stock-still and for a second I think that they're zapping him with so much current that his brain has short-circuited. A moment later he holds his arms out in a way that brings back bad memories. Bodyguard or not, I'm not getting anywhere near him.

Lucifer, once upon a time the greatest angel of them all, conjures up not one, but two flaming gladius swords. He sweeps them down in a smooth, simultaneous overhand attack that slices both Tasers in two. The swords are between the shooters and down low. He brings his arms up at an angle and hits the gunmen just above their waists, but he doesn't stop. He keeps going until he's drawn the swords all the way through them. Their bodies are nothing but towers of burned meat and they fly apart like suicide bombers at a backyard barbecue.

Lucifer stands with his head bowed, staring at the ground, studying the smoldering mess. I wonder how long it's been since he's used those swords. They probably bring back funny memories for him, too. Finally, he looks up and heads toward me.

On instinct, I snap the rifle up to my shoulder, sighting in on his left eye. He freezes. Looks at me hard, wondering what I'm doing and why I'm doing it. Finally, he lowers his arms and the swords flicker out. I drop the rifle to my side.

He comes over like he's going to say something, but two unmarked vans are roaring down the street toward us. Backup for the first team. I toss the empty rifle away and sprint to the limo, start it up, throw it in reverse, and floor it.

The vans are doing about forty and I'm doing the same when we hit. Van number one smashes through my back bumper and up onto the trunk. Then van number two crawls right up number one's ass, knocking it and the limo another ten feet down the road. Good thing I wasn't doing anything important with my vertebrae or my neck would probably hurt.

Both vans are smoking and silent, but the men inside won't be for long and I'm not waiting around for Lee Marvin and the Dirty Dozen to come out shooting.

Half a block from us, two limos are at the curb to take other guests home from the party. I gesture for Lucifer to head for the lead car and I take off after him.

I can feel it now. The heat in my muscles and bones whispering to me like an old forgotten friend. I'm not Lucifer's anymore. I'm not the Vigil's night janitor, sweeping up bloodsuckers and demon fuckers. I'm back in the arena where the air tastes like blood and dust. Something is screaming at my feet because I'm making it scream. Then I make it stop. I throw its head into the grandstands to remind the crowd what a real monster looks like and it's just like coming home.

I get to the limo first and put my fist through the driver's-side window to pull out the chauffeur. A jelly-bean-size chunk of my frontal lobe is firing just enough to remind me that the driver is probably just a terrified slob doing a shitty job. I pull him through the window and shove him hard enough that he lands on the opposite curb, out of harm's way. Lucifer is already in the limo when I slide behind the wheel. As we take off I can hear gunfire popping behind us. The crowd from the party is screaming and running back toward the water.

Overhead, there's the *whup-whup* of helicopter blades and a floodlight hits us from above. At the far end of the reservoir, two vans are parked side by side, blocking the road. I turn off the headlights and look at Lucifer.

"I hope that's not your favorite suit."

"Why?"

I floor it and crank the wheel right, fishtailing the limo up over the curb and across the grass. While we're still under the trees, I push open my door, grab Lucifer, and roll left. We hit the ground hard, but not as hard as the limo when it hits the water. The hood snaps back and smashes through the windshield. It only takes a few seconds for the car to disappear into an oily froth of bubbles. The helicopter hovers over the crash, its bright belly light turning the scene into a Vegas floor show.

By then, Lucifer and I are hunkered down behind the cars on the opposite side of the street. While the vans and chopper concentrate on the spot where the car went into the resevoir, we head down a side street into a residential area. I must have pulled a muscle or something when we rolled out of the car. My side is cramped and burning.

Down a block or so, I spot an old Jeep Wrangler in a weekend warrior's driveway. I get it open with the knife, but don't start the engine. Just pop it into neutral and Lucifer and I push it into the street. Then we hop in and coast. It's slow going with no engine and no headlights. I don't see any better in the dark than you do, and my Batman night-vision scope must have gotten lost in the mail, so we pretty much crawl down the hill.

When we hit Fountain, I start the engine and steer us onto Sunset Boulevard, where we're immediately lost in the city's bumper-to-bumper nightlife wonderland. I've never been so happy to get stuck in traffic among a million other assholes in my life. I glance at Lucifer to see how he's doing. He's frowning and fingering a spot on his jacket cuff where he lost a button.

BACK TO THE Chateau it's no big surprise when we find that Amanda and her coven pals took off a few minutes after we left and there was never any trouble there.

We take the elevator up to Lucifer's floor, get out, and squeeze through the *Alice in Wonderland* clock. My neck and left side where I landed after jumping from the car is numb except for spasms of pins and needles. My right side is burning and leaking red all over my nice suit. I want a drink and a real cigarette.

I start to sit down and Lucifer says, "Don't get blood on my couch."

"It's not your couch."

I sit.

There's a black hotel phone on almost every flat surface in the room. Lucifer sits across from me and picks up the one on the coffee table between us.

"Desk? Would you ring Dr. Allwissend's room and tell him to come to my suite immediately? Thank you."

"If you're doing that for my benefit, don't bother. I've got my own doctor."

"Do you mean the little girl or the missing old man?"

"Sounds like Kasabian's been earning his keep."

"He told me about the girl. As for Kinski, it's part of my job description to keep track of all of Heaven's rejects. You never know when you might need an archangel."

"Maybe you can hire him for a party like those idiots tonight. He can turn your guests into pillars of salt."

Lucifer takes off his jacket and tosses it onto a chair. Gets a cut-crystal bottle from the end of the table, fills two glasses, and slides one in front of me. When I reach for it, I can feel the wet spreading from my stomach down to the tops of my legs.

"Does it hurt?"

"Is this Aqua Regia?"

"Yes."

"Then it won't hurt for long."

"Was it a bullet or the jump from the car that did that?"

"A lucky shot from the rifle, I think. I'd still be on my back if it was the shotgun. It's not too bad. He hit my side, so the shot went through and through. No bullets inside me this time. But I seem to be losing a lot of blood."

"The doctor will be here soon."

"I want to call Kinski."

"Be my guest."

Both of my hands are covered in blood. Not helpful when you're trying to dial the tiny keypad on a cell phone.

Surprise, surprise. I get Kinski's voice mail.

"Goddamn it, doc. Where are you? I'm bleeding to death and all I've got here is Lucifer, a stapler, and a couple of cocktail napkins. You said to get help from Allegra, but she doesn't know how to handle stuff like this. Please call me back."

I go back and drop down onto the couch.

"Did you have a nice chat?"

"Do you know where he is?"

"No."

"I don't believe you."

"I have a general idea, but he's a powerful fellow. Angels are very good at not being seen or heard when they don't want to be."

"Then what use are you?"

"None. We angels have outlived our time. We're superfluous. But I thought you already knew that."

"The pyx is gone. It's back in the limo. So much for my bonus."

I pick up my drink. Something reflects off the glass and for a second I see Alice's face. I turn quickly and the pain in my side is blinding. There's no one there.

Why can't I forget anything like regular people? Is it because I'm a nephilim that my brain hasn't dissolved by now? I've swallowed an ocean of the red stuff and Jack Daniel's, but I still remember everything. Every woman looks like Alice and every cigarette smells like my skin burning down below.

Memories are bullets. Some whiz by and only spook you. Others tear you open and leave you in pieces. Someday the right one will catch you in between the eyes and you'll never see it coming. There'll just be a flash of a face or a smell or her touch. Then bang, you're gone. The only rational thing to do is kill memory. Get it before it gets you. One more drink should do it. It hasn't worked before, but what the hell, maybe I'll get lucky this time. I finish the Aqua Regia.

"I don't want you to worry, James. I'm going to make sure you're taken care of. I know with the way your mind works, that must sound sinister, but you're just going to have to live with it."

"You're only worried 'cause I owe you money."

He ignores this and points to my stomach.

"You're still leaking. You need to keep pressure on the wound."

"I'm not made of rubber. I've got the front, but I can't reach the hole in back."

He gets up and comes around the table.

"Turn around so I can see your back."

I slide around and feel him press one of the throw pillows against the wound.

"I'm bloody and drunk and a strange man is holding a pillow over me. It's like summer camp all over again."

"You did a good job tonight. You saw the attack coming before I did. I hope you know how embarrassing that is for me."

"It'll be our little secret."

"A century ago, I wouldn't have missed it."

"A century ago, they'd have been coming by steamboat and horse-drawn buggies. Helen Keller wouldn't have missed it."

Someone steps through the clock with a leather satchel in his hand. It's an old man in a wrinkled shirt and a severe case of bed hair.

Lucifer barks at the old man.

"You took your time, you old fool."

"Ich schlief. Es tut mir leid, mein herr."

"Take care of his wounds."

The old man nods and sets his bag on the table as Lucifer goes back to his chair. I start to take off the jacket, but Dr. Allwissend waves at me to stop. He takes an oversize cut-throat razor from his bag and, with a couple of smooth Jack the Ripper slashes, cuts the jacket and shirt so he can lift them right off me. I wouldn't want to be dating this guy's daughter. He wipes the blood from my wounds and takes some bottles from his bag. He spreads them on the table and begins mixing a potion.

"So, which one of them did it?" I ask.

"Which one?"

I look over the doctor's shoulder so I can see him.

"Which one of everyone who hates your guts set you up? Mason? Aelita? Some civilian who doesn't want his soul on a hook in a Hellion butcher shop? Maybe Bruce Willis is scared your movie will be bigger than his?"

"You're hilarious. I have no idea."

"Guess."

"Not Mason. He wouldn't have done it like that. He would have gone for something more . . . baroque. Winged snakes. Fire from the sky."

"Yeah. Lizzie Borden with a death ray stuff."

"Exactly."

"At first I thought it was the Vigil, but—and don't get offended, I'm just the messenger—you're not on Aelita's radar. She thinks you're all buggy whips and syphilis. Quaint old antiques."

"Lucky me."

"That only leaves one candidate. Someone at the party. A Sub Rosa?"

"How's that?"

"Who else knew where you were going tonight?"

"Just you and Kasabian."

"Kasabian didn't know when you were leaving. If I was the one who arranged the hit, I could have just let those guys take you. That means either I arranged to get myself shot again or it was someone else."

"There were a lot of people at the party. Including civilians."

"Yeah, but how many of them have the contacts to arrange a hit like that? They came at you with nonlethals, so they wanted you alive. That means someone has the contacts to set up a snatch-and-grab that size and the balls to think that they can hold you. That doesn't sound like a civilian to me. At least not a civilian on his own."

"I don't imagine they wanted ransom. Whom would they ransom me to?"

"One of your generals? Mason? God?"

Lucifer laughs.

"If Father wanted me, he wouldn't send a SWAT team. A rain of toads or plague of locusts, maybe, but not children in ninja pajamas."

"What about a civilian who wants his or her soul back?"

"Hmm."

The doctor pours the potion he's put together into his hands and smears it on my wounds. It's thick and smells like diesel oil. From a battered wooden box he pulls a couple of fat, glistening beetles. Puts one on my stomach and the other on my back. They start eating the oil.

"Shit!"

I try to twist away, but the doctor grabs me.

"Nicht bewegen."

"He's telling you not to move," says Lucifer.

"Being shot is one thing. Bug food's another."

"Be quiet and take your medicine like a good boy."

As the beetles eat the oil, they nibble the dead skin around my wounds, leaving a filament behind. When they're done, both wounds are closed with a kind of thick spiderweb patch.

The doctor puts his beetles away and says something to Lucifer.

"He says that you've already stopped bleeding internally and that you won't even have scars. He says that all your scars, including the burn on your arm, are healing very nicely."

"Does he know any way to stop them?"

Lucifer says something to Allwissend. The doctor looks at me and laughs.

"I know. Only an idiot doesn't want to heal. Forget it," I say.

After the doctor puts away his tools, he and Lucifer talk for a couple of minutes. Allwissend looks at me and nods a good-bye.

Lucifer takes two Maledictions, lights both, and hands me one.

"To answer your question, I don't know which Sub Rosa or civilian would want to kidnap me. If they're working for one of my enemies, why not just kill me? I'd go straight back to Hell, to where whatever general hired them could pick me off."

"What about the missing guy, Spencer Church? Do you own his soul?"

"No, I'm not sure I even met the man."

"Seems like there's other people around town missing. It's practically all Lurkers at Bamboo House. Do you know anything about that?"

"No."

Now that my right side feels better, I can feel my neck and the pins and needles on my left side more.

"You need to be careful. And you need more help than just me. Who else do you have here?" I ask.

"I'll make some calls. But until this is resolved, I'll be doing most of my business from this suite."

"Good, 'cause I think I'm going to want tomorrow off."

"Of course. We can stay in touch by phone and through Kasabian. Let's talk and I'll let you know when I need you again."

I pick up the shirt the doctor sliced up.

"Can I borrow something to wear?"

Lucifer gets up and goes to the bedroom. It lets me get a good look at him and confirm what I thought I saw earlier.

He comes back and drops a pile of neatly folded silk dress shirts onto the table.

"Take whichever you like. Take a few extras, too."

I go through the pile shirt by shirt, dropping each one onto the table.

"You like these colors, don't you? Black, dark reds, and purples."

"Why do you ask?"

"They're good colors for hiding blood. You're bleeding, aren't you?"

He stares at me for a while. Long enough that I start to wonder if I've finally said the wrong thing and he's going to have to tip the maid extra to peel my skull off the ceiling. Eventually, he nods.

"Yes, I am."

"But you didn't get hurt tonight. You always wear these colors, so I'm thinking you've had the wound for a while."

He smiles.

"Keep going. You're impressing me."

"That's why you're here and not in Hell. You got hurt in a tussle with one of your generals who went bad on you, but you don't want anyone to know. It's better to come up here and play an egomaniac dick than it is to stay Downtown and hide all the blood."

He cocks his head and puffs his Malediction.

"Not bad. You're not entirely right, but you're closer than I thought you'd get."

"What did I get wrong?"

"No one in Hell did this to me. I received these wounds in Heaven."

Lucifer stands and opens his shirt. Most of his body, from his waist to his chest, is wrapped in linen bandages. Here and there, yellow lymph and blood have soaked through. There's a large bloody patch near his heart. That's the blood I noticed earlier.

"There are some things even an angel can't endure. A father's disapproval is one." He sits down and winces. "His thunderbolts are another."

He buttons his shirt.

"You think you were scarred in the arena? You should have seen my face before the surgeons had their way with me. Of course, in those days we had no medicines or medical instruments in Hell. My doctors attended to me with obsidian knives chipped from the walls and slivers of sword blades that had fallen from Heaven with us."

"You've always been like this. The whole time you've been in Hell?"

"Daddy showed me the door with a face full of fire."

"Do your generals know you're hurt?"

"They fought beside me. Of course they know."

"If they know, that means Mason knows."

"I suppose so."

"The wound is getting worse, isn't it? It's bleeding more than it used to and you had to leave to hide it. What happened? Did you get hexed?"

Lucifer gestures at the table.

"Pick a shirt and get dressed."

I take a red one so dark it's almost black. He stares at me as I put it on.

"The front desk will call you a cab."

He pulls a few hundreds from his pocket and hands them to me.

"This will get you home and buy you some drinks to stop the pain. We'll talk later."

I go to the clock and lean over to step through. I pause and look at him.

"You're the one who told me to get smarter about what I do, so don't get weird because I start asking questions."

I push open the door on the other side of the clock and am stepping through when he says, "I think I liked you better when you just killed things."

"So did I," I say, and pull the door shut.

THIS IS SOMETHING I haven't felt for a while. This is pain. Real pain. Fire ants gnawing their way out of the stitches over my bullet wounds. Some use their pincers, but the twitchy speed freaks are going at it with chain saws and jackhammers. I remember this feeling from my early human-punching-bag days Downtown and later ones in the arena. I don't like remembering it and I sure as shit don't like feeling it. This is how regular people feel, not me. I'm home and my body is developing a mind of its own. It thinks it gets a vote in how things work around here. It wants my scars to heal and it's taking away my most basic weapon— my armor. My body is staging a revolution and it no longer recognizes me as its great and glorious dictator. Pain is how it's burning me in effigy.

It's not just the bullet wound, but also the road rash from bailing out of the limo. I didn't even notice it last night when I was busy leaking all over the stolen Jeep and hotel. My pants are shredded and Lucifer's shirt is stiff with dried blood. I may need to rethink my priorities.

Maybe put off the not-killing-everyone thing while I work on shielding hexes. Getting hit without my armor just isn't fun anymore.

As sweet as it feels, I can't lie here forever curled up in a big ball of fuck-the-world.

If I was really smart, I'd go online, take an aptitude test, and change careers completely. Work around soft things and away from bullets. A marshmallow factory or a plush-toys sweatshop. Maybe dress like a clown and learn to make balloon animals for kids' parties. I know some beasts the kiddies have never dreamed of.

"You're awake," says Kasabian.

"If you say so, Alfredo Garcia."

"What happened to your pretty Sunday school clothes?"

"I jumped out of a car."

"Of course you did."

I get out of bed slowly, stagger into the bathroom to piss and brush my teeth. I wash my face in cold water, but it doesn't help. I'm as zombied out as last night's golems. I hope someone has the courtesy to burn my chewed-up head-less corpse when I die. The thought of ending up a billion-aire's Muppet makes me want to shoot every Sub Rosa I can find, starting in East L.A., heading west, and not stopping until I hit the ocean. I'd need a pickup truck to carry that many bullets. I wonder if Kasabian can drive shift?

Still on autopilot, I flop back down on the bed. It hurts, but I don't have to move again for a long time. Glad I told Lucifer I was taking the day off.

When I was a kid I plucked magic out of the air. Didn't even think about it. It was just there, like breathing. I was naked last night without my gun. I can't live without my weapons and I'll never give them up, but I can't rely on guns to get me out of every scrape. I need to make friends with my inner brat, get back to when magic was as easy as getting bit by the neighbor's dog. Ever since I got back, I've been in arena mode. I picked up the habit of weapons there and I have to get out of it here.

Time for a drink. Something to loosen up and let little Stark out of the basement, where he's been locked up playing five-card stud with Norman Bates's mom. She cheats, of course. The dead think they can get away with anything because you'll feel sorry for them. If you play cards with the dead, make sure you deal and don't let them buy you drinks. They'll slip you a formaldehyde roofie and pry the gold fillings out of your teeth.

I pour a tumbler of JD and take a long sip. Whiskey doesn't mix well with toothpaste, but I already filled the glass, and once whiskey's been let loose you have to deal with it, like love or a rabid dog.

There's a crumpled bag from Donut Universe on the floor. I drink and Kasabian likes glazed chocolate with sprinkles. We're the trailer trash that Dorothy never met in Oz.

I tear a square from the bag and fold it over and over again, trying to remember the pattern. When I'm done, I have a lopsided origami crane. I put it on the bedside table, tear another square, and start folding. It takes a couple tries, but I end up with a kind of thalidomide bunny. Now I'm on a roll and make a fish, a dog, and an elephant whose legs are too long. Like he escaped from a Dalí painting.

I set up my inbred critters around the whiskey tumbler

like carousel animals and whisper a few words to them, not in Hellion, but in quiet English, like I'm trying to coax a cat out from under the bed.

My mother once told me a story she said got left out of the Bible. It's when Jesus was a young boy. He snuck off from the fields where His family was working and Mary finds Him on a riverbank making birds out of mud. The little sculptures are lined up next to Him, drying in the sun. Mary yells at Him and tells Him to come back to work. Jesus gets up but before He goes He waves His hands over the mud birds and they come to life and fly away. A great way to let your folks know you're not going into the family business.

The origami animals start to move. The elephant takes a step. The crane tries its wings. I lean in close and blow on them. That does it. They march and flutter around the glass like a special-ed Disney cartoon. I pick them up, set them on the floor, and point at Kasabian. They start the long Noah's Ark march across the room.

I take another sip of my drink and see Lucifer's stone on the table next to the money he gave me last night. Is it a seeing stone? Chewing gum? Am I supposed to start carrying around a slingshot because he knows I'm going to run into a giant who never went to Sunday school and doesn't know how the story ends? I stare at it and the stone lifts from my hand and hovers about six inches over it. I tap it with a finger and start it spinning. Maybe Lucifer is supposed to take the stone back from me like David Carradine in *Kung Fu*. Or maybe he was fucking with me and it's just a stupid rock.

"Shit. What is this?" asks Kasabian.

The animals have made it across the floor, up the table legs, and are clambering onto Kasabian's skateboard.

"Get 'em off me!"

"Don't move, man."

I crook a finger and imagine a peashooter. When I flick the finger, the bunny flies off Kasabian's deck like it stepped on an origami land mine. The fish and the dog get the same kill shots. When I try to sniper the elephant, it seems to see it coming and the shot knocks Kasabian's beer over onto his keyboard. He kicks the bottle off the table as the elephant legs it for the window. The crane might be lumpy and not very aerodynamic, but it's no dummy. It flutters out the window after the elephant.

"What's wrong with you, goddamn it?" yells Kasabian.

Luckily, the beer bottle was mostly empty. I point to it.

"Come on, I'm open. Hit me!"

He doesn't need that much encouragement. Kasabian half turns and kicks the bottle at me with six of his legs. It goes somersaulting at my head.

When it's a foot away, I bark some Hellion and the bottle explodes into a million pieces. Okay, it wasn't exactly shield magic, but I didn't get hit.

"Don't even dream of asking me to clean that glass up."

"I'll get the maid to do it. Come on. Boot something else. I need to practice."

I don't have to tell him twice. He kicks an empty DVD case, a wire-mesh penholder, and a pile of printer cartridges at me.

This time I hold back and throw a big mental marshmallow around me. The DVD case bounces and ricochets off the ceiling. The penholder bounces and flips into the bathroom. I block two of the printer cartridges.

"My wings are like a shield of steel!"

I'm so pleased with myself that I miss the third cartridge and it hits me over the eye.

"Touchdown!" yells Kasabian.

"Damn. That hurt."

I take another sip from my tumbler. The pains in my stomach and side aren't getting any better, but they're getting farther away. Like I'm looking down at them from the third floor. My cell phone rings. It rings again. Kasabian is back working on the computer. After the third ring, the phone stops. A second later, the phone at Kasabian's desk rings. He picks it up and gives me a look.

"Yeah, he's here. Sure it rang. He's just being a little bitch today."

I have a pretty good idea who's on the other end of the call. Kasabian mostly listens and grunts every now and then.

He has *Black Sunday* playing on the monitor with the sound down. Some very bad men are nailing a devilish witch mask to Barbara Steele's pretty face. I've seen that done for real. I'm glad this version is in black-and-white.

A couple of "okays" followed by a "yeah" and Kasabian hangs up.

"Guess who that was," he says.

"Unless it was about me winning the lottery, I don't care."

"Lucifer says for you to answer your damned phone."

"What did he want?"

"He doesn't need you today and maybe tomorrow, too. Ritchie and some bigwigs are coming to the Chateau for a meeting."

"Does he know them all? Does he trust them?"

"He said you'd ask that and says not to worry. He owns all their souls. They wouldn't dare cross him."

"Those are exactly the people who are going to cross him."

"He says he's got it under control."

"I hope he has fun and only agrees to tasteful nudity."

"You know, you've been drinking a lot lately, even by your standards."

" 'There was moonshine, moonshine to quench the devil's thirst. The law they swore they'd get him, but the devil got him first.' Robert Mitchum wrote that for *Thunder Road*, the year of our Lord, 1958."

"You're not Robert Mitchum, this isn't *Cape Fear*, and the devil is pissed at you. You might think about spacing out the Jack with, I don't know, anything that's not Jack."

"You heard anything new about Mason?"

"Nope."

"Ever hear of a guy named Spencer Church?"

"Should I?"

"Probably not. He's a rich junkie who's turned up missing."

"There's a first."

"What about the Sub Rosa. The families. Are they in the Codex?"

"Everything is in the Codex."

"Except what I want."

"Try asking the right questions."

"It's my fault, then. You're not holding out on me."

Kasabian ignores me and watches his movie.

"What does it say about the families?"

"It's boring. It's mostly histories. Family trees. Who begat who. There's one fun fact to know and tell. Whenever a lot of families are in the same geographic area, each family specializes in a different kind of magic. It's like a franchise. Supposed to keep down the hillbilly feuds."

"The Springheels were blue bloods, so I suppose they'd have first dibs. What kind did they do?"

"Past-tense blue bloods. They didn't have much by the end. I don't know what magic they started out with, but even at the end they were pretty respected charm makers. Amulets. Talismans. Protective runes."

"What about the Geistwalds?"

"Scryers. Fortune-tellers. If you ask me, the whole so-called art is a joke. I've met maybe two or three scryers with enough nickels in their pockets to make a quarter. The others I'd second deal at poker and take all their money. They couldn't even see me cheating. What kind of seer is that? The whole so-called art is for rubes."

"The Geistwalds look like they're doing all right. Their house is about the size of the San Fernando Valley. Someone said they advise studios on what movies to make."

"Still sounds like a gaff."

"What does it say about the Ashes? Cabal and his sister."

"Another old family. They pulled something shady back in the old country, took off, and ended up here. No one's sure if Cosima, the chick, is Cabal's sister or his wife. Hell, they probably don't even remember anymore, which makes it even worse if you've ever seen them."

"I have."

"My condolences. The Ashes are into the Black Sun. Chaos magic. Technically, it's about controlling elementals to bring you luck and your enemies bad luck. It's power yoga for the ruling class. Tycoons and politicos love it. It's sketchy, but no one's getting attacked, so it's all legal. Everyone knows the Ashes keep the big-money stuff off the books. Revenge. Banishments. Maybe even vaporware."

"They're soul merchants?"

"Soul trading is bigger than hookers and drugs combined in L.A. So many people have lost theirs or the one they have is so rotten they need a transfusion."

"Think they'd murder someone for a particular soul?"

"There's stories."

"Working with elementals means they'd probably have hotshot demons on their Christmas-card list."

"Along with their T-shirt size and favorite Beatle."

"They ever been caught playing rough, demonwise?"

"The Inquisition has made some moves, but never found enough to do more than fine them. The Ashes are one of the oldest families in the world. They know how to cover their tracks."

"Unless they don't want to cover their tracks. Unless they want to make an example of someone."

"What do you mean?"

"Nothing."

I mentally walk through the Springheel house, from where Marshal Julie was pulling doorman duty to Santa

Muerte standing guard over bones and gristle, to the broken magic circle that was really a hexagon drawn to call dark forces. One dark force. The eater. Did Cabal and Cosima know that Enoch Springheel was a Bone Daddy and sent him something special delivery? But why bother? From what everyone is saying, the Springheels were about as low as you could get and still have indoor plumbing. If you wanted to off somebody to make a point, why not go for the Geistwalds? But the Ashes are too smart for that. And if they just wanted to have fun, they'd go for civilian rubes, not another Sub Rosa. Still, there is a dead guy and the demon that ate him.

I don't even know why I care. I didn't know the guy. I don't know any of these people. But I don't like being lied to, especially if being lied to gets me shot. Springheel gets eaten. Lucifer gets bushwhacked. Another Sub Rosa named Spencer Church is missing. Carlos lost his pal, Toadvine, and that woman at Bamboo House is missing a kid. Probably none of this has anything to do with me, but as long as Lucifer means to drag me along into the Sub Rosa's billion-dollar outhouse, I know there's a gun pointed at the back of my head.

"Give me the Walter Cronkite on Hell. What's the weather like down there?"

Kasabian turns from the movie and looks at me. He sighs.

"There's nothing to tell. It's the usual mess. Guys stabbing guys. Women stabbing guys who just stabbed guys. It's rerun season down there. Nothing new."

"The other night I was walking around East L.A. and for a second I thought I saw Mason."

"You didn't. That's impossible."

"Then he's down there. You've seen it."

"I don't have to see it. I know."

"From Lucifer?"

"I just know."

"That's not good enough. I need to know what's happening. Lucifer is here for a reason and it's not to make a damned movie."

"Can't help you. Speaking of movies, shut up. The two traveling doctors are about to open Barbara Steele's coffin and bring her back to life."

When you make a threat, make it big. When you make it big, make sure you're prepared to go all in if someone calls you on it.

I go to the table and hit the power switch on Kasabian's monitor.

"Hey, I'm watching that."

I grab Kasabian and his deck under one arm, pull open the door, and carry him downstairs.

He stage-whispers, "Put me down! Take me back!"

I carry Kasabian straight out the back door to the alley. If any customers caught a glimpse of a head on a deck, they would just think I was throwing away a mannequin or an old movie promotion.

Kasabian is pretty discreet considering his situation. He doesn't start screaming until I close the back door.

"What the fuck are you doing, man? Take me back inside."

"It's time for you to leave the nest, Tweety Bird. The world is your oyster. I saw a 'Help Wanted' sign at Donut

Universe. With your managerial skills, you'll be running the place by the end of the week. *Vaya con Dios*, Alfredo Garcia."

"Are you out of your mind? What if someone sees us?"

"People will pay big bucks to see you. Maybe you should go to Griffith Park and sign up at the petting zoo. Hell, you'll be their star attraction."

"Is this about the money? I wasn't embezzling. I was investing it for us. The store is on its last legs, man. We're going to need a stake when it goes under."

"It's not the money or the attitude or you shitting beer out your neck hole. You've outgrown the place. You're a lone wolf, not a team player, and I don't want to hold you back."

I reach into my pocket, wad up one of Lucifer's hundreds, and toss it at him.

"Go buy yourself some platform shoes. Tall people always get the best job offers."

When I go back inside, he's still sitting there with his mouth open, the hundred lying at his metal feet.

I pull the door closed and wait. Right away I hear scratching, like a stray cat trying to get in after it got locked out of the house at night. Kasabian is cursing me through the door, but not loud enough for anyone else to hear. He doesn't want that. The kicking and cursing goes on for thirty or forty seconds, getting louder the whole time. Then it stops. I listen. Nothing.

Okay. That's something I didn't count on. That moneygrubbing jack-o'-lantern isn't crazy enough to go around to the front, is he?

I run up the stairs far enough that the customers can't see me, and step through a shadow into the alley.

At first, I don't see him. Then I hear a scrabbling from overhead. Fuck me. The little centipede is halfway up the wall, climbing for the bathroom window on his prehensile legs. He's slow, but he's moving steadily. I had no idea he could do that. Something else he's been hiding along with all the other information he's locked away?

I start to say something. When he looks down his eyes go wide. He screams and starts to fall. I throw up the shield I used earlier in the room. Kasabian is right over the Dumpster, so I vault the side and catch him when he bounces off the shield.

He yells, "Get out! Get out now!"

"Calm down. You've been in plenty of dirtier places than this."

"Look down, asshole."

I move Kasabian's deck to the side and look at my feet. At the bottom of the Dumpster, on a pile of JD bottles, boxes, and worn-out DVD cases is a man's hand. There's a few inches of bone sticking out past the torn and ragged wrist. It looks like rats have been having a Sunday buffet.

"Please take me back inside."

"What are you so upset about? It's not yours."

I get out of the Dumpster and set him on the ground.

"Sorry. I can't go carrying you through there naked again. You're wearing a disguise this time."

There's a Disney box lying on top of the Dumpster junk. I grab it, drop it on top of Kasabian, and carry him inside and up to the room. I punch the power on his monitor and set him down in front of it. *Black Sunday* is still playing. He stares at it for a moment like he's never seen a movie before, and then turns it off.

"Is there any beer left?" he asks.

"I think so."

I take one from the minifridge, pop the top, and slide his bucket under him. Kasabian is still staring at the blank monitor screen.

"Did you see that fucking thing?"

"It was pretty much on my foot."

"Where do you think it came from?"

"A guy's arm."

"I mean did you recognize it. Did it look familiar?"

"It looked like a hand. You want to be Sherlock Holmes? I'll drop you back down there and you can play patty-cake with it all day."

"Body parts lying around. That's a bad omen for me. I can't afford to lose anything else."

"That's right. The universe stopped by our trash to personally deliver you a message from the great beyond. Get a grip. Some wino probably died in the neighborhood and the dogs got at him. Or there's medical trash on the beach again and kids are leaving legs and eyeballs all over town."

"What a waste. A perfectly good hand like that."

"I'll look for the other one. You can wear 'em like angel wings."

"I'll never have one again. Lucifer'll never let that happen."

"You mean a body."

"It's humiliating, you know. This whole situation. I'm

not even a dog. I'm half a dog. On top of that I got you and Lucifer surrounding me, gnawing my ass like it's filet mignon. You both want information and I know someday I'm going to tell one of you something you don't like and you're going to throw me into the wood chipper without a second thought."

"I can't help you get a body. The black blade is a mean Hellion hex machine. Whatever it cuts stays cut and all the king's horses and all the king's men can't, you know."

Kasabian picks up his beer and chugs the bottle. It drains out of his neck and into the bucket, sounding somewhere between a light summer rain and someone peeing in a Dixie cup.

"So, my options are: I can go back to Hell, be damned and tortured forever, but at least I'll have a body, or I can be Zardoz on a skateboard up here with you forever. You'd think this would be an easy choice, but it isn't."

"Does the Codex say anything about someone in your situation putting a body back together?"

"No, but I'll tell you one thing I've learned. Any spell cast can be broken. Any spell broken can be put back together."

"If you want I can have a word with the boss."

He shakes his head and drops the bottle into the recycling bin.

"Forget it. The last thing I need to get into is office politics."

"I can see how your situation sucks, but in case you haven't noticed, neither one of us is exactly free to go drink mai tais in Maui. Maybe if we don't shank each other in the shower, we can do something to improve that stupid situation. I don't know what exactly, but maybe something."

"You're going to improve things? I'm so fucking relieved. Just remember to tell Santa I'll need a stepladder when he brings me that pony next Christmas."

I get up and look for some clothes that don't have blood on them. When I'm pulling on my boots, Kasabian says, "Beelzebub is the only one of the big generals left who hasn't joined up with Mason's bunch. He has all the other generals, but Beelzebub's army is almost as big as all of theirs put together. But if he gets offed or switches sides, that's it. Mason wins."

"And Lucifer has nowhere to go."

"Allegra can teach him to run a cash register. He can be night manager and we'll be his bosses."

I check the drawers in the bedside table looking for something to smoke. I check my pockets for the electronic cigarette and then remember that I tossed it into a canal in the ballroom. Sometimes we do dumb things to amuse women.

"There's something else."

"Don't tell me. Mason has a herpes gun. Or a bomb that gives everyone a fat ass and they get depressed and sit around eating ice cream all day while he takes over."

"Mason is working on something all right. He's got his own Manhattan Project going with alchemists, sorcerers, witches—human and Hellion—all working together. One of Beelzebub's spies found out and passed the word along. From what I heard, right after that, he ended up in Tartarus."

"You can hear things when Lucifer talks with other Hellions?"

"Not always and not everything. But I heard enough of this."

I shrug and give up on finding smokes. That's okay. I need to get out of here and walk off some of the knots in my legs and side.

"This isn't news. Mason's always got two or three things going at the same time."

"Yeah, but nothing like this before."

"What is it?"

"He's trying to make a new key to the Room of Thirteen Doors."

I don't know what I was expecting to hear, but that wasn't it. But it makes sense. What's worse is that the prick is talented and relentless enough to actually do it.

"Is that what you didn't want to tell me?"

"You shot at me once. You threatened to drop me in the ocean and throw me to the coyotes, so I had some concerns you might overreact."

"You weren't holding back because you thought you could cut a deal with Mason?"

"Make a deal with the guy who blew me up and left me like this? He's right at the top of my people-to-trust list."

"Okay. Thanks for coming clean."

"You're taking it pretty well."

"No. I'm not."

I head for a shadow next to the closet door, stop, and turn back to Kasabian.

"No one's going to look out for us but us. We're just bugs on God's windshield. You need to get serious and work with me on this or we're both going to end up in Tartarus."

"What the Hell is in Tartarus? Even the Codex doesn't say."

"I don't know, but I figure anything that scares Hellions ought to scare me. We need to talk some more, but I need some alone time to clear my head."

"Me, too."

"By the way, what happened out back? I wouldn't have left you out there."

"Yeah, you would have."

"Only if I thought you were going to dick me around forever. Then yeah, but only then."

"Lucky me some schmuck lost a hand."

"You were wrong, see? Turns out it was a good omen."

Kasabian scuttles around and hits the eject button on the DVD player.

"You got enough devil movies for tonight?"

"Suddenly I'm out of the mood for those. Maybe I'll watch *The Great Silence*."

"Do one more devil movie. *Bedazzled*. The original. It makes facing down Lucifer easier if you picture him in a Brit burger joint in a silly cape."

"Maybe I'll do that."

"I'll be going by Bamboo House later. Want me to bring you back something?"

"A burrito. *Carnitas*. Hot. Not those old-lady ones you get. Lots of salsa and green peppers."

"Anything else, boss?"

"Thanks for not doing a slice-and-dice when I told you about Mason cooking up a new key."

"You've got good timing. I was going to try and not kill

all those other people out in the world, but that's on hold
since they're trying to kill me. That means you get to be my
no-kill project."

"Lucky me."

"Lucky us. We might be doomed, but we're not in pieces
in a Dumpster."

I STEP OUT of a shadow into the hallway by Vidocq's apartment. Vidocq and Allegra's. I need to start thinking about it
that way. I love the old man, but the thought of him rattling
around in there alone used to bother me. Now that he's with
Allegra, it's different. I don't know why. Yeah, I do. I don't
want that place to be something else Mason has ruined.

I knock on the apartment door and Allegra answers. She
looks at me.

"Since when do you knock?"

"Last time I was here, you said I only came over when I
wanted a potion or needed to get sewn up, so I thought I'd
come over and try to act like a person for a while."

She steps back and opens the door more.

"Come in."

Vidocq comes over, wiping his hands on a black rag that
I'm guessing didn't start out that color. He grabs me in a
bear hug.

"Good to see you, my boy. And look, no blood. We need
some wine to celebrate."

"Thanks."

As he grabs a wine bottle and glasses off the counter, he
says, "Allegra was going to call you. Tell him."

She smiles at me.

"The Cupbearer's elixir is ready. We finished it maybe an hour ago."

Vidocq comes back with the bottle, hands out glasses, and pours wine for everyone.

"Allegra figured it out. Often, when those old witches wrote their potions down, they would leave out a step or two to preserve their secrets. We worked all night, but the mixture wouldn't hold together. Then Allegra intuited a solution. You want to preserve your body, so that's what we gave it. I found one of your bloody shirts in the trash, cut a piece, and dropped it in. That's the trick. The elixir must be made for each individual. And this one is yours."

He hands me a small amber-colored antique apothecary bottle. Like something Mattie Earp would use to hide her laudanum from Wyatt.

"Thanks. I mean it."

Vidocq stands next to Allegra, puts his arm around her, and kisses her on the temple.

"She will replace us all soon. And you, you'll be back to yourself, as scarred and lined as Lucifer's scrotum."

What can you say to that? I hold up my glass.

"To the devil's balls."

Allegra and Vidocq hold up theirs.

He says, *"Pour les bourses du diable."*

Vidocq and I drain our glasses. Allegra sips hers politely.

She says, "Speaking of the devil, is it true you're working for him?"

I put my hand over the wound where the bullet went in.

"Looks that way. I saved the bastard's life last night."

Allegra is looking at me like a disapproving schoolmarm,

but Vidocq leans in for a close look at the bullet hole.

"Saint Raphael's silk. *Les petites araignées* do beautiful work, don't they?"

"I wouldn't know. I had my eyes closed."

He laughs and pours us more wine.

"I don't blame you. They're ugly little buggers."

Allegra shakes her head when he offers her some.

"How can you work for him?"

"I work for him because he pays me, same as the Vigil."

"Taking his money doesn't bother you?"

"Does taking mine when you get paid? Some of your salary comes from what he gives me. A salary for a job you don't even do anymore."

"I'm no Bible-thumper, but I don't think it's right."

"A little while ago you were begging me to meet him. Now, all of a sudden, you're Cotton Mather. What is this?"

"Wanting to see him isn't the same as working nine-to-five for someone who's pure evil."

"He isn't the one who sent me to Hell. He isn't the one who wants to destroy the world and Heaven and everything in between. That's Mason. Lucifer has always played pretty straight with me. It's humans I worry about. Besides, he's had me on retainer pretty much since I got back, so I owe him."

"Do you really think he would worry about what he owed you? You think he wouldn't trick you so he could take your soul?"

"I don't care what he would do. I was raised to pay my debts. Besides, I'm Pinocchio, remember? Not exactly a real boy. No one knows if nephilim even have souls."

"That's right, stick up for the old man, daddy's boy."

"What does that mean?"

"You said Lucifer helped you when you were hunting Mason and the Circle. Up till now he's been paying you money for doing nothing but being a drunk. Now he's here with a job he could easily get other people to do, which means it's really an excuse for keeping you around."

"I pulled his ass out of the fire last night and I've got the holes in me to prove it."

"How many cops do you think Lucifer owns? How many politicians, soldiers, spies, and corporate billionaires just in California? And you're the only one who can protect him?"

"You think I can't?"

"Think about it. Your mother was a pretty, lonely woman and your father was an angel."

Vidocq sniffs the wine in his glass and shrugs.

"Surely the possibility that Lucifer is your father has crossed your mind before."

"A lot of things cross my mind, but I let go of the stupid ones."

Allegra gets closer and puts her hand on my arm. I know she's trying to be kind, but it feels like a cop about to snap on the cuffs.

"The more you're with him, the more he'll suck you down into his world so that you start really acting like his son, and when you do that you'll be like him and you won't be Stark anymore."

"For someone who says she's not a Bible-thumper, you've got a lot of opinions on the subject of the devil."

"I don't care about the devil. I care about you. He's going

to manipulate you and trick you and make you into something you'll hate."

I move my arm away from her hand and pour myself more wine.

"You're just jealous 'cause everyone knows my daddy's name and no one's ever heard of yours."

"This isn't a joke."

"Everything is a joke if you come at it from the right angle and that's the angle I'm coming at this conversation."

I swallow the wine and set down the glass.

"I spent eleven years Downtown and you think Jake the Snake is going to twist me around in the few weeks it takes to make a movie? I don't care if he's my father. All that means is he fucked my mom. I grew up with another guy who fucked my mom and he wanted me dead every day of my life. Hell, in the world's greatest dad contest, Lucifer wins just for not wanting me laid out with pennies on my eyes. Like I said before, he isn't what keeps me up at night. It's humans I worry about."

Vidocq steps between us and puts a hand on both our shoulders.

"Why don't we all sit down, have some more wine, and forget this talk of devils and fathers. Neither of those subjects ever leads to anything pleasant."

I look at Allegra. Her heart is going like crazy and her pupils are dilated. Her breathing is steady, but she's having to work at it.

"Thanks. But I've got to be somewhere."

"Please don't go," she says.

She puts her hand on my arm again. I pull away and go to the door.

"Thanks again for the elixir. What do I do with it?"

"Just drink it," says Vidocq. "But mix it with something first. It tastes a bit like turpentine."

"I'll pick up some margarita mix and little umbrellas. Thanks."

"Come back soon, okay?" says Allegra.

I open the door and go out into the hall. I don't have anything to say to her, so I don't say anything.

Of course, it's occurred to me that Lucifer might be my father, but how do you even begin to wrap your mind around something like that? Is he the secret to my whole sorry life? Why I had so much power when I was a kid and why I never did a damn thing with it when I got older? Is it that simple? Maybe it's why it was so easy for Mason to send me to hell. And why I get everyone I care about killed or hurt on a regular basis. The worst thing is having to admit that maybe Aelita is right. Maybe I am an Abomination. Daddy's boy, just a chip off the old brimstone.

TEN MINUTES LATER I'm talking to Carlos at Bamboo House of Dolls. Tak Shindo's "Bali Hai" is on the jukebox.

"On a scale of one to ten, how evil do I come off? Let's say one is Santa baking cookies for orphans and ten is Hitler eating babies with Freddy Krueger."

"You're sure not Santa. But I don't see you dipping babies in ranch dressing. To me how evil you are depends entirely on how much blood you track on my floors."

"You don't think I'm trying to trick you into becoming a serial killer or working for the IRS or something else horrible?"

"No. You just need to remember to wipe your feet sometime between when you kill things and when you come in here."

"That's good to hear. I trust you because you're a businessman and I know you wouldn't want Hannibal Lecter hanging around your bar."

"What do I care? 'Cause of the business you bring in, I'm going to be able to retire early. If you have to eat a few people to make that happen, I'll turn my back."

"You're a saint. You're Mother Teresa with a happy hour."

"I just call 'em like I see 'em. You might be crazy, but you're just not that evil, bro."

"Thanks. I just wanted a second opinion."

"Want something to eat?"

"Maybe just some black beans and rice. And I'm going to need a burrito to go. Spicy enough to melt an engine block. It's for a friend, not me, so I'll give you cash for that."

Carlos shakes his head.

"Don't be stupid. You want some of the red stuff?"

"A double. I'm drinking for two today. My scars and me."

Carlos brings the bottle and a glass and pours me two healthy shots. I take out the apothecary bottle and look through the amber glass.

"What's that stuff?"

"Medicine."

"You sick?"

"Not for long."

I upend the bottle and pour the whole thing into the Aqua Regia.

"*L'Chaim*," says Carlos.

"*De nada.*"

I knock it back in one gulp. My mouth, throat, and stomach are very unhappy about that. I squeeze my lips together to make sure I keep it all down.

"That good?"

"Worse. It's like a dog with cancer ate a rat with leprosy and shit it down my throat."

"I had one of those in El Paso once. You're supposed to chase it with goat piss, but I'm fresh out."

"Next time."

"That old lady is back."

"Which old lady?"

"The one with the missing kid."

"Aki."

"Yeah, that's him. She's over with Titus. I hope he's not stealing all of that lady's money."

"He always leaves them enough to cover his drinks."

"Seriously, I don't like people messing with old ladies. *Mi madre* had cancer and gave all her Social Security money to a faith healer."

"What happened?"

"He gave her a homeopathic cure and she felt better. Of course, the homeopathic cure was just sweet wine with ginger and some low-grade morphine. When she ran out of money, the cure stopped coming. She went back to the regular doctor, but by then the cancer was everywhere. Let me tell you, having cancer sucks, but being broke and having cancer is the shittiest fate that can land on a human being."

"I'm sorry, man. You want me to go over and have a word with Titus?"

"Don't sweat it. I'm just talking out loud. I've got my eye on him."

"Titus might string things out a little, but he's good at what he does. If the ring is real and the kid's here, he'll find him."

"He better get his bloodhounds barking if he wants to keep drinking here."

Carlos goes off to serve other customers. I can see a few of them staring at me in the mirror behind the bar. It's a good crowd tonight. No one tries to talk to me.

I drain the dregs of the dog shit cocktail and set down the glass, feeling queasy. The things we do to stay ugly. I check my hands hoping that maybe I'll be able to see the scars grow back in front of my eyes like Lon Chaney Jr.'s hair in *The Wolf Man*. Nothing. I can't live without scars. I bet if I asked nicely, someone around here would tie me to their back bumper and drag me a few blocks. I'm like a marathoner coming off an injury. Only I need to get my wind back by peeling off a few layers of skin. Is that too much to ask? Where are Mason and Aelita when you need them? They'd drag me to Alamogordo and back.

Enemies kill you with a knife in the back. Friends kill you with kindness. Either way you're dead.

I didn't need to stomp out on Allegra like that, but I couldn't just stand there after she opened her mouth. There are things you think and things you say out loud and they're very different things. You'd think someone like her, six months into hoodoo lessons, would know that. You don't ever say "The devil is your daddy" out loud. It doesn't matter if you and everyone else in the room are thinking it. You don't say the words. Words are weapons. They blast big bloody holes in the world. And words are bricks. Say something out loud and it starts turning solid. Say it out loud enough and it becomes a wall you can't get through. The last thing I need is a big brick Lucifer in my way.

What kind of kid would want Lucifer for a father? He'd give you the shittiest Christmas presents ever. On the other hand, he'd throw great Halloween parties.

Carlos comes back with the bottle.

"You want another one to wash the taste out of your mouth?"

"Just a half. Thanks."

A woman says something to the guy on the stool next to mine.

"That pretty redhead in the Gucci blouse? She's been looking at you the whole time I've been here. Why don't you go and say hello?"

This guy looks around and gets up. The woman slides into his seat.

I know that accent. I turn and look at her.

"Brigitte?"

"I wanted to tell you that you're not an easy man to find. That I had to scour the back streets of Los Angeles to track you down. The truth is that you're ridiculously easy to find. All of Simon's friends know where you drink."

"But do they know where I get my donuts?"

"I'm not sure I know exactly what those are."

"Frosting and grease with a little cake in between. Sometimes chocolate on top. Sometimes they put in industrial waste that tastes like cherries or apples. They're like eating sugar land mines."

"Ah. You mean *koblihy*. Yes, I'm fond of them."

"No. What you ate back home probably resembled food. You're not in America until you've eaten an American donut."

"Then I'll have to try one. You'll take me?"

"If you promise not to tell Ritchie's friends. I don't mind if they know about Carlos's place. It's more money for him. But a man should be able to enjoy a fritter in peace."

"It will be our secret. Is that red wine? I'm famished. Do you mind?"

"It's not wine."

She sputters and spits it out. Curses in Czech.

"What awful thing is that?"

"Aqua Regia. It's an acquired taste."

Carlos appears with a glass of water.

"Drink this or you're not going to have any taste buds by morning."

"Brigitte, this is Carlos. Carlos, Brigitte."

"Nice to meet you, Brigitte. Have we met somewhere?"

"She's in the movies. Maybe you saw one of them. She goes by the name of Brigitte Bardo."

"Oh yeah."

He nods. Half smiles, apparently not sure what to do with his face.

"Sure. Okay."

Another customer flags him down for a drink.

"I think you made him blush," I say.

"That's sweet. I didn't think California people could blush."

"They're an endangered species. The government tags them like condors and pandas."

"You're not what I expected. You're a very silly man, James."

"I come from a long line of tall-tale talkers. Our family crest is bullets over crossed fingers and underneath it says, 'Bullshit *Über Alles.*' "

She takes cigarettes from her purse, but Carlos stops her.

"Sorry. You can't in here."

"I'm in a bar full of vampires and witches, but what people are afraid of is my cigarette."

"Welcome to America, where everyone lives forever and everyone is beautiful if you have the money."

"Why do you drink that horrible drink?"

"It's a bad habit I picked up along the way."

"When you were gone?"

"Gone, yeah."

"And you still drink it? I'd think you'd want to forget about that place."

"No. I don't want to forget anything. Not one second of it."

"Why?"

"Because someone owes me for it. Every second I was there. Every beating. Every bad habit and every shitty dream. And for Alice."

"There you are. That's the man I was looking for. He was hiding in your eyes. A killer's eyes."

"What are you doing down here, Brigitte? Shouldn't Ritchie be buying you France or something?"

"Simon is with Mr. Macheath just now. I don't expect him back for some time. He says they're discussing the movie, but I think he's lying."

"He's trying to renegotiate his soul deal? I'd love to hear that conversation."

"Simon can be very persuasive."

"That I believe."

It bugs the hell out of me how beautiful she is. I've seen friends go through this. Falling for porn girls can be like mainlining Twinkies. It's usually more about addiction than nutrition. Both are sweet and oh so irresistible because they can't help it. Then you get jealous or she gets bored and the sugar rush ends. The crash hits and there you are, depressed, toothless, alone, and with crumbs in your sheets. I don't need to take Brigitte to Donut Universe. She *is* Donut Universe.

Or maybe I'm just full of shit, spooked by her ballistic beauty, and looking for an excuse to run away like a kid who's never figured out how to talk to girls.

"You still haven't told me why you came down."

"I wanted to see more of L.A. than the inside of a limousine. And our conversation was cut short at the party. I heard that I missed all the fun when you and Mr. Macheath left."

"Fun like a bullet hole in my side."

Her eyes widen.

"Really? Let me see."

Okay. Maybe I was too harsh. Maybe she's more than donuts after all.

I stand and pull up my shirt. She gets off the stool and squats on her haunches so she can get a better look at the damage. We're getting a lot of looks from around the bar and this time I can't blame them. This crowd probably thinks I get medical exams from porn stars every night. It's better than them knowing most of my social life is drinking and watching *The Killers* with a dead man's head.

"Do you always heal that quickly?"

"Not lately. But I'm hoping that's fixed."

"So do I."

"Do you know anything about the guy they were talking about at the party, Spencer Church?"

"Why do you want to know about him?"

I shrug.

"Because I've been drunk and out of touch for a long time and I've missed a couple of hundred things. A woman came in here asking me about her missing kid. Then I hear that other people are turning up missing. The truth is, I don't give a rat's ass about Spencer Church, but someone tried to make my boss disappear the other night and I got shot for it. If Church did disappear, I want to know who took him or if he did it on his own."

"I'm afraid I didn't know him well. I know that some of Simon's friends bought drugs from him."

"Did he burn any of them? Take their money and not deliver?"

"Not that I know of."

"I never heard of a Sub Rosa dope dealer before. I guess they had to be there, but I never thought about it till now."

Carlos sets down two glasses of brown beer nearby and comes over to us.

"Did I hear you talking about Spencer Church?"

"You know him?"

"Hell yes, I know that prick. He's an ice-cream man and a bad one. He used to sell his shitty product out of my bar, meaning when people came back to complain, I'm the one that had to hear about it, not him. He is totally, one hundred percent banned from any building I happen to be in."

"Good policy."

"Except that that ratfuck *concha* piece of shit just walked in."

"Spencer Church is here?"

"A couple of minutes ago. He's at the end of the bar. You can't miss him. Skinny blacked-eyed junkie that looks like a scarecrow with a migraine."

I look at Brigitte.

"I'm going to go talk to this guy."

"Do you think he will tell you anything?"

"Ritchie isn't the only one who can be persuasive."

I push through the crowd to the end of the bar. It's not hard to spot Church. He's taking up a lot of real estate. No one wants to get near him. Once upon a time his clothes were nicer than Cabal Ash's, but he smells worse and he looks like he's been sleeping under freeway overpasses for a week. Both of his hands are flat on the bar. His nails are long, dirty, and broken. He's got a thousand-yard stare aimed at the far wall. Between a hundred voices yammering and the jukebox, he doesn't hear me coming. I motion for Carlos to come get his attention.

I'm right behind Church when Carlos eyeballs him.

"What the hell are you doing here, man? I told you you weren't welcome here."

Church doesn't move. Doesn't blink. He just stares straight ahead. I nod to Carlos to try it again.

"Hey, asshole. You need to get out. Like now. Like five minutes ago. And don't come back."

This time Church seems to notice he's being yelled at. He slowly raises his head, like a Sphinx waking up after a thousand-year nap. He moves his lips and makes a small sound.

"What?" Carlos asks. He moves closer. "What?"

Church growls and half leaps across the bar, grabbing at Carlos with his filthy claws. His mouth is open and he's craning his neck like he wants to bite him. Carlos is yelling and bracing his arms against the bar. Church makes a gurgling growl. The floor clears as people try to get away from the chaos.

Church snaps black teeth at Carlos's face, missing it by an inch. I grab the back of Church's head and smash it down on the bar. I can feel his jaw crack, but it doesn't even slow him down. He turns and lunges at me. He's growling and biting the air, only his mouth isn't working too well anymore. His shattered lower jaw flaps around like a baggie full of oatmeal. His teeth and tongue are black as tar. Someone must have slipped something interesting into his syringe. But even meth won't rot your mouth that fast. What's he on?

Church grabs my arms and opens his black pit of a mouth. He's strong for a skinny guy. Must have pumped out a year's worth of adrenaline in the last thirty seconds.

Cue my own little panic attack. What if Church only seems strong because I've got a Samson hair thing going on and I'm getting weaker as my scars fade?

His teeth snap next to my ear.

One way to find out.

I grab Mr. Oatmeal Jaw's shoulder, spin, and toss him like a bag of trash. He flies the full length of the bar and smashes into the back wall, leaving an extremely satisfying dent in the plaster. While I'm admiring my work, feeling a warm, giddy sense of relief that I can still do unreasonable amounts of damage to my fellow man, Church rolls onto his side and stands up. He's holding his body at a funny angle. It looks like his back cracked when he hit the wall. His left arm is badly dislocated. It hangs by his side, as limp as his jaw. If he's in pain, he doesn't show it. He teeters, gets his balance, and rushes me.

His head jerks back and then explodes. Not all of it. Just the back. An exit wound.

I spin around to see who fired and there's Brigitte, up on the bar, kneeling and holding a weird little pistol in a double-hand cop grip. A white wisp of CO_2 curls out of the gun barrel.

I'm thinking *When the hell did you turn into Emma Peel?* but before I can say it, two more hungry-black-mouth scarecrows come stumbling in. Brigitte turns and blasts one before he gets more than three steps inside. The other one lunges for a woman by the jukebox. A blond civilian wearing her girlfriend's oversize leather jacket. Lucky for her that her girl rides. Scarecrow Guy latches onto her shoulder, but can't bite through the thick leather. The blonde's girlfriend pulls her one way while I get an arm around the guy's throat and pull him the other. It doesn't help. He's not choking and he won't let go of the jacket.

"Break his neck!"

It's Brigitte.

"Don't let him scratch her! Snap his neck!"

I slip my arm from around his throat, grab his jaw and the back of his head, and twist sharply. You can hear the crack of vertebrae and his spinal cord snapping over the music. I know this because everyone in the bar groans at exactly the same time. He drops to the ground near the scarecrow Brigitte shot. The crying blonde falls back on her girlfriend, who pulls her away. They bump into a table and a bottle smashes on the floor. The sound is like a starter's pistol going off. Everyone in the bar decides to go batshit simultaneously and stampede over each other trying to get outside. In less than a minute it's just Brigitte, Carlos, the corpses, and me. Except for a couple of drunk Deadheads slumped at a corner table in their purple necromancer robes.

The less drunk one shakes his head at us.

"Big deal. The soccer games at necromancer school were rougher than that."

"We're closed," says Carlos.

The Deadheads stagger out while Brigitte and I drag the corpses into the back. Carlos goes to the doors and locks them.

"Can one of you tell me what the goddamn hell just happened?" I ask.

I look at Brigitte.

She says, "Don't worry. Whatever you think you saw, no one died here tonight."

"You're saying Church and the others were already dead?" asks Carlos.

Brigitte nods.

"You're saying they were a bunch of High Plains Drifters?" I ask.

"High Plains?"

"Zombies."

"Yes."

"How did you know Church and his friends were going to be here?"

"I didn't. I came here looking for you."

"You go everywhere with that gun?"

"Of course."

"Why?"

"It's part of why I came to Los Angeles. My real work. I kill the dead."

Carlos is leaning over Church's body.

"Your friends are starting to leak on my floor. Should I be worried?"

"Is the back door unlocked?"

Carlos nods.

I grab Church and one of the other Drifters by the ankles while Brigitte grabs the third. We drag them into the alley behind the bar. The Dumpster is about half full, but I can make them fit if I push hard enough.

"Don't bother," says Brigitte.

"Why?"

Brigitte walks to the next building. Water is leaking from

an outdoor spigot. She turns it on harder and washes her hands. I follow her over and put my hands in when she's done, letting the frigid flow rinse black gunk from my palms. When we're done, I wipe my hands on my jeans. Brigitte is wearing a red T-shirt with the name of a Czech band, a black miniskirt, and boots.

She gives me a questioning look.

"Go ahead," I tell her.

She's not shy. She happily wipes her hands all over my jeans and even kneels down so she can use my cuffs to clean between her fingers. Wish I'd thought of that.

"I take it that you don't know a lot about revenants?" she asks.

"I've never even seen one until last night."

"Do you know how to kill one?"

"I thought I just did."

She shakes her head.

"We haven't killed any of them. Just their brains. The rest of them is still alive and will awaken soon. That's why it's pointless to put them in the trash. They will just crawl out. A revenant without a brain can still hold you while others attack and kill. Or bite or scratch you, passing on their disease."

"Okay. How do you kill it?"

"The nerves are the key. You must completely destroy its nervous system by ripping out its spine."

I should have stayed home and watched *Bedazzled* with Kasabian.

"I did that to a Hellion once. It peeled all the skin off my fingers and knuckles, and really hurt."

Brigitte makes a "why bother teaching a retard to juggle?" face.

"Don't be stupid. There are tools for it. I don't have mine with me, but look here."

She takes a broken slat from an orange crate and draws something on the ground. It's like a spear, but with a kind of claw and long backward-facing barbs on one end, like a hand with the fingers pointing the wrong way.

"The Hellion weapon you use. A na'at? Can you shape it into something like that?"

"I've never tried, but probably. Give me a couple of minutes."

"Don't take long. Depending on their injuries, revenants will revive in five to ten minutes."

She paces back and forth while I rework the na'at. The clicking of her boots echoes down the alley. She isn't like the woman I was talking to in the bar. More like a tiger waiting to eat an antelope it took down.

"What kind of gun was that?" I ask.

"Compressed CO_2, like at an amusement park. Mine is more powerful and fires sharpened silver-coated stainless-steel bolts."

"Why silver?"

"It's not necessary for revenants, but the silver allows you to also use them against verdilacs, beast men, and other undesirables."

"You'll have to let me try it sometime."

"After you take me to your donut shop."

"Are you really here to get into the movies?"

"Of course. I've wanted to come to Hollywood for a long

time, but I was needed at home. My erotic career was going well. I made money and had ample time to do my family's real work. Now, though, I'm needed here. It wasn't hard to get Simon to invite me. I'm going to be in a big-budget Hollywood movie and still have time to do my other work. This is what you call a win-win, yes?"

"You think there's more Drifters out there?"

"If there are three here, there are many more. How many is the question. We believe the numbers must be dealt with now before things become intolerable."

"How do you know about all this?"

"My family has done this work for centuries. In the old world and the new. I'm Roma."

"Gypsies."

"My grandfather would shoot you for using that word."

"I've been shot for less."

"So I've heard."

"Let me make sure I have this straight. The cavalry just now rode into town and it's a Czech Gypsy porn-star zombie killer. Have I got that right?"

She crosses her arms and looks at me like if we weren't on a timetable she'd kick my ass.

"Forgive me. I didn't think my life would seem so strange to Lucifer's alcoholic cowboy assassin."

"I wasn't criticizing. I'm just trying to get everyone's résumé straight. Last night you were a pretty girl at a party and tonight you're Catwoman."

She shrugs.

"Secrets quickly revealed often seem more profound than they really are."

"Everything's profound when there's guns and zombies."

She taps her wrist.

"Ticktock, Wild Bill."

"Done. How does that look?"

I hold out the na'at to her. She takes it and spins it easily, making thrusts, jabbing the air. She drops into a strong forward stance, mimes pushing it through a body and yanking it back out. Whatever else she is, she's comfortable with weapons.

"Church will revive first. Bring him to me and I'll show you how it's done."

I kick the other two aside and pick up Church. He's already starting to twitch.

"Lean him against the wall, facing away from us."

I do it and get behind her.

"Your weapon isn't perfectly designed yet, but you'll fix it when I show you a real one. It's best to go in through the back so you aren't forced to rip out the rib cage and organs. Thrust the weapon at heart height through the back with an upward motion so you slide between the ribs. Try not to pop it out the front of the body. The blades will expand inside the body and grip the spinal column. Spin the blades to cut away connective tissue and pull sharply using your body weight. Only when the spine is out is the revenant dead."

Church groans. His body straightens as much as it can, but stays facing the wall. Without its brain it doesn't occur to it to turn around.

"You can do the next one," she says.

Brigitte collapses the na'at as small as it will go. Stands at a forty-five-degree angle to Church's body, resting most of her weight on her back leg, and then swings the na'at over her head. On the third rotation, she snaps the na'at out like she's throwing a blade. The weapon extends in a second, spearing Church in the back. That wakes him up. He groans and wiggles around like a fish on a line, reaching back with his one good arm to grab at the na'at. Brigitte gives the na'at a sharp snap to the right. Church stiffens. The blades are a Veg-O-Matic in his dead guts. Brigitte crouches and jumps, not an easy thing in her boots. When she comes down she shouts something in Czech and drops her weight back. Church's back splits open and his spinal column pops out like the handle on a one-armed bandit. This time he goes down and stays down.

"Now you."

Brigitte retracts the na'at and hands it to me.

The second Drifter is dressed in brown shorts and shirt. Some kind of delivery guy. He's pulling himself to his feet hand over hand, using the Dumpster like a ladder. His back is to me. When he's upright, I spin the na'at and toss it.

It goes all the way out his front and one of the barbs hooks on the edge of the Dumpster.

When I pull the na'at, the Dumpster moves, too, and the Drifter has to do a little soft shoe to stay upright.

Brigitte sighs and walks to the Dumpster. The Drifter lunges for her and she calmly spins and catches him with a roundhouse kick to the head. While it's dazed, she climbs onto the Dumpster's lid and kicks the na'at free.

"Thanks."

"Don't talk. Kill it."

That might be the sweetest thing a woman's ever said to me on a first date.

I snap my wrist the way she did, but the barbs are still out the front of the guy's body. The spinning helps dig through his chest, but I get stuck on his rib cage. I'm pushing and pulling the guy all over the alley, like I'm the worst puppeteer in the universe.

"You've shit it all up. There's no finesse here. Use your strength. Just rip it out."

I take half a step forward and then snap back, using all my body weight to pull. The Drifter's back explodes as its rib cage, lungs, heart, and spine spill out onto the alley floor. The stink is worse than a Hellion outhouse.

"Now you know why we try not to do that," Brigitte says.

"Thanks, Nurse Ratched. Haul up the other one. I'm getting a feel for this."

Brigitte sets the third one upright. It takes one drunken step toward her. As she steps back, her left boot heel comes down on a chunk of the delivery guy's liver. Brigitte wobbles for just a second, but it's just long enough for the Drifter to lunge forward and grab her wrist.

She lays into the guy hard with fists, knees, and elbows, hammering him and twisting her arm to break his grip. A living guy would have let go just from the pain. The problem is that Drifters don't feel pain and none of her shots are quite hard enough to lay him out because she's still ice-skating on the guts of the other Drifter.

I swing the na'at and throw. It hits the Drifter square in the back and this time it stays inside. Wrist snap and pull. His spine pops out of his back like a bony jack-in-the-box.

I run over to where Brigitte is leaning on the Dumpster, scraping pieces of lungs, muscle, and who knows what else off her boots.

"I'm really sorry about that."

"Do you know what these boots cost? Of course you don't because if you did you'd be shitting yourself."

"Sorry. I don't have money, but I can walk into any store in the world and steal you another pair."

"I'm not worried about the boots. Simon will buy me all the fucking boots I want. I'm worried about what I'll tell him happened to them."

"He doesn't know about your hobby?"

"Simon can be a sweet man, but ninety-nine percent of his IQ is in his cock. I'm his trophy fuck and he can't conceive of me as anything else."

"Too bad. He's missing out."

Brigitte looks around at the gore-filled alley.

"I've seen neater kills, but I've also seen worse."

"I need to call someone about this. I can't leave a bunch of corpses lying around Carlos's back door. I know some people, the Golden Vigil. They have all kinds of resources. They can handle this kind of thing."

"I have people, too. They know how to dispose of revenants. Besides, I don't much like your Vigil."

"What do you have against them?"

"They're the government. They're police. That's enough."

Can't argue with that. I let her call her people.

I go back into the bar. Carlos is closing up, putting glasses in the washer, dumping ice in the sink, and wiping down the bar top.

"Brigitte is finishing up out back. The bodies will be gone soon."

"I never thought I'd see anything in here scarier than those skinheads that used to come in, but you always manage to surprise me."

"Don't worry. We're going to check this out and make sure it doesn't happen again."

"*Está chido*. I'd appreciate that."

"This is probably a bad time to ask, but can I still get a burrito to go?"

Carlos looks at me for a second.

"I'll see what I can do."

I go into the men's room and check myself in the mirror. I don't look too bad, but there's more blood spatter than I'd hoped. I slip off my shirt and hang it on a hook on the back of one of the toilet stall doors. I turn on the spigot in one of the sinks and wait for hot water.

A minute later, Brigitte comes in, slapping her cell phone closed.

"My people are on their way."

"Who are your people?"

"Friends."

"Roma?"

"Some."

She goes through the same routine I just did. Looks in the mirror. Doesn't like what she sees and turns on the water in the other sink.

"Where did you hang your shirt?"

"There's hooks on the toilet doors."

She takes off her blouse and comes back to the sink in just her bra and skirt.

I keep my eyes to myself, scrubbing the last drops of dead guy off my arms and face. I should probably do something about my boots, too, but I'd feel kind of stupid shining my shoes next to a half-naked woman. I can wait until I get home.

Brigitte dries her face with a paper towel.

"How do I look?"

"Like thrill-kill Mona Lisa."

"No, you fool. Look close. Is there any blood? On my neck? My arms? Check my back."

"You're fine."

"Good," she says, and pushes her hair back with her wet hands.

"Now I'll do you."

She turns me into the light and inspects my face.

"You missed a spot."

"Where?"

"Lean down."

She uses her thumb to rub something off my cheek. Then my forehead. Her fingers move around and hold the back of my head. Her arms ripple where the muscles work underneath her skin. So different from the pretty girl at the Geistwalds' party. And the rancid meat we just left in the alley. Her heartbeat and breathing are up. She runs her other hand over my chest.

"I like your scars."

And just like that, we're kissing.

My hands move down her back and up her sides. I can barely remember what it's like to be this close to another body without trying to punch or stab it. Brigitte's skin is smooth in a way that feels brand-new. Is all skin like this? Have I really forgotten everything about bodies that isn't about killing them?

I run my hands up Brigitte's belly to cup her breasts. She reaches back to undo her bra and tosses it on the sink. We catch ourselves in the mirror and how ridiculous we look. Making out in a bathroom. Tracking gore on the floor. Brigitte smiles up at me and pushes me back with surprising strength into the stall where I hung up my shirt.

I sit down on the toilet and she follows me in, closing and locking the door behind her. She drops down onto my lap, straddling me, and we're kissing again. Her skirt is pushed up and she's moving her hips up and down over the hard-on that's been tucked away in my pants for eleven years.

Maybe she's part mind reader because she reaches down, unzips me, and lets my cock flip back against my belly. She reaches down and wraps her hand around it.

"What about your pal Ritchie?"

"You talk too much."

She lets go of my cock and stands up, reaches under her skirt and slips her panties off, balancing on one leg at a time with the sure and practiced motion of a sniper taking aim.

"You should know I haven't done this in a long time."

"Shut up."

She lowers her hips, grabs my cock, and slides me into her. The feeling is both familiar and strange, in the same way that everything happening is both familiar and strange.

The good news is that bodies are bodies, and even if your brain is on overload, sense memory takes over when you feel her body start to move. After a couple of fumbling tries, we fall into a gliding rhythm and our bodies seem to sync up, Brigitte coming down deeper and deeper as I move up into her.

My hands move back up her body, cup her breasts, and pinch her nipples. She leans back, pressing her hands and arms against the stall walls while thrusting down hard with her hips. Every few strokes, I put my hands on her waist and hold her there, deep inside her, then let her go and we fall back to our rhythm.

We're both panting and covered in sweat. Gutting Drifters was a walk on the beach. This might kill us.

Something blares from across the room, bouncing off the tile walls. It's a short loop of Johnny Cash singing "Ring of Fire."

Brigitte slumps for a second.

"Shit."

She grabs my hair as her hip thrusts come harder and faster. She moans, wraps her hands around my neck, and kisses me hard. Her breathing gets ragged. Her nails dig into my shoulders. Just as Johnny reminds us one last time that it burns, burns, burns in the ring of fire, Brigitte presses down hard onto me and stays there. Her hands shake on my shoulders and she's about to draw blood. Then she slowly relaxes, letting out a long, breathy "oh," and starts breathing normally again. We stay that way for a while, her forehead resting against mine. It's sweet at first. We're both panting, but sweat keeps running into our eyes and burning. She laughs, brushes my cheek with her palm, and stands, reaching between her legs to slide me out of her.

Brigitte unlocks the stall and goes straight for her phone. I don't have to ask who has a "Ring of Fire" ringtone. I tuck my softening cock back inside my pants and go to the sink to wash up again.

Brigitte is staring at her phone, reading a text.

"The call wasn't important, but the text is my people saying that the truck is nearby. We should be somewhere else before they begin their work."

"Fine by me."

Brigitte comes to the sink to wash next to me. She bumps her shoulders into mine. I bump back. It's a very strange sensation, not having seen a naked woman in all these years and now being next to one whose profession is being naked, so she's completely relaxed and in no rush to put her clothes back on. But she does. Still relaxed. Still content. And I know that half of her fun is knowing she has done and is doing serious damage to my brain.

"Do you always finish off zombie hunts by seducing a virgin?"

She smiles at me in the mirror.

"How long has it been since you've done that?"

"Eleven years."

"My God. Now you can tell your friends at school that you've seen a real live naked girl."

"I don't talk to most of the people I know. The rest either aren't human or they're dead."

"You can tell Carlos."

"I kind of think he knows."

"You didn't come back there, did you?"

"No."

She smiles.

"We'll have to do something about that next time."

We go into the bar. The chairs are up and the lights are off. The front door is open. Carlos is out front smoking.

I say, "I thought you gave those up."

"I started again. Tonight. I knew this thing, riding your coattails and making money off you, was too good to be true. I just didn't think it would end with me almost getting eaten in my own bar."

Brigitte goes over and puts her arm around Carlos's shoulders.

"The secret world behind the world is always strange at first, but seeing James's friends must have been strange, too, yes?"

"That's true."

"Don't be afraid for your business. Customers will be back. By the weekend, you'll be making more money than ever. People love the exotic, but they love danger even more. And danger they escape is the best of all."

"You think so?"

"I've seen it with my own eyes. You'll have a line outside. You'll need a doorman and pretty girl waitresses."

He looks back at me over his shoulder.

"I never liked the velvet rope thing, but I guess there's worse fates."

"Definitely."

Like ending up in a Dumpster. Seen that twice today. None of the sushi out back is missing any limbs, so someone else lost a hand near Max Overdrive in the last couple of days. Wonder if it belonged to the eater or the eatee?

"I have to go. Simon is waiting for me." She turns to me. "I'll call you. We have a lot to talk about."

She pecks Carlos and me on the cheek and gets into a cab waiting at a stoplight at the corner.

"Interesting night," says Carlos.

"That's one word for it."

"Don't forget your burrito."

He hands me a brown paper bag.

"Thanks. See you tomorrow."

"Don't get eaten on the way home."

"That's my mission statement."

By the time I make the corner, my adrenaline is dropping and all the pain I felt when I woke up is coming back hard. The bullet wound throbs and I slip into an alcove half doubled up. Even with the pain, I'm thinking straighter than before. I lean against the wall and chant some healing hoodoo. Nothing too heavy. I just want to turn the pain down a few decibels, but not erase it. I don't want to forget I'm hurt, but I don't want to be stumbling around like a cripple. It's stupid I didn't think to use the spell when I woke up. What is it about me that it takes a massacre to clear my head?

I stop by Donut Universe on the way home and get coffee and a bag of glazed old-fashioneds. Waiting for my change, I remember New Year's Eve and kissing Candy in the middle of the bodies, blood, and the smell of cordite the night we took down Avila and wonder why I seem attracted only to women who enjoy carnage.

I'M SITTING IN bed with Alice. She's smoking and flipping through a magazine.

"Something happened last night. There was this woman I met."

"I know. I'm dead. I'm not blind, dear."

"That's the thing. You're dead, but I still feel guilty. Like I was cheating on you."

"You're such an idiot. That's why I love you. It's been eleven years since we last touched each other and I didn't exactly die a virgin queen. I mean, I waited for you and hoped, but after a while it got clear that you weren't coming back. A girl can't rely on her Hitachi Magic Wand forever."

"You always cheated on me with technology."

"Technology is more reliable than boys or girls."

"You're okay with what happened?"

"You're alive and I'm dead. Of course I'm okay."

"Thanks. It feels like I'm coming off a six-month bender. Things aren't straight in my head yet."

"You *are* coming off a bender. Want me to tell you the secret of life?" she asks.

"Please, no."

"Everyone in the world is a Charlie. The trick is to figure out which Charlie you're going to be. Charlie Manson. Charlie Starkweather. Or Charlie and the Chocolate Factory."

"Charlie Chaplin."

"Charlie Parker."

"Charly."

"Who's that?" she asks.

"The retard from *Flowers for Algernon*."

" 'Retard' is not a nice word."

"How would you know, retard?"

"Whatever you say, Charlie Brown."

"I am not Charlie Brown."

"Denial isn't just a river in Egypt, Chuck."

"Did I ever tell you I thought I saw an angel when I was a kid?"

"What happened?"

"I'd left my bike on the lawn again and the old man yelled at me to move it. I went outside and there was a woman staring at me from across the street. Really intensely. She had dark skin and bright green eyes. For a second I thought that I'd died in my sleep and she was there to take me to Heaven, but she just shook her head, turned, and walked away."

"Why did she do that?"

"I think she knew what I was and was there to tell me that no matter what I do, Heaven isn't interested."

Alice shakes her head.

"What a morbid little bastard. Your poor mother."

"Mom was worse than me. She saw angels everywhere. She looked for them like other women in the neighborhood looked for two-for-one sales at the booze warehouse by the freeway."

"Charlie's Angels."

"Forget it. Charlie's Angels is three people and none of them are Charlie."

"I was going to say your girlfriend Mason is Charlie

Manson, but that's too good for him. He's Charlie Douche-bag."

"That's exactly who he is."

She kisses me. I can taste the cigarette and her lips and tongue.

"When you thought you saw Mason the other night, it wasn't him. But he's still looking for you. You should find him first."

"Am I really talking to you?"

"I doubt it. Not with the whole being-dead thing and all."

"Yeah."

"But that doesn't mean I can't tell you real things."

"Like what?"

"That something bad is coming."

"What do you mean?"

"Something really bad."

"She's right."

Brigitte is sitting in the doorway of the bedroom on one of Carlos's bar stools and cleaning her gun with one of my old T-shirts.

"Something bad is coming," she says.

"What do you mean?"

Alice says, "Just remember who you are."

"What the fuck are you two talking about? Why are all dreams and prophecies so goddamn obscure?"

"Because, dumb-ass, if any one of them flat-out told you what was coming, you'd try to stop it or change it. Some things you can't stop. You just have to go through them. At least with a clue, you'll be able to recognize it when it gets there."

"If a bus hits me I'm pretty sure I'll notice. But it would be more help if you told me when to get out of the way."

"You ask a lot, James," says Brigitte.

"Sometimes you need to get run down," says Alice. "It could keep something worse from happening."

"Now you're both trying to piss me off, but that's okay because I feel a lot less guilty than when this dream started. Thanks for that."

"See you around, Charlie."

"*Dobrou noc,* Sandman."

I KICK THE sheet down by my feet and roll out of bed the moment I wake up. I'm still naked from the long shower I took last night. Kasabian stares at me from the desk, his little legs poised over the keyboard.

"Morning, sunshine."

"Do you smell anything funny?"

"No. What's wrong with you?"

I know it's in my head, but I swear I can still smell Drifter gunk all over me.

"Nothing. Just a funny dream."

"Good for you. Get dressed. I don't need your junk staring at me while I'm trying to work."

Last night's clothes are getting burned as soon as I get some lighter fluid. I find a pair of jeans tossed over the back of a chair and one clean and folded T-shirt in the drawer. Thank the gods of laundry for wash-and-fold places.

"You've got some donuts left over from the last night, but the coffee is cold."

The crumpled donut bag is on the floor near the head of

the bed. I open it, take out one of the old-fashioneds and take a bite. I can't taste it. I'm afraid to breathe because I might get a whiff of Drifter. I go in the bathroom, gargle, and wash my face in cold water.

"You didn't talk much when you got back last night. You're no fun when you go to bed sober."

The bullet wound in my side still looks pretty raw. It doesn't hurt, but it should have faded to just another scar by now. I'll have to ask Allegra about that. If she's talking to me.

I sit on the bed and eat the rest of the donut. I can sort of taste it now.

"What happened last night? All you did was grunt when you got back and then you were running a marathon all night in your sleep. Chasing bunnies again, Lassie?"

"There anything in the Codex about Drifters?"

"Lots. Why?"

"I think I killed some with a friend last night."

"Is that what they're doing in Hollywood instead of aerobics? Who did you hunt coffin jockeys with?"

"I just met her. Name is Brigitte Bardo. She's supposed to be kind of an actress in Europe."

Kasabian looks at me for a minute.

"Are you shitting me? The star of *Cosmonauts of Sodom* Brigitte Bardo?"

"I have no idea."

"You'd know her. She has a tattoo of an angel that starts on her stomach and the wings wrap around her and up her back."

"I wasn't looking at her stomach."

"Oh man. She does this scene with these two other chicks."

"I don't need to hear about this from you."

"No, listen. All the chick cosmonauts quit the space program and joined a traveling circus. They're all dressed like clowns, only their noses are dildos—"

"Stop right there and tell me about Drifters."

He stares at me. If he had regular hands, he'd give me the finger.

"At least get me her autograph."

"If you promise not to talk about clown fucking, I'll get her to Xerox her ass for you."

"Think I could meet her?"

"Are you crazy? She kills Drifters. What's she going to make of you?"

"I'm not a zombie."

"You're undead. She'll think you're a new model Lucifer just invented."

"Do you know anything about zombies at all?"

"Yeah. They smell like an abandoned slaughterhouse when you pull their spines out."

"You know about spines. That's a start. What else do you want to know?"

"Everything. But I don't need a Ph.D. Just give me the Trivial Pursuit version."

"Okay."

He looks at me.

"You're really going to get me her autograph?"

"Christ."

"Forget it. Tell me about the zombies last night."

"They stank. They were stupid. They drooled and grunted and tried to bite us."

He nods.

"Zeds and zots."

"What?"

"Zombie shoptalk. They're zeros. Dumbest of the dumb. Nothing more than a mouth with legs. What most people call golems."

"It sounds like there's something besides golems."

"See? Who says you have a learning disability?"

"Yeah, who says that?"

"There's another kind of zombie. Lacunas. You don't want to meet them."

"What's the difference?"

"Lacunas have some brain function left. They can talk, walk, and dress themselves. You might not even notice one in a crowd. But don't get close enough to smell their breath. They can't really think for themselves, but they can take orders. The other thing is they're mean. Old-timers called them St. George's Pet, like all that's working upstairs is their speech centers and their lizard brains. Because they're such little shits, they mostly get used for muscle work."

"Like Mason with Parker."

"Exactly. You don't usually see them unless there's Dead-heads having a turf war, but sometimes they make money renting them out or selling them to street gangs. Lacunas are pretty much the perfect thug."

"How do you kill them?"

"Like the others. The spine."

"That's it? Nothing else?"

"Whatever fucks up the nervous system. Run them through a wood chipper. Nuke them. Chase them down the street like an angry mob in *Frankenstein* and burn them."

"I wonder if I could mount a wood chipper on the front of a Bugatti?"

"What happened with you and Ms. Bardo last night?"

"You're talking your way out of an autograph fast."

"Asshole."

I offer Kasabian the last donut, but he shakes his head. There's a half-smoked cigarette butt in the ashtray and I light it up. That he wants, of course. I let him have a couple of puffs and then kill it off.

"Does the Codex say where zombies came from?"

He shakes his head.

"Not really. Hellions have plenty of blind spots and their own tall tales to fill in the missing pieces. Most Hellions say that Cain was Patient Zero. After he killed Abel, God sent him out to wander the earth forever and put a mark on him so no one would stop his wandering and torment. The Hellion smart set think zombieism was the mark. When Cain got into beefs with pushy civilians, he'd just bite them. They became the first golems and Lacunas."

"The ones who don't think it was Cain, what do they say?"

"This is bullshit, man. There's facts and there's fairy tales. None of this is going to help you kill them any better."

"Who says I'm going to kill them? I killed those ones last night because they attacked us. I don't have anything against going on a Drifter safari, but I want to get paid for it."

"Goddamn it, you don't get to be a brat when it comes to zombies. They're like jackrabbits. They make new zombies, eat everything in sight, and then migrate down the road and do it again."

"What do you care, Alfredo Garcia? You don't owe this world anything either."

"No, but I happen to live here and I like beer and burritos and cigarettes. Last time I checked, zombies don't deliver."

Alice and Brigitte's voices come back to me. They're telling me that something bad is coming. Is this it? I hope not. That would be about the lamest prophecy in history. I don't exactly need a vision to explain how everyone getting eaten, including me, would be a downer. No, it can't be this and that's bad news. It means there's something even worse coming.

"What's the other Drifter story?"

"You're like a dog with a bone. Let it go. Go chase a ball. Hump a stranger's leg."

"Tell me the story and I will."

"The story? You're the story. You and your kind. You fucked-up angels. The Codex says that when Lucifer's army was cast out of Heaven, one of the fallen didn't make it all the way to Hell and landed in a valley on earth instead. It was burned and broken, but humans still recognized it as an angel. The local blue bloods sent their doctors to help it, but the angel was sick and bloated like a tick by then. It attacked anyone who came near it. All of those people ended up turning into zeds. Those zeds attacked their families and friends. The ones they didn't eat became zeds and attacked other people. The people who lived in the hills saw that things were getting out of control, so they started fires and burned the whole valley. They thought they'd gotten everything, but some of the zeds supposedly escaped into caves. Mostly they stay underground, but every now and then one wanders out or gets summoned by a necromancer. That's it. They all lived happily ever fucking after. The end."

I wave him off.

"You were right. This isn't any help. Might as well say Muppets did it."

"You asked and I answered. You still owe me an autograph."

"You'll get your scrawl. I wonder who'll pay me more to hunt zeds and zots? Lucifer or the Vigil?"

"You don't actually have to say 'zeds and zots' all the time. You can say one or the other."

"I'll stick with Drifters. Those other names make them sound like candy."

"Lucifer and the Vigil both have a stake in keeping humans in general and L.A. in particular alive. Get them both to pay."

"That's what I was thinking. But there's one thing bugging me."

"What?"

"When those Drifters came in, I knew one of them. I mean I knew who he was. A guy named Spencer Church. I only heard of this guy the day before when someone said he was missing. I asked a couple of people about him. Then, out of nowhere, the guy shows up at Bamboo House like the place is a zombie salad bar."

"That's a hell of a coincidence."

"Isn't it? And if golems can't think . . ."

"It means someone sent him there. Probably walked him right up to the door and pushed him in."

"Somebody who knew where I was and happened to have a few spare Drifters lying around."

"You know the most interesting people."

"Guess I do have a vested interest in this after all. But I still want to get paid."

"Hell yeah."

"I need to set up meetings with the Vigil and Lucifer."

My phone buzzes on the nightstand. I pick it up and listen. It's a short call.

"Cool. See you there."

"Who was that?"

"Speak of the devil. He's out at the studio. Wants me to swing by and squint menacingly at the help."

"Next he'll have you doing his taxes."

"I've never been to a movie studio. How many guns do you think they'll let me take inside?"

"You? All you want."

The .460 pistol is too big to carry in my waistband, so I wear it on my hip in a tool belt I colored black with a Sharpie and modified into a speed rig. I can have it out and cocked before an angel can say "amen."

The knife and na'at hang snug inside the coat lining.

"Does the Codex say anything about Lucifer having a family?"

Kasabian gives me a curious little smile.

"Like is there a Mrs. Lucifer?"

"Yeah. Or kids."

"Not that I've ever seen, but the Codex isn't exactly easy to use. It's all stories and allusions, not a PowerPoint presentation. But I can look if you want. Of course, Lucifer has been fucking around on earth since the Fall, so he probably has a load of sprogs earning their keep as warlords and priests. You looking for a cage match with the Antichrist?"

I shake my head and go into the bathroom. I check myself in the mirror to make sure I look presentable and that the weapons don't show.

"No. It's just more trivia. I'm going to go and find a ride."

I'm closing the door when Kasabian says, "Can you imagine him for a father?"

"Uh. No."

"He's such a jerk, it would be torture ninety-nine percent of the time, but, come on, parent-teacher night would be fun. 'Little Bobby took half the class's lunch money.' 'Only half?'"

I nod at him.

"I'll pick up some cigarettes while I'm out."

THERE'S A VINTAGE car lot on North La Brea. Big glass showroom up front. A lot full of classics and a service bay right around the corner. Cars come out of the lot, make a quick right, and are double-parked by the garage until another car pulls out. A situation like this is all about shopping and timing. I don't love T-birds or Corvettes. However, when a mechanic double-parks a red '67 GTO, I start across the street.

I mumble a little Hellion spell. There are boxes stacked around the side of the garage waiting for garbage pickup.

The oil- and gas-stained cardboard goes up fast. It takes about thirty seconds for the crew to clear the garage, some to gawk and others to hit the flames with fire extinguishers.

The moment they're out, I'm behind the GTO's wheel, knife jammed in the ignition and the V-8 engine growling like a Tyrannosaurus rex. I aim the beast out into traffic and take the corner as white smoke from the dying fire drifts into the street.

I pull onto the Hollywood Freeway, heading north toward Burbank. The time on my phone is 3 P.M. Should I give Brigitte a call? There's a better-than-even chance that she'll be at the studio with Ritchie, so I wait.

It's not a long drive. I'm kind of sorry when I see the exit for the studio. For a second I think about not turning. Just hitting on the accelerator and heading north until there's nowhere left to go. What would stop me first, a moose, an oil pipeline, or a glacier? I'd sit on the shore of the Arctic Ocean and let the snow pile up around me in my GTO igloo. Curl up in the backseat with a radio, turn on a news station, and listen to the world ending.

There's a guard station at the studio gate. A tired-looking guy in a blue rent-a-cop uniform leans out of the guard-house as I drive up.

"Sweet ride. We don't get many V-8s on the lot anymore. It's all rice-rocket hybrids."

"L.A. is going to be under water in twenty years. As an American, I figure I should do my bit to help out."

He eyes me before deciding I'm joking. He takes a clip-board from the wall inside his hut.

"Name?"

I have no idea what name Ritchie or Lucifer gave the guy.

"Stark."

The guard scans the list and nods. He hands me a plastic parking permit about the size of a hardback book.

"Keep that on your dashboard in plain view."

He pulls a white paper map of the lot from the back of the clipboard and hands it to me, pointing to landmarks with his pen.

"Follow the outside road around the edge of the lot. The soundstage you want is all the way on the far side. There are some producers' bungalows nearby. That's where you can park."

"Thanks."

"Looks like there's a hell of a production going on out there."

"That's the idea."

I follow the road around the outside of the lot. On my left is the freeway. On the studio side, there are forklifts and sweaty guys putting up scaffolding outside soundstages. Men and women in khakis and button-down shirts cruise by them on golf carts. The stages look like blimp hangars, giant humpback Quonset huts with huge posters of the studio's new releases. The place is about as glamorous as dental surgery.

I park the car outside the bungalows, take the knife from the ignition, and slip it back inside my coat.

There's a soundstage across the road. Outside, a hundred people are unloading trucks, telling other people how to unload trucks, or sitting in trucks waiting to be unloaded. Ritchie and Lucifer are at the edge of the chaos, with Ritchie pointing at some papers and then at the stage, where they're building something huge. Old women in elaborately decorated robes carry incense among the workers. Others walk around the perimeter with bottles in each hand. From one they sprinkle sacred oil on the ground. From the other they sprinkle what smells like animal blood.

Ritchie waves me over. He nods at the car when I get close.

"She's a beauty. How long have you had her?"

"A half hour, give or take."

"You know, if you leave the windows down like that, the sun is going to bleach the upholstery."

"That's okay. I only drive cars once."

Ritchie looks from me to the car and back. It takes him a minute, but he finally gets it.

"I see."

"Keep it, if you want. It drives like a dream. There aren't any keys, but I'm sure someone around here can change the VIN and slap in a new ignition."

Lucifer watches the old women make their rounds. Ritchie's eyes flick down to my waist. He's spotted the gun and smiles.

"Have you ever been on a movie lot before?"

"Can't say that I have."

"Then this ought to be pretty interesting for you."

"Okay."

"Let me give you a tour. We're shooting all the Heaven sequences first, so that's what's being built right now. I guess you'll have to take my word for that since you're better acquainted with the other place."

"Heaven for the weather and Hell for the company."

"Who said that?"

"Mark Twain. Or Jim Morrison. Or Stalin. One of them."

Lucifer turns to me.

"When did you start quoting Twain?"

"It was in a fortune cookie. I've been saving it up."

Lucifer stops and looks at Ritchie.

"Simon, why don't you let me show James around. We need to discuss some work details."

"Yeah, we do."

"Sure. Good seeing you. Stop by and say good-bye before you take off. I still want to pick your brain about life down in the hot country."

"Before you go, let me ask both of you something. What exactly is my job right now? Am I here all day every day you're shooting? How is this going to work?"

Ritchie shakes his head.

"We won't need you all the time. Mr. Macheath won't be on set every day. Unless he wants you, you don't need to be here the whole time. I'm sure you noticed that we've brought in a planeload of Chinese nyu wu witches to work special security. Mean old bitches, but they know tricks and charms older than dirt. Stuff most of the local talent has never even heard of."

"I'm well protected here," says Lucifer. "Mostly, I want you anytime I'm in public and not at the hotel or the lot."

"Maybe when you're not here, you should stay at the hotel. I mean you're pretty much royalty. People can come to you."

"Considering the drama after the party, I have to show

my face around. I don't want people thinking I'm Howard Hughes."

"Okay. Just be smart about when and where."

Ritchie checks his watch and looks around with a sour expression.

"You two have fun. I need to find someone and see if these goddamn union guys can possibly unload my fucking trucks any slower."

Lucifer heads for the soundstage and I follow him inside. The Heaven set is pretty skeletal, but it's still impressive. The floor is fake marble inlaid with complex star patterns. There's a gold vaulted ceiling encrusted with jewels and subtly shifting lights. In the middle of the fake room is a throne decorated with intricate celestial, animal, and plant shapes.

I ask, "So, is this what it looks like?"

"Not in the slightest. But for the purposes of the movie, it's uncannily accurate."

"You trust Ritchie and his imported Golden Girls with security?"

"Simon knows what he's doing. He's been protecting himself and his stars for a long time. And he knows that his soul is at stake."

I follow him as we circle the interior of the stage.

"Did he ever have to protect anyone from Drifters?"

Lucifer raises his eyebrows.

"Zombies here?"

"Last night. Three of them came into the Bamboo House of Dolls. What's worse is that one of them was Spencer Church, a guy I heard about at your party and had been asking about since. I'm going to go out on a limb and say that wasn't a coincidence. That means that not only do we have Drifters, but someone is running them."

"A situation like that right now could be very bad publicity. With something that extraordinary happening while I'm in town, I'll end up being blamed for it."

"Then hire me to go after them. Take what you've paid me so far, tack on a bonus, and I'll find them and get rid of them for you."

"You killed three of them?"

"Actually, I only took out one. A friend killed the other two."

"Maybe I should hire your friend."

"Ritchie wouldn't like that."

"Why?"

"It was Brigitte. Turns out the aspiring actress and porn things are her playing Clark Kent. The rest of the time, she's a trained Drifter killer."

Lucifer nods.

"I noticed that you two were getting along well at the party. When you're not killing zombies together, you aren't doing something reckless and stupid, are you?"

"When have I ever done that?"

"You don't want Simon for an enemy. He has a lot of resources at his disposal and a bad temper. There are bodies buried all over this lot and he's responsible for more than a few of them."

"Don't worry. No one is running to Vegas for an Elvis wedding."

"Be smart for once. Remember, you're still under contract to me."

"About that. What's really going on? Why did you hire me for the job? Is there something I should know? Or am I still your science project, like Jesus in the desert?"

"Temptations are a bore. I only played that game with the kid and a few of the more annoying saints. Read the Book of Job. One of my jobs was to test self-righteous mortals for Father, but everyone has conveniently forgotten that."

"That's what the movie is going to fix."

"Among other things. I learned early on that tempting you people was unnecessary. How does the song go? 'I'm waiting for my man, twenty-six dollars in my hand . . .' What I have is better than crack, heroin, money, or love. I don't have to sell it. People come to me to buy."

"What exactly is it you sell?"

"Same as Father. Hope. For a better life. A brighter future."

"Only the back ends of your deals are pretty harsh."

"I can make your dreams come true here and now or you can hold your breath, click your heels three times, and hope that it's all cruise ships and finger sandwiches when you die. It's one hundred percent your choice."

"What about the world? What about wars and famines and AIDS? Watching a million people die is probably a Marx Brothers double feature for you."

"'I form light and create darkness, I make weal and create woe; I the Lord do all these things.' That's Father talking about Himself, not me. And I never started a war except the one I lost with him."

"That's pretty hard to believe."

"I'm not saying I'm an innocent, but on earth I've never directly instigated or fired a shot in anger."

"So, it's just us, then."

As we walk down a short staircase to a lower level of the set, Lucifer bumps me with his shoulder. I miss a step and almost fall.

"What the fuck was that?"

"That's what I do. I nudge. That's the extent of my vast power in the affairs of mankind. I nudge. I jostle. I whisper."

"Your nudges have a little more juice behind them than when civilians do it."

"True. But as I said, it's always your choice. That's one rule I've never broken. In your old stories, I'm always tricking or cheating you people, but that's something I refuse to do. Cheating you would be an admission of weakness. I would never give Father the satisfaction."

There's a short silence.

Lucifer asks, "When did you decide to become the loyal opposition? Conventional morality isn't your strong suit."

"Nothing. It's just something someone said."

"Let me guess. 'Why are you working for Old Scratch?' "

"Something like that."

"What did you say?"

"That I owe you money."

"That's what I've been talking about. You made a free choice to take a deal with me. But unlike some people, you've chosen to honor your debt. Did it occur to you that accepting responsibility for your actions is in itself a moral act? It certainly makes you a better man than fools like

Ritchie who think they can deal and scheme their way out of anything."

"About how many human women do you think you've fucked over the years?"

"That sounds like the old you. Subtle as always."

Shit. I didn't mean to blurt that out.

"Forget it. So, how about giving me the Drifter gig? Between Brigitte and me, we can clean up your zed and zot problem fast."

"You shouldn't see Brigitte again, even for work."

"I know, but I'm going to. Give us something to pass the time. Maybe it'll keep us from doing something reckless and stupid."

"I'll think about it."

An alarm goes off outside. Not an alarm. It's like fifty sets of truck brakes screaming as they all lock up at once. It takes me a few seconds to figure out that it's human voices colliding in a terrifying animal wail. The old Chinese witches are screaming and running, converging at one point of the stage perimeter where they'd splashed oil and blood. The sun glares off raised knives and white banners scrawled with ancient spells.

Ritchie sprints onto the stage and right at us. A big man, he looks more like an ex-cop than ever. Without a word, he loops one arm around Lucifer's shoulders and half drags, half pushes Lucifer to the back of the stage. I get on the other side and push them into a small office in back. Ritchie kicks over an armchair leaning against the far wall revealing a barely visible crease running up the seam between two sheets of paneling. He slams the heel of his hand on a point halfway up the wall and it pops open. Ritchie pulls Lucifer inside. I follow them and Ritchie slams the door closed.

Ritchie huffs his words, winded and bent over.

"You'll be safe here."

Lucifer turns in a slow circle. There are comfortable chairs. A stack of five-gallon water jugs. Packets of dried food. Two queen-size inflatable beds. A cabinet against the far wall is marked MEDICAL. I open it. The cabinet is divided into two tall vertical compartments. The left side is stocked with enough drugs and medical junk to open your own hospital. The right side is all guns. Mostly flashy action-movie hardware. HKs, Berettas, and Desert Eagle automatics. There's a foot-high stack of ammo at the bottom of the cabinet.

I say, "Shoot, a fella could have a pretty good weekend in Vegas with all that stuff," but no one gets it.

Lucifer nods. Ritchie drops down into an office chair in front of a bank of video monitors.

"I never took you for the panic-room type, Simon."

"You weren't here for the riots in '92. Hollywood looked like Dresden after the bombs. We kept waiting for the mob to get this far north, but they never made it. Lucky for us. Back then our security was a gate, a few off-duty cops, and a new sprinkler system. All we were safe from was shoplifters and people smoking in the bathroom. I swore that would never happen again."

"Good for you," says Lucifer. "I love a take-charge coward."

Ritchie flips a switch on the console and all the video screens come on, giving a 360-degree view outside and inside the soundstage. The witches are on the center screen.

They're manhandling someone who looks almost human, but not quite. His arms and legs are too long. His skull is too flat. Uniformed security people push through the mob, cuff the Lurker, and perp-walk him away. The old women still yell and slap his shoulders as he goes by.

A couple of minutes later, a phone on the console chirps. Ritchie picks it up.

"Yeah? You're sure? Take him to one of the special cells downstairs. No one gets in or out until I get there."

He swings around in the chair and smiles at us.

"Looks like a false alarm. A Lurker maintenance worker, one of the water nixies we keep around to clean the pipes, decided he wanted a closer look at the set and crossed the old ladies' protection circle. We'll question him and probably let him go with a warning."

"At least you know you're getting your money's worth out of the old dears," says Lucifer.

I ask, "What's to keep a magician or a few of your witches from marching up to the door and lobbing hexes in here?"

Ritchie shakes his head.

"The room is shielded from outside spells. We're like a roach motel. Magic goes out, but it doesn't come in."

"That makes us the roaches," says Lucifer.

"I guess so," says Ritchie.

"At least they're survivors."

"Are we done in here or do we need to show a permission slip to the teacher?" I ask.

Ritchie nods to the gun on my hip.

"Slow down. Not all of us are packing as much heat as you."

"That's why I have it. So I don't have to drag our boss into Fort Knox every time a pixie farts."

"Holster your dicks, boys," says Lucifer. "Everything went smoothly. Everyone did their jobs, and no one had to get shot. Unless you need to wing someone to feel useful."

He looks at me. I look at Ritchie.

"I wonder how your room would hold up if a few Drifters came knocking. Is it soundproof?"

Ritchie's eyes widen.

"Zombies? Not the ones at the party. You've seen zombies in the streets?"

"Less than a block off Hollywood Boulevard. It was just some shamblers, so don't pop a cork. Mr. Macheath is hiring me to do a search-and-destroy on the whole glee club, right?"

"We'll see."

Ritchie is staring at the monitors. Things are pretty much back to normal outside. The old ladies are laying down a new layer of oil and animal punch where the Lurker smudged their circle. The sweaty guys are back unloading the trucks and the office types who were standing around before snap right back to standing around. Ritchie shakes his head. I didn't think the news would hit him so hard, but he's not like my friends and used to this kind of shit.

"We haven't had any walking dead since I was a kid. Not wandering the streets. It only lasted a few days. They were supposed to have crawled out of an old Pasadena gold mine after a quake."

"What does 'not wandering the streets' mean?"

He shrugs.

"They pop up every now and then, like any dark magic. But they're always contained, not strolling to Whisky A Go-Go."

"When was the last time someone used Drifters to settle an argument?"

"The last I heard about was when Regina Maab and Cabal Ash were going at each other. I don't know about what. It sounded like it was old-world stuff. That's maybe why it escalated so far. You know how those Europeans get. Some Cossacks stole Grandma's beets five hundred years ago and they're still bitching about it."

"Where's Regina Maab now?"

Ritchie shrugs.

"Gone. No one's seen her in years. Whatever the argument was about, I think Cabal won."

"Ash is into Black Sun hoodoo. You think he's hooked up with Drifters?"

"Not directly, but chaos magic attracts a lot of freaks. He wouldn't be above hiring an alcoholic Deadhead who can't pay his rent. God knows there are enough of them around."

Lucifer is examining the drugs in Ritchie's cabinet, pretending he's not listening to us.

"You ready to hire me to get on this?"

He doesn't say anything for a minute.

"I'm more interested in who shot at us when we were leaving the Geistwalds' party. Find me something on that."

"You're the ones with cop connections. They do hit men. I do monsters."

"Who says they're not connected?"

"Hire me and we'll find out."

He slips a bottle of pills into his pocket and puts the rest back.

"Go talk to Cabal and then call me. I'll decide then."

"Fine. You want to hang here or do you want me to ride back to the hotel with you?"

"I'll stay here for a while. You'll find the Ash clan in the Linda Vista Hospital. You'll love it. It's been closed for years, but they still shoot movies and television there. You get into Cabal's place through the big freezer in the morgue."

"I'll come by the hotel after I talk to him."

"Call first. And take a shower and change your clothes before you come over. Smelling Cabal every decade or so is quite enough. And one more thing."

"Yeah."

"Take your new partner with you. Cabal can be difficult, but he's an important man. Maybe your friend can keep you from shooting his place up."

"She carries a gun, too, so I wouldn't count on it."

NOW I'M ON two missions. Three if you break them down the long way:

1. Weasel information out of Cabal.
2. Kill Drifters, zeds, Lacunas, whatever.
3. Get paid. That one's mine and it gets taken care of first.

I'm in no mood to waste time on door monkeys, so I walk through a shadow and out into the Vigil's compound. One of the gate guards sees me and starts yammering into a talkie. I give him a friendly wave and head inside. You might be fast on the button, but don't count on a raise this year, pal.

The warm Jell-O hoodoo barrier at the warehouse door always makes my skin crawl. For the second it takes to pass through it, it's like you've been body-snatched into a German oatmeal-fetish video.

People have seen me here before, so no one bats an eye when I get in. I walk like I'm heading for an appointment in one of the offices at the other end of the building. I almost make it, too.

A gaggle of Vigil hall monitors closes in on me from all sides. They have their guns on me and they mean it, but they're too disciplined to start blasting. Marshal Julie, the newbie from the Springheel house, is part of the posse. I walk over to her. Her heartbeat goes up, but I keep enough distance between us so she doesn't get too twitchy and open fire.

"Good to see you, Marshal. Did they let you see any dead bodies yet or are the boys still making you bring them coffee and play junior high drinking games because tough guys think vomit is hilarious and only pussies die of alcohol poisoning?"

"Why can't you enter a building like a normal person, Stark? It would simplify everyone's life."

"My life is simple and getting simpler by the minute. Did you ever wonder if they haze men as hard as they haze women around here?"

"You're trespassing on a restricted federal site. If you want to get arrested, why don't you go and do something interesting first?"

"I'm a paid consultant to this organization who took a shortcut inside. Mea culpa. Get Wells down here and he can put a nasty note in my personnel file."

"You don't have a personnel file because you're not a person."

It's Wells. He's behind me.

"You're an entity. Not the same thing as a person by a long shot."

"Why don't you have your crew put their guns down? I have a business proposition for you."

"That's funny because I have one for you, too."

He comes around into my field of vision and stops in front of me. He looks tired. Like he's been pulling a lot of late nights. He motions for the G-men to lower their guns.

"We're fine here, everyone. Go back to what you were doing."

He glances at Marshal Julie as she holsters her gun and walks away.

"Don't talk to my people like you know them. Especially the new ones. It confuses them. It makes them think you're on our side."

"I *am* on your side when I get paid. I've done every job you asked me to do."

"So does my dog when I tell her to. She does a trick and gets a biscuit, same as you."

"Do you take taxes and Social Security out of that? How many biscuits does it cost her a month?"

Wells walks to the edge of the warehouse. I follow him. Gray plastic storage crates marked with diamond-shaped chemical warning stickers are stacked against the wall. He sits down on one and glances at his watch.

"You said you wanted to talk to me about something."

"Yeah. High Plains Drifters and what you want me to do about them."

"In Los Angeles? Not possible. I'd have heard about it."

"You'd think so. It's funny that you don't. I thought you had some supercharged radar that tracked us magic types. Or was that another Vigil fairy tale?"

"It's real all right. I know where you go, who you go with, and what you do."

"Then why don't you know about the dead men who wandered into Bamboo House of Dolls for human sushi?"

"Never. I'd have heard and we'd be on alert."

"I guess omnipotence isn't what it used to be. But I can fix that for you. I've already killed three Drifters. Give me a contract and I'll get the rest. There's probably a lot of them, so I ought to get time and a half on this one."

Wells scowls. He looks around like he's expecting someone.

"If you killed three, then where are the bodies?"

"A friend got rid of them for me."

"And where did this friend put them?"

"I didn't ask. She has people who know how to dispose of people eaters."

"It was just one other person you worked with a minute ago and now it's people. How many people exactly?"

"I couldn't say."

He takes a tired breath and rubs his eyes.

"So, you let someone I don't know call people you don't know to haul away the remains of some of the most dangerous creatures walking the earth. And you want me to hire you to kill a whole pod. How many do you think are left? One? A dozen? Fifty? What are you going to do with those bodies? Maybe your friend's friends can take them down to the Farmers' Market and sell the bones to tourists. You can start a co-op. Make friendship bracelets and wind chimes and share the profits."

"Let me ask you something, Deputy Dawg. If the Vigil isn't onto the Drifters, what's keeping you up nights?"

His frown goes to a smile and back to a frown.

"Things are going to change. In this town and beyond. Far beyond."

"What? You going to raid all the Valley hipsters having ghost swinger parties? Let me know if you need to use condoms with things made of ectoplasm. I've always wondered about that."

"How's the movie business treating you? Have you gotten to hobnob with the stars? Maybe your new best friend can get you an agent and a part in his movie, then you can leave all this behind."

"What's the matter? Getting jealous of Lucifer? Don't be mad, baby. You knew this wasn't an exclusive thing. We agreed we could see other people."

"I tried to give you the benefit of the doubt. I thought your foul mouth and your shitty attitude were part of a post-traumatic stress reaction to being back on earth. Now I have to ask myself whose side are you truly on? The light or the dark?"

"Why is it you can say 'shit' when you're mad, but I get yelled at for it?"

Two of Wells's men in black wheel in a crystal ball the size of a Volkswagen Bug on a metal dolly. The blurry outline of a demon is just visible inside the ball as it beats itself against the walls.

"Why would you work for an animal like Lucifer?"

I shake my head.

"I've already had this talk once today and I'm not doing it again with you."

"I'm going to tell you something and then I'm going to ask you something. I want to listen to both things carefully, as if your future depends on them, because it does."

"Say it, then."

"Under the provisions of the U.S. Patriot Act, the Department of Homeland Security has declared Lucifer an unlawful foreign combatant as well as a suspect in a number of terrorist activities around the world. I have a federal warrant for his arrest. You're going to help me serve the warrant."

"I am?"

"I understand that this is a high-risk situation and I don't expect you to do it for free. Work with me. Serve the warrant and help me arrest Lucifer. With your unique experience and abilities, I can offer you a full-time position at the highest government pay grade."

"Does that come with dental and a company car?"

"This is a onetime offer. You can be my friend or you can be my enemy. It's your choice."

"Is this Aelita's idea? If she's that bored, hire me to find what's left of the Kissi and bring them back. She can have fun fighting them."

"Were you even listening? This isn't Vigil business. It's DHS."

"Bullshit. In L.A. they're the same thing."

"Let's say you're right. It doesn't alter your situation. New DHS policy says that we can no longer work with questionable outside vendors."

"I was right. This is all Aelita."

"Lucifer's name is on the national terrorist watch. The classified one. You're not yet, but you'll be happy to know that your friend Kinski is on there, too."

"Why?"

"We can't let fallen angels run around the countryside any more than we can allow terrorists to drive around with vans full of kerosene and fertilizer."

"When do I go on the list?"

"That all depends on whether you're my friend or my enemy."

"It was you who ambushed us after the party the other night, wasn't it?"

"It wasn't the Little Rascals."

"For a while I thought it might be you, but then I remembered what Aelita said. That you don't care about Lucifer. He's past his prime." •

"Don't try to think. It doesn't look good on you."

"Ever since then I've been trying to figure out who would be a better candidate. I was starting to think it was Ritchie, the guy who runs the studio. He hires off-duty cops to work security and has the money to throw his own *Apocalypse*

Now ambush. But it was the simple answer all along. Serves me right for trying to be creative."

"You still haven't answered my question."

"I thought you people were all about keeping the universe in balance, not handing the whole thing over to one side. This is definitely Aelita's idea. You haven't got the guts to think this big. So, what's she getting out of this? A shinier halo? A transfer off this rock?"

"Answer the question."

"I gave Aelita my answer six months ago. None of you own me. Go ahead and put me on your list."

His lips tug up in a little smile.

"I've already drafted the memo. I knew you couldn't respond reasonably to a reasonable offer. You're just like my dog. Entirely predictable."

"What happens now? Do you have snipers on me already? Or do the two of us go outside and have a Tombstone showdown? If you'd told me we were going to party, I'd have brought Wild Bill's gun."

"Nothing like that. You just walk on out of here and don't ever walk in again. You and I will settle this in time, but right now the grown-ups have bigger fish than you to fry."

He gets up and nods to someone, then heads back to his office. When I turn around, six of his people are spread out in a semicircle around me. No one is pointing a gun at me, but together they look like little Grim Reapers reincarnated as bouncers at a Beverly Hills yuppie bar.

"Admit it. You used canned olives in your martinis."

Nothing. Tough room.

Maybe Wells is right and it's time to pick a side. If I'd

said yes to him, do you think any of these dour cocksuckers would have cracked even a polite smile? I'm not holding my breath. Lucifer wouldn't have laughed either, but at least he wouldn't be morally superior about it.

We're just bugs on God's windshield. No one owns me.

These are the good and righteous people who sat on their fat asses and let Mason and Parker murder Alice and send me to Hell. And then they let him waltz away. I might not have been a good guy before, but I loved someone and I wasn't broken into a million little pieces. I wasn't as hollow and dead inside as a locust husk.

I know whose side I'm on.

Mine.

I walk outside and leave through the front gate, Wells's gunsels trailing behind me like a line of black ducklings.

THE PHONE RINGS four times. I'm about to hang up when she answers.

"Hey. What are you doing?"

"Nothing important. I'm reading the *Light Bringer* script, trying to learn my lines. What do you think it tells us about the world that I have less to say as Eve than I do when I make my pornographic films?"

"Want to go talk to a guy with a rep for using Drifters to do his dirty work?"

"Drifters?"

"Zeds. Golems. The dead boys from last night."

"Ah. *Prázdný,* you mean."

"Zed has less syllables, so I win. Do you want to meet the guy?"

"Who is it?"

"Cabal Ash."

She spits out something in Czech. I can't understand it, but I don't think it's "yippee!"

"Sure."

"Where are you?"

"At Simon's. Where are you?"

"At Max Overdrive. I could get a car and pick you up."

"No thank you. Simon told me about you and cars. I'll pick you up."

"Okay. Don't forget to bring the toy you were going to show me. The Drifter de-boner."

"Ah. I was waiting for you to say something sexy. I thought for a moment that all you remembered about the night was the business behind the bar."

"I remember the business inside the bar, too. You always remember losing your virginity."

"Good boy. I'll see you in half an hour."

"I'll be out front."

Kasabian looks up as I thumb the phone off. While I was talking he was pretending to work.

"That was her, wasn't it?"

"Who?"

"Don't be cute. Bring her up when she gets here."

"Next lifetime maybe."

"At least get her to sign these."

He holds up a couple of DVDs he was hiding on his table.

"I found a couple of her movies from when I was bootleg-ging discs to make ends meet."

"Poor you. Forced to steal porn."

"Hey, there weren't any American versions. They were all European. PAL format. The wrong region code. By reformatting them, I was performing a public service."

"For horny old men and bonehead teenyboppers."

"Who needs more help than them?"

"I'm not bringing her up. But I'll get her to sign your discs."

"Have her make it out to 'Aldous.' "

"You sure you don't want to go with 'Alfredo Garcia'?"

"Fuck you. It's an old family name."

"That'll be our little secret."

"Fuck you twice. I'm not taking name abuse from someone called Sandman Slim. That sounds like a diet shake with roofies."

I look at him perched on the desk, his little legs on his keyboard. He frowns back at me, a defiant head on glorified skateboard.

I hate it when Kasabian is right. I take the DVDs and put them in a Max Overdrive bag.

"You're a cruel man, you know that, Aldous?"

"I'd give a rat's ass if you weren't running off with the love of my life."

"This week's love."

"That goes without saying."

BRIGITTE PICKS ME up in a very new pale blue Porsche Targa. She's wearing jeans and a T-shirt, plus a leather jacket for protection.

She greets me with a deep kiss when I'm inside. I kiss her back, but keep an eye open. I have to admit that after Lucifer and Wells, I'm starting to feel black helicopters circling. Ritchie seems like the kind of control freak who might have Brigitte followed. Or the Vigil could be back there. I can slap Ritchie into shredded wheat or hex him into a bowling trophy, but if Wells gets a bug up his ass, the world will get ugly fast.

Brigitte uses her thumb to wipe lipstick off my lower lip. Maybe Romany are psychic after all because she says, "Relax. No one is watching. You're not the only one trained to look for these things."

"Point taken."

"Where are we going?"

I read her the hospital's address on South St. Louis Street off my phone. She punches it into the GPS on her dashboard and we head out. I always thought those boxes were for losers, but it shows us a quick, direct route through the traffic. I make a mental note that in the future I should only steal cars equipped with the boxes.

There are TV trucks parked across the street from Linda Vista. Can you go ten minutes in this town without seeing some idiot running down the street in a Steadicam rig like he has a giant robot hard-on? I hope the hospital is haunted so when the director has the cinematographer zoom in on a really interesting bloodstain on the floor, he gets a late-night Christmas-carol visit from the blood's owner.

"There will be security if they're filming. How do we get in?" asks Brigitte.

"I found a map of the place online. We can use a trick I have for getting in places without using the door. But you don't get to ask any questions about it."

"Now you absolutely have to show me."

We walk across the street, pointing at the building like a couple of tourists. I get Brigitte to snap pictures with her phone while I look for out-of-the-way shadows. We find some by the old emergency entrance.

"Take my hand and don't let go until we're all the way inside."

"All right."

She resists a little as I pull her into the shadow. And then again when I pull her out of the Room and through the Door of Restless Ardor.

"What was that place?"

"What did I say about questions?"

"You're no fun."

"Yes, I am."

We follow the map to the rear of the hospital, beyond where the crew is filming. We're on a side hall and can see the lights and cameras where they're shooting in the wide central corridor. The director yells, "Action!" A woman screams. Voices moan. A bloody nurse runs by, chased by a mob of filthy, groaning patients. Fuck me. They're making a zombie movie.

One more turn and we're in the morgue. The white tile walls are cracked and streaked with grime. There's a banged-up gurney against one wall. Someone went at the padding with a knife and left it scattered on the floor like white tumbleweeds. I don't want to know what's inside the pullout coolers in the walls.

We head into the big freezer. It's dark inside and—surprise,

surprise—the lights don't work. Just as I'm trying to think of some hoodoo that makes light without blowing something up, the place brightens. Brigitte's turned on a small LED flashlight she had in her pocket.

She asks, "What are we looking for?"

"We're not. *I* am. Unless someone left the door open, you need to be Sub Rosa to find these things."

I feel along one wall and then another. It's between the seams running down one row of tiles. The wall swings open silently.

Brigitte coos.

"I love magic. You must show me more."

"I think you'll see plenty before this is over."

The door swings shut behind us and we're in a low stone passage. Yellow light outlines a curtain up ahead. I go through first and hold the curtain back for Brigitte.

Cabal understands Sub Rosa chic. This location is even shittier than Springheel's shack.

The place looks like the house of the month in *Better Homes & Monsters*. It's all dark stone walls. There's a huge fireplace with andirons the size of parking meters. The furniture is made of old stained mahogany. Most of the varnish has been worn off the armrests on the chairs and they're covered with water stains and glasses and cigarette burns. Traces of half-eaten food and empty liquor bottles are scattered on every surface of the room. There are tapestries of hunting parties and war scenes hanging on the walls. One shows horsemen with scimitars slicing up a village of women and children. The men are already dead, tossed on a bonfire in the lower right corner of the tapestry. Cabal is going for a Vlad the Impaler look, but he's ended up with a Slayer album cover.

Cosima, Cabal's sister or wife or both, comes through a curtain that runs the length of one wall. On the curtain is an image of a Black Sun wheel. Ancient, hard-core hoodoo that supposedly gives dark mystics power over the material world. The Nazis loved the Sun wheel. Of course, things didn't work out so well for them, so maybe they forgot to plug theirs in or something.

"You can't just walk in here without an appointment. Cabal won't like it," says Cosima.

"We met at the Geistwalds' party."

"I know who you are and he still wouldn't like it."

"I don't like having to walk in here and I'll like having to walk out even less, so you can let him know I'm here or I will."

Cosima looks Brigitte up and down and goes back through the curtain. Brigitte and I follow.

The next room is similar to the one we just left, but the furniture is a lot more comfortable. Plush sofas, love seats, and pillows on the floor. At least a dozen people are passed out asleep around the room, some dressed and some not. They were really living it up. Wonder what they were celebrating?

Cabal comes out of a door that looks like it was looted from Lucifer's broom closet. He's wearing a stained floor-length black robe, a little like a cassock. He looks skinny out of his rags and is cleaner than he was at the Geistwalds', but he still smells like he uses sewage for aftershave. He's holding a half-empty wine bottle in one hand. Cabal smiles, showing big yellow teeth, and holds out his hand. He knows I don't want to shake it. I've met guys like this before. Everything is a test with them. Will I shake his hand? Do I get mad when he makes a dumb joke at my expense or weepy when he insults me? Alpha-male bullshit. But I can't get too mad. I've done it plenty myself. I take his hand and shake like we just bought Manhattan for some M&M's and a carton of Luckies.

Cabal waves us back into the other room and away from his snoring guests. He stumbles and sways trying to step over them and almost dumps his wine on a naked kid sleeping in golf shoes.

Cabal waves us over to the big table and drops down into the head seat. Brigitte and I sit next to each other. He offers us the bottle.

Brigitte puts up a hand and I shake my head.

"To what do I owe the honor of such an unexpected, but charming visit?"

"I wanted to ask you something."

"Goodie. I love twenty questions."

"You can drop the drunk act. If you were drunk, I could smell it in your sweat. All you did was take a hit off the bottle and swish it around your mouth so your breath would smell of wine."

He gives me a wink.

"Clever boy. Cuts right to it, doesn't be? We can't put anything past this one, can we, young lady? I didn't catch your name."

"Brigitte Bardo."

"Of course. Ritchie's darling. Forgive me, my dear. I only know you from your work and I didn't recognize you without a cock or two in your mouth. It's lovely to finally meet you in the flesh."

"And you."

"If you don't mind me inquiring, do you have just the tiniest bit of Gypsy blood in you?"

"I don't mind you asking. And yes, I do."

"I thought so. You people play some glorious music. Of course, you weren't so appreciated where I'm from. Most likely it was all the stealing."

"If there's anything missing after our visit, send a bill to Simon's and I'll have it taken care of."

He laughs and takes a swig from the bottle.

"Love your Nazi curtain," I say.

Cabal turns in his chair and looks at the Black Sun like he's never seen it before.

"Oh, that. One has to keep up appearances. Clients expect a bit of the scary-scary when they call on me."

"Is that why you have a slaughtered village hanging on your wall?"

He moves his eyes to look at the tapestry.

"Sadly, no. That's more of a family portrait. We're not the ones on horseback but the ones on fire."

He has a pretty strong magic barrier set up around his thoughts, so I can't tell if that's a sad damned story or a pretty effective lie.

"I wanted to talk to you about Drifters."

Cabal shakes his head.

"It breaks my heart to disappoint you, but the resurrected are not within the purview of my business dealings. I toil in the more prosaic fields of demons and elementals."

"But you've used them, haven't you? Maybe you don't use them on a regular basis, but how about in some kind of rent-to-own deal?"

He shrugs.

"As I said, one has to keep up appearances. When a competitor or social upstart oversteps the clearly demarcated boundaries of my sphere of influence, they must and will be dealt with swiftly and in as decisive a manner as it takes so that they might serve as an object lesson to others with similar rash inclinations."

"So, you have used Drifters against your enemies."

"Once or twice. I won't deny it."

"When was the last time?"

"I can't recall with any great clarity. One gets old. Many of the things that were so crystalline clear in one's youth become misty and difficult to plumb from the depths in our later years. Though I work hard to keep up appearances, I'm afraid I'm not the man I once was."

Brigitte says, "In my experience, that's what men say when they're exactly the man they used to be, but hope to deny it with age and excuse it with youth."

Cabal claps his hands in light, quick applause.

"Well said, young lady. You've ensnared me in a petite prevarication. Which, unhappily for you, doesn't alter the fact that I have not consorted with the resurrected, either deliberately or inadvertently, in many, many years."

I say, "It doesn't help Regina Maab that it was a long time ago. Eaten is eaten and dead is dead."

"Regina? What does she have to do with this?"

"Nothing, other than the fact that when she stepped on your toes you sent some Lacunas over with a jar of barbecue sauce and charcoal briquettes."

His eyes narrow and he sits up. All traces of the drunk act are gone.

"Listen to me closely, young man. That's not the kind of thing I'll tolerate being murmured about me, not by you or any other soul in this sunny burg. Regina and I had our differences, yes. And there came a moment when she required the administration of a lesson that she would remember on a molecular level. And yes, I vainly and foolishly employed a gaggle of resurrected in what you might term a professorial manner to deliver said lesson, but when Ms. Maab took leave of Los Angeles, she was most exceedingly and annoyingly alive."

"Why should I believe you when everyone else is positive you had her snuffed?"

He leans back in his chair and takes a box from his pocket, opens it, and pulls out what looks like a wriggling earthworm.

"Do you have a light?" he asks.

I reach for Mason's lighter and Cabal picks up the earthworm, running a grimy finger along the length of its body several times. The worm straightens and stiffens until it looks like a pink chopstick. I hold out the lighter and flick it. Cabal leans in, holds my wrist, and puts the worm's head into the flame. He puffs a few times and the worm catches, the end glowing cherry red. As Cabal smokes, he takes out a small black book and a pencil. He flips through the book, writes something down, and slides the piece of paper across the table to me.

"That is Regina's number in Mumbai. That's far away in a country called India. You might have heard of it. If you adjudge to ring her, please give the old girl my best."

I hand Brigitte the number and she looks it over. I let her hold on to it because her clothes probably don't get destroyed as often as mine.

"What kind of problem did you have with the Springheels?"

He looks genuinely puzzled by that. It caught him off guard and I can feel the edges of his mind sifting through old memories.

"None. They were like water buffalo shitting in the streets of Kathmandu. Like any lifelong resident of that fair city, they were something I neither noticed nor particularly cared about."

"They were an important family once."

"Virgin sacrifice and bloodletting were considered of the utmost importance once, but when they outlived their efficacy they were abandoned along with the other discarded refuse of an earlier, though in some ways more graceful, time."

"You old Sub Rosa families are pretty concerned about your place in the social pecking order. The Springheels were the first family in America. You didn't think that kind of history might overshadow you just a little?"

"The Springheels were a dusty diorama. A museum display illustrating Neanderthal man's first crude efforts to control fire and not shit themselves at every opportunity.

The only reason the Springheel family still existed was as a concession to nostalgia and sentimentality. They might have begun their days well in this green and verdant land, but through shrewd planning and incandescent gamesmanship, they managed to metamorphose from ancient royalty into dirt-scrounging hillbillies. They threatened my house as much as this luminous worm."

He holds up his pink cigarette.

"What happened to them?"

"Time. The world. Charles Springheel, the one who repatriated the family to California, designed and constructed exquisite charms, protective objects, talismans, and the like. He was, at heart, a tinkerer. And a brilliant one, but sitting in your ivory tower fiddling with Lilliputian cogs and thingamabobs is no way to maintain one's standing in the world. Many of us purchased Charles's contraptions over the years, both to bolster the old boy's sense of purpose and to add a bit of lucre to the family's dwindling fortune. But there's only so much one can do. A fool determined to saunter off a cliff will find his way around even the most formidable barricades."

I'm learning to really hate Cabal. I don't want to believe the words coming out of his skull-white face, but after seeing the pathetic and maybe deliberate death scene at the Springheel house, I can't argue with what he's saying about the family.

"Since you're our resident demon expert, did Enoch Springheel ever ask you for advice on how to summon or control them?"

"Enoch seldom discoursed with anyone. Certainly not

with me. The few times a year he would deign to appear at Sub Rosa soirees, he left the distinct impression of a man marooned in the Sahara of his own psyche."

"Who would we go to if we wanted to learn about Drifters or perhaps hire one?" Brigitte asks.

Cabal shakes his head.

"No one mucks about with the resurrected these days. Too dangerous. You'd be making yourself vulnerable to a veritable avalanche of peril, both from the families and our lovely local Inquisitor, Medea Bava."

"So, there aren't any Drifter experts in L.A.?"

"There are a number; however, by publicly acquiescing to such a dubious practice, they would be aiming a gun to their own precious skulls. To put it in blunt terms that you'll understand, they won't talk to you. I'm not so rude as to call myself an expert, but I have more than a passing knowledge of the resurrected. Is there something specific you wish to know?"

"Unless you know someone in town who runs with them, no."

Cabal drops the last few inches of the burning worm on the floor and crushes it out with his bare foot.

"I'm curious about the depth of your knowledge concerning our hungry friends. If I had a sense of your understanding, perhaps I could speed you along in your investigations."

"Out of the kindness of your heart?"

He smiles.

"To get you off my fucking back."

I look at his eyes. It doesn't look like he's lying. And he's genuinely interested in hearing what I'll say.

"Brigitte is the expert, but she'll talk longer and I'm in

a rush, so here's what I know. There are Drifters and Lacunas. One is dumb as dirt and one is maybe as smart as a
house-trained poodle. They bite and they won't stop until
you rip out their spines."

Cabal looks at Brigitte. She clears her throat.

"I could recite a thousand years of lore and list the ana-
tomical and biological differences of the species, but for the
purposes of our mission, James is right."

Cabal kills off the wine and drops the bottle on the floor.

"I see that I can aid you children with your quest, after
all. When I place this bauble of knowledge into your greedy
hands, I'd be immoderately grateful if you would quietly
exit the way you came and leave me to my guests."

"Deal."

"Most Sub Rosa don't have any greater understanding of
revenants than you. They memorize a few salient facts and
drop them into conversations at cocktail parties to make
themselves sound more interesting than they really are. I
know this because most people believe that the resurrected
are a binary species, but the truth is they are tripartite. You
mentioned golems or Drifters, as you call them, and Lacunas. They are a formidable pair but there is also a tertiary
species known to those with a deeper knowledge as Saperes
and to the man in the street as Savants. The peril with this
particular resurrected is that you will often not perceive
its true nature until it's eating your guts au gratin. Savants
appear to be fully functional members of the brotherhood
of man. They can chitchat, hold a job, dress themselves, and
they possess, or seem to possess, the power of thought as
clearly and intoxicatingly as you or I."

"So, a Savant is a Lacuna that can call for pizza delivery. I don't get it. Why are they so special that no one knows about them?"

"The first, most obvious reason, is panic. Admitting the existence of a strain of resurrected invisible to even adept Sub Rosa would have dire consequences. Human history is strewn with the corpses of those entangled in the panicked slaughter of mobs. This is especially true if the person or people perceived by the general population is different. Wouldn't you agree, little Gypsy?"

"Definitely."

"That was the obvious reason. What's the other?"

"Saperes are special because nature or God or some other entity has chosen to make them so. You see, at any one time there are exactly twenty-seven of them in the world. No more. No less. If one is destroyed, a new one appears somewhere else. It then becomes the burden of those of us, as you say, in the know, to find it. It's not unlike Buddhist monks searching for each new incarnation of a Lama subsequent to the death of the old one."

"Is that all?"

"You're one of those dark souls impossible to satisfy, aren't you?"

He wants to start an argument. I just smile and shrug.

"The number of Saperes appears deliberate. If you add two and seven, you get nine. Nine is a holy number. Three times three. The Trinity times the Trinity. I could go on, but you see the pattern."

"What does it mean?"

"I have no idea. No one does. And that's another reason

Saperes are such a closely held secret. We haven't a clue as to how they befit the everyday workings of the world."

"How does knowing any of this help us find last night's Drifters or who's controlling them?"

"We care for Saperes by seeding them strategically around the globe. If one is destroyed in Sumatra, the others remain safe while we scour the globe for its replacement. The three most proximate Saperes are in New York and Mexico City. Can you guess the location of the third one?"

"In Los Angeles," says Brigitte.

"*Bellissima.* I assure you, the twenty-seven cities were not chosen willy-nilly. Each is a magical crossroads. Each is a power spot, Los Angeles being a distinctly active one."

"You think if we find the Savant, it can help us?"

"If it wants to."

"How can we make it want to?"

Cabal grins like a naughty little boy.

"Give it what it wants. What all the resurrected want."

"You're fucking joking."

"I'm not telling you to gut some hapless soul. Go to an abattoir. Go to a *boucher*. Their desire is simply for fresh flesh. Human is the preferred fare, of course, but pig is close enough to man-flesh."

"How do we find the Savant?" asks Brigitte.

"Call the number on the piece of paper I gave you."

"You said that was Regina in Mumbai."

"I lied."

"Where is Regina?"

"Well, she's certainly not chained up in my basement.

That would be wrong of me. Still, Regina does tend to inspire the desire to lock her away somewhere deep and dark and full of more than an immoderate amount of spiders."

I look at Brigitte. She shakes her head. I look back at Cabal.

"If you're sending us into a trap, it's not going to work. And even if it does work, just because I'm dead doesn't mean I can't get to you."

"I'm exceedingly aware of your reputation, Sandman Slim. The phone number is true and leads to no trap that I know of. You'll want to call soon. If anyone can point you to true north, it's Johnny Thunders."

"The singer?"

"No. The zombie, you dunce. Johnny Thunders is your Savant."

He waves a tired hand in my direction. "Johnny's minders will explain."

If Cabal is lying, he deserves a teddy bear from the top shelf and the Publishers Clearing House Sweepstakes. I've heard world-class whoppers and told a few of my own, but this guy is spinning sable from shit.

Or he's just let Brigitte and me in on one of the world's weirder secrets. If he's lying, it would be a fun excuse to come back and punch holes in Castle Grayskull. But if he's telling the truth, it would make life a lot easier.

"One more thing," says Cabal. "There's someone else you might chat with concerning the resurrected. Rainier Geistwald, Jan and Koralin's son. He's a clever boy, and while a genuine brat, his brains are more acute than he cares to let on. He'll be an important man one day."

Cabal stands up. This time he doesn't offer his hand.

"I could say it's been enchanting, but I've already told you one lie today. I couldn't bear it if you lost all faith in me. You know the way out. Feel free not to linger. Ta-ta."

He turns and disappears through the Sun wheel curtain without looking back.

Brigitte asks, "Do you think he is sending us to people who will try to kill us?"

"I don't know. What would be more fun for him? Killing us right away or watching us bump into things and skin our knees?"

"True. Would you like me to call the number?"

"Let me. It's my town. I should be the first one through closed doors."

"How chivalrous."

"That's French for stupid, isn't it? That's okay. If we have time, I'll give you a demonstration of naked jousting."

We leave through the Room and back to her car. She doesn't ask any questions this time.

BACK IN FRONT of Max Overdrive, Brigitte leans over to kiss me, and this time I'm not shy about kissing her back. Cabal's act sucked the paranoid jitters right out of me. Sometimes annoyance will keep you going when booze and fear and hope are as dead as the Big Bopper.

Brigitte says, "I could come up for a while if you like."

"I would like, but you wouldn't like. I have a roommate."

She smiles.

"Does he like to watch?"

"He'd love it. But he's a kind of a spy and that means Lucifer would be watching us, too."

"What do I care? Lucifer probably has my calendar in his office in Hell."

"It would be awkward for me."

How do you tell someone you want to fuck that you can't do it in front of the devil because you don't want your dad spying on you?

"All right. I should probably be getting back anyway. But you owe me."

"Before I forget, my roommate loves you more than beer and cigarettes. Would you sign these for him?"

I hand her the DVDs. She smiles and takes a pen from the glove compartment.

"Who do I make it out to?"

"Aldous."

"What a lovely old name."

"I'll tell him you said that. It'll make his week."

"There's something for you under the seat."

I reach down and feel along the carpet until I touch a box. I pull it out and open it. Inside is a collapsed metal weapon.

"The gift that keeps on giving."

Brigitte hands me the DVDs.

"I want to go back to Springheel's house and look around soon. Want to come with me?"

"Is there a bedroom?"

"I didn't see one, but you can help me look."

"Then count me in."

She blows me a kiss, pops the clutch, and burns rubber back onto Hollywood Boulevard.

KASABIAN IS GOING through online video catalogs when I get back. *Death Rides a Horse* is playing on the other monitor.

"Did you remember cigarettes?"

"We didn't get to a store. I bummed one off one of the kids working the register."

"Which one?"

"I have no idea. They all look alike to me."

I set the DVDs on his table.

"Don't say I never gave you nothing."

He grabs them in his little metal legs.

"You are my goddamn hero, man."

"One more thing off my bucket list."

The DVDs have him in a good mood and I don't want to spoil it yet. I'll wait to tell him that Wells fired me and either I start knocking over gas stations or we set up shop in the Dumpster next to the hand.

"How was your date?"

"It wasn't exactly a date. We talked to a guy who yammered like he was gangbanged by a thesaurus. It's all a big act, but he's had a lot of practice. I don't think I ever met a human before who could stretch 'pass the peas' into a hundred and fifty syllables. I once killed a Hellion who talked like that just to shut him up."

"When Brigitte dumps you, you might not want to include 'kills people who use big words' in your personal ad."

"What makes you think Brigitte's going to dump me?"

He cocks his head in my direction.

"Gee, I don't know. She dates billionaires and you live in an attic over a video store. She wants to get into big-time movies and you can get her free beer and tacos. You're a monster and she's a person. I can e-mail you a spreadsheet if you want to see the other five hundred reasons."

"She won't dump me."

"Why not?"

"She hasn't told me her real name and I haven't told her what the Room is."

He takes a beer from the fridge under his table and cracks it open.

"So, you're finally done mooning over Alice. About time."

Kasabian's beer flies across the room and hits the wall before I realize it was me who knocked it out of his hand.

"Do not ever fucking say her name. Not now, not ever, unless you want to go back in the closet. And while you're playing spy, tell Lucifer not to pull that shit with me either. People are after him and all I have to do is step out for a sandwich and let it happen."

Kasabian is staring at me, shit scared. A deer head in the headlights. He's quiet for what seems like a full minute.

He says, "I'm sorry, man. I overstepped."

I take the cigarette from where I'd stuck it behind my ear and light it. Take a couple of puffs. Kasabian is still staring at me. I go over and hold the filter end of the smoke out to him. He doesn't move for a second and then takes a tentative puff.

"Thanks."

"Yeah."

We finish it in silence.

I take beers from the fridge, give him one, and take the other to the bed.

Where did that slap come from? I haven't heard Alice's name out loud since I sent Mason Downtown. I'm trying not to think about her every time I close my eyes or make a decision. Not thinking about her is the same as getting over her, right?

"Tell me something. When you were doing Zombie 101 earlier, why didn't you tell me about Savants?" I ask.

"What's a Savant?"

I look at him. He's not lying.

"Just something I heard. It might be a wild-goose chase, but it might not. When you're in the Codex, keep your eyes open for Savant or Saperes."

"Sure. In the meantime, I think I know something that's going to make you feel better."

"What's that?"

"Whatever you said to Lucifer at the studio shot a bottle rocket up his ass. He's been sending me into the Codex all day. Looking at sections I didn't know were there. Digging through footnotes and diaries and commentaries. Some of the writing is old. Like beginning-of-time old. Some of it's written in an angelic script I bet even Mason never saw. I think it might be the first one. The original script. The first writing for the first language in the universe."

"Hallelujah. I'll buy the cherubs a lap dance when this is done. But right now, I'm up to my ass in little fortune-cookie facts and I don't know how any of them go together."

"Here's something. The big man had me do a brain dump on you and he saw the drawing you did of the belt-buckle thing. Know what happened?"

"He ordered one from QVC?"

"He freaked the fuck out. It was so strong I felt it. I mean, we're supposed to have a one-way communication system. I send and he receives. But when he saw that drawing, the blowback out of his brain went all the way up the line and back into me."

"So, what is it?"

"I don't know yet. The writing around the edges is more of that old angelic script. I can't read it yet, but I'll figure it out."

"Whatever it is, this means that Lucifer knows that I know about the belt buckle."

"Yeah, but I can block things from him. All he knows is that you saw the image. He doesn't know you really saw the thing or know where it is. If I were you, I'd move my ass and get it. Whatever it is, the buckle is strange enough to scare Lucifer and it's definitely connected to the zeds."

"Let me finish my beer."

"Of course. The end of the world can wait."

No, I GUESS it can't. I go through a shadow and into the boarded-up movie theater with the bottle in my hand, finishing the last dregs of the beer. The place is dead black when I get inside. The owners must have done a better job sealing the place up after the cops came by. I just hope they didn't clean it. I throw the bottle at the wall and wait for the crash. But there isn't one. Just a dull thud as it hits something soft. I get out Mason's lighter and spark it.

The beer suddenly tries to come back up my throat. It's not like wanting to puke. It's more like the beer is smarter than me and it wants to run away and leave my dumb ass where it's standing.

The bottle didn't smash because it didn't hit the wall. It didn't hit the wall because it hit a zed. Or a Lacuna. I can't really tell the difference, but this would be a good place to learn about them because there are about a hundred Drifters mobbed together maybe twenty feet away.

I lurch halfway back into the shadow when I realize that I don't have to. None of the shamblers are looking in my direction. Not even the one I hit with the bottle. They're just standing in a big circle among the seats. A few moan quietly, but it doesn't seem to have anything to do with me. They're all looking down at the same spot on the floor. I think I know what they're looking at.

The gun and the na'at aren't going to do me much good in these close quarters and I don't want to use any hoodoo on the off chance it'll break the buckle's hypnotic hold on these meat sticks. What I really need is about a hundred pounds of C4, but I must have left it in my other coat. I get out the black blade. It'll be hard to use, but better than nothing. If the belt buckle is at the center of the mob, I'll have to put away the knife to get it. But until I'm sure, I'm staying ready to slice and dice.

I take a couple of steps closer to the mob. It's a mixed bunch. Some of the dead are very recent. They look like regular civilians who've missed a night or two of sleep. Others aren't much more than gristle and bones in decaying rags. A lot of the older ones are eyeless, so whatever brought them here must be pretty powerful hoodoo.

I'm right behind them now. I could touch the one in front of me without stretching my arm. He's wearing shorts and sandals and an orange "I'm Not as Think as You Drunk I Am" T-shirt.

I put the knife to the back of his neck. If he so much as twitches, I can take his head off and slice up the nearest ones enough so the others will trip on them when they come for me. But I don't have to do anything.

Slowly and steadily I shoulder my way between the stinking dead, inching toward the center of the room. I keep the knife up, but none of them have the slightest interest in me. They're all hypnotized by what's on the floor.

It feels like it takes a week to get to where they're all looking. And there it is, lying on an altar of broken glass and crushed Mickey's malt-liquor cans. Eleanor's belt buckle.

I'm sorry I ever doubted you, Eleanor. I should have known that the stunt in public with the flamethrower and the mad dash home to the theater weren't accidental. You wanted to get caught. You wanted someone to find you and whatever it was you'd stolen and kill you for it so Mommy and the rest of the Sub Rosa would know what you'd done and what happened to you. That's a lot of pain for a kid to be hauling around. It makes me not mind you frying my arm so much. I know what it's like to want to cook the world. I'm sorry I didn't figure it out sooner, but, for what it's worth, I'm here now, and if I don't end up a Quarter Pounder with cheese in the next few minutes, I'll take your buckle and do something with it. If I do end up eaten, well, I'll buy you a Happy Meal in Hell.

At the center of the crowd, the Drifters are so packed together I have to knock a zed on his face to squeeze through. I freeze, waiting for the crowd to lunge. But the zed on the floor just stands up and goes back to staring. I know they can smell me. I'm sweating like a three-legged racehorse, but even now when I'm about to pick up their holy grail, they ignore me.

I'm in too deep to back off now. I put the knife back in my jacket and hold the lighter close to the floor so I get the buckle without wasting time. Crouching, I touch the edge, ready to back off at the slightest reaction from the Drifters. Nothing. I get my hand around the buckle and slowly lift it a few inches, then a foot off the ground. Still no reaction. Either I was wrong about the buckle or Drifter brains are so slow to process information it'll take them a while to notice that the family jewels are gone. I hope it's the second one.

I slip the buckle into my coat pocket, but keep one hand under my coat. Slowly, I push my way through the Drifters back the way I came. They stay put, though the moaners are getting louder.

Without warning, they all step forward at once. They sense that the talisman is gone and want to get closer to where it was and soak up the residual hoodoo. There's a hundred or more of them trying to squeeze into a space about the size of a phone booth. I lean forward and put my shoulder into them. I have to use all my weight to move forward. I'm getting through, but the farther back I go, the more they press forward.

The mood is changing. The place was a church when I got here. Cool and contemplative. Getting the buckle wasn't much worse that pushing to the front of the stage at a hardcore club. Now the air is getting bad. Jittery with panic and confusion. I've been here before. I know what's coming. Time to de-ass the premises.

Fuck close quarters. I pull the .460 from its holster and pop a shoulder-level shot between two zeds I want to move. The blast knocks one off its feet and rips the other's arm loose, so it's hanging by a few strands of tendon. With just the loose limb in my way, I push past them without slowing down. I need out of here ASAP and get into a rhythm about it. Take a step. Blow open a porthole. Take a step. Fire. Step. Fire. It's working. I'm moving faster now. My only worry is slipping on corpse leakage or a severed arm.

Just as I'm about to step out of the circle, it tightens. Pins me where I am. I can't even raise my arm to shoot.

Then the mob relaxes. The magic in the center of the room is gone and they have no reason to crowd there anymore. I break free of them and head for a wall. It's taken me longer to get out than I counted on. Plenty of time for even these rotten brains to figure out that something is going on and look around for what. I have a bad feeling that if I turn around, a hundred pairs of dead eyes will be aimed straight at me and what's in my pocket.

"Who the fuck are you, motherfucker?"

I know it's stupid, but I can't help it. I turn and look.

So that's what a Lacuna looks like. Cabal was right. I wouldn't notice him in a crowd. He's in a double-breasted gray suit, and if it wasn't for all the dried blood on his jacket from the ragged bite mark in his neck, I wouldn't look at him twice. He's looking at me like a starving wolf. Like he's trying to read the theater marquee through my chest. Blank-eyed shamblers behind him are turning this way.

"I said, 'Who the fuck are you?'"

I take a step back and hold the lighter so he can see my face.

"You can't catch me, I'm the Gingerbread Man."

He rushes and the mob follows; a tsunami of black, broken teeth and putrid meat crashes down on me.

But chatty and bright as the Lacuna is, he's still a dumb, dead piece of shit. When he rushes me, my back is already to the wall and I'm stepping through it. He's not going to make it in time. He's going to be the smartest deli slice in the slaughterhouse when those other hundred Drifters splatter him against the wall like a car crusher. Good thing he's dead or it might hurt.

RITCHIE'S PLACE IS in Laurel Canyon. Back in the sixties, rich hippies, movie moguls, and famous bands lived up here. Between the dope, their biker friends, the Manson wannabes, and all the free love that was never really free, the place turned into *The Killing Fields* with a Jefferson Airplane sound track. Don't you want somebody to love? They were Khmer Rouge in designer jeans, and when the dope and the money ran out the canyons and deserts bloomed over the bodies they buried there.

I drive up the winding road to the address Brigitte gave me. I'm in a stolen Lexus because I want to be boring tonight. And I don't want to take Brigitte back through the

Room if I can help it. Eventually she's going to ask questions I don't want to answer.

It's about 2 A.M. when I stop in front of Ritchie's gates. I can see the house at the end of a long circular drive. It looks like a claw machine in an arcade plucked an Italian villa off a hill in Rome and dropped it down in the middle of the manzanita and coyotes. The place is pretty, but looks ridiculous here. Like something you'd build to win a bar bet.

Brigitte is waiting for me in the shadow of a eucalyptus. She's holding her leather jacket tight around her to keep out the canyon cold. She should have something heavier, but when you're sneaking out of the house in the middle of the night like a teenybopper running off for backseat groping with your boyfriend, you can't exactly take the time to squeeze into Lancelot's armor.

She gives me a quick kiss when she gets in and immediately starts playing with the car heater.

"How does this work?"

"I have no idea. How is Ritchie not going to notice you're gone?"

"I put a powder in his drink. An old family mix and not at all harmful. He'd probably approve if he knew. It's all organic."

I take her down the hill the way we came, then head for Springheel's place. The heater is going and she starts to relax. She opens the glove compartment and pulls out the contents into her lap, like a kid going through her Halloween candy. I spot a pack of cigarettes.

"Score."

"Take them. I quit before coming to L.A. Rich men like their girls pure inside and out."

"Darlin', purity has nothing to do with why Ritchie went for you."

"You know what I mean. Trophy girlfriends have to make you look good in front of your friends. Here that means no smoking. The next place I go hunting, it will be somewhere like France or Japan. Somewhere they don't believe they'll live forever if they give up everything that gives them pleasure."

"Speaking of you hunting, I still don't know much of anything about you. You're like Van Helsing in drag, but you have a whole public life on video. How does your life go that way?"

"What don't you understand? The revenants or the pornography?"

"I understand the porn. Lots of Sub Rosa and Lurkers do it out here. But I've never met a professional Drifter exterminator before. How does that end up the family business?"

"The Hussites ate my grandmother."

"That was going to be my second guess. What are Hussites?"

"Protestants. They were angry over corruption in the Church and the Church rewarded them by burning their leader, Jan Hus, at the stake. My village didn't care. They were all fools to us. But the Hussites and the government went to war, and monsters, which love nothing more than chaos, came with them. One evening, a Hussite band came to our village. They took as much food as they could carry and some goats and left. We cursed them, but would have saved our curses if we had known what was to follow. More soldiers came, but these were different. They were ragged and stank of death. Some were little more than bones and none of them spoke. Grandmother was a *čarodějnice*. A witch. She and the other old women, with nuns from a local convent, went together to drive off the ghost soldiers. They carried Bibles and my grandmother and the old women carried potions and magical objects. None of them ever returned."

"Damn."

"Two days later, a few of the women and the nuns returned, including Grandmother. But it was not really her. She was nude. The flesh from her breasts, her belly, and her legs had been eaten away. Most of her face was gone, but Grandfather recognized her and went to her. She gouged out his eyes and devoured him in the main room of our little house, under the crucifix her mother had given them at their wedding."

"You didn't have to kill them yourself, did you?"

"This happened six hundred years ago, so no, I didn't, but we still remember."

"So your people decided to go after the ghost soldiers."

"The bravest, boldest men went after them that night. They all were eaten or turned into revenants themselves. Other men were able to capture a few of the beasts and, over time, we learned how to destroy them. After that, my family were no longer farmers. We were killers. Like you. And like you, we do whatever we have to do to live and continue our work."

"You don't have to justify anything to me."

"I know. That's why I'll tell you this. Normal people, Simon's sort of people, wouldn't understand."

"You definitely win the deep-dark-secrets competition. I never hid anything that good."

"What about your magic? You must have kept that secret."

"I didn't know any better when I was a kid, and by the time I figured it out, it was too late."

"Poor Jimmy. Full of magic and happy to use it. Doomed to beat the boys at all their games and do tricks for the girls to make them kiss you."

"I didn't have a car. I had to do something."

"I'll light a candle for you."

"Don't waste the wax. They don't take my calls anymore."

I get Brigitte to hold the wheel while I tap out a cigarette, light up, and take a big puff. Instantly, I'm Doc Holliday trying to cough up a lung.

"God. They're menthols."

I toss the rest of the pack, including the one I'm smoking, out the window. I'm doing the Lexus owner a favor ditching those nerve-gas sticks. He'll whine when he realizes they're gone, but sometimes tough love is the only answer.

The street across from the vacant lot on East Sixth is empty. I kill the engine and the lights and we sit for a minute watching the place. In the moonlight the Springheels' hovel looks like a cardboard cutout left out in the rain. I don't see anyone standing guard.

Brigitte leans across me and looks out the window.

"That's the house of an important family?"

"The most important once upon a time."

"I think you Sub Rosa have a different sense of beauty than other people."

"You get used to it. Like herpes or a missing leg."

"I want to see inside."

"Not yet. I need to do something first."

I grab a bag from the backseat, get out of the Lexus, and go around to the passenger side. Brigitte watches as I dump a pile of powders, plants, and the piece of lead I use for certain kinds of circles.

"Lovely. I get to see magic?"

"You get to see magic. I hope these ingredients are still good. They're Kasabian's. My roomie's. He hasn't done this kind of hoodoo in a long time."

"What kind does he do?"

"He shits out of his neck."

Brigitte stares.

"I'll explain later."

There's a mortar and pestle in the bag. I pass them to Brigitte along with a bag of ingredients.

"Take these leaves and seeds and grind them up into a powder. I need to go be da Vinci."

I take the lead and draw a circle in the car's shadow so it will be hard to see if someone wanders by. The image isn't complicated. A pentagram facing north inside a double circle. Outside the circle I scribble words in Latin, Hebrew, and Hellion. Not a spell. More a friendly "hi and thanks for stopping by" kind of stuff. It's pretty random, but better hoodoo than it sounds. If you think it's easy saying anything in Hellion that doesn't come off as a veiled threat, you'd be wrong. I suck at milk-and-cookies magic, but I need to attract as much wildlife as possible without blowing it up.

"Your powder is ready. What kind of magic are we doing?"

"The Vigil will have left an alarm on the house. Probably angelic, and those detect conscious life. That's animals, insects, and us. Anything can go inside or be magically controlled to go inside. We can't turn the alarm off, but we can give it a migraine."

The powder goes into the center of the circle and I lean over it to whisper some bits of greeting magic I sort of halfway remember. Brigitte is smiling, trying not to laugh. I look like I'm whispering sweet nothings to a pile of dirt, not exactly the two-fisted hoodoo she was counting on.

When I get tired of cooing to the pavement, I dump powdered sulfur onto the pile and mix it all together with my hands. Get out Mason's lighter, spark it, and throw the mess up into the air as hard as I can. I touch the flame to the tail end of the cloud and the sulfur catches, igniting a twenty-foot pillar of fire.

The fire is gone as quickly as it came, but by the time the last powder embers hit the ground, I can already hear what I was hoping for.

Around us and above us there's a rustling sound. The birds arrive first, settling into the vacant lot by the house, chirping, cawing, and pecking at the ground. Rats and mice swarm out of the sewers and warehouses, followed by insects. The crawlers cover the ground like a massive undulating carpet and the fliers drop from the sky like a black, glittering fist. Cats and dogs, the smartest animals of the bunch, so the hardest to convince, get there last. They head right for the house, circle it, mark the boards, and climb onto the roof. The birds and insects finally get the idea and head in that direction. As soon as they're moving, I grab Brigitte's hand and we start to run. The animals know we're coming. Yeah, they're dumb, but this is hoodoo and it would be a pretty shit spell if you ended up crushing all the wildlife you'd just called.

The bugs and mice and rats part like the Red Sea and Brigitte and I run through the field to the house. By the time we're there, the walls and roof are a solid mass of feathers, fur, and shiny carapaces. There's no way the alarm can read and separate this much life at once. I pull out the na'at as we go up the steps and slash the lock. The door swings open on its own. It's dark inside. Brigitte gets out her flashlight. I take her back to the kitchen and out through the missing porch. She gasps when she finds herself in the Springheels' sprawling California ranch house.

"This is beautiful."

"If you're Ronald Reagan, I guess."

"The idea of it, I mean. The beauty hidden within the rot."

"Sure. That's what I meant, too."

I find the lights as Brigitte wanders around the living room touching the furniture, then going to the big windows that open out over the desert.

"I'd like to see the desert."

"It's not hard to get to from L.A. Maybe I'll show you sometime."

"Maybe."

There's a big side table against the wall across from the windows. I go through all the drawers. I'm not looking for clues. I'm looking for the half pack of stale Marlboro Lights I find in the middle drawer. I take a long sniff and I'm in love.

"Junkie," says Brigitte.

"I'm not addicted. I just want to be able to inject these directly into my brain."

"We didn't come to the house so you can loot it, did we?"

"No. I did a demon reading where Springheel died. I just want to make sure I was right."

"Why wouldn't you be?"

"It was crowded and noisy. Good distractions if you want to keep someone from finding something."

"Why would you be invited and asked to examine something if you weren't supposed to find the truth?"

"I've been wondering about that. Maybe it was a test to see if a crime scene was covered up well enough. Maybe I'm being set up to be the fall guy if it wasn't demons back there."

"I have tools with me that will tell us if revenants were present."

We go to the room where Enoch Springheel was chewed up like human jerky. I keep an eye on Brigitte when I flip on the light. The Vigil tidied up a bit, but Springheel's sex magic altar is still there and the bloodstain on the floor is as wide as a king-size bed. Brigitte doesn't flinch. Her heart and breathing are rock steady. She's walked into a lot bigger messes than this. That means she's been telling the truth. Also it means that whatever we find, I won't have to babysit her.

"What sort of demons do this damage?"

"Eaters."

She nods.

"This wouldn't be the first time someone has confused demons and revenants. Or used one to cover up the other."

"It would be a first for me and it better be the last."

Brigitte sees Springheel's altar and heads right for it.

"These things are for very dark magic. Do what you are going to do. I want to watch."

"It's not hard, but it's messy. You might want to step back."

She goes and stands by the door. I get out a plastic bag of dry skin I scraped off Kasabian's Hand of Glory and use the black blade to cut my palm and let a few drops of blood fall into the bag. I squeeze the bag to work the blood into the skin, pour the mess into my hand, and then scatter it over the magic hexagon. I take the bottle of whiskey off Springheel's altar, get a mouthful, and spit it onto the Hand of Glory dust and wait. In a few seconds green and black smoke curls up from the floor like miniature prairie fires.

I look over at Brigitte and shrug. "I wasted your time. I was right. There were demons here."

Brigitte takes a glass vial about the size of a lipstick container from her pocket. She shakes it and says, "Turn off the light."

She throws the container as I hit the switch. The vial crashes somewhere on the other side of the room and something begins to glow. Pale blue spots glimmer on the floor like blood spatter. They're all over the hexagon and extend away into the dark room.

"What is that?"

"The essence left behind by a revenant."

"Demons and Drifters were both in here? Can you tell how long ago it was?"

Brigitte kneels beside the glowing pattern and smudges some onto her fingers.

"A few days. Less than a week. That's as close as I can judge."

"Same thing with the demon marks."

I flip the light on.

"I'd like to know which was here first and who came after."

"Does it matter? You have proof now that you were right," says Brigitte.

I take a shot of the smoke with my phone.

"But I was wrong, too. Demons fade to the immaterial world when they're not summoned, but if Drifters were in here, where are they?"

"They could have wandered out or been led away."

"What the hell is going on? None of this makes any damned sense."

"Let's discuss it somewhere else."

"Like where?"

"Somewhere more comfortable. We're done here, but Simon won't be up for hours. Take me home. I want to see where you live."

She reaches down and grabs my cock through my jeans, gets up on her toes, and kisses me. I lean down to her, slip my hand around her ass, and pull her into me.

I see Kasabian's beer bottle crashing into the wall and me yelling, "Don't say her name."

No. I'm not going to feel bad every time I touch another human being. I'm the one who's still alive on this rock. I won't apologize for wanting to feel like a person every now and then.

But this is pretty fucked up even for me, making out in the room where someone was ripped to pieces and eaten a few days ago. We're standing where his blood was pooled like black custard.

"I can't do this here."

"Are you sure you're the man who lived in Hell for all those years? You're awfully delicate sometimes."

"And you're pretty hard core. Does anything get to you?"

"Not this. I was helping my father hunt when I was seven. I've seen bodies in every state imaginable."

"Well, I've been the guy torn up on the floor. I don't want to kiss you here. Let's get out. I'll get Kasabian some beer and smokes and he can spend the night in the closet."

I loop my arm around Brigitte's shoulder and steer her toward the door. We're just about clear when she stops.

"What?"

"I want to see something on the wall."

She swings the door half closed and doesn't move for a moment.

"This is a very old sigil. A revenant clan. People who took revenants into their families with dreams of immortality."

"Let me see."

I step around and there's the sigil. The writing is different, but the design looks a lot like Eleanor's belt buckle. But the paint job isn't right. Everything else in the room, as screwy as it might be, is put together well. The big, toothy monster face on the wall was spray-painted fast and sloppy, like a kid tagging his school at lunch.

"Are you sure?" I ask.

"Definitely."

I push the door closed to get a better look. When it shuts, there's a sharp metallic click. Brigitte gives me a funny look. A thin metal strand leads from the top of the door frame across the ceiling. A tripwire rigged to go off when the village idiot closed the door to look at the wall. This is why I hate working with other people. They see things. I don't look, so I don't set off traps. Curiosity didn't kill the cat. Other people did.

There's a grinding and the floor vibrates as a section of the far wall slides away. Fluorescent lights blink on in the deep black. It's just a basement. Springheel's secret room. The walls look like they're carved out of solid rock. Someone's been working down there. A wall is open and fresh dirt and rocks are scattered on the floor.

I hold up my phone to get a shot of the room, but someone gets in the way and it's not Brigitte.

I don't have to look to know who. I can smell them.

Zeds pour out of the basement like army ants protecting their territory. There's just enough time to get out the na'at and collapse it to a couple of feet, leaving the thorns exposed so that when I swing it, it's like a morningstar.

I catch the first one on an upstroke, crushing its face and jamming its jaw up into the bones around its eyes. The second gets it on a downstroke. One of the barbs catches his skull just above his forehead, his head opens up, and everything inside spills out. After that, I don't notice individual blows anymore. I'm swinging the na'at like a street sweeper, trying to clear some room on the floor so that I can actually fight. With each swing, the na'at sends bone and meat flying.

"Get the door open," I tell Brigitte.

"It is."

There are just too many of them and more pour from the room. I could slash and smash all day and I'd end up right where I am.

I yell, "Get down!" and bark some Hellion arena hoodoo.

All the air in the room gets sucked into a central point above our heads, pulling the Drifters back with it. I knew it was coming, so I leaned the other way, and when the vacuum lets up, I drop to the floor. Brigitte is already down.

"Cover your eyes and hold your breath."

Above us, all the oxygen sucked up to the top of the room explodes. A fireball blows down from the ceiling, frying everything that's more than a couple of feet off the ground.

Even with my eyes closed, the flash leaves me seeing spots. The Drifters are a pile of crispy, twitching Manwich meat. I look around for Brigitte. She's on the floor where she dropped. She shoots me a sooty killer's smile. She never sees the little girl coming up behind her.

The girl looks like she's around five or six. She's in a long pink-and-yellow party dress and there's a wilted pink rose in her tangled hair. When Brigitte pushes herself up to her knees, she's just level with the princess's head.

I'm running, but I know I won't make it. The princess is too close. She opens wide and digs her rotten teeth into the back of Brigitte's neck like a dog trying to break a rat's spine. Brigitte falls and screams with the little girl on top of her.

I swing the na'at like a baseball bat. The princess rears up growling and the na'at slams into her mouth, snapping her head back and shearing it off at the upper jaw. The top of her head rolls away, but the rest of her hangs on to Brigitte. That doesn't work out so well for her. Brigitte braces her legs against the floor and slams her back into the wall, pinning the headless princess. She spins and pulls her CO_2 gun, locks the kid's writhing body against the wall with her knee, and fires a bolt straight down into the baby Drifter's spine. Her back blows out and she stops moving.

That's the good news. The bad news is that more Drifters are stumbling out of the basement. Some trip over their friends' burned bodies. Some fall to their knees and gnaw on them. Some of the crispy critters on the floor start to move. Charred arms and legs pull away from the pile of scorched bodies and haul themselves across the floor like spiders. This is why fighting corpses sucks. They're too dumb to know when they've lost and dead enough not to care.

"She bit me."

It's Brigitte.

"She fucking bit me, James. She's killed me."

"We've got to get out of here."

I say it really reasonably, but Brigitte's mind has gone bye-bye. She wades into the Drifters, kicking and pistol-whipping the ones walking point. She catches others as they come out of the basement, blasting bolt after bolt into their heads. I let her blow up a few skulls figuring it'll calm her down, but the falling bodies just make her crazier, so I grab her shoulders and pull her to the door. She shoots until her gun is empty.

I get her as far as the living room before she faints. She's bleeding bad. There's a kind of shawl on the back of an old chair. I tear off a long section, wrap it around Brigitte's neck like a scarf, pick her up, and head for a shadow. But there's no door there. Just wall. Fucking Springheel must have put an antihoodoo cloak on the house. I carry her out through the kitchen.

Extra-crispy and original-recipe Drifters shamble from the back into the living room. Most of them get lost in the furniture and bounce around like pinballs, but some of the smart ones that can follow a straight line stumble after us. Eventually, the pinballs will bounce their way out of the front door, too. Nothing I can do about that now. I get Brigitte to the Lexus, put her in the passenger seat, and buckle her in. I get to the driver's side cursing Kinski for being gone. We could use you and your magic glass right now, you prick.

Maybe a dozen Drifters are wandering around the vacant lot and there are more behind them. This neighborhood is all warehouses and pretty deserted even in the middle of the day, but it won't take them long to wander into populated neighborhoods. Someone left them there like a land mine. It was going to go off sometime and I'm the asshole lucky enough to have set it off. How many more bombs did whoever spray-painted behind the door leave around the city?

Brigitte moans. I hit the gas and point the Lexus in the direction of Vidocq and Allegra's.

I BEACH THE Lexus half on the curb outside the building, run to Brigitte's side, and pull her out. The streetlight casts a fat shadow on one wall. I step through and come out in the apartment.

I don't know what time it is. Probably three or four. All the lights are off. In my head, the room is still the same as when I left it eleven years ago, but it's not my place and Vidocq has changed everything. I want to put Brigitte down on the couch, but I keep stumbling over chairs and piles of books. Fuck it. I start kicking anything that makes noise.

"Wake up! Wake up! Wake up!"

A light comes on in the bedroom. Allegra wanders out in an extra-extra-large Max Overdrive T-shirt. Vidocq follows, tying his robe.

"What time is it? What's going on?" asks Allegra, rubbing her eyes.

Now that I can see, I carry Brigitte over to where they're standing.

"She's hurt and she's lost a lot of blood."

"Who is she? If she needs blood take her to an emergency room."

"She isn't hospital hurt. She's Kinski hurt, but he's gone, so you're Kinski tonight."

"What happened to her?"

"There was a metric assload of Drifters. One of them bit her."

"What the hell? What's a Drifter?"

"A High Plains Drifter."

Vidocq clears his throat.

"He means revenants. Zombies."

Allegra's forehead creases in a frown.

"There really are zombies? Why doesn't anyone tell me these things?"

"They're extremely rare. I've only seen an outbreak once in this country and it was put down quickly."

I say, "History later. A chunk of her neck is missing."

Allegra points past me.

"Put her on the kitchen counter."

She and Vidocq grab plates, utensils, and a cutting board and toss them on a nearby table. When there's a clean spot, I lay out Brigitte, facedown. Allegra pushes the hair back from Brigitte's wound. I put a kitchen towel under her so her face isn't right on the tile.

"Eugène, get the first-aid kit from the bathroom. And the pharaoh grubs."

He leaves. Allegra turns on a metal desk lamp she keeps there for reading cookbooks and potions. As she tentatively runs her fingers around the edges of Brigitte's wound, she holds the light by her face.

"Who is she? Is she from the store? I swear I've seen her somewhere."

"She's Brigitte Bardo. You two probably watched some of her movies together."

She pauses for a few seconds.

"Right. That's it." Her tone is slightly embarrassed. "What's she doing here?"

"She's in Lucifer's movie."

"Lucifer is making a porn movie?"

"She's a trained zombie hunter, but she stays dressed for that, so there's not that much money in it."

Allegra hands me the lamp, goes to the sink, and washes her hands. By the time she's finished, Vidocq is back with a canopic jar and a small white metal case stamped with a red cross. She opens a plastic bottle of Betadine and squirts it all over the wound, then takes a couple of big gauze pads from the first-aid kit and gently cleans it out. When she's done she presses her ear to Brigitte's back.

"It looks like the bleeding has stopped, but you're right. By her color and heartbeat she's lost a lot of blood. I can give her a general healing potion for the wound and a restorative for the blood loss."

"She was bitten by a damned zombie. How about something for that?"

Allegra ignores me. She takes the lid off the canopic jar and I get hit with a smell that reminds me of the Drifters at Springheel's. She upends the jar and a pile of fat, wriggling worms falls out. Each one is the size of my thumb.

"What are those?"

"Pharaoh grubs. They're like maggots. They eat dead skin and leave clean, healthy tissue and they're about ten times faster about it than maggots."

Allegra puts several of the grubs on Brigitte's wound. They go right for her discolored flesh. Vidocq puts his hand on my arm and raises it so I'm holding the lamp at a better angle for Allegra to work.

"Thank you, dear."

"Of course."

I look at Vidocq. Lit from below by the lamp, he looks old and tired.

"You've been around two hundred years, man. Tell me you know something to fix this."

"I do know something. But I know that what you want doesn't exist. There is no cure for the bite of a revenant."

"You have all these books. How do you know there isn't something you've missed?"

"I've read all these books many times and more besides. I've traveled the world hoping to cure my own involuntary immortality. I learned from magnificent alchemists, witches, and magicians. The few times the subject of revenants came up, all were in agreement. There is no cure. The best you can do is leave the afflicted in the Winter Garden."

"No way."

"Where's the Winter Garden?" asks Allegra.

I say, "It's not where. It's what. He wants to put Brigitte into a fucking coma. Like suspended animation in a science-fiction movie."

"It will stop the infection from consuming and killing her. It will halt her transformation."

Allegra picks up a couple of the grubs.

"How long can you keep her like that?" she asks.

"In theory, forever. It will give us time to look for other possibilities."

"You just said there weren't any possibilities," I say.

"There aren't. But that doesn't mean we shouldn't look."

"I don't like it."

"No one ever does, but there's nothing else to do. Unless you want to do nothing, wait for her transformation, and release her yourself."

As Allegra packs the wound with cotton, Brigitte opens her eyes. Allegra gently holds her shoulders so she doesn't try to get up.

"James?"

"Brigitte."

"Where are we?"

"With friends. You're all right. They'll fix you up."

"Bullshit. I've been bitten. Kill me, James. You can do it."

"No I can't."

"I would do it for you. Please. Do it before I change."

"No."

"How many people have you killed? I'm going to be much more of a monster than you soon. Kill one more. Please."

"Maybe. But not right now."

Brigitte closes her eyes. I look at Vidocq.

"Do it. Freeze her."

"Stark?"

It's Allegra. Her voice is odd.

"What?"

"You're bleeding."

I look at my hands. Both are bitten and scratched. There's a sliver of skin missing from my left palm. All the wounds are closed and scabbed.

"How 'bout that."

Vidocq says, "Jimmy, we must do it now. Both of you must go to the Garden."

"Look at her and look at me. Her skin's going blue. Her eyes are bloodshot. She's dying. Look at me. Do I look any different from when you saw me earlier?"

"No."

"I feel fine."

"For now," says Allegra. "What if you're wrong and you change later?"

"Then you have my permission to kill me. You've got to kill the central nervous system. You don't have the right tools, so the easiest thing for you would be to cut off my head and burn it and my body."

"That's what's easiest? Great."

Vidocq takes the lamp and shines it in my eyes. Checks my face.

"There might be a simple reason you aren't changing. The Cupbearer's elixir."

"You think it's keeping his body from changing?"

"It's possible. There are accounts of similar occurrences. During the Great Plague there are stories of people who drank the elixir for various ailments. These people survived while whole towns died around them. You might be all right."

Allegra goes to the shelves lined with potions and alchemical mixtures and brings a few bottles back to the counter. She looks at me and shakes her head. I don't know if it's because I won't let Vidocq put me to sleep, because I dropped a half-dead woman in her lap, or because who knows what the devil's kid is really up to?

"My offer still stands. If you think I've gone bad, take my head. But I'm not lying down for this right now. Someone told me that any spell cast can be broken and any spell broken can be put back together. Someone is making all this happen and I bet they can unmake it."

"What if you can't?" Allegra asks. "What if Brigitte is stuck like this forever?"

I look her in the eye.

"What would you want? Would you want to be Sleeping Beauty for the next thousand years until maybe perhaps pretty please someone figures out how to fix you or do you want to get it over with fast?"

"I don't know."

"Well, you think about it. You're a woman and about her age, so you think about it and tell me what you'd do."

"I don't want that responsibility."

"Too bad."

I head back to the wall I came through earlier.

"Allegra, I might need you to come with me later and play Kinski one more time, but just to look. Not cut anyone up."

"Whatever. Eugène and I will plant your friend in the Garden for now."

"Text me when she's under. And don't leave the apartment for anything. It's going to get dangerous outside. I'll talk to you later."

When I'm back on the street I dial Carlos.

"Hola Hula. You've got the Bamboo House of Dolls. Talk to me."

"Carlos, it's Stark. You need to listen to me."

"What's up, man? A buddy just brought me fresh *sesos* straight from the butchers. Swing by. You gringos don't know shit about food till you've had *auténtico* street-style brain tacos."

"Shut up and listen. Something's happened. Close the bar. I don't know if things are going to completely melt down out here, but there's a real good chance."

"It's the fuckers from the other night, isn't it? Those dead motherfuckers."

"Yeah. There's a lot more of them and I don't know exactly how many. Until I do, stay off the streets. When you close, if any of your friends want to go home, let them. But once they've gone, lock up, barricade the place, and don't let them back in."

"*Ay Dios mío.*"

"Yeah, pretty much."

I COME OUT of a shadow by the anime section in Max Overdrive. It startles two kids pawing through the cutout bin where the used and extra discs get dumped for a couple of bucks each. They look at me, more surprised than scared. I grab a couple of handfuls of movies and give them to each kid.

"Take 'em and go home. Stay there and don't let anyone in. Things are going to get weird."

I walk them to the door so none of the counter people tries to stop them.

"We're closing early," I tell the closest kid working the registers. He's a pale pretty boy with a lopsided haircut that hangs over one eye. He's wearing a T-shirt that says THE GOVERNMENT KILLED TUPAC AND ALL I GOT WAS THIS LOUSY T-SHIRT. I've never seen him before.

"Let these people take the damned movies. Just get them out of here. Then you and the rest of the crew take off. You'll get paid for a full shift. If you're smart you'll go home. If you go somewhere make sure you know where all the exits are. Lock up on the way out."

He just looks at me.

"Who the hell are you?"

"I own the place."

He turns to the guy working the other register.

"Is he for real?"

The second kid glances at me.

"Yeah."

"Cool."

I head upstairs as guy two whispers to guy one. They don't know that my hearing is better than theirs.

"I told you about him. He's Mr. Kasabian's boyfriend. Did you see all those scars? They never leave upstairs. No one knows what they do up there all day, but there's always bloody, torn-up clothes in the trash."

When I'm upstairs I lock the door.

"The revenuers onto you selling moonshine?"

I drag the bedside table over and wedge it under the door-knob. Get my lead out of the top drawer and sketch shield circles on the door and table.

"What's going on, man?"

I open the closet that's Kasabian's bedroom.

"I know that running your board is most of the hoodoo

you're into these days, but can you use anything else in here, like a weapon or some antispirit rune stones?"

"What are you talking about? What's going on?"

I sit on the bed, suddenly tired.

"We were ambushed tonight by a load of Drifters. Brigitte got bit. I got her out and over to Vidocq's. But most of the Drifters got out in the streets. I don't know how many, but by morning there are going be a lot more. I'm going to be running around trying to take care of this, which means you're going to have to look out for yourself."

"Fuck me."

I'm hot and my head is throbbing. I toss the coat, the belt, and the gun on the bed and go to the bathroom. Half my face is smeared with soot from the barbecued zeds. I run water in the sink and wash my face. Drying off, I remember the wounds on my hand. I get an Ace bandage from the medicine cabinet and wrap it up. I don't really need to. The cuts are all scabbed over, but I learned a long time ago that hand wounds and scabby knuckles tend to make people nervous. Since it's vaguely flesh-colored, an Ace can keep people from noticing. And it isn't as much trouble as throwing a glamour on the hand and trying to keep it there when you're punching people in the brain.

"What are you doing in there? Talk to me."

I bring a big bottle of Pepto with me and go back to the bed and down half of the pink sludge right away. Then I stretch out and drop the bottle on the floor because I moved the goddamn night table to the door. Rolling over to pick up the bottle, I get dizzy.

"What's that on your hand?"

Kasabian might be dumb, but he's not stupid.

"Oh shit. You got bit, too."

"I'm fine."

"I've got to get out of here."

"Where? You going to call a cab to take you to LAX? Maybe the airline will give you a discount because you can fit in the overhead compartment."

He looks at me.

"That's cold, man. And for your fucking information, I'm going into the closet. You think I haven't been waiting for you to flip out this whole six months, you crazy drunk motherfucker? I've been scratching spells in the walls. And I've been online loading up on protection charms whenever I ordered videos. I'm Fort Knox, man. I'm the goddamn Death Star."

He looks at me. I nod.

"Actually, that's a pretty smart idea. Go and lock yourself in. You have a phone in there?"

"Yeah."

"Good. Stay in there until I give you the all clear."

"What if you don't come back?"

"I'll get Allegra or Vidocq to come and get you if anything happens to me."

"Do they even know about me?"

"Sort of. No."

"Great."

"Don't worry about it. Nothing is going to happen to me. I'm not human, remember?"

"Part of you is."

"Not enough to matter. And all it means is I have a migraine. You don't look any more appetizing to me now than when I first met you."

"You've always been my dream date, too, Penelope. Just stay over there on the bed, dead man."

"Do you remember where I hid the belt buckle?"

Kasabian rolls his eyes.

"You really are in good shape. It's under the mattress at the foot of the bed."

I move the mattress and pull it out. Toss it onto my coat. I don't know what to do with it, but I want it nearby.

"Did you ever figure out what the writing on this thing was?"

"A little. Lucifer can read it and I used the bits and pieces I grabbed out of his head to find more stuff like it."

"What does it say?"

"It's a warning and a blocking curse. It's keeping something from getting in somewhere. But I don't know who or where."

"Drifters?"

"Or Jehovah's Witnesses. Or census takers. Or the Fuller Brush man."

"When you figure it out let me know."

"Sure."

I go to the nightstand and find some aspirin in the top drawer. I pour out four and sit there for a minute.

"Your JD is under the bed, in case you forgot."

I shake my head.

"I don't want that. You have any water in your fridge?"

"Oh shit. You really are dead."

"Do you have any water?"

"I have beer. That's kind of like water."

"No. That's kind of like beer."

I go back into the bathroom, dry-swallow the pills, and drink water out of my cupped hand.

"There. I'll be fine once those kick in."

"That's what Jeffrey Dahmer said when his doctor gave him Valium."

I find my phone and dial the number Cabal gave me.

"McQueen and Sons bail bonds. We can't come to the phone right now. Leave a number and we'll get back to you as soon as we can. If you already have a bond with us, don't even dream about leaving the jurisdiction. Have a nice day."

I go back to the bathroom and drink a little more water. Then I dial the number again. It goes straight to the message.

I go back to the other room and lie down.

"You're going to break the news to Lucifer about this shit," I say.

"Am I?"

"Yeah. I'm Dirty Harry. You're Paul Revere. It's called division of labor."

"It's called having a Martian's grasp of history."

"Just let him know."

"I mean, one of those people isn't even real."

"Of course they're real. I saw them on TV."

I dial the bail bondsman again and get the message. Fuck it. I need to close my eyes.

"I'm going to lie down and wait for a callback. You should go lock yourself up."

Kasabian does his bug thing, crawls down to the floor

and over to the closet on his little legs. He stops by the door.

"Seriously, man, are you going to go cannibal crazy?"

I sit up.

"When I dropped Brigitte off, she was already turning. Do I look dead or hungry?"

"I don't want to have to break in a new roommate is all I'm saying."

"Don't open the door for anyone but me. The secret word is 'swordfish.'"

He closes the door and I can hear him throw the lock. He's never done that before. A TV comes on. I'm waiting to hear Lucha Libre or an old movie, but it sounds like the news.

I close my eyes and drift in the dark for a few minutes, letting the Pepto and pills have their way with me. I'm already feeling better, though my head still throbs behind my eyes. That will stop soon. I can tell.

I lied to Kasabian. I can feel myself dying inside, but just the Stark part. He flickers in and out of focus, like a strobe light losing power. The intervals of darkness get longer and longer. Soon the flashes will stop and Stark will be gone.

The phone rings. I ignore it.

Rest in peace, asshole. Maybe someone will miss you, but it won't be me.

The phone stops ringing, then starts up again a second later. I pick it up.

"What the hell is wrong with you, boy? Have you gone full time into the getting-people-fucked-up business? I swear, you could open a goddamn franchise."

I sit up and swing my feet onto the floor.

"Hi, doc. What do you want? I'm just a little busy."

Kinski says, "I'm an archangel, remember? The aether all of a sudden started smelling like blood and it was coming from your direction. Some girl of yours got hurt tonight, didn't she? And it wasn't Allegra."

"It's kind of late to be pulling out your little black bag right now, don't you think? You got secrets you want to keep, that's fine with me. I can respect that. But don't go calling me when you're road-tripping on the dark side of the moon getting all high-and-mighty. I thought you were one of the few people I could count on, but it turns out to be just one more reminder of how I should never trust an angel."

"Did it ever cross your mind that taking off in the dead of night and dragging Candy along was about the last thing I wanted to do? That it would take something pretty important for me to do anything like that?"

"Like what? You need to get your harp restrung?"

"Like someone trying to kill us. Me, mostly, but they seem fine with killing anyone in my vicinity."

"Is Candy all right?"

"We're both all right, but we've been lucky and that's not going to last forever."

He doesn't say anything for a minute. I never heard this kind of stress in his voice before. There's noise on the line behind him. Wind and rumbling. It sounds like he's calling from the side of a freeway.

"Exactly what happened?"

"We were out one night at a Thai joint we like and six masked heavies came in. They make like they want to rob the place, but I could read them and knew they were there for something else. They told the girl at the register to give them the money, but kept getting in her way. They told the customers not to move, but they kept tripping over them. The whole thing was an act to start a fight. When no one took the bait, they got real agitated and just started shooting up the place. These boys weren't thieves. They were a hit squad."

"How do you know that?"

"Street punks don't have Dragon's Breath rifles and quantum street sweepers. All around us people were burning up and gassing out into subatomic particles."

"Shit, that sounds like Vigil gear."

"Or Lucifer's. He has a whole stable of state-of-the-art friends. Though why they'd come after me after all these years, I can't say."

"I know you're Mr. Self-Control, but did Candy do anything to piss them off?"

"When the shooting started she went into full Jade mode and, no, it wasn't easy holding her back. She took down a couple of them before I could stop her. All I wanted was to get both of us out of there while we were still on our feet. The longer we were in there the more civilians were going to be collateral damage."

"Are you safe where you are?"

"We're safe for now because we keep moving. This is a throwaway cell, but I'm still not wild about talking even this long."

"Why did you call?"

"To tell you to get out of there. That city is about to be hit by the shit storm of the century. I can feel it. The dead have wandered out before and the Sub Rosa have always taken care of them, but this feels different. I don't know that they can cork the bottle this time."

"How is it different? What do you know?"

"This isn't going to be a few zeds and Lacunas wandering out of some abandoned mine shaft. This is going to be big. I never felt anything like it before. It's a damn sight too big for you to handle by yourself and don't tell me you're not going to try 'cause that's exactly the kind of thing you do."

"Thanks for the warning, but I have things to do here. There's that hurt girl, remember?"

"Dammit, boy. This isn't the time to be bullheaded. I'm telling you to get Eugène and Allegra and get out of L.A. Bring the other girl along if you need to."

"I'll tell them what you said, but I'm going to stick around."

"You saved the city once already. You don't have to make a habit of it at the expense of dying."

"Trust me, I know. But I'm staying anyway. See, I was bumming a smoke off a zed tonight and got bitten."

There's a long silence this time.

"That when the girl got hurt?"

"Yeah. Her name is Brigitte. She got bitten, too. Vidocq's planted her in the Winter Garden. I got the feeling it wasn't safe to be dragging her around in that condition."

"Okay, but getting bit doesn't necessarily mean anything for someone like you," he says. He says it quietly. I can barely hear him over the noise on the line.

"I was just explaining that to someone. But the truth is I don't want to risk it. And even if nephilim don't start seeing everyone as finger food, I'm feeling sick and not very good company right now. It'll be better for everyone if I stay."

"Maybe Candy and me ought to come back."

"Yeah, the two of you getting shot will fix everything."

"I'm not going to just leave you there."

"Stay the hell out of L.A., doc. This isn't your town anymore. It's mine and I'll burn it to the ground if I have to. You take care of yourself and Candy. Thanks for calling and thanks for the offer. Tell Candy hi for me."

I hang up before he can say something else stupid about coming back. I'm not afraid. I should be, but my head is a little funny, so I'm not.

My head is clear, not clear like before the drinking got out of hand. Clear for the first time in my life. I feel like a blind man who traded up for new and better eyes. The world has never looked like this before. Like deep, bottom-of-the-ocean fish. They're so far down there isn't any light and their skin is transparent. You can see the fish and through the fish at the same time. That's the way the world looks to me. I can see it, but see inside and through it, too. This is how the world looks to angels. Real, but only as real as the souls of the almost-dead waiting to be the completely dead. We're a world of ghosts to them. That's how angels can turn cities to salt and rivers to blood. To them, we're already 90% corpse and the part that's alive is made of glass. And glass is meant to break.

When Stark is gone the angel is all that will be left.

Check me out now, boys and girls. I am become Death. The destroyer of worlds.

I dial the bail bondsman again.

The line clicks.

"Yeah?"

It sounds like a woman's voice.

"Is this McQueen and Sons?"

"Is this the guy who calls over and over in the middle of the night and never does anything but breathe into my voice mail?"

"That was probably me."

"I don't recognize your number and caller ID says you're not dialing from lockup. What do you want?"

"I want to meet Johnny Thunders. Don't say no. I didn't remember your name at first, but I do now because it was on a matchbook I had in my pocket when I crawled out of Hell. We're connected somehow. You're going to get me an audience with Pope Johnny because if you don't this whole city is going to die and I guarantee that you're going to be among the first."

Someone else says something. McQueen and Sons puts her hand over the mouthpiece. More muffled talk. Then she's back again.

"Come to the office at nine-thirty. You know what to bring?"

"I know what to bring."

"Good. Don't cheap out on the jelly beans."

I HIT ALLEGRA'S number and she picks up on the second ring.

"Sorry. Did I wake you up?"

"Hell no. With a friend like you, no one expects to sleep more than a few hours a night."

"Is Brigitte under yet?"

"Yeah. Eugène is watching her. Making sure the potion took and she's doing all right."

"Thanks."

"No problem. But you owe me a story about how you hooked up with Pussy Galore."

"Sure. Listen, I need to read someone's meter. Do you have an animascope?"

"A couple of different kinds. But I thought you were off chasing zombies. Why do you need the scope?"

"I'm meeting someone new and I need to know if he's dead or alive. If I have the scope, you don't need to come along. It'll be safer that way."

"Fuck that. You and Eugène are going to protect me to death. If you want the scope, I'm the one who's going to work it. That's the deal."

"Okay, but you have to tell Vidocq. And don't leave out the part where I said you could stay home."

"When should I expect you?"

"I'm supposed to meet the contact in Hollywood at nine-thirty this morning. I'll come by a few minutes before that."

"I'll be ready."

The Grand Central Market doesn't open until nine, which is still a few hours away. I lie back on the bed, close my eyes, and sink back down into the angelic dark. It already feels like home. The place I should have been my whole life. If I'd seen and felt like this when I was a kid, I wouldn't have grown into someone who let Mason play him for such a fool. I wouldn't have lost a third of my life in Hell. I wouldn't be living with a dead man in an attic and covered in scars. Normally, going over all the ways I've fucked up my life turns my brain to swamp gas and bleeds my vision red. I need a cigarette and a drink to keep my heart from gnawing its way out of my chest. But now my heart beats fine. I don't want a glass of the red stuff or a smoke. The world is a perfect white diamond. Transparent. The facets glowing with internally reflected light. And it takes just one tap in the right place to shatter the whole thing.

I GET UP a few minutes before nine and walk through a shadow to come out in a corner of the Grand Central Market. I haven't seen the place since that day with Eleanor. It looks a lot nicer when it's not on fire.

I buy a Styrofoam cooler and dry ice at the liquor store where Eleanor torched herself. I have to stop at three different butcher stalls to make sure I have enough pig guts to bribe Johnny. At a Filipino market near the Hill Street entrance, I pick up pork blood to fill out the feast.

Of course, if I'd felt this way earlier and hadn't fucked up in just the right way so I landed exactly where I was at exactly the right time and place, I might never have met Alice. Without that, why would I be doing anything at all?

I pick up a couple of pound bags of jelly beans and step into another shadow.

And out into Allegra and Vidocq's living room.

They're sitting around the kitchen counter drinking coffee. Allegra is dressed, but there's something wrong with her proportions.

"Did you gain twenty pounds since I've been gone?"

"Ask him," she says, and nods at Vidocq.

"I simply want her to be well padded if your friend should try to make a snack of her."

"I'm wearing like three shirts, a sweater, and a coat."

I look at the Frenchman.

"You couldn't have just sprinkled her with holy water or shark repellent or whatever it is that scares off Drifters?"

"I did that, too. But spells can be broken. Potions counteracted. I would rather she didn't look so pretty for a while if it means she comes home."

Allegra smiles and leans across the counter to kiss him on the cheek.

"Where's Brigitte?"

"In the bedroom for now, until I can find a safe and more permanent place for her."

"Thanks."

"None are necessary."

"I'd invite you along, but it's dicey enough bringing one more person. I don't think this guy's handlers would go for two."

Vidocq waves off the comment.

"I should stay and watch your Sleeping Beauty anyway. And, as my dear has explained to me several times this morning, she needs to see and experience the kinds of things that I have experienced to become the alchemist she will someday be."

"Good answer," says Allegra.

"Are you ready to go?" I ask.

She stands and pats a nylon bike-messenger bag slung across her shoulder.

"Got the scope right here."

I hand her the bags of jelly beans.

"What are these for?"

"Tribute."

"What's in the cooler?"

"You'll see soon enough. Then you'll be sorry you asked."

She goes around the counter and gives Vidocq a real kiss. He looks at me.

"You will look after her the way you would Alice, correct?"

"I won't let anything happen to her."

"And you yourself. You're feeling all right?"

"I'm fine. You were right. The Cupbearer elixir is keeping me from changing one little bit."

"Excellent."

Allegra takes my arm. We step through a shadow on the wall and out onto Hollywood Boulevard.

McQUEEN AND SONS Bail Bonds is at the end of the block next to a used medical supply store. Prosthetic arms and legs are hung from a cord and propped up in the window like today's specials in the world's worst butcher shop.

A couple of LAPD cars blast by, lights flashing. Are they heading to grab some gangbangers or to check out the first reports of strange cannibal killings?

The bail bond office is a clone of all the dismal DMV offices and bus stations in the world. It's a wide single room with fluorescent lights and a white tile floor. Dented metal desks piled with papers that the last people who used the desk never bothered to file. There are message boards around the room covered in flyers for classes, cheap moving, and drug counselors who just have 800 numbers and a Web site. Everything else is calendars and wanted posters. If you shot time in the gut, this is where it would crawl off to die.

It looks like the place just opened. Someone in a white button-down shirt with the sleeves rolled up sits at a desk at the far end of the room talking on the phone.

"Get him to give you the money or take his car, Billy. I know it's not legal, but so the hell what?"

I recognize the voice of the woman I talked to early this morning.

"The way to keep a parolee's attention is to threaten to call his PO or to show him that his testicles are soccer balls and you're David Beckham. Beckham. He's a Brit who kicks the holy hell out of things for a billion dollars a year. Look, just get the money he owes or don't bother coming back to the office."

She's wearing a white shirt, black Dickies, and a black tie she might have stolen off Joe Friday's corpse. Her upper body and shoulders are wide, like someone taught her to box when she was pretty young. She doesn't like us strangers in her office. She doesn't like anyone who isn't ready to turn over the title to their car or the deed to their house.

I use the cooler to push some papers out of the way and set it on her desk. Now she really likes me.

"You must be McQueen, but I don't see any sons."

She looks at me steadily.

"McQueen was my dad and he's dead. And there aren't any sons. Daddy was an optimist, but all he got was me."

"I know the feeling."

"I didn't say you could put that there," she says, pointing a pen at the cooler. "It'll leave a ring."

"Then we should get going."

She cranes her head around to look at Allegra, who's hanging a step behind me.

"I invited Bert. I don't remember inviting Ernie, too."

"She's my technical adviser. I don't know you and I don't know your Drifter boyfriend. She's here to confirm that he's what you and Cabal say he is."

She nods.

"Cabal sent you. No wonder my ass started burning the moment you walked in. That guy is one big rectal itch and so are his friends. Why should I let you see Johnny?"

"Haven't you heard? I'm Clark Kent and I'm here to save the world."

"It's not my job to take care of the world. I take care of Johnny."

"Introduce me and maybe I can help with that."

"We don't need your help."

The office is still the abandon-all-hope bunker I saw when I came in, but to my new angelic vision, it's an X-ray of shimmering, vibrating molecules. Everything is made of the same microscopic particles and they're almost weightless.

I turn and hand Allegra the cooler, turn back to McQueen and Sons, hook two fingers under the rim of the desk, and flip it into the air. It goes high enough to graze the ceiling tiles and lands upside down with a deep hollow metal *thunk*. A snow of bail forms follows it to the ground.

McQueen and Sons looks at me from her desk chair.

"I guess you really are the guy they said would be coming."

"Who said?"

"The rectal itch."

I nod and take the cooler back from Allegra.

McQueen says, "Sorry about the attitude, but you're not the first person to walk in here claiming he was Saint George, the angel Gabriel, or the devil himself and start asking questions."

"I thought Johnny was a secret."

"He's supposed to be. Hence, the attitude."

"I understand. If you want I'll put your desk back."

She shakes her head.

"Let Billy do it. It'll be his penance for the mortal sin of lameness."

"Hi. I'm Allegra."

We both turn.

I say, "McQueen and Sons, this is Allegra. She's an alchemist and my medical specialist."

Allegra frowns at me and turns to McQueen.

"If you don't tell him your regular name soon, I guarantee he's going to call you McQueen and Sons for the rest of all our lives."

"Tracy."

"Hi, Tracy," says Allegra.

Tracy focuses back on me.

"So, you're really that Sandman guy people talk about."

"I don't know. I don't talk to that many people."

"Did you really come all the way back from Hell for a woman?"

"Wouldn't you?"

"Shit, man. I do it every day."

TRACY LOCKS THE office and walks us around the corner to an apartment building a couple of blocks away. It's one of those peculiar L.A. complexes supported on a series of metal legs, with an open parking area underneath and the apartments above. It's like Hannibal Lecter hired an architect to design something guaranteed to turn into a human trash compactor in any quake higher than a 3.0.

She has a corner place on the top floor. It was probably the old owner or manager's place because it looks like someone knocked down a wall and made two small apartments into one decent-size one.

A small blond woman lets us in.

"That's him? I thought it was just going to be one person coming."

"It's okay, baby. The chick's a doctor and she brought the candy."

Tracy ushers us in and closes the door behind us.

"This is Fiona," she says, going over to the blonde. "Fiona, this is Stark and Allegra."

"Hi."

"Thanks for letting us in on such short notice," says Allegra.

Fiona gives her a nervous smile.

"It's just that Johnny doesn't get a lot of visitors and we know most of the people who come to see him."

"So, why are you here to see Johnny?" asks Tracy.

I say, "Because Johnny may be top of his class, but his friends cut school and they're hungry."

She stiffens.

"There's going to be an outbreak?" asks Tracy.

"There already is, but it's early. Maybe Johnny can help us stop it from getting out of control."

"We haven't heard anything about rogue zeds and we know some important Sub Rosas," says Fiona.

"People have been disappearing for weeks, but just one or two at a time. Last night was the first breakout of Drifters into the streets. If the Sub Rosa isn't being chatty about it, it's probably because someone in the Sub Rosa is behind it."

"Are you sure?"

"Yes."

"Who?"

"Cabal is my guess. He's got the background, the family chip on his shoulder, and his public drunken crazy act has most of the other families scared. And they should be. Just because Cabal pretends like he might be crazy doesn't mean he's not."

Tracy gets a bottle of blue Mexican soda from the refrigerator, twists off the cap, and tosses it into the sink.

"If no one is talking about escaped zeds, how do you know about it?"

"Because I let them out. They bit a friend of mine and they escaped while I was getting her away."

"You let them out? So this is all your fault."

"They got out when I was trying to save a friend. Someone who came halfway around the world to stop exactly what's happening and save all your asses. You want to start working on whose fault it is those Drifters got out last night, how about finding out who put them there in the first place?"

"I suppose," says Tracy. "Where were they?"

"At the Springheels' place."

Tracy and Fiona exchange a look, but neither says anything.

I hold up the cooler.

"This is getting heavy. Think we could meet Johnny?"

Tracy sets the soda on the counter and gestures for us to follow her to a closed door at the far end of the apartment.

"Don't come in until I tell you to and don't say anything until I tell him who you are. Savants are kind of obsessive-compulsives. Don't take it personally if he ignores you for a while."

"Got it."

She opens the door and says, "Johnny?" like she's talking to a nervous six-year-old. "There are some friends here to see you. Can I let them in?"

I don't hear anything, but Tracy waves us in.

"Johnny, this is Allegra and Stark. They brought you some presents."

She nods at us to put the cooler and jelly beans on the floor near Johnny.

Johnny Thunders is hunched over a metal folding table wearing a magnifying visor on his smooth white head. He's studying something microscopic in his left hand while his right hovers above it with a delicate paintbrush. He's wearing black sweatpants and nothing else. He looks like an albino mantis about to strike. Johnny is beyond skinny. He's Auschwitz thin. You can count each of his ribs. Practically strike a match on them. But he doesn't look sick or weak, more like he's a separate breed of minimalist humans designed to take up as little physical space in the world as possible.

"Can you say hello, Johnny?"

"Just a minute," he mumbles.

His right hand moves almost imperceptibly. I'm not sure Allegra or Tracy saw it. I barely caught it and I can see down to the quarks in his fingernails.

Johnny holds his microscopic object at arm's length, studies it for a second, blows on it, and sets it down in a small upturned box lid. There are dozens of other flea-size objects in the lid. Apparently satisfied, Johnny turns and looks at us. He smiles and for a minute looks sort of human.

"Hi. I'm Johnny."

He stands and puts out his hand. It's reflexive. Something he's learned or remembers from another life. Allegra shakes and I follow. He holds on to my hand and looks at me, cocks his head like a dog listening for a strange sound.

"They brought you some goodies," says Tracy.

Johnny touches the cooler and bags of candy with his toes.

"Thanks."

"Glad to," I say. "Mind if we sit down?"

"Of course not."

Tracy gets us a couple of folding chairs from the closet.

Johnny crosses his long legs and waits for us to start. I heard that the dead are usually patient. What else do they have to do?

Allegra takes an old Polaroid camera out of her shoulder bag.

"Do you mind if I take your picture?"

Johnny smiles and sits up.

"Is this all right?" he asks.

"Perfect," says Allegra. She presses a button and the flash goes off. The camera's motor grinds and ejects the shot. Allegra takes the photo and rests it on her lap while it develops.

I ask, "Do you know about the other dead people in the city, Johnny?"

"Not really."

"Some got out into the streets last night. They're probably going to cause a lot of trouble."

"I'm sorry. But I don't know anything about them. I know I'm one of the twenty-seven, but I don't know much about other revenants."

It was a long shot that the smart ones might have a sense about or a psychic link to the dumb ones.

"What are the twenty-seven?"

"I don't know. It's my understanding that no one knows."

"Do you like being here? Do you ever want to get out of this room?"

"I like it here. Tracy and Fiona are wonderful and the people who come to visit are mostly very nice."

"Mostly, but not always. Who hasn't been nice? Cabal?"

Johnny shrugs.

"He tried to be nice, but I don't think it's in his nature. I think he's a very troubled person."

"Did Cabal want to take you out of here and away from Tracy and Fiona?"

"No. We just talked."

"About what?"

"I don't remember."

Is this how I'm going to end up if the Stark part of me dies off? Like a psych patient drooling on Thorazine. Or will I be something else? I'm already something else, I think. Not that that helps much. The stronger this angel vision gets, the deeper I can see inside things. But I still can't be sure if Johnny is a well-spoken Drifter or a P. T. Barnum scam.

Allegra leans over and hands me the photo. The animascope built into the camera can catch the life essence on film. Johnny's isn't there. The photo is a normal shot of a boring room except for the Johnny-shaped black hole in the middle. It's true, then. Johnny is as dead as corn dogs.

What would that camera show if I let Allegra shoot me?

"Did you ever bite anyone, Johnny? Did you ever kill anyone and turn them into something like you?"

"That's completely out of line," says Tracy.

Johnny raises a hand.

"It's all right. The truth is I don't know. I think I was dead for a long time before I woke up and became what I am now. I suppose I might have hurt some people back when I was a zed."

I didn't expect him to even know that word, much less use it.

"No one's taken you out of here recently? Even if it was just for a little while?"

"That I would remember. Why would I go? I have everything I want right here."

"Not free-range flesh. You like Tracy and Fiona and you'd never hurt them, but what about a stranger? What if someone took you out of here and let you loose on someone you didn't know?"

He looks at the floor. Crosses his legs and shifts in his seat like it's suddenly uncomfortable.

"I'm not sure," he says. "But as I said, I haven't left the apartment in a long time."

"Maybe it's time to take a break," says Tracy.

"Just one more thing. If a regular person like Tracy here got bitten by someone like you, or maybe a zed, is there some way to fix her?"

"You mean so she doesn't die and return?"

"Yes."

"No. There's nothing for that."

Tracy comes over and stands between Johnny and us.

"That's it for now. Let's let Johnny have his snack, and if he feels like it, he can answer a few more questions."

As Tracy talks, Johnny takes off the top of the cooler and looks inside. He goes to a dresser and takes a plastic sheet from the top and spreads it on the floor like a picnic blanket. He rips off the top of one of the bags of jelly beans and pours the candy into the pig guts and blood, stirring it with his fingers. He looks at us and grins.

"I have a bit of a sweet tooth."

"Let's go have some coffee and let Johnny eat," says Tracy, shooing us out of the room and closing the door.

"He likes to eat by himself. He knows his food bothers living people. It's his way of being polite."

"He's not what I expected. He's like a kid."

Fiona started the coffeemaker while we were in with Johnny. It smells good. She pours cups for all of us.

"He isn't always like this. None of the undead sleep, but they still have bodies and bodies need rest. Every few weeks, Johnny goes into a kind of fugue state. Sleepy. Vague. Uncommunicative. Like he's suddenly autistic. After a couple of days, he starts coming out of it. That's what he's doing now, so he's a little slower than usual."

"How's his memory?"

"Look, if you still think someone's been sneaking him out, you can forget it. Johnny's tagged with one of those house-arrest ankle bracelets. If he tried to leave here or if someone tried to take him, alarms would go off all over the place."

"Someone could disable it with tools or magic."

"Yeah, but they'd have to know about it. The bracelet isn't on his ankle. It's inside him. Sewed inside his stomach cavity."

Dammit. Cabal using Johnny as a blunt instrument was a nice neat package, but Johnny seems to be off the hook. Cabal, on the other hand, is still homecoming king to me. I just need to connect a few more dots.

Allegra pours cream and sugar into her coffee.

"How'd he get the name Johnny Thunders?"

Fiona smiles like a mother remembering her kid's first step.

"Johnny was in one of his fugues when they brought him here. I think moving when he was zoned out was hard on him. He ignored us and didn't talk for days. He just stared at the wall. We used to leave the TV or music on when we weren't in the room so he'd have company. Usually one of us was in the apartment, but this one night Tracy's car broke down and I had to go and pick her up. When we got back, Johnny was bouncing up and down singing along with the stereo. It was the Murder City Devils song 'Johnny Thunders.'"

I drink the coffee straight. It feels good to have coffee for its own sake and not to cure the night before.

"Why was he staring at his hands with a magnifier when we went in?"

Tracy says, "He wasn't staring. He was working. I said it before, Savants are obsessives. They do something really well and they do it over and over again. They'll do it forever, I guess."

She pours herself more coffee.

"Johnny likes words and he likes geology. He's transcribing the entire *Oxford English Dictionary* onto grains of sand. The last time I asked, he was up to 'farraginous.'"

I take my coffee, go back to Johnny's door, and open it. He's bent over the cooler on his knees, a fistful of pig guts in each hand. His mouth and chest are smeared with blood and half-dissolved jelly beans. Not exactly a yearbook photo, but I saw plenty worse Downtown. Hell, I did worse. When Johnny notices me he smiles.

"These are really good. Thanks."

"Before Tracy told me to bring the candy, I didn't even know Drifters could taste anything."

"That's what most people think. They bring smelly meat and old, clotted blood. That's zed food. This is better."

"You're welcome. Who comes to see you?"

He shrugs.

"A few Sub Rosas. I think they're important, but they're not very interesting. They always ask about what I remember. I tell them the same thing I told you. I don't remember anything before waking up, but I think they think if they keep asking, I'll remember and they'll win a prize or something."

"Even if you do remember, you don't have to tell them anything. They're your memories, not theirs."

He nods and shoves more pig into his mouth.

"If you don't mind, I'm going to finish my coffee and come back and talk a little more."

"Okay," he says through a full mouth.

I go back to the kitchen and Fiona pours more coffee.

Tracy stares at me.

"You must walk on goddamn water. Johnny never just talks to people like that, especially when he's eating."

"I get along pretty well with monsters."

"Johnny's not a monster," says Fiona in a tone that tells me I'm not getting any more of her coffee.

"Yeah, he is. Look out your window. Johnny's the worst nightmare most of those people will ever have."

"That's only because they don't know him."

"They don't want to know him. Or you. You feed the monster and hide his leftovers in the trash under the pizza boxes. Don't get me wrong. I like monsters. But to people who don't like them, people who help monsters are monsters, too."

"What are you getting at?" asks Tracy.

"How did you end up being Johnny's stepmoms?"

"Granddad was Sub Rosa, but Dad wasn't born with the

gift and neither were any of us. After Granddad died, the family kind of went to shit. You heard about Enoch Springheel?"

"Yeah."

"He was a distant cousin. His part of the family used to look after Johnny. When there was just Enoch left, well, he couldn't take care of himself, much less a Savant. That's when we got him."

"I'm going to see if Johnny's finished," says Fiona, and goes to his room.

"A few of the big families kicked in and pay us to look after him," says Tracy. "They make like they're doing us a favor because all us Springheels are such losers. The truth is that none of them want Johnny around. For all their money and power, they're a bunch of pussies."

She looks over her shoulder.

"Don't tell Fi I said it like that."

"We'll keep your secret," says Allegra.

Tracy looks at my coat, then at me.

"Are you packing?"

"Always."

"Can I see?"

I take out the Smith & Wesson and hand it to her butt end first. She weighs the .460 in her hand.

"What are you planning on shooting with this?"

"You never know when Hannibal is going to come back with his elephants."

She hands me back the pistol.

"Years ago I was a cop. I'm glad I don't have to carry anymore."

"With Drifters loose, you might want to reconsider that. At least for the next few days."

She shrugs.

"I'll think about it."

Fiona comes back with a plastic trash bag filled with something wet.

"Johnny is finished and cleaned up. You can talk to him for a few more minutes, but then I think that's enough for today."

She means she wants us out of here, but she's too polite to say it.

We go back to Johnny's room and sit down. He looks a lot better than when we first came in. Alert and awake.

"I just want to ask you a couple more things and then we'll leave you alone."

"That's okay. I like talking to you."

"Tracy tells me that you used to live at the Springheels' house. I've been there, too. Did you ever go into the basement behind the wall?"

"All the time. Enoch liked us to play down there."

I seriously don't want to know anything about the games an autophagia freak would play with a zombie.

"Last night a group of Drifters came out of the basement. There was a big hole in one wall. It looked new and like it might have led to a tunnel. Do you know where it goes?"

"A lot of the old family houses were built over the caves in case they needed to run away. Of course, they don't use them anymore. Enoch didn't have much common sense, but even he wouldn't go down there. Live people never go into the Jackal's Backbone."

"Tell me about the Jackal's Backbone, Johnny."

"It's where the dead people live. It's where everybody lives."

"What do you mean 'everybody'?"

"Everybody who dies in Los Angeles goes into the Jackal's Backbone and stays there. Unless they find one of the tunnels that leads out or unless someone comes and gets them, like me. I guess it's pretty crowded down there these days."

A sick, cold feeling rises from my stomach.

"When you say 'everybody' do you mean all the people in the cemeteries? What about the people before that? Before the city was here. Are they there, too?"

"Everybody. The Jackal's Backbone has been around for a long time."

"What if someone wasn't buried? What if they were cremated and their ashes scattered in the ocean?"

He thinks about that for a minute.

"I don't know. I only remember a little of the caves from when I woke up and before they took me away. The rest I learned from people who come by to talk to me."

"Like Cabal."

"He knows a lot about them. He said there's someone else who knows even more and told him about the Backbone after he did something for them."

"Do you remember what he did?"

"No."

"If I wanted to go into the Jackal's Backbone, would you go with me? You could show me where you woke up."

"I don't remember it very well."

"Maybe you will if you go back."

"Maybe."

"Would you go with me?"

"Hey," says Tracy. "You can't ask him that."

Johnny says, "I don't think you should go into the Backbone. It doesn't seem right."

"I have to. Someone is using Drifters to kill people they don't like and now some are loose in the city. I have a feeling more are going to get loose. I need to understand why it's happening. And there's someone I need to look for and see if she's in the Backbone."

"You won't be able to find one person. There's about a million people there."

"I still have to try. Will you go with me?"

Tracy says, "Johnny, don't listen. You don't want to go out there where people will be afraid of you."

"No one will know I'm there if I go into the Backbone."

"You can't leave," says Tracy. "That's final."

She whips around at me and sticks a finger in my face.

"And you, asshole. I knew I shouldn't have let you in. Get out."

"Johnny is one of the twenty-seven. I think if he wants something, he should get it. Including going home."

"Get out."

"It's your choice, Johnny."

"You need to leave now."

I turn around. It's Fiona. She looks very determined. The .45 automatic in her hand is probably helping with that.

I turn to Tracy. "Let me guess. Your old cop gun, right?"

Tracy says, "It's a big bad world out there. A lady needs to know how to defend herself, doesn't she, Fi?"

"Herself and her loved ones. You two need to leave."

Allegra is frozen in her seat. I think it's been kind of a long day for her. I take her arm and pull her to her feet.

"Okay, we're going. You be careful with that."

Fiona cocks it.

"Go to hell."

Allegra tugs on my coat.

"Let's go."

We start for the door, Fiona behind us, an angry righteous mom defending her brood.

"Fi?"

It's Johnny calling.

"Yeah?"

Fiona pushes us the last few feet and throws the dead bolt to let us out.

"I think I want to go."

"No you don't, Johnny. It's dangerous and you can't trust these people."

"I think I want to go."

"Let's talk about it after they're gone."

"I don't think I want to talk about it. I want to go."

Fiona keeps the gun on us. She looks back at Johnny standing in the doorway to his room.

He says, "I want to go."

"You can't."

"Stark's right. I'm one of the special ones. Sometimes I get to say what I do."

She sighs and says, "Johnny, the twenty-seven thing is made up. It's a way to keep you smart ones together and controlled."

"I still want to go. We'll go tonight. It's too bright out now. It hurts my eyes. Come back tonight. When is it dark, Tracy?"

"It gets dark late, honey. And you want it real dark if you go out. Don't go out before eleven."

"Come back at eleven," says Johnny.

"I'll be here."

Johnny goes back into his room and for a second I think that Fiona might shoot us on principle. Finally she puts the gun on the kitchen counter. Tracy puts her arm around her.

"Get the fuck out," she says.

When we get outside, Allegra wants to run but I hold her back. Even with people, running makes you look like prey and we don't want to look like prey to an angry mom with a .45.

"Now you know some of the kinds of things Eugène and I have seen. What do you think?"

Allegra holds a hand over her mouth. I can feel her trembling under all the shirts and sweaters Vidocq made her wear. Get ready for the waterworks. Get ready for her to puke. This is when it always happens. People get away from danger, start to relax, and it all comes out at once.

"What do you think?"

She lowers her hand.

"That was the most awesome thing ever."

She grabs me and hugs me as hard as anyone ever has.

"Let's get home. I want to blow Eugène's mind."

We head back to the Boulevard. I scan the backs of stores and sides of apartment buildings for a decent shadow shielded from the street. The sun is so goddamn bright at this time of day it's bleaching the shadows to frail patches of gray. Those pale shadows are no good to get to the Room, but they're beautiful. I can see each burning photon and trace it all the way back to where it emerged from the sun.

We could call a cab to get home, but in the morning in this part of Hollywood we could wait an hour. I could steal a car, but that might be one colorful adventure too many for Allegra. I'd rather float home through the sewer on a raft made of medical waste than take the bus.

Fuck it. I turn back and forth looking for a likely car. That draws my attention away from the rest of the street until they're right on top of us.

I smell them from ten feet away, but am distracted enough to think it's restaurant trash that's gone ripe. I know what a complete fucking idiot I am when I hear Allegra give a little yelp.

There's two Lacunas. A man and a woman, if you can call them that. They're pretty obviously dead. Their skin looks like bruised sandpaper wrapped around fat and muscle. The male wears a camouflage baseball cap. The female wears wraparound shades. They both have knives and are holding them at Allegra's throat.

Even with it pressed right up to her carotid, I know I could get the knife away from one of them and pry its skull open with it before it could hurt her. But I'm not sure about two. Especially two somethings that feel no pain, are kind of dumb, and aren't afraid of ending up any more dead than they already are.

"You going to do something, tough guy? Save the day, cocksucker," says the female.

"No. I think I'm going to stand right here and admire the view."

"Good cocksucker. Smart cocksucker. First smart thing you've said in a week," says the male.

"Is that it? Did you come by to hurt my feelings or are muggers getting paid by the word these days?"

The female is next to Allegra, pinning one of her arms to her side while pressing the tip of her knife into her throat. The male holds Allegra from behind. He has his arm wrapped around her neck with the side of his blade ready to slice her jugular. He presses the knife harder against her neck.

"Watch your tone, cocksucker. One of us might twitch."

"It's nothing personal. I'm just trying to get the conversation rolling and find out what it is you walking garbage heaps want."

"We want you to go to Disney World," says the female.

"It's called Disney*land*, you stupid cunt," says the male.

"No. There's another one. In Florida, I think."

"If you two want to go get a map, we can come back later," I say.

"Shut up," says the male. "You need to take a vacation. Stop everything you're doing and go away. Right now. This goddamn minute."

"I'm kind of booked up. How about Labor Day? We can all go to Hawaii together. Get a cabin on the beach and burn you two for firewood."

The female is jumpy. She really doesn't like not stabbing anyone. When I have to move, she'll go first.

"That's the wrong attitude. For you and her, but especially her. You don't want her to end up in pieces like the Fiddler, do you?"

"I don't know any fiddlers, but I've never been into blue-grass. Either of you ever listen to Skull Valley Sheep Kill? Now, that's music."

"He's too stupid to get it. Cut her," says the female.

I say, "No. Don't. Don't move at all. Stay exactly where you are."

I'm a little surprised and extremely relieved when they do it.

"Put down your knives. Let go of her and move away."

The Lacunas do that, too. I grab Allegra, pull her away, and push behind me.

"Throw your knives into the street."

They toss them.

I turn to Allegra.

"Are you okay?"

She steps up beside me.

"Fine. Who are they? And why are they just standing there?"

"Take a deep breath. Smell that? They're Lacunas, pit-bull Drifters. And I think they're standing there for the same reason that Johnny said he'd come with me tonight. Because of this."

I take Eleanor's belt buckle out of my pocket and show it to her.

"What is that?"

"I have no idea, but it's honey to Drifters. They can't get enough of it and it seems to have some control over them."

"So, you didn't know they'd listen to you when you started calling them names?"

"After Johnny said yes so fast, I had a hunch."

"I'm pretty sure I hate you right now."

"But you're not positive. I can live with that."

Allegra goes to the gutter and retrieves the Lacunas' knives. She pockets the male's, but holds the female's, a black KA-BAR. She points the tip at the male.

"What did they mean I don't want to end up like the Fiddler?"

"It's a kind of hoodoo. Titus Eshu is a Fiddler and this maggot pile just told me that he's dead. Titus was looking for some lady's kid and he's been murdered for it. That's one more person fucked up by whatever this is."

"How did they know where we'd be?"

"Good question. You, Dark Phoenix, how did you know where we were?"

The female takes something the size of a matchbox from her pocket and hands it to me.

"What is it?" asks Allegra.

"It's a tracker. This is Vigil tech. It has to be."

I hold up my arms.

"Pat me down. See if there's anything on me."

Allegra stands behind me and runs her hands down my arms and sides and around my boots. She starts one leg, but stops.

"There's something on the bottom hem of your coat."

"Let me see it."

I feel a tug and she hands it to me.

It's the size of my thumbnail. A matte black beetle with six pincer legs. I check the screen on the matchbox the Lacuna gave me. The GPS map shows our exact location. Great.

The Vigil is dealing in Drifters now. Are they running this show or just piggybacking on someone else's apocalypse, taking the opportunity to knock off people they don't like and make it look like someone else's fault?

"What are we going to do with them?" Allegra asks.

A garbage truck is moving our way. It looks like it's picking up commercial loads from stores and apartment buildings.

I tell the Drifters, "Come over here," then lead them to the parking lot attached to a self-storage place. There's a double-size commercial Dumpster hidden from the street by a low wood-slat fence.

"Open your mouth," I tell the male Lacuna.

He does. I toss the tracker down his throat.

"Shut your mouth and both of you get into the garbage." I look at Allegra.

"Go back to the street. Let me know when the truck is close."

She knows I just want her away from here and she's happy to oblige. When she's out of sight I take out the na'at, twist it to expose its sharpest edge, raise it, and bring it down hard, splitting the male Lacuna from head to crotch, making sure to slice his spine in half. The two halves crumple onto the trash bags. Its blood has long since turned to dark sludge, so there's almost no spray from the cut.

I do the same thing to the female, and when both of their bodies are laid out in the garbage, I slice them in half at the waist. Smaller parts are easier to hide and harder to recognize if some citizen happens by. The barbs on the na'at are good for hooking trash bags. I stamp the Lacuna giblets

down into the can and camouflage them by piling garbage
on top.

Just in case they aren't dead, I lean over the Dumpster
and say, "If you don't get crushed and make it to the dump
site, you're going to stay wherever you fall. You're not going
to bite or scratch anyone. Just lie there and wait for the
crows to pick your bones clean."

Allegra and I go across the street to a real estate office.
We check our phones. Look around. Check the wrist-
watches neither of us owns and generally try to look like
we're waiting for someone.

The truck rumbles to a stop across the street. Two bored,
sunburned men hop off the back and wheel the Dumpster
into place so that the truck's hydraulic lifts can upend it.
When it's twenty feet up, the garbage slides into the big
compactor. I think I catch a flash of the female Lacuna's
legs, but no one else seems to notice. One of the men hits
the button that activates the compactor. It grinds through
its cycle, stops, and resets. The driver guns the engine and
the truck moves on to the next pickup.

I'm sick of regular people who can't see what light is
made of. I don't care what they think or what might give
them bad dreams. I take Allegra's hand and pull her into
a shadow in the real estate office doorway. An agent inside
sees us coming and opens the door just as we disappear.

AFTER I DROP Allegra back home, I wander the streets for
a few hours. I can't go back to Max Overdrive. Kasabian's
fear will leak through the door and give me a headache.

Too bad. I'd like to see him. I'm definitely seeing beyond the normal spectrum. I might be able to see in the dark. The streets are made of light. People are the most interesting thing to watch. Their glow is different. Their light doesn't come from the particles of their physical form, but from silver-colored balls of plasma inside each of them. I think it's their souls. I'd like to see if Kasabian has one of those balls bouncing around behind his eyes. I'm careful to avoid mirrors and windows as I walk. I don't want to see my reflection and what might or might not be there.

I walk down to Wilshire and follow it all the way out to Sunset, where it skirts the hills leading up to the canyons and the strongholds of the old super rich.

I hit Lucifer's number on the cell. After a few rings it goes to voice mail.

"The Vigil is using Drifters. I just got braced by two of them. Stay inside and don't let anyone in. If you have to let someone in, make sure it's someone you know a hundred percent. I'll check in later."

If the city falls apart, will the elites be better or worse off in their hilltop mansions than the rest of us down here in the flats? The Drifters will clear us out first, but at least there are possible escape routes on the freeways and even the ocean. When the dead are through with us, they'll wander into the hills and the canyons will fill up with nouveaux Drifters. The civilians up there won't have anyplace to go. The mansions won't hold and the woods will be death traps. Once again the future has screwed us because we never got the jetpacks we were promised as kids.

I dial Kasabian. He won't answer when he sees it's me,

but I leave a message about the Vigil and tell him to keep calling Lucifer until he gets through.

I circle back into Hollywood. Bamboo House of Dolls is closed, so I go to Donut Universe.

Someone is smoking in the parking lot. The part of me that isn't Stark smells the industrial processes that created the cigarette, the injected nicotine, the fog of carcinogens. The Stark part of me smells whiskey, music, and pretty girls. He'll be gone soon enough.

"What's fresh?" I ask the counter girl. Everyone on staff at Donut Universe wears springy antennae. Hers bob charmingly as she answers.

"The apple fritters and the bear claws just came out."

"I'll take a fritter and a black coffee."

As she gets my food I wonder if I should tell her what's coming. That she should turn off the lights and close early, but I know what she'd think. The concept of zombie hordes is something regular people have to experience to believe. Maybe she'll be one of the lucky ones who gets to see it from a distance and makes it home in one piece. Maybe I'll be ripping out her spine tomorrow. I hope she makes it home first. It would suck to be killed and reanimated while wearing corporate antennae. Though, it wouldn't be as bad as reanimating dressed like a crab or a taco because you were pimping a new restaurant when you died. There's a difference between a bad death and the universe stopping by to take a great big shit on you.

I pay her and sit in a booth by a window at the far end of the place where it's quiet. I sip my coffee and dial Lucifer again. No answer.

There are sirens in the distance. Cops and fire trucks. Three, then four plumes of black smoke curl into the sky south across the city. The aether twitches and twists, giving off a metallic smell of panic. If I hold my breath and sit very still, I can hear the Drifters moving underground. They sound like ants scratching at the packed dirt walls of their caves, digging out new tunnels, undermining the soil until they pull the whole city down into the Jackal's Backbone.

"Are you okay?"

I look around.

Antenna Girl is standing by the booth.

"What?"

"Are you okay? Do you know you've been sitting here for two hours and you haven't moved? I mean totally haven't moved."

I glance up at the clock over the counter. She's right. Two hours have passed. My coffee and fritter have long since gone cold.

"I got lost. I have a lot on my mind."

"I guess so. I've never seen anybody sit that still that long before. I couldn't decide if you were high or meditating."

I smile.

"Both. Neither. If I told you something unbelievable, would you listen without running away?"

"Okay."

"You hear those sirens? See that smoke? Something is going to happen. Maybe tonight. Maybe sooner. But something is going to happen and it's going to be bad. Go home. Lock the door and turn on the TV. Call your friends and tell them to do the same. Most of them won't listen, but some will and later you'll know you saved them."

She squints.

"Are you a cop?"

"Never."

She curls her lips in a smile.

"Maybe you're my guardian angel."

"Could be. Of course, not all angels are created equal."

"What does that mean?"

"There's those kinds of angels."

I point up.

"And those kinds of angels."

I point down.

She leans her hip against the table.

"Which kind are you?"

"I haven't decided yet. Probably neither. But please don't tell Dad I said that."

"Angels have daddy issues, too?"

You have no idea, Antenna Girl. The silver light inside her glows brightly.

I say, "You think I'm crazy. What else can you think? But being crazy doesn't automatically mean I'm wrong. Stay in tonight and be safe. What have you got to lose? It's one night. By tomorrow night, it'll be done one way or another."

"Are all angels as serious as you?"

"I'm sober and I think I just quit smoking. That'll depress anyone, even an angel."

"Please don't tell me you're vegan, too."

"Even God isn't vegan."

"That's a relief."

She looks at me. The wheels are turning in her head. I can almost hear her thoughts, but not quite.

"Okay, Johnny Angel. Maybe I'll order in Chinese tonight. How's that?"

"Or you could pick some up on the way home. Don't want to put the delivery guy in danger, right?"

"Fine. Go and tell Freddy I said to refill your coffee. The stuff you have is turning to paint varnish."

"Take care of yourself, Janet."

"How did you know my name is Janet?"

"You're still wearing your name tag."

She looks at her blouse. Unclips the tag.

"For a second I thought you were psychic."

"No. I just like donuts."

A helicopter shoots by overhead heading south toward the smoke.

Janet puts on the coat hanging over her arm, gives me a little wave, and leaves.

I KNOCK ON the apartment door at exactly eleven.

Tracy opens it and lets me in without a word. Fiona is by the kitchen counter, standing conspicuously close to the gun she held on Allegra and me that morning. I walk over to her.

"I'm not staying long, so if you're going to use that, you might want to get started."

She shakes her head.

"Go to Hell."

She wants to stop me from taking Johnny. The Stark part

of me understands her wanting to protect someone she cares about. The not-Stark knows how easy it would be to kill her and Tracy and how simple it would be to justify. What are their silly lives worth versus a whole city? But it won't come to that. They won't try to stop me. The resignation is in their eyes and body postures. Their breathing. It's hard for them. They're both brave and they want to be heroic, but they know they've already lost. Johnny said he wants to go and they know I can take him. The gun is just a gesture. More for their benefit than mine. It's something Stark would do. Use a prop and bluster to cover up for what he knows he can't do.

"I'm ready to go."

Johnny is standing by his door in clean sweats and sneakers. He has a wool skullcap pulled down almost to his eyebrows. He looks like an emo kid who went off his meds.

"You look good, Johnny. I'm glad you're coming."

"Me, too. I haven't seen the Backbone since they took me out."

"You remember the way?"

He laughs.

"I remember where Beverly Hills is. Do you have a car?"

"I can get us one."

"Great."

He turns to Fiona and Tracy.

"How do I look? Will I pass?"

"You look good, Johnny," Fiona says. "Stick close to Stark, especially if there are people around. And don't talk to anyone. If anything happens, you come right back here. Okay?"

Tracy looks at me.

"He hasn't been outside without us since he's been here. I don't know if he's ever been outside without one of his minders. You'll take care of him, right?"

"We're going to his territory, so he'll be fine. In between here and there I'll look after him."

Tracy gets close and whispers.

"As far as I know, Johnny's never seen one of his kind get put down. If you gut a zed in front of him, I don't know how he'll react."

"I don't think it'll come to that. I'm getting better at talking to Drifters."

"I hope so."

I try to ignore them as they say their sappy good-byes. I look out the window and listen to corpses digging L.A. out from under our feet. Maybe we've been lied to all these years. The San Andreas Fault doesn't exist. Maybe earthquakes are just the dead turning over in their sleep.

Johnny is next to me.

"Should we go?"

I nod.

"Sure."

He follows me outside. A moment later the door closes and someone throws the dead bolt. I take Johnny downstairs and boost a Hummer parked in the lot by McQueen and Sons. Normally, I hate these suburban G.I. Joe land barges, but tonight seems like a good night to be surrounded by three tons of metal.

"Where to?"

He gives me an address on West Pico at the edge of Bev-

erly Hills. I pull out into traffic and head for the Jackal's
Backbone.

THE FIRES AREN'T just to the south anymore. They're
spreading all over the city. LAPD chopper searchlights rip
up the sky. I turn on the radio. It's exactly what you'd expect
at the end of the world. Panicky chatter about mass murder.
Something new and bad running wild in the streets. Is it
a CIA experiment gone wrong—super crack seeded into
"undesirable" neighborhoods—or a new strain of Book of
Revelation rabies? The freeways are bumper-to-bumper.
Nothing's moving. Just one big box-lunch buffet for flesh
eaters. Cop cars and ambulances tear through the city like
speed-freak banshees. I turn off the radio. People sprint
through the traffic in ones and twos. Sometimes small
groups. They aren't going anywhere. They're just running.

My cell rings. I know it's Kasabian or Lucifer, so I don't
bother checking the ID.

"Where are you? Why aren't you home?" comes a harsh
voice.

"Doc?"

"No. It's Jim Morrison's ghost," says Kinski. "Tell me
you aren't running around in that goddamn madness out
there."

"I'm not running around in the madness. I'm driving.
Tell me you aren't in L.A."

"I could, but I'd be lying. Did you know there's a head
living in your closet? And it's pretty pissed off."

"That's Kasabian. Be nice to him. He has a hard enough
time just existing."

"He's doing fine. We were chatting about finding him a body so he doesn't have to crawl around this room forever."

"Where's Candy?"

"She's having a beer with the head. He's telling stories about you. He's a real cutup."

"Why are you in town, doc? I told you to stay away."

"Candy and I came back to drag your ass out of here. You can't stop what's coming. This isn't about zombies or the Vigil or Lucifer. It's about the city eating itself. This train's been coming for a long time and you don't want to be here when it crashes into the station."

"Thanks, doc, but a dead buddy and me are on our way to the Jackal's Backbone for drinks and a lap dance."

"Dammit. If you go in there you're never coming out. Do you understand that? You've been bit. You're already halfway to becoming one of them. Come back and we'll see what we can do for you."

"You're wrong and you're wrong. I'll come out of the Backbone and I'm going to stop whatever's going on because whoever's doing it has really pissed me off. You're wrong about the other thing, too. I'm not turning zed. I'm turning into you. Stark's going bye-bye. In another day or so, the angel part is all that's going to be left."

That shuts him up.

"Listen to me. You've got to stop whatever it is you think you're doing and come back here right now. We can fix this and put you back like you were."

"Why would I want that? Get Allegra and Vidocq out of town. If you can't take Brigitte or Kasabian, then hide them someplace safe."

He doesn't say anything.

"Doc?"

"Hi, Stark."

"Candy?"

"You need to come home. Kasabian and I are drinking all your beer."

"Just remember to empty his bucket every bottle or two."

"I've missed you."

"Hobbies are a good way to forget your troubles. I've heard needlepoint is relaxing."

"Doc says you're sick."

"No. I've *been* sick. Now I'm getting better. Soon I'll be perfect."

"Please come back."

"I can't. We're here."

I park across from the address Johnny gave me. We're in front of a ten-story office building shaped like a cake box sitting on top of a shoe box. The only interesting thing about the place is that it doesn't seem to have any windows.

I say, "Good-bye, Candy," and hang up. Good-bye to everyone. Been nice knowing you.

Johnny leans over and stares up at the building, as curious as I am.

"Do you have a way in?"

"You got us the car. I thought you could do it."

"You're more awake than this morning."

"Yes. Almost back to my old dead self. That snack you brought hit the spot."

"You have a sweet tooth."

"I have a sweet tooth."

I look the building over, wondering about the best way in. I've never tried to take a dead man through the Room and this doesn't seem like the right time to turn Einstein and run experiments.

"I guess you twenty-seven Drifters really are special. How did they put your soul back in when they made you a Savant?"

He shifts his gaze from the building to me.

"What do you mean?"

"I can see souls and you have one."

I point at the ball of light behind his ribs.

"How did they put it back in after you died?"

"No one put it back. It never went anywhere. I told you before. The dead live in the Jackal's Backbone. Everyone who's ever died in L.A. is down there."

"Right. I got that."

"If everyone is down there, where else would their souls be? What's the use of holding on to the bodies if you don't have the souls? The Backbone is here because L.A. is a power spot. We're here because it needs to be fed."

"It feeds on the souls."

"That's what I said."

"What happens to the souls when the city sucks them dry?"

He shrugs.

"They're gone. Poof. Dust in the wind."

"I'll get us inside."

I gun the Hummer, crank the wheel, and hit the gas. The Hummer blasts over the curb and up the stone stairs, and smashes through the glass front doors. Yeah, I just set off a shitload of alarms, but LAPD has more to do tonight than check out a B&E. Johnny gets out of the Hummer with his big kid grin plastered across his face.

"Cool."

"You lead the way from here."

We go through an atrium and paneled doors that look like they lead to business offices. But it's not offices on the other side. It's machinery. The interior of the building is hollow and it's full of generators and pipes. Huge fucking pipes that come out of the ground and twist around each other like Gigantor's intestines.

"Where the hell are we?"

Johnny's smile grows wider.

"In the pumping station. Right over the Backbone."

"What's it pump?"

"Oil. I looked it up. This is the largest station, but there's ninety-seven active wells in this field pumping almost a million barrels a year. One of them is right by the football field at Beverly Hills High School."

"I'll call my broker when we get back. Take me to where the dead people are."

"Sure."

He takes us down a couple of levels to the bottom of the place. The stairs and railings are splattered with dried blood. There are bones and shredded clothes on the catwalk above us.

The oil pumps must either be buried deep or sound-proofed well. I can feel the machinery through the soles of my feet, but it's quieter on the bottom level. On the other hand, it smells a lot worse. Probably it's all the zombies.

It's like the shift change at Grand Central Dead Guy Terminal. Drifters wander in from every direction. They come out of offices and maintenance rooms. From behind machinery. Lacunas, a little more agile than your regular shamblers, climb up pipes dug deep into the ground. The Drifters shoulder their way up a ramp to a big room at the top. A loading dock. The steel doors are shredded and Drifters pour out into the streets.

None of them even look at Johnny. They don't rush over to rip me apart, but I get checked out every now and then. One stops. Bares its teeth and moans. I hold the belt buckle tighter and say, "Keep moving," and it does.

"That's a nice trick," says Johnny.

"Thanks. Later I'm going to make balloon animals. Let's keep moving."

"The fastest way is down the pipes."

"Is there another way? I like to see what I'm walking into so I can strategically run away if it looks too meat grinder-ish."

"Sure. You can see where I came out."

I get out the Smith & Wesson and follow him into what looks like the shift boss's office. There's a bank of video monitors and a lit-up layout of the place on the wall. A desk in the middle of the room is covered with papers stiff with dried blood. It must have come from the pile of bone and gristle on the floor. I guess we found the shift boss. It looks like he was following safety procedures and had his hard hat on when was eaten. Good news for the company. At least their insurance rates won't go up.

"Here," says Johnny.

He's by a filing cabinet that's been moved a couple of feet away from the wall. There's a hole in the floor. I stay where I am, waiting to see if anything decides to crawl out. When nothing appears, I go over and push the cabinet out of the way. Johnny politely stands aside and waits for me.

"No fucking way I'm going first. You walk point, Lazarus."

Johnny nods, bends over, and drops down into the hole. I don't want to follow, but I do it anyway. Brigitte needs whatever might be down there. And if Alice is here, well, I'll deal with that when and if I find her. But if she is here, it means that from here on out, everyone I have to kill is going to die at half speed so they remember it when they wake up in the Backbone.

There are no lights in the tunnel. It's dark enough that I shouldn't be able to see, but I can. Every swirling electron cloud around every atom of every object in the Backbone gives off a dim neon glow. And there's a hell of a lot of atoms down here. The walls are lit up like New Year's in Time Square. Even the Drifters are made of light. Ugly, smelly, decayed, dry-bone, flesh-hungry light. I hold the buckle and send out a general "be like the Red Sea and split" message and they move out of the way.

I haven't been a hundred percent sold on the whole "we're the magic twenty-seven" thing, but I'm becoming a believer. People pull the new Savants out of the Backbone and there's definitely been a lot of human traffic down through the place. The walls are covered with hoodoo symbols and bone murals. Not something these brain-dead maggot factories could pull off.

A series of leg-bone chandeliers runs the length of this

tunnel. There are niches carved in the walls and lined with bones. Some niches hold skulls. Others have vases or burned-out candelabras. There's a huge bone crucifix at the first tunnel junction. The skeleton Jesus is André the Giant–size. He has to have been wired together from the bones of two or three bodies. Someone's attached articulated hand bones to skulls and suspended them around Jesus' head like graveyard cherubs.

Most of the Drifters are headed up and out, the opposite of where we're going. There are thousands of them. They fill the tunnels we're in and every other tunnel we pass. The only reason Johnny and I aren't crushed by all the bodies is that there's a lot more room down here than on the pumping-station floor.

Very few of the Drifters even notice us. I relax. Stark's fading away fast. I don't have to keep doing things the way he does. I holster the Smith & Wesson.

"I think they brought me up from down here," says Johnny, and starts down a set of stairs cut into the rock.

The steps lead to a metal catwalk bolted to a wall hundreds of feet over what looks like an underground Grand Canyon. Dozens of other catwalks extend below us and dot the far side of the cavern. How far does this place go down? How many people have died in L.A. altogether? Or died along the river before L.A. was a city, a town, or even orange groves? I never thought about it before seeing the Backbone. Tribal people and travelers have probably been dying here for thousands of years. It's a whole sister city of corpses and each one of them has a soul bouncing around inside its leathery hide. There have to be a lot of vacancies in Heaven and Hell. Apartment rents must be great.

Johnny steers us off the catwalk and into another tunnel. There's a strange sharp light ahead. It slices through the cavern's internal atomic glow like a laser beam and plays over the bodies of each passing Drifter. Something is holding and examining them. The outline gets clearer. It's a man wearing an insulated suit to hide his body heat from the shamblers. The sharp light is the infrared beam from a set of night-vision goggles.

I open my mouth to yell when something slams into me. All I see are teeth and nails clawing at my face. It's a Lacuna. Mr. Laser Eyes distracted me from the buckle and the Drifters long enough for one of the smart ones to get ambitious. I smack him against the stone wall with one of the hexes I practiced on Kasabian. It starts to get up, and without thinking about it, I pull the Smith & Wesson and blow its spine out its back with three quick shots.

Shit. I guess there's more Stark left inside than I thought.

I look for Mr. Laser Eyes, but he's hauling ass the other way. I grab Johnny and start running.

Laser Eyes has a decent lead on us, but my funny angel vision picks out wisps of his body heat leaking from around the edges of his suit. I keep hold of the buckle with one hand and Johnny with the other. He has a hard time keeping up. I don't think he's run anywhere in awhile, but like everything else tonight, he seems to be enjoying himself.

A couple of minutes later, we emerge into another cavern. Big, but not as big as the bottomless sinkhole I saw from the catwalk. It feels like we've run out of the Backbone completely.

The cavern looks like the back of a museum or the world's biggest junk shop. Johnny wants to stop and stare at things. I have to pull him behind me like a badly trained Chihuahua. We go through a slit canyon made of gargoyles on one side and temple dogs on the other and come around the edge of a stone labyrinth. I let go of Johnny and run for a familiar set of stone steps carved into the rock a hundred yards away.

When I'm in spitting distance of the steps I yell, "Muninn!" and the echo bounces for miles into the distance.

I wait and listen. A sound to my right, coming from behind shelves piled high with melting Mexican sugar skulls.

The little man peeks around the side. He's holding an impressive iron morningstar over his head.

"You planning on tenderizing some steaks? Are we going to have a barbecue?"

He lowers the weapon.

"Stark? What in the name of all the gods living and dead are you doing here? And how did you end up in the Backbone?"

Mr. Muninn is probably the oldest man in L.A. I hope he is. The guy talks about ice ages the way most people talk about lunch. He's a merchant to the stars and connoisseurs of esoterica. He can find you anything old, discarded, or forgotten and a few things from worlds I don't even want to know about.

"I was about to ask you the same thing. Why are you dressed like Diver Dan and giving Drifters physicals?"

Muninn likes silk bathrobes and dapper little suits. Right now he's dressed in a skintight rubber getup, like something a scuba diver would wear. On his round little body it makes him look like a boiled egg with legs.

Muninn shakes his head, tosses the night-vision gear and morningstar aside. He pulls a bottle and glasses from a shelf and pours a couple of glasses of wine. I go over and sit down across from him.

"You scared the devil out of me, young man. In all the centuries I've been looking after the dead, I've never encountered another living being. When you introduced yourself with a gun, I should have known it was you."

"You still haven't answered my question. What were you doing back there?"

Muninn unzips the top of his bodysuit and takes a gulp of wine.

"I was looking for specimens. You know I collect and preserve ephemera from the world outside of here. When I realized that the Backbone might empty completely, I went looking for a few interesting examples of these lost souls to keep for archival purposes."

"So what are you, like a caretaker for shamblers?"

"Something like that. The resurrected are technically dead, but still ensouled beings. Someone should look in on them every now and then, don't you think? Now let me ask you a question or two. How did you find your way into the Backbone and why would you go there? Oh, and there's the small matter of you not being eaten alive."

I sniff the wine. Stark wants to drink it, but not-Stark doesn't and is still annoyed about using the gun. The wine stays put.

"Johnny over there is how I got in."

I nod toward Johnny as he wanders to where we're sitting. He's having a good time looking around. He has a plastic Visible Man model kit in one hand and an old leather-bound dictionary in the other.

Muninn stares at him.

"Hello, my boy. You don't seem to be alive, but those are interesting choices you've made. You wouldn't happen to be a Sapere, would you?"

Johnny nods and grins, but doesn't talk. He's overwhelmed by Muninn's gewgaws.

"I've never really seen one up close before. Saperes, of course, leave the Backbone. They don't come in."

"Johnny's doing me a favor. I'm trying to learn everything I can about Drifters."

"Why?"

"Because someone is using them as a weapon. And one of them bit a friend of mine."

Muninn sets down his glass.

"Oh. I am sorry. Is she . . . ?"

"Turned? No. Vidocq has her in the Winter Garden."

"That's the best thing for her, I'm sure."

I look at the table for a minute. My brain is churning with questions and answers that don't hook up and don't make any sense.

"Mr. Muninn, do you know what's happening in the Backbone or up in the city?"

"I'm afraid not. A few of the dead wander out every now and then, but never before in this number. How did you and your Sapere friend find each other?"

"Cabal Ash sent me to his minders."

"Ah, Cabal," Muninn says. He chuckles.

"What a charmer. He must be feeling generous these days. He paid off a sizable debt recently. It was very unlike him. My impression was that he'd fallen on some hard times."

"Did he say where he got the money?"

"It never occurred to me to ask. Do you think he has something to do with our migrating wildebeests?"

"Definitely. I was thinking that he'd released the Drifters to settle some old scores, but if he's suddenly rolling in cash, maybe he did it for someone else."

"Who would want that?"

"If I could figure out what they wanted, maybe I'd know who's doing it. Releasing all these dead fuckers in the tunnels will make it even harder to tell who had a hit out on them and who just didn't run fast enough. At first I thought this was a Sub Rosa feud that had gotten out of hand, but today I got mugged by a couple of Lacunas and I'm pretty sure the Golden Vigil sent them."

"That is a strange collaboration."

"What's this?" asks Johnny.

He holds up a sculpture that looks like a tarantula with wings.

"That's a spider deity worshipped by natives on a small island lying between Japan and Russia. They used to capture larger spiders, sew wings onto their backs, and toss them off cliffs so they could fly up to the great Spider Mother in the sky. The spiders, of course, didn't fly so much as plummet into the sea. They weren't a particularly bright people and disappeared along with their island in a volcanic mishap."

"Has anyone else who had a debt with you paid it off recently?"

"There was a strange one just the other day. Do you know Koralin and Jan Geistwald?"

"Sure."

"Their son, Rainier, purchased some potions from me a while back. Later, there was some talk that had me concerned about payment, but then he appeared out of nowhere and settled the entire debt with some very lovely Etruscan gold."

"What's so strange about that?"

Muninn finishes his wine and pours himself another glass.

"It's strange because what I'd heard was that the boy was dead."

"Are you sure?"

"Fairly. I'm certain I'd seen young Rainier in the Backbone with my own eyes."

Johnny is moving around behind us. Pawing through Muninn's shelves. Knocking things over and laughing at what he finds. Can you give Ritalin to a corpse?

"What was he buying?"

Muninn shrugs.

"An assortment of potions. A few rare plants and extracts. None of it particularly sinister. I got the impression that he wasn't buying them for himself since he didn't seem to know what any of the substances were for."

"I saw the Geistwald kid at his parents' party just a few

nights ago. Are you sure it was him you saw in the Backbone?"

"As certain as anyone can be in the tunnels. The dead appear and disappear so quickly. But I'd met the boy before and I'm sure it was him."

"So, if the kid really is dead, then the Rainier who paid you is impersonating him. If he can fool you and the family, he must be using a pretty potent glamour. That's some tight hoodoo."

"Maybe not so tight as all that. Some of the potions I sold him, when combined with other more common ingredients, could be used to create a very powerful disguise, more powerful than your average young Sub Rosa could conjure up with simple spoken magic."

"I'm going to need to talk to him and Cabal. Making glamour for a con man sounds exactly like the kind of job Cabal would be good for. If he paid you off, he's done some work for someone and it sounds like the fake Rainier has some coin to spare."

Muninn laughs quietly to himself.

"You're becoming quite the gumshoe, aren't you? When Eugène first introduced you, I thought you'd only be good for walking through walls and punching people very hard, but here you are puzzling through clues like a champion. If we were drinking tea, we'd practically be Holmes and Watson."

"I feel like both these days. I had a kind of accident recently, and there's a couple of different me's punching it out in my head. Sometimes it's me and sometimes it's this better, stronger, smarter me, but even more pissed off and with a massive stick up its ass."

"And which one of you am I speaking to now?"

"I'm not always sure, but I'm pretty sure it's not the Stark me putting all these clues together because whenever it starts, I sort of go out for a mental cigarette and let not-Stark talk."

"Fascinating."

There's a loud crash behind us.

"Sorry," says Johnny.

"You know if you break the Holy Grail, you have to pay for it, right?"

"Don't be too hard on him. He's a lovely boy. Much more interesting than the tall, dark, silent types in the tunnels."

"What's driving me crazy is that none of this feels like any of it is getting me any closer to helping Brigitte."

Johnny asks, "Is she the one you said was bitten?"

"That's her."

"Why don't you just cure her?"

"There isn't a cure. You told me so yourself."

Johnny turns and gives me a puzzled look.

"Did I? Wow. I must have really been out of it."

"You're saying there's a cure for a zombie bite?"

"Sure. It's simple. It's my blood. Well, any Savant's blood."

"What do you do with it?"

Johnny drops a papier-mâché devil's head he'd been holding and comes to the table.

"It's super easy. You just mix my blood with a little Spiritus Dei and goofer dust—graveyard dirt—and boil it over a fire made from white oak. Scoop off the clear liquid that floats to the top and inject it into her heart."

"Johnny, can I have some of your blood?"

He looks at Muninn and me.

"Sure. I'm not using it."

"I'll get you a jar," says Muninn, heading for the shelves. "I believe you have your own knife."

I get up and let Johnny have the chair. He examines the Visible Man model while I get out the black blade.

"You probably want to cut the femoral artery up here near the thigh."

He points to the Visible Man's upper leg.

"If I remember right, there's a lot of blood in there and the skin is easy to bite through, so it should be easy with a knife."

"Thanks, Johnny. I appreciate this."

"It's okay. You're fun."

Muninn comes back with a smooth pearlescent black flask with a gold stopper.

"That looks like it's worth more than the space program. Don't you have a regular bottle?"

Muninn shakes his head.

"The boy is right. You're a fun addition to our collapsing city. If it makes you feel better, consider the vessel a gift for poor sleeping Brigitte."

I kneel down by Johnny's leg and roll up his sweatpants. He's still studying the model.

"You ready?"

"Sure."

I lay the blade on his inner thigh and press. He doesn't react. I press harder until I break the skin. Still nothing. His surface nerve endings probably died off a long time ago.

I shove the blade in until it hits bone, then slice down his thigh until the skin falls open. He doesn't flinch.

Johnny's blood is dark and thick, like black maple syrup. It isn't easy scooping it out, and getting it into the flask is just as hard. I have to sort of trowel it in. I don't want to rip into Johnny's leg too much. He still needs to be able to walk. It's slow going.

"Don't be shy," he says. "I don't know how much you'll need, so take a lot."

I scrape out his arteries and veins until the bottle is almost full. When I'm done I look at Muninn. I have no idea what to do with the dissected leg. Muninn hands me a roll of duct tape.

"Can you hold the skin closed for me?"

Johnny puts down the model and holds the two halves of his thigh together. I run tape around his leg from the crotch to just above his knee. When I'm done, he flexes and nods.

"Good as new."

I stopper the bottle and press it down, making sure it's tight.

"Mr. Muninn, I have a feeling that your handwriting is better than mine. Would you write down what Johnny said to do with the blood?"

"Certainly."

He gets a quill pen, purple ink, and an old Fillmore West flyer and scribbles the formula on the back.

I can barely think. There's something like relief rumbling in my gut, but I push it down. I can't deal with it until I see what happens with Johnny's magic juice. I didn't see Alice in the Backbone and that's both a disappointment and a relief. I don't know what I would have done if she'd been there. I'm not a hundred percent sure I could have survived that. There must be a lot more of Stark left in here than the angel wants to admit, because the guilt and fear and anger and hopelessness are squirming around my skull, making the few seconds of relief I felt earlier easy to ignore. I have to keep it together and keep thinking. I want to kill my way out of all this confusion, but that won't work this time. Going after Mason was simple. Chasing the Kissi was simple. I knew who they were and what they wanted. I'm lost at sea right now, but I have to see this through. Too many people I care about are locked in their apartments hoping they make it through the night. I don't want to lose any more friends. The Kissi killed a waitress at Donut Universe last New Year's to get my attention. I don't want any more dead donut girls on my conscience.

"There you are," says Muninn.

He takes the flask, holds the note against it, and wraps them together with silk ribbon.

He says, "Go and help your friend. And when you finally figure out what all this business is, your only debt will be to come back and tell me the whole story."

"It's a deal."

Johnny puts the Visible Man down.

"Keep it," says Muninn. "We can't send you home empty-handed."

"Thank you."

"Come on, Johnny. I have to get this to Brigitte and take you home."

"No thank you. I'd rather stay down here."

"You sure?"

He puts his hands in his lap and looks down at the floor.

"Yes. I don't know what's going to happen next, but I think I'm tired of being alive. I'll miss Tracy and Fiona and I'll never get to finish the dictionary, but I like it down here. It's quiet. I don't think I want to answer anyone's questions anymore. I want to smell the dirt and be in the dark for a while."

"You're welcome to stay here with me," Muninn says "You'll have access to all my toys and the Backbone is just a stroll away."

Johnny looks around the piles of junk that seem to stretch forever in every direction.

"Do you want to ask me things?"

"I've been down here for a long time and will be here for quite a bit longer. Life and death don't interest me terribly much."

Johnny nods.

"Okay. I'll stay."

He turns to me.

"Will you tell Fiona and Tracy that I'm sorry and that I'll miss them and to not worry about me?"

"Sure. Thanks again, Johnny. When I come back I'll bring you some jelly beans."

"That would be nice."

"Thanks, Muninn. If you don't hear from me in the next couple of days, look for me out in the Backbone."

There's a good shadow by the bottom of the stairs. I step through and leave behind the nicest dead guy I've ever known.

I COME OUT in the old apartment. Vidocq and Allegra are studying a pile of books.

"Jimmy, are you all right?" asks Vidocq. "Allegra told me about what happened with the revenants."

"I'm fine. Everything is fine. This is for both of you, but you in particular."

I hand Allegra the flask.

"You want to be a healer? Here's your chance to be a famous one. Follow the instructions on the paper and you'll be the only person alive who can cure a Drifter's bite."

Her eyes widen.

"What's in here? Where did you get it?"

"I've gotta go. We'll have lunch after the apocalypse. Have your people call my people."

I go back out the way I came in.

I COME OUT on the corner in front of the building just to see what it's like in the street. It's not pretty.

I can see a couple dozen Drifters from where I'm standing to the next corner. Most are just doing the dead-guy shuffle, but a couple of dumb-ass civilians are belly-crawling behind parked cars. What is it with regular people? They don't seem to get the idea that extremely bad things can happen to them until they're on fire at the bottom of a ditch or handcuffed in the back of a cop van on their way to central lockup and their first night as a prison bride to a three-hundred-pound crack dealer.

Plus, they don't know how to do anything. These geniuses think they can scuttle along like crabs and not get spotted. A good belly crawl is slow and steady, moving like a tree sloth. Why? Because you're simultaneously moving and fucking hiding from the fucking enemy. Zeds might have kitty litter for brains, but I've seen them in action, and like all predators, they have a good sense of smell and their eyes pick up motion before they see anything else. The moron twins doing the dog paddle from the VW Bug to the Camry are sending out every prey signal in the book. Just ask the Lacuna who's spotted them and is scrambling over the Camry's hood.

Whoever owns the car keeps it in good shape. It must be waxed because the Lacuna is slip-sliding back and forth and lands right on his head between the cars. Even if he's clumsy, he's fast enough to run down a couple of panicky idiots.

When the civilians stand, the Lacuna finds his footing, which alerts the other Drifters, who move in on them. I pull the Smith & Wesson and turn the Lacuna's head into a pretty pink-and-bone-colored cloud, which gets everyone's attention.

"Run home, assholes. And don't go out again or I'll feed you to these shit sacks myself."

I don't have to tell them twice.

At this point, I could just use Eleanor's buckle to get the Drifters to lie down, crack each other's skulls, or square-dance. But I don't. I put away the gun, get out the na'at, and let them come at me.

I'm not too subtle, but I'm not too greedy either. I only gut a few of them. The angel inside me is getting impatient, but Stark loves the sound of their spines snapping and watching them fold in half when there's nothing left to support their upper bodies. Seeing a Drifter come at you with just its legs working, dragging everything from the waist up on the ground like a bag of dirty laundry, is a sight I recommend to anyone who gets the chance to see it.

But the angel finally wins the argument and I grab the buckle and tell the Drifters, "Sit," and they do. "Good doggies. Now wait there until someone comes along to burn you like Yule logs."

I step through a shadow under a streetlamp and come out by the hospital that's the entrance to Cabal's place. It's dark enough that I can only make out the hospital's outline with the angel's vision. The darkness extends for blocks in all directions. A blackout. That means no decent shadows to get inside. No problem. This place has glass doors, too.

The locks are strong, but the doors are the usual crap aluminum that most institutional places use. One good kick and they swing open like the saloon doors in *My Darling Clementine*.

I'm halfway to the morgue when my cell rings. It's Kasabian.

"*Druj Ammun.*"

"Gesundheit. You might want to put the snakes down. You're speaking in tongues."

"Actually, I am. *Druj Ammun* is from the same old angelic language I saw on your belt buckle. It means 'Sleepless Aegis.' It's a seal of protection that was on the gates of Heaven."

I duck and go around TV cameras and microphone booms the crew left in the hall.

"Protection from what?"

"Who else? Lucifer and the fallen frat boys. God put it there to keep them from sneaking back into Heaven. It mind-fucks any fallen that get near it. Turns them into Muppets."

"You dug all this out of the Codex?"

"Well, Kinski helped. He pretty much knew what it was when I showed him the drawing. I found the rest after."

"So what's the *Druj Ammun* doing here?"

"You know how the Kissi like a little chaos with their morning coffee? The story is that they stole it off the gates and dropped it on earth just to see what would happen."

"Okay. That still doesn't explain how Eleanor got it or why it affects Drifters."

"I don't know about Eleanor, but the zed thing makes perfect sense. Remember the story that the first zombies were civilians who'd been attacked by the fallen angel that landed on earth? It must be true. Zeds were made by that dying angel's blood and saliva. They have a direct blood link to Hellions, so the *Druj* affects them the same way it affects any of Heaven's rejects."

I make it to the morgue, but don't go in since I might lose the phone signal.

"Nice work. It's good to know what this thing is. I'd hate to end up gnawed to death because the batteries ran out."

"Hey, man. I don't know if you're zeroing in on the big picture. Not only can you control those coffin jockeys from skull-fucking tourists, but the *Druj* is kryptonite to Hellions. That means you can stroll into Hell, make one of Lucifer's generals tell you where Mason is, go right up to the son of a bitch, and put a bullet through his head and no one is going to stop you."

I get out the gun, push open the morgue door with my foot, and take a look around. I don't want any surprises when I step inside. The room is empty.

"Speaking of strolling into Hell, have you talked to Lucifer?"

"No. He's not answering his phone. I've left messages, but the way things are, I don't even know if my calls are getting through."

"Okay. Thanks for the spook story. I'll swing by the Chateau Marmont when I'm done making Cabal cry."

I hang up and push open the wall to Uncle Cabal's Haunted Mansion ride.

I don't get more than a few steps inside the front room when my heart is broken. I'm not going to make Cabal cry. Someone has beaten me to it.

Cabal's body is scattered in about fifty pieces around the table where Brigitte and I first talked to him. If Drifters didn't do it, then it was someone doing an A-plus impression. I follow a trail of bones and splintered furniture through the curtain and into the room where Cabal's party guests had been asleep the last time I was here.

It's the same story. Shredded bodies spread across the floor and furniture and splattered up the walls. There's one Drifter left. A female at the back of the room. She's hunched over the body of a naked boy. His chest is cracked open and someone has been gnawing on his exposed ribs. The female has the boy's heart in her hands and she's working on it hard, trying to bite through the tough muscle. A couple of her teeth are embedded in the shiny meat. It's a good few seconds before she sees me and gets up to attack. That's when I see her face. It's Cosima. I hoodoo her back against the far wall and pull out her spine fast with the na'at. Even though I never really knew Cosima, ripping apart someone whose face you recognize isn't as much fun as gutting a stranger. Go figure.

Bottles are scattered around the furniture and bodies. I rescue an unopened bottle of Jack Daniel's from the depths of a beanbag chair and a bottle of wine from a moldering stack of Italian *Vogue*s. Go back to the room where Cabal lies in peace. He was nice enough to die on the other side of the room and not get blood or meat all over my chair.

Stark and not-Stark are going at it inside my skull. Jack Daniel's versus no-name wine. Stark is too weak. Wine wins. I slice off the top of the bottle with the black blade and drink a toast to my dead host.

"You were a prick and a crook, but no one deserves to go out the way you went. I hope it was over quick and that you tasted like ass all the way down. Amen."

So much for suspect number one. Under other circumstances, I might think Cabal ending up a Hot Pocket was just a case of bad juju or karma coming home to roost, but he was too good a magician to let some dumb Drifters wander in here. And he just came into a load of money, which sounds like he'd done some iffy magic for someone. I'm sure he's the one who sold the glamour to Rainier, which makes him suspect number one in Cabal's death.

But Cabal isn't the only Sub Rosa who's been fucked by Drifters. Someone let loose a roomful of eaters on Enoch

Springheel. The Vigil sent two after me. I bet whoever sicced them on Cabal and Springheel rented Aelita my pair.

Then there's poor Titus. The guy never hurt anyone. The worst thing Titus ever did was pad his hours when his client had money. And he was small-time. He never had a big-time or dangerous case in his life. He was just doing a back-of-the-milk-carton job. He must have seen something he wasn't supposed to. What was it? Maybe whoever has the local zombie franchise? And now every flavor of Drifter is running—well, stumbling—down every street in the city. Was that the plan all along or is someone making a bigger mess to cover up the mess that Titus found?

Why would anyone bother to kill a loser like Enoch Springheel? And—sorry, Cabal—take out another loser like Cabal? Cabal might mix a good glamour cocktail, but he can't be the only Sub Rosa in town who could do that. Vidocq could do it in his sleep. There have to be others as good as Cabal and more reliable. So, the glamour might have been only half the reason the buyer came to Cabal.

What did Cabal Ash and Enoch Springheel have in common? Nothing except that they were the heads of two important Sub Rosa families. But who fucking cares about that? No wonder Sherlock Holmes did all that coke. Math is hard.

I get out my cell and call Kasabian.

"Listen, is there anything online or in the Codex about old Sub Rosa families?"

"Yeah. What do you need?"

"Spencer Church. Are the Churches a big deal? In the history of L.A.?"

"Wait."

The line goes quiet. I can hear typing and low voices.

"Yeah. The Churches were one of the first four families in the area."

"That's what I thought."

"What are you looking for?"

"Connections. Cabal is dead. So's Springheel. Church went missing and then turned up dead and hungry at Bamboo House. What do they have in common? They're all from heavyweight households. Someone is using Drifters to go after all the original families."

"Why?"

"A grudge? Social climbing? I don't know how those people think. But if I'm right, it means that the Geistwalds could be next. Hell, even without Drifters they're in trouble. It looks like their son is an impostor. A con man. He might be the one behind this whole ballistic cluster fuck."

"You know, sometimes I'm glad I never leave this room."

"I'm going to stop by the Chateau before heading over to the Geistwalds'."

"Don't get eaten, man. Your friends are nice, but they've never even heard of *Once Upon a Time in the West* or *Le Samourai*."

"I make no promises."

I GO OUT through the broken front doors. There are no shadows and no decent wheels to steal, so I head back toward the city lights on foot. How do regular people ever get anywhere?

I almost do a header into an open manhole in front of

the hospital. Another manhole is open farther up the street. And another beyond that. I want to get mad at the teeny-bopper clever kids who would do something like that, but I can't because it's exactly the kind of asshole move I would have found hilarious when I was fifteen.

The empty streets are getting crowded ahead, but no one is going anywhere. Great. A Drifter block party. They're crawling up out of the sewers, but there's nothing to eat in this part of town but me and I'm off the menu. I broadcast a general "Fuck Off" message through the *Druj* Emergency Broadcast System. That doesn't leave the shamblers much to do but shamble. They look like little kids at their first dance class, turning in vague circles, swaying back and forth, and bumping into each other. If it wasn't for the murder, cannibalism, and trapped, tormented souls in their rotting carcasses, they'd be almost cute.

I could go around the Drifters, but even the angel part of me is fresh out of reasonable behavior where they're concerned. I follow the white line down the middle of the street, shoving Drifters out of the way, knocking over the slow ones and walking over them.

More open manholes and more Drifters crawling out.

Being a salaryman bad guy must really suck. Lex Luthor and Dr. Doom get to come up with the crazy schemes, but then some poor schmuck has to actually corral the giant radioactive ants or put exactly the right amount of poison in exactly the right water treatment plants at exactly the right time. And an entry-level bad guy probably doesn't even have a helicopter. He has to drive the poison from treatment plant to treatment plant on city streets in his second-hand

Civic, hoping there isn't a flock of ducklings or a broken-down minivan blocking traffic.

Case in point is the loser up ahead prying up another damn manhole with a crowbar. Does he have gloves? Is he wearing a lower-back brace like warehouse workers use? Are there OSHA rules for supervillain henchmen?

"Lift with your legs, not your back. Didn't Dr. No teach you anything?"

He looks up and starts running. Right into a wall of wandering Drifters. I catch up in about two seconds. He swings the crowbar a couple of times. I catch it on the third swing, tear it out of his hands, and jam it through the skull of the nearest zed. Yeah, it's a little showy, but a move like that can save you from having to waste time making a lot of boring threats.

He went down on his ass when I snatched the crowbar, so I grab his jacket and haul him to his feet. It takes me a minute to figure out what exactly I'm looking at. There's a face superimposed over another face, like two ghost faces stacked on top of each other. The angel's eyes take over and separate his real face from the glamour. I recognize one immediately. The other takes a few more seconds. I smile, but the Thug Number Six doesn't smile back.

"Nice night, fake Rainier. How's it hanging?"

He doesn't say anything. His hands fumble at his waist. He has another weapon. I let him look for it.

"Is this how you got the Drifters into Cabal's place or did you walk them in yourself? I know you were in there because he put on that glamour you're wearing right now. I couldn't see it back at the party, but now I can see both of your faces."

He finally pulls his backup weapon. A cute little Sig Sauer P232. It's a compact, toylike pistol that will blow substantial holes in you at close range. I let him get it out of his belt, but catch his arm as he's swinging it up to shoot. Fake Rainier is a big bundle of twitchy fear, so when I grab him, the gun goes off and blows a hole in his foot. He screams and I let him fall. I take the Sig and put it in my pocket.

I look around and spot a Drifter bouncing off a chain-link fence across the street. He looks brand-new, like he was bitten and turned tonight. I go over and rip off his shirt and take it back to Rainier.

He's on the ground rocking back and forth, whimpering and clutching his foot in both hands.

"Relax. You've got another foot."

He says, "Fuck you," through gritted teeth.

"You might want to watch your tone with the man who can bandage you or let you bleed to death."

"Get away from me. Do you know who my family is?"

"Yeah, and the Geistwalds aren't your real family, are they, Aki?"

He blinks at me. His hands open and close around his bleeding foot. I tear the Drifter's shirt into strips and wrap them around the wound.

"I remember you at Bamboo House of Dolls. You came over to the bar like a snotty little prince and ordered me to do my portaling trick. When I told you to go away and you wouldn't, there was almost a scene. But it was all an act, wasn't it, Aki? Your mom was there hoping to find someone who could track down her lost boy. Someone told you she was going to be there. You weren't in the bar to impress your friends or get under my skin. You were testing your glamour. You knew if you could walk by your own mother without her recognizing you, you were home free. No one would ever see anything but Rainier Geistwald."

"Keep talking, asshole. You're dead."

I pull the bandage tight and make him wince.

"If Cabal did such a good job with the glamour, why did you have to kill him?"

"Have you smelled the guy? Besides, I never killed anyone."

"Right. You just opened the door and let your friends do the dirty work. I bet you didn't even go inside to watch the fun. You stayed by the door until the screaming stopped and then shooed your friends back out. One thing. I know why Drifters don't eat me, but why don't they eat you?"

The kid shrugs. Hits me with a very professional sneer. I bet he practices in a mirror.

"Maybe I was good in Sunday school and Jesus loves me."

"Or someone threw a protection spell your way."

He shrugs.

"There's so much going on right now, who can remember?"

I flick his bleeding foot with my finger.

"You still haven't told me why you killed Cabal. Mind if I take a guess? Cabal and Cosima had hit some hard times, so when he found a ripe young rube like you on his doorstep asking for illegal hoodoo, he had to say yes. Not for the fee, but so he could blackmail you later. Isn't that what happened? He threatened to let slip that you weren't really Rainier?"

Aki shakes his head.

"You have no goddamn idea what's going on."

"I know you're impersonating the Geistwalds' son and that someone is gunning for the old families. I have to give it to you. Hiding with an old family while you take out the others is pretty slick. You already got Cabal, the Spring-heels, and Spencer Church's family. Probably others I don't even know about. Tell me, when do the Geistwalds get it?"

"Gee, I don't know. You're the one with experience killing Geistwalds. You tell me."

I look at him and keep looking until he turns away.

"You're not a Geistwald, so don't give me any family outrage over Eleanor. And she was a vampire. She was already dead when I got to her."

"But she was still walking and talking. That's an okay kind of dead. Not the best because she needed blood to keep going, but it's better than nothing. And you had to take that away from her. Were you jealous that for all your supposed powers, you're still going to die like all those anonymous sheep back in town? You should have been smart and let Eleanor bite you. Or do you have something against living forever?"

Interesting question. I hadn't thought about Eleanor's death beyond it being one more thing I regretted. But Aki has a good point.

"I don't have anything against immortality, but I'm not begging for it either. Are you? Is that what this is about? You think you found some way around death? How? As one of these things? Jesus, kid, I hope your brilliant idea isn't to somehow get yourself turned into a Savant."

"You don't understand one damned thing that's going on."

The angel whispers something in my ear.

"Are you sure, Aki? If you're not going to night school to become a Drifter, what was Eleanor doing with the *Druj Ammun*? Where did she get it? From you?"

"How do you even know about that?"

Aki thrashes around. Almost grabs me before falling back down.

He says, "You're dead. You are so fucking dead. And not like Eleanor. You'll be the kind where your soul is trapped in your rotting flesh while the city sucks it dry. L.A. belongs to the Death Born. It always has and it always will."

That's interesting.

"Who are the Death Born, Aki? Not you. You're just a suburban brat. You learned your magic from watching *Bewitched*. Who are the Death Born?"

"Your ass is grass, man. I cannot believe how fucking dead you are."

The angel speaks again and things fall into place.

"How's Mutti doing? Not your birth mom. Your fun mom. Koralin. Is she all right? I hope she's somewhere safe and sound."

He blinks, slowly.

"Eleanor wanted me to apologize to her mom for her. To tell her that Eleanor was sorry and she only took the *Druj* to scare her mom the way Mom scared her and Daddy. Is what Eleanor said right? Did Mutti own the *Druj*? Was she controlling the Drifters? Is she the one behind this? What does she want? Does she want to join the Death Born, too?"

Aki looks away. He's talked too much and he knows it.

I bark a couple of Hellion words. A Drifter behind Aki bursts into flame. I say the word again and another zed goes up. I tell all the dead in the neighborhood to close in on us. I start burning them all. Aki and I are in the middle of a walking bonfire.

I slap the kid and hold him down on the pavement as the temperature rises.

"She knows you're not Rainier, doesn't she? What is she up to? What does she want? Tell me!"

Aki's head swivels back and forth and he's letting out a kind of high-pitched moan that hurts my ears.

I haul him to his feet and turn him around so he has to look at burning Drifters closing in around us. Thirty more seconds and it's officially un-fucking-comfortable in the circle. The air ripples and greasy corpse smoke hurts every time I suck in a breath. The kid goes limp in my arms and starts screaming.

"It's Mother. Mother runs everything. Who else? Father is useless. Hiding and weeping for poor dead Eleanor. Boo-hoo."

I turn Aki around so I can look at him. His crazy fear has turned just plain crazy. He snarls when he talks.

"We'll own this place soon and the rest of you are going to be gone or you're going to be food."

I could let Aki go and turn the Drifters back, but I don't. I hold him and let them close in. My skin turns red and starts to blister. So does Aki's. Stark likes the pain. The angel doesn't care.

Aki starts doing the panic moan again, so I drop him and shout another Hellion word. The Drifters fall to the ground, sizzle, and ash out. Gray flakes still red-hot at the edges float away like dirty snow.

I nudge Aki with my foot.

"You have a car around here?"

"A block up."

"Get up. I'm taking you someplace safe and then we're going to invite Mommy over for tea."

"She knows who you are. She's not afraid of you, you know."

"Not yet. But if she knows I have her little boy, she'll come over. And if she doesn't, I'll kill you and find her myself. Where's your car?"

He points behind us.

"It's the silver Beamer."

"Give me the keys."

He does. I pick him up and toss him over my shoulder in a fireman's carry.

The BMW is a silver four-door coupe. I open the rear driver's door and toss Aki in so he can straighten out his leg and bleed somewhere that's not on me.

It feels funny to start a car with its own key. Blasphemous almost. Who would want to own something like a BMW? You'd have to take care of it like it's a pet. The whole idea of owning things makes me queasy.

I adjust the mirrors and look back at Aki in case he has another pistol hidden under the seat. If he does, he's not pulling it. He's flat on his back, sweating and bone white.

"I don't want to drive around in a puke-smelling car, so if you need me to stop, say so."

"Okay," he says. "Thanks."

I turn the ignition and we head for the Chateau Marmont.

IT'S ONE LONG, wet shit storm from the hospital to the hotel. Drifters and civilians fill the streets. Civilians run and the slow-moving Drifters bring them down in groups, like hyenas. They grab people at gas stations and all-night markets, off buses, out of cars, and chase them off the roofs of nearby buildings.

The pack is the Drifters' real weapon. A motorcycle cop in the intersection manages to get away from one group and runs straight into the arms of another. There are just so damned many of them. I have to drive on the sidewalk and over a few stop signs to get around all the abandoned cars. The Beamer is heavy enough that it makes a pretty good battering ram, so along the way I splatter as many Drifters as I can on the hood. Mostly I go for Lacunas, the vicious little pricks. They're easy to pick out. Zeds lumber like windup toys, but Lacunas can run and climb and hunt specific people. And they're intelligent enough to understand what's happening when I crush their spines and skulls under my wheels. By the time I get to the Chateau Marmont, the front of the car is a slaughterhouse spin-art painting.

Aki moans and whines every time the car bumps into something.

"Aaaah! I'm losing a lot of blood back here."

"If you were losing a lot of blood, you wouldn't be able to talk, so feel free to bleed faster."

I steer us into the hotel parking lot, minus a headlight

and with a lot more dents in the hood and skull fragments in the radiator than when we started. Fuck me for having too good a time on the way over. I don't spot the vans following us until I kill the engine and the vans are moving into position to block the only exit to the street.

"The cavalry is here. Want to give yourself up, kid?"

Aki pulls himself up into a sitting position using the passenger-side headrest. He looks outside through the windshield.

"Who's that?"

"That's a law enforcement combo pack. The Golden Vigil and Homeland Security."

"Golden what?"

"God's G-men. If you think I'm bad, see what happens when those feds and sky pilots get hold of you."

"No way, man. No cops and no preachers."

"At least we agree on that. Keep your head down and don't make a sound."

The doors slide open on the sides of the Vigil vans and they make a big show of moving their troops outside. There are a dozen true-blue men in black. None are holding guns, but all have the distinctive jacket bulge that says they're packing. There will be more and heavier artillery in the vans.

I recognize the two guards on the gate from a few days back. I'd taken the Shut-Eye, Ray, on a roller-coaster tour of Downtown. Most of the others I recognize from when Wells tossed me out of his clubhouse and off the Vigil's payroll. Even Marshal Julie is there, though she looks like she'd rather be on an ice floe wrestling polar bears.

Wells stands in front, hands behind his back, a corn-pone Napoleon.

"Hold it right where you are, Stark. Put your hands behind your head and move away from the vehicle."

"Are you arresting me?"

"I sure as shit am, junior."

"For what?"

"General assholery in the face of God and reason."

"You know, just because you're in love with that angel hiding in your van doesn't mean you have to be her monkey on a chain."

He shakes his head.

"You heard stories about Gitmo? We have black prisons over in the Arctic that make Gitmo look like the penthouse at the Bellagio."

"Does that come with a continental breakfast?"

Aelita steps out of the van and into the green fluorescent glare of the parking lot. In the flat light, everyone looks like a corpse. Only Aelita looks alive. The jittery fluorescent light doesn't seem to affect her like the rest of us. It sort of flows around her, leaving her looking more alive and human than anyone in the lot.

"Good evening."

"Good nothing. Did you happen to notice what we just drove through? Why are you people here playing games with me when you should have your troops and firepower out there burning down those Drifters?"

"Los Angeles isn't our concern anymore. These lost souls will be dealt with by God. Or not."

She gives me a conspiratorial wink.

"My guess is not."

"It's every man for himself now? I must have missed that Commandment. Why did you send those Lacunas after me? They almost sliced a friend of mine."

"Whoever the friend was, I'm sure they deserved it. And I didn't send any golems after you. Marshal Wells was good enough to put a tracking device on you, but that's all. Trust me, if I had sent something, it wouldn't have been to frighten you."

She's telling the truth. I can't read angels like civilians, but the angel inside me can and it isn't picking up any lies. So, who would want me to stop what I'm doing? Cabal? Aki? His mother or someone working for her? Maybe. Maybe it's Brigitte's people wanting me to stay out of their business. Hell, Fiona and Tracy might have talked to some of the other zombie minders. They all have reasons for wanting me not to get too close to a Savant. Not that worrying about it really matters. Cabal is already dead. Aki, Koralin, or whoever else it might have been won't get another chance to ambush me. Everything ends tonight. All debts paid. All accounts closed. Tonight is the end of someone's world. If it's mine, it's going to be messy.

Wells turns to someone in his crew.

"Marshal Sola, arrest this man."

Marshal Julie looks even more uncomfortable. But she reaches under her jacket and pulls out a set of handcuffs.

Aelita shakes her head.

"No. We've discussed this. We're not doing that. Not with his type. He's a walking heresy. An Abomination, and anywhere he stays or stands becomes corrupt, even prison. Kill him."

Wells looks at her for a minute, then at me. He turns to his people and gives a small nod. Suddenly I'm looking down the barrels of an awful lot of guns.

"Did you forget what we talked about a few months ago over donuts? The dead man's switch and the Mithras?"

She nods.

"Yes, if you die, the Mithras will be loosed and it will set fire to all creation. I remember. And I know you're lying. You're too attached to this world to let that happen."

"You silly bitch, you're going to kill everyone in L.A. because you're too good to help them? How many Deadly Sins is that? Pride. Anger. Greed. Envy, too, maybe?"

Aelita turns away from me. I take a couple of steps toward her and a bullet rips into my right arm. It's Ray, the Shut-Eye, getting back a little of his own. I look at him and he seems as surprised as anyone else that he fired. Without a verbal order, the other marshals are unsure if they should follow up.

Ray's bullet is just a grazing shot. It ripped off a lot of skin near the deltoid. Surface shots can tear up a lot of nerves and nine times out of ten they hurt more than a killing shot. This one burns like a hot wire pressed against my arm from the shoulder to the wrist. I hate to admit it, but the pain catches me off guard. It comes quickly enough that I close my eyes reflexively when it hits. I don't see Aelita turn to her people, but I hear her voice.

"You are the Golden Vigil. Holy Crusaders on a mission

from Heaven. You have no reason or right to hesitate. Kill the Abomination."

It's her voice that hits me, not the threat. Something about the deep and beyond-time certainty of her tone. It's like she's shouting my death from the bottom of a well halfway across the galaxy and a billion miles deep. When she tells the marshals to kill me, she's really giving the order to kill the world. She's an angel. She's seen stars and worlds come and go. We're just mayflies living on this one. Maybe humans really are made in God's image. That makes us harder to kill, but sweeter, too. Angels want revenge. Everything alive wants revenge, even if it's simply for the affliction of existence. The sound of my death sentence and the death of everything I've ever known, cared about, or hated rattles and clangs in my skull, getting heavier every second as the weight of all the aeons it took to get from the Big Bang to my ears drops down on me. God went to all the trouble of creating the universe, the angels, the stars, and this world just to murder us. Alice and me and everyone else.

Even angels want revenge. Everything alive wants revenge.

The moment the thought crystallizes, Aelita wins. The solar winds and deadly vacuum freezing the empty space between the stars blows the last of Stark away. He falls into the dark. He doesn't make a sound. He's not surprised. He saw this moment coming. He fixes his eyes on me as he falls. That's the last I see of him, the light reflected in his eyes as they go from white orbs to pinpoints to nothing. Then he's gone and I'm alone.

Only the angel left in here. No humans allowed.

My eyes are still closed. The world has gone electric. I hear the rustle of fabric and the stretching of muscles and tendons as the marshals adjust their stances. Their heartbeats and breath go from fear to resignation. Ripples spread out like waves in a pond from their fingers as they increase the pressure on gun triggers. Metal shifts against lubricated metal. The muscles in their arms tighten. They're already anticipating the explosions when the guns go off. The sound. Muzzle flash. Recoil. The pleasant reek of cordite.

I'm not angry or concerned. Time is slow and cold and it never stops. What's going to happen will happen and nothing will stop it.

My arm burns and the heat throbs all the way down to the bone.

I hear a rattle of explosions as the marshals fire.

I'm not afraid. I see all this happening from the bottom of a well halfway across the galaxy and a billion miles deep.

The pain in my arm makes me double up. I'm burning alive.

When I open my eyes, the marshals' bullets glide toward me in slow motion. I sweep my arm across them and my arm is made of fire. The bullets glow red, then blue, then white, and disappear like they're made of steam. I swing my arm back and a dozen human faces gape at me. I look at my arm. It's not burning, but it's glowing red from the heat of the flaming Gladius in my hand. An angel's weapon. Something Stark would never be capable of summoning, much less holding, but it's my birthright.

The marshals don't know what to do. They're here for Stark, but Stark shouldn't be able to manifest the sword.

They don't know that I'm not Stark anymore. I'd try to explain it to them, but they're busy pulling triggers, filling the air with more slow-motion metal snowflakes. I brush them away like moths and keep moving.

I kill Ray first. He started the bullet party, so he deserves the first dance. His eyes open wide. He expects a high blow, that I'll slice him from above, so I swing the fire blade under and up, taking off his legs. Before his torso hits the ground, I swing again and give him the downward stroke he was looking for. I take two more Vigil agents in the time it takes for a hummingbird to flap its wings. I cut each of them in half at the waist and let them collapse onto each other, the top half of each man trying to hold the other up so he won't follow the other down. I catch the next marshal with a thrust into his gut. He'd already moved into fighting position while I was killing the first three, and when I stab him, his gun goes off by my ear. The ejected shell bounces off my temple. Before it hits the floor, I've pulled the blade up and out through his head. As I kill the others, each gets off one or two shots. In their confusion, most of their bullets hit each other. Ejected shells arc through the air and bounce off my cheeks and chest. The last few marshals all fire at once. The shots I can't sidestep, I vaporize with the blade. When eleven are dead I move in to kill the last one, but when I raise the Gladius my arms stay up. She's not like the others.

I stare at Marshal Julie for a moment and lower the burning sword to my side.

"You're Sub Rosa," I say.

She nods.

"We try to be like them. To have a few eyes everywhere,

like them," she says, inclining her head toward Wells and Aelita.

I look down at the gun in her hand. The steel barrel is black and cold. No trace of warmth there. She didn't fire. When she sees that I've seen, she shakes her head.

"I wouldn't hurt you. You're one of us."

"No. I'm not."

That scares her, but it's not what I intended.

"You should go now," I tell her.

"No she shouldn't."

I turn and there's Wells with a big .50 Desert Eagle pointed at my head. He gives me his Clint Eastwood stare. He's scared to death, but disciplined enough that it doesn't matter. He'd kill me without hesitation or regret if I let him.

He says, "If she's a pixie spy, she can rot in prison alive and in Hell right next to you when she's dead. You killed my people and she just stood there. Fuck both of you."

I'm running at him with the Gladius at throat level, but Aelita is already moving to him and she's closer. She's as fast as I am, so while she's a blur to others, to me she looks like a normal woman walking to a man and plucking a gun from his hand. She holds the pistol with the barrel up to indicate she isn't going to shoot. I stop, but keep the Gladius high.

In real time, human time, Marshal Wells looks at his empty hand and starts. He turns, looking for his weapon.

Aelita shows him that she has it. He doesn't say a word. His gaze is as puzzled as it is wounded.

"We're done here," she tells him.

"What?" shouts Wells.

She tosses the gun aside and points at me.

"He can manifest the Gladius. How is that possible? The answer is: it's not. But there he is and there it is. This is a divine sign."

"We can't let him walk away. You said that with the others gone, stopping him was the most important thing."

Aelita smiles. She goes to Wells, puts a hand on his cheek.

"Things have changed. Look at him. He has no purpose. He won't survive what's to come. Soon enough, he'll be back in Hell, where he belongs. The other rogue angels were the dangerous ones and they're being dealt with."

I move with angelic speed and grab Wells. Hold the Gladius in front of his face.

"What about the other angels? What have you done?"

"This day has been a long time coming. I know that the marshal explained it all to you. I heard him tell you the story. The one set in Persia about the troubled man who went away and left his family behind. But his shadow remained and became head of the house and took care of them. I look at you, an Abomination with the Gladius, and I know for certain that our Father has truly abandoned us. But I am the shadow on the wall. I will become the Father and I will never leave my family behind. The troubled Father has lost his way and must be dealt with: mercifully, lovingly, but he must be dealt with."

"Where are Kinski and Lucifer?"

"Alive as far as I know, but they'll both be dead soon enough. One might already be. Who knows? Only one will die by my hand."

I press the Gladius closer to Wells's throat. The flame

singes the hair on the side of his head. Instinctively he tries to move away, but I don't let him.

"Which one are you going to kill?"

"Go to your master's room and see for yourself."

I toss Wells across the parking lot and charge Aelita. She manifests her sword, swings it easily, and meets my blade. The jolt throws me back onto the Beamer's trunk, where I leave a Stark-size dent. I roll off onto the ground, seeing stars.

"Just because you have a Gladius doesn't make you a true angel. It merely confirms that you're a freak."

Aelita helps Wells to his feet. He looks like he still wants to put a bullet in my head, but he'd have to be able to stand up on his own to do that and he won't be doing much of anything for the rest of the night.

Aelita says, "Stark, I know you won't believe me when I say thank you, but I mean it sincerely. The scales have fallen from my eyes. You've opened the Glory Road and shown me that it was finally time to act. I'll always be grateful to you for that. Bless you."

She guides Wells back to the lead van and helps him into the passenger seat. He's limping and holding one arm across his chest. I hold on to the Beamer's bumper and haul myself to my feet. My Gladius has gone out, so I pull the Smith & Wesson. It's empty, but still looks intimidating.

"I'm not going to let you leave and kill an angel."

Aelita smiles at me. Exactly the kind of beneficent smile you'd want from one of God's chosen ones.

"I'm done with this world, you, and the fallen angels who wallow with you in humanity's filth. Sin, destroy, and corrupt this world to your heart's content. I'm called to something more beautiful than you can imagine. I will become the Father and I will take care of my family. But before I do, I'm going home to kill God."

Aelita closes Wells's door, goes around to the driver's side, starts the engine, and drives away.

I DRAG AKI from the BMW and push him ahead of me into the lobby. He limps and whines and I'm seriously thinking of hurting him some more, but the Chateau's lobby shuts him up.

The place is a meat market. The streets looked bad, but seeing the remains of what must be twenty to thirty people in an enclosed space is shocking even by the standards of what I saw Downtown. The scene is made merry because groups of zeds are still working on the human leftovers. They notice Aki and me coming in, drop the femurs and livers and brains they'd been snacking on, and come for us. I send out a "Sit, Stay" order with the *Druj* and they go back to eating the hotel's guests.

I spot a metal cane by the check-in desk and hand it to Aki.

"Use this and be quiet."

Before we head up to Lucifer's room, I find a janitor's closet in an alcove on the far side of the lobby. I fill a trash bag with duct tape, a gallon bottle of liquid soap, and all the lightbulbs I can find. I push Aki out of the closet and over to the elevators.

I say, "Here, kitty kitty," and the Drifters come to us, but under my control this time. I shove Aki to the back of the elevator, herd the drifters inside, and squeeze in last. I hit the button for Lucifer's floor and look over my shoulder at Aki. He's squeezing his eyes closed so hard, I'm surprised they don't pop.

We get off on the third floor. I leave the zeds in the hall and take Aki through the grandfather clock into Lucifer's room. Even though he's in considerable pain, Aki is impressed. He might be Sub Rosa, but he's only seen hick hoodoo before.

"This is amazing," he says, limping around to look over Lucifer's room.

I point to a sturdy wooden chair with arms.

"Sit."

Aki comes over slowly and sits.

"You don't have to do this. I'm not exactly going to run off. What if those things get in here?"

"Don't worry. They will. But not now."

I take away his cane and toss it across the room. I take my time duct-taping him to the chair, but I'm not thinking about it very hard. I'm wondering why Lucifer hasn't shown up or yelled at us from another room. The suite is big, but I'm not trying to be quiet. He must have heard us come in.

When the kid is secure, I drag the chair into the middle of the room onto the hard marble floor and leave him.

I go into the bedroom carefully. I have the knife in my hand and keep my head low. Even though it's dark, each object is perfectly outlined. Still, the two crumpled piles of something on the floor aren't distinct enough to see in detail. I find the light switch and throw it.

There are two bodies at the foot of Lucifer's bed. The tailor and Dr. Allwissend. Each has been shot three times.

Twice in the chest and once in the head. A triple tap. It's a little excessive considering that they're a glorified seamstress and a sawbones. There's no sign of Lucifer except for a bloody patch on the bed.

I sit down and look at the bodies. It hadn't occurred to me until now that Lucifer's attendants would be human. Even though I know none of the Hellions can crawl to earth from Downtown, in the back of my mind I'd always imagined that they'd be Sub Rosa or at least Lurkers. But the two men on the floor are just a couple of common ordinary everyday dead men. Lucifer must have owned their souls. Or maybe they were members of Amanda's devil groupie cult. Whatever they were, they aren't that anymore. I want to feel sorry for them. Stark would have, but from where I sit, they're too small and human to matter.

I go back to the living room. Aki is moaning again.

"I'm really hurting here, man. Can I have a drink or something?"

"Say another word and I'll staple your lips shut. Understand me?"

He nods, biting his lips like they're alien animals stuck to his face and he has to get hold of them before they do something stupid.

I circle the room looking for something, anything that might tell me where Lucifer is. The light on his phone isn't blinking, so he doesn't have any messages. His desk is neat and there's nothing interesting in the drawers. Most of what's in the wastebasket are notes and set sketches for *Light Bringer*. Someone from the studio was here. And they had lunch. I smell a turkey sandwich and roast chicken. That narrows the suspects down to everyone in L.A. who eats meat.

On the table by the sofa where Lucifer showed me his wounds is an open bottle of wine and his jewelry-store tray full of objects confiscated from people whose souls he owns. The watches, lighters, reading glasses, and rings are laid out in tidy rows. But there's a blank spot. Something is missing. A child's rosary necklace with a gold unicorn charm.

I get the bottle of liquid soap and pour the whole thing around Aki's chair. I toss the lightbulbs next, so Aki is surrounded by a moat of soap and glass.

"I'm leaving for a while, but I'll be back. I don't think you can get out of that chair, but on the off chance you do, with that bad foot of yours you're going to slip on the soap and fall on all the broken glass and end up a bloody mess. Sooner or later those Drifters in the hall are going to find a way in here. I think that you lying on the floor helpless and covered in blood is going to be enough to overpower whatever hoodoo has been keeping the Drifters from eating you. So, you can try to break out, crawl through the soap and glass, slip by the zeds in the hall, and make it home with all your limbs, or you can sit there like a good boy, and when I get back, we'll call your mutti, get her over here, and make a deal to end all this. Do you understand me?"

Aki nods, still biting his lips.

"You can talk now."

"Okay. Yeah, I understand."

"Good."

"You're leaving me here to go after Lucifer? Why would you do that?"

"Because you have to rescue family. Even asshole family."

He starts to say something, but before he can get it out, I tear off a length of duct tape and slap it across his mouth. I don't have to do it. There's no one around to hear him if he starts screaming. I do it because I enjoy it.

I check to make sure he's securely fastened to the chair. When I'm sure he is, I step into a shadow and come out by the studio bungalow where I abandoned the GTO. The *Light Bringer* soundstage is across a wide parking lot full of construction equipment.

I work my way past the machinery and onto the stage to the little office where I remember the panic room is located. The chair Ritchie pushed out of the way the last time we were in here is on its back across the room. I lean on the wall where it opens and I listen. I can't hear anything, but I can feel something alive just beyond the hidden door. Light throws shadows against the wall. I slip inside and emerge in the panic room.

Lucifer is on his back on the floor. His shirt is open, revealing his seeping bandages and wounds. He looks drugged, but I'm pretty sure that what's keeping him down is the silver athame dagger sticking out from between his ribs.

Ritchie is sitting with his fat cop ass on the lip of the control console and his feet propped on an office chair. He's chain-smoking and covered in flop sweat. The air is thick with Marlboro smoke. He's flicking ashes and dropping his butts on Lucifer. There's an HK assault rifle across his lap. He looks lost in thought. He checks his watch. Shakes his head. He looks like he's expecting someone.

I speak softly so I don't startle him so much he'll start shooting.

"I don't think Aelita's coming."

It doesn't work. Ritchie starts and jumps off the console, spraying the room with the HK on full auto.

I don't have to hit him or grab him or do anything. I just hit the deck and stay there.

The shots that don't embed themselves in the furniture and video monitors ricochet back and forth off the blast-proof walls. Ritchie just invented a new game. Ballistic handball. Too bad that he's the ball.

I keep my head flat against the cool concrete floor as he blows the whole clip. Ritchie is taking the name "panic room" way too literally.

A three-inch chunk of heavy glass is blasted from one of the monitors and into my arm just below where Ray shot me. The coating on the back of the glass itches and burns. The shooting only lasts a few seconds, and then Ritchie is out of ammo.

When he stops shooting, the room becomes unnaturally quiet. My ears ring from the noise of the HK blasting in the confined space. The only thing I can hear is Ritchie's slow and labored breathing. He's on the floor next to Lucifer. Ritchie is full of holes from his own bullets. They must hurt like hell. Most of what hit him ricocheted off the steel-and-concrete walls, so he was slammed with heavy, flattened lead discs the size of quarters and traveling faster than a jet fighter.

I go to where he's lying and take away the rifle. Pat him down and take a .45 from his belt. Then I leave him on the floor, bleeding.

"Brigitte is fine, by the way. She got what she needed. Or did you even notice or care that she was gone?"

Ritchie doesn't say anything and I didn't expect him to. He's on his back, opening and closing his mouth, spitting blood and gasping like a fish.

I pull the monitor glass from my arm and toss it so that it bounces off his forehead before smashing against the wall.

I grab Lucifer's feet and drag him out of cigarette ashes and blood and pull the silver dagger from between his ribs. There's a sudden intake of air as he gasps and coughs, like pulling out the knife kick-started his lungs. When he looks awake enough to sit up, I help him onto the office chair. He picks up the athame from where I set it on the control console.

"Thank you," he says. "That was getting uncomfortable."

He sets the knife delicately back onto the console.

"What was this? Was he waiting for Aelita to come and finish you off?"

"Yes. But she never appeared."

"How the hell did you let this prick do this to you?"

"We were having a nice chat about the movie at the Chateau and he caught me off guard. It's my fault for taking his fear for compliance. Aelita gave Ritchie the athame. It's not exactly an ordinary knife. It's straight from Michael's own armory. She could have killed me with it. Truly killed me. Not just this body. But she missed their appointment and poor Ritchie had been getting steadily more and more panicked."

"Ritchie doesn't strike me as the type to help an angel out of the kindness of his heart."

"Aelita promised him his soul back if he incapacitated me."

I nod, pick up one of Ritchie's cigarette butts from the floor, sniff, and drop it again. It smells like hot tar and cancer. A little echo of Stark's compulsions.

Lucifer cocks his head and gives me a sidelong look.

"What's wrong with you? You sound different, James."

"James isn't here. It's just me now."

Lucifer rolls his eyes.

"I was wondering when this was going to happen. Nephilim are so unstable. Now it's time for you to have a little psychotic break and imagine you're a true angel. How sweet. Sad, but sweet."

"You knew that something awful was going to happen, didn't you?"

I sit down on the console near Lucifer.

"You knew about the Geistwalds. And maybe even that Aelita would use the chaos to pull something, didn't you?"

Lucifer nods.

"You never intended for *Light Bringer* to get made. The movie was just an excuse to hang around and see it play out. Tell me that you didn't know it was going to be a Drifter shit storm."

He reaches into his pocket, pulls out a pack of Maledictions, finds one that isn't broken, and lights it.

"Are you interrogating me? Remember who it is you're talking to."

"A half-dead old man who hides his seeping wounds and bloody bandages under dark shirts."

"Playing angel is fun, isn't it? You feel powerful. Omnipotent. Don't let it go to your head. Even if the Stark part of you is gone, it doesn't make you an angel. At best it makes you half. You're a novelty toy like a talking doll or sea monkeys."

I pick up the athame and shove it back between Lucifer's ribs. He doubles over and collapses onto the floor. I leave him there and go to Ritchie's gun cabinet to look for bullets. I find the right ones on the top shelf and reload the Smith & Wesson. Take that box and another box of shells and put them in my pocket.

"You knew all about it. You knew about Koralin and Aki and how they were going to murder the city."

From the floor he says, "What if I did?"

"Why? You own half the place. Why would you let that happen?"

Lucifer tries to sit up. It gets annoying watching him flail around, so I pull out the knife. He breathes deeply, leaning on one elbow on the floor.

"Remember when I came to your room after you stopped the angel sacrifice at Avila? I joked that you were my science project."

"Yes."

"You still are."

"You sent Spencer Church into the bar the other night."

"I had to. You'd missed so much in your drunken self-pity these last months. You didn't notice people disappearing or sense the presence of golems in the aether. I sent Spencer to nudge you in the right direction."

"Why me? Why am I your damned project?"

He draws on the Malediction and coughs. Smoke leaks from the wound in his side.

"Weren't you a Boy Scout when you were young? I'm helping you earn a very special merit badge."

"Explain."

Lucifer shakes his head and laughs.

"There's that tone again. You're beginning to sound like Aelita. I don't like you towering over me. Help me into the chair."

"I think you look good right where you are."

"Have your fun, then. However, I might point out that if you don't help me, Mason is going to win and you're going to die and that if you think that tonight is Hell on earth, kiddo, you ain't seen nothing yet."

I holster the gun, take him by the shoulders, and set him on the chair. I can't tell if he's smaller than I remembered or if I'm getting stronger. Maybe both. Lucifer has to lean on his arm to stay upright. He sets the Malediction on the console and lets it burn into the plastic top.

"I'm not the angel I used to be. I showed you my dirty little secret back at the hotel for a reason. The truth is that my wounds are getting worse, not better."

"And you don't want Mason or your generals to see you getting weak. I get that."

"When Father threw us out of Heaven, all he gave us was a hole in the ground. I built Hell out of my sheer will, the same way he created Heaven. But now I'm falling apart."

"And so is Hell."

"The king is the land. The land is the king. The dying king is the death of the land. It's an old story."

"If you want a damned doctor, why don't you go to

Kinski? He has God's divine-light punch-bowl glass. Wouldn't that help?"

He laughs.

"Uriel is just sentimental enough to help me. That's why he fell for you people in the first place. But the truth is, I'm not looking for that kind of help. What I want is to go home. But I can't simply abandon Hell. The fallen are my responsibility. I can't leave them to Mason and chaos and self-destruction. When I'm gone, Hell will need a new Lucifer."

"If this is going where I think it's going, then fuck you and every other blackhearted angel in the universe."

"Careful with those curses. Don't forget. You're one of us now."

He laughs at his own joke and stubs out the Malediction.

He says, "Don't get me wrong. I'm not going home to fall on my knees and beg Daddy for forgiveness. I still believe in the argument. Angels shouldn't be slaves to God or man. But I regret how I made the argument before. All the slaughter. I won't ever be one of Father's sycophants like Michael. I'll be the thorn in Heaven's side as much as I ever was. But I'm not a child anymore and I don't want to burn the house down."

"The way Aelita does?"

"You know about that?"

"She told me. She was practically bragging about it. She said I set her on the right path when I manifested a Gladius."

He raises his eyebrows.

"That I hadn't expected."

"So, you want to go home and help out dear old Dad. Who's the sentimental one now?"

Lucifer's lips curl into a weak smile.

"Whatever else happens, I don't want Aelita and the Sisters of Perpetual Smugness taking over. She's such a bore. My war with Heaven had some style to it. You should have seen my golden armor. It was brighter and more beautiful than the sun. So bright that even after Father blasted the golden metal with a thunderbolt, driving us rebels into the dark, I still shone like the morning star. I was the light that the other fallen followed as we plunged from Heaven to the bottom of the abyss.

"Aelita's war, on the other hand, will be drab and vicious, and Heaven will be worse than Hell if she wins. If Mason wins down below, then there will be all-out war between Hell and Heaven, and when it's over there won't be enough of either left to matter. Do you think this fragile world of yours can survive that? Can Alice and all those other help-less souls up there strumming their harps?"

"Thanks for the offer, Dad, but I'm not really interested in going into the family business."

He looks at me, his eyebrows creasing.

"Good lord, boy. Do you seriously think I'm your father?"

"It's obvious. My father is an angel. You've helped me over and over, when I was Downtown and now that I'm here. Now you come back to L.A. and invent some lame excuse that you need a bodyguard just to keep me around. And you've never for one minute stopped messing with my head. That sounds like a father to me."

"First of all, considering that you just pulled a knife from my side, your 'not needing a bodyguard' argument falls spectacularly short. And second, if I helped you it was just to occasionally nudge you in the right direction. You did the rest yourself. If I 'messed with your head,' it was to challenge you to get past any obstacle in your way. You've seen Hell, so you should understand that ruling and surviving there takes cunning, insight, creativity, a little bit of luck, and a fair amount of ruthlessness. You had the kernel of all those qualities, but you lacked focus. You needed training."

"You're my Mr. Miyagi."

"I've been called worse."

"I'm not through with Mason, but I'm not interested in being you."

"Too bad. It's a package deal. Whatever you decide, I'm going home. None of my generals is equipped to run Hell on their own. It will fall apart in months if one of them takes my place. There are only two candidates with the power and knowledge to take over: you and Mason. One of you will live and lead. The other will die. I'm on your side, James, but if Mason is better than you, I won't be able to stop him from taking over."

"If you're not my father . . . ?"

"Uriel is your father, you imbecile. But you always knew that. I know your mind, James. You liked the idea that I might be your father because it fit your image of yourself and would let you continue to cultivate your anger. You have to stop fighting yourself if you're going to survive what's coming."

My mind ices over for a second. I shake it off. Now's not the time to think about any of that.

"If I'm not your son, why does this come down to Mason and me? Is Mason your little monster, too?"

Lucifer winces and touches his side. There's blood on his hand when he pulls it back, thick and so dark it's almost purple.

"Hardly. I've had a million children over the centuries and they're all like Mason. Even when I've had them with good, smart, kind women, they always came out the same. And no, none of them are nephilim. Not the way you are. Whatever the deformity in my blood that produces such little bastards also makes my progeny human. Powerful humans, but nothing more than mad, cruel little Caligulas. They're more the way the Church has painted me than I ever was. Isn't that funny? I wanted to keep this transition in the family, but none of them was ever worthy to take the throne. That was truly humbling. I'd been God's favorite. More than Gabriel, Michael, Raphael, or even your father. But I couldn't produce a single heir who wasn't a miserable piece of scheming human excrement."

"What you're really asking me to do is clean up your mess."

"No. I'm going home to clean up my mess. I'm giving you a chance to save your world."

"This isn't my world any more than it's yours. I've changed and everything is different. Nothing is solid. The world is all motes of light. Random nodes vibrating on long strings of existence. Fireflies in a jar. Who could love that?"

I almost want a cigarette. Stark screams in my head. I have to concentrate to keep him locked in the dark.

"I think about the Mithras more and more. I'd solve everyone's problem by releasing the first fire and burning down the whole universe."

"I tried that with Heaven, remember? Talk to your father before doing anything rash. Unless you want to be exactly like Mason."

I look over at Ritchie.

"What are we going to do with him?"

"Nothing. He's dead."

"And you don't even have his soul. He's on his way to the Jackal's Backbone."

"I'm perfectly happy to let him wander and rot for a while. I'll have his soul eventually."

"You can't go back to the Chateau. I'm using your room to finish things with Koralin Geistwald."

He shakes his head and tries to stand. He doesn't make it.

"I wasn't going back there anyway. I need to return below and ready things for my departure. Do you think you might take me through the Room? It's the quickest way and I'd like to rest before leaving Pandemonium. The elevator is out of service and it's a long walk up to Father's place."

"The *Druj Ammun* controls the Drifters. Is it true it will control Hellions?"

"I expect so."

"That could be a nice weapon if I decided to take you up on your idea."

"It could be, but don't count on it. Magical weapons have a way of revealing a fatal flaw at exactly the moment you need them the most. The *Druj* is powerful, but don't ever get dependent on a single weapon. Who knows? You might not be able to keep it."

"What do you mean?"

"You figure it out, nephilim."

"Am I still being trained?"

He pushes himself up and manages to stand this time. I put out a hand to steady him.

"Consider it a last homework assignment before graduation."

"Hold on to my arm and I'll take you through the Room."

He pulls me back.

"Don't leave the athame lying there. Just because you shouldn't rely on weapons doesn't mean you shouldn't have as many as possible."

I get the athame and slip it in my coat next to the black blade.

"That goes for my armor, too. At some point you'll need it. If Mason has it, you'll have to take it from him."

"I'll only need it if I go back to Hell and I'm not. Ever."

"No. Of course you aren't."

"Let's take you home, old man."

"Thank you for this, James."

"I'm not James."

"I know. But I liked James better. I hope I get to see him again someday."

I LET HIM through the door, but I don't go in with him. He's on his own Downtown. I honestly don't know if I want him to make it to Heaven or not. Like me, he'll have to rise or fall on his own.

Only one of the angels will die by my hand, Aelita said. She was coming here, so she had to have meant Lucifer, right? But she didn't come.

I dial Kasabian. No answer. I dial Kinski and the call

goes to voice mail. Shit. I should feel something more than this. Fear. Rage. But I don't. I just see the microscopic elements of the universe vibrating. The clockwork wheels turning behind the stars.

I can go and look for them or I can go back and deal with Koralin. I suppose Lucifer was right about some of the things he said about me. Especially now with these angel's eyes, ruthlessness seems like good common sense.

I step through a shadow and back into the hotel lobby. A few of the hotel guests, who were bitten but not completely eaten, are awake. Adorable baby zeds. I herd them into the elevator, punch three, and take a few of them into Lucifer's hotel suite with me.

Aki's eyes go wide when he sees us.

I tear the tape off his mouth, cut one of his hands free, and give him my phone.

"Don't worry. The Drifters won't bite. For now. Call Koralin. Tell her where you are and that her prodigal son is going to be tonight's all-you-can-eat buffet if she doesn't get her ass down here fast."

When he's done, I tape him back up and go through a shadow to Vidocq and Allegra's place. I need to get things ready.

KORALIN STEPS THROUGH the clock and into the room slowly, like she's expecting a firing squad.

I turned off most of the lights, just leaving on the ones that illuminate Aki and the area by the sofas.

She spots Aki.

"Rainier, darling, are you all right? Has he hurt you?"

"I didn't hurt him, but the genius shot a hole in his own foot."

She starts to go to him, but I cut her off.

"He isn't taking visitors and he isn't Rainier. Don't call him that."

"He's my son. I'll call him whatever I like."

"Your son is dead. So's your daughter. I know. I killed her."

She looks at me for a moment like she doesn't believe me and then turns back to Aki.

"That was a terrible thing for you to do. Still, she was lost to me a long time ago."

"It's funny you should say that. You're the last thing she talked about. She wanted me to tell you that she was sorry. She said that you scared her and her father and she wanted to get you back for it, but now she was sorry. What was she so sorry for? Taking the *Druj*?"

"She was always her father's daughter. They were just alike. Always weak and worried. Always apologizing."

"But not Rainier."

"Rainier was a good boy. He was strong like his mother. He understood how the world was and what was necessary for the family."

"He was that important and you let him die. Take you off the mother-of-the-year list. What happened to him?"

She walks back and forth, looking past me at Aki. But she doesn't try to go to him.

"It was an accident. Rainier was reckless and headstrong, like all children. He went to a chemical plant and stole a large amount of ammonal, aluminum, and ammonium nitrate. He was going to use it to blow up the Springheel home. Can you imagine? It would have been such a merry thing, ending that ancient family line not with sorcery, but with something so mundane. But Rainier didn't know how to properly handle the material. There must have been a spark or a flame. Perhaps one of his witless friends lit a cigarette. There was an explosion. That was the true tragedy of his death. It was so common and petty as to be obscene. It was a human death."

"That's got to be a bad way to go for you."

She turns to me, looking every bit the ironclad matriarch that frightened Eleanor so much that she'd rather be a bloodsucker than a daughter.

"It's the worst possible way for a Geistwald."

I look at Aki and back at Koralin.

"I see Aki over there and I see a pampered little prince taped to a chair. His heart is beating like a scared rabbit and his soul is bouncing around like a Super Ball in his chest. Then I look at you and I don't see anything. You're hollow and I can't help noticing that you don't seem to have a soul."

"The Geistwald line discarded them centuries ago. They're done away with at birth."

"Are you dead by any chance, Koralin? Are you Death Born?"

She shoots Aki an angry glance.

"*Der Todes Geboren.* Yes. All Geistwalds are. It's our gift. The source of our strength."

"You're Drifters. Your whole fucking family. That's your secret. Savants might be special, but you're something else entirely. I bet no one even knows there's a fourth kind of Drifter."

"Not many. The few who do either work with us or they die quickly."

"I bet. That's a big secret to hide for centuries. Is that why you came to America? You couldn't stay in the old country without someone finally figuring out what you were? Pretty soon you'd have to wipe out every Sub Rosa in Europe. Not the way to make friends and influence people."

"Something along those lines. But we also came for the same reasons as the Springheels. There was no room for new dynasties at home. Here it was open land and fertile soil. The East already had settled families so we followed the Springheels to the West. It was paradise for many years, but then things changed."

"Other Sub Rosas came and started crowding you out?"

"Of course not. We encouraged them to follow us. You can't build a true dynasty in the wilderness. A dynasty must be appreciated and acknowledged."

"Then why are you doing this? How many old families do you have to kill off to prove you're the best? How much more wealth and power do you need? What the hell is it that you really want?"

"The next million years," she says. Koralin paces as she talks. I've hit a nerve.

"This land is ours. It belongs to *Der Todes Geboren*. The other families can stay as long as they understand who rules here. But not you. Not your stores or industry or cars or noise. When we came here, the Indians living along the river didn't trouble us. They recognized what and who we were. They respected our privacy and we respected theirs. Then others came. Traders from Mexico. Spaniards on ships.

European trappers and settlers. They ran out the Indians. We poisoned the river. We called down the haze from the ocean. We froze and choked them, but they wouldn't go away. They planted trees and brought their stinking cattle. They built their cities and bred like rats. They changed the land completely. We hardly recognized our home."

"But they learned to keep out of your way, so you must have made contact sometime."

"Charles Springheel was a fool. He decided that we should coexist with you people, and being the oldest family, he convinced the others to go along with him."

"So, you decided to kill off everything to get back at Charles for snubbing you. It sounds convincing except that when I look outside I don't see any kind of organized attack. All I see is chaos. I mean, Aki here was running around prying open manholes by hand like some teenybopper playing pranks on Halloween. This isn't how it's supposed to go, is it? This isn't your plan. It's Eleanor's revenge. Stealing the *Druj* screwed up your timetable and you weren't ready."

"It doesn't matter. Tonight. Tomorrow. This has been coming for a long time and now it's here."

"It's going to end tonight."

"Yes, it is. The golems we've released should make the situation clear. You people can leave now and live, or you can die here and wander the Jackal's Backbone until the stars burn out."

"I wonder what would happen if I held you down and pulled your head off your pretty shoulders."

She smiles and touches a hand to her lips.

"Aelita said that you would make threats when you didn't

get your way. She gave me something that's valuable to you. A Jade named Candy."

"Anything else?"

"A head that won't stop talking."

She waits for me to say something. I don't. I stand still.

"Interesting. Aelita told me that this is when you would attack. She said that you would erupt at anything resembling a threat."

"I'm not like that anymore. Getting all theatrical is only about making the attacker feel better."

"I couldn't agree more."

"Then why don't you put down whatever else Aelita gave you and let's figure a way out of this together."

She takes an athame from inside her sleeve.

"Do you know what this is?"

"I have one just like it."

"Good. I'll keep it out where you can see it, but I don't think I'm ready to give it up quite yet."

"Whatever. Here's the deal. I'm willing to give you back the *Druj.* You use it to put the Drifters back in the Backbone. When you do, you get Aki and I get Candy and Kasabian."

"Why wouldn't I just use the *Druj* tomorrow and all this would begin again?"

"Once the Drifters are back inside, I'll get Muninn to seal the caves good and tight. The dead will stay put for a thousand years. Assuming you don't blow yourself up like Rainier, you can try your plan again then."

"Let me have the *Druj.*"

"Get my friends over here and I'll hand it over. Do anything stupid and your fair-haired boy is dead and you won't be able to do a damned thing about it."

"This is an angel's knife. It might just kill you."

"I think I can outrun your knife, but I'm positive Aki can't outrun mine. Make the call and everyone gets to go home and sleep in their own bed."

"I don't have a phone."

"There's one on the desk over there."

She goes to Lucifer's desk and dials.

I give Aki a once-over. The tape is still good and tight on his arms and legs. There's a small pool of blood around his foot. Enough to make him light-headed, but not enough to worry about.

Koralin says, "They're on their way. It will be a few minutes. Traffic is a bit heavy tonight."

I go to one of the sofas and sit down.

"Take a load off. The room is comfy enough. For us. Poor Aki must be hurting pretty bad right now."

I look back at him.

"How are you doing, champ? Foot throbbing?"

He garbles something through the tape. Even gagged, I can recognize a sincere "fuck you."

Koralin perches on the sofa opposite me, barely resting her ass on the edge. She holds her knife upright, the point between her breasts.

"Since we seem to have struck a bargain, I'll put down my knife if you lay down all of your weapons."

I take out the Smith & Wesson and put it on the table. I set the black blade and athame next to it. I put the na'at at the end, where she can get a good look at it.

"So what was it between you and Eleanor? She must have really hated you to run off with your secret weapon."

"She was a troubled child."

"That's an interesting way to put it because the moment you bring her into your story, it doesn't add up. You Geistwalds are Death Born. But Eleanor was bitten by a vampire and turned. That means she had to be alive."

"Eleanor wasn't *Der Todes Geboren*."

"I thought so. Was your husband?"

"Of course. He was the patriarch. And Rainier. Eleanor, however, was like you. The family grotesque."

"She was Daddy's girl, wasn't she? It's his fault Eleanor wasn't dead like Mommy."

Koralin doesn't say anything for a couple of minutes. Just stares at Aki. I wait. I count the molecules that make up the pearls in the necklace.

Finally, she says, "Not being alive ourselves, we can't produce our own children. Jan conceived Eleanor with a living woman."

"Was she pretty? Was she nice? Did he fall in love with her?"

A slight smile plays around her mouth likes she's found a pleasant memory.

"Tell me about your father," she says.

"Which one? I seem to have a lot."

"The human one."

I shrug.

"He was all right. I wasn't an easy kid. He tried his best, but he never really took a shine to me."

"What a surprise. And your other father?"

"Until an hour ago, I thought it was Lucifer."

"That would be almost as good a family secret as ours."

"So, Jan was in love with a pretty human and they had a girl. Then what?"

She looks at her hands and then starts.

"Jan was a romantic. He loved the woman and didn't want their daughter to be Death Born. The Geistwald children receive the death bite at birth when the head of the family removes the umbilical with his teeth. Jan refused. He stole the child, and by the time he brought her back, it was too late for her to be reborn."

"So you tortured and tormented Eleanor and her father every day of her life."

"They deserved worse. I would have killed her, but she was still a Geistwald and there would have been talk."

"Rainier was born right, though. And you weren't going to let him get away."

"Rainier was a good boy and I took care of him."

"But he was still too stupid to live. Even with all your torture, I think Eleanor and Dad got the best of that deal."

"My new Rainier will be born properly and become the new head of the family."

She waves to him.

"I love you, dear. Hold on just a little longer. Daddy is on the way."

"You just said you have to be Death Born at birth. Aki is at least twenty-five."

"There are ways around that. Sorcerers who can remove his spirit and put it into the body of a newborn. I'll personally make the child *Der Todes Geboren* and Rainier will be reborn."

"But he'll still be Aki. You keep choosing fuckups for sons."

She leans forward on her seat.

"Now tell me about your real father."

"I don't know him that well. He's a doctor, but it's a second career. He used to be an archangel."

"Kinski? How funny. And you only just discovered this?"

"If Lucifer was telling the truth. I think he was. It's more fun for him to kill you with the truth than with a lie."

"I wish I'd been there to see your face."

"It wasn't all that dramatic."

"Seeing you in any amount of pain would be a joy."

"I cut my arm on a piece of glass earlier."

"Did it hurt?"

"It stung."

"Good."

The phone rings. Koralin goes to the desk and exchanges a few words with the caller.

"Jan is here."

"Tell him to take the elevator to three."

I pick up my gun and go to the door.

"Our deal is still on, but if you get near Aki while I let them in, I'll blow his head off."

I push open the door just as the elevator arrives.

"In here."

Candy comes through first. She throws her arms around me and holds on tight.

"He's dead. Doc is dead," she says. "That angel bitch Aelita killed him."

"I know. It's all right. We'll get through this."

Jan comes in after her with Kasabian's bowling bag.

I gesture to him with the gun.

"Go over to the table and let him out. Then sit down next to your wife."

Jan unzips the bag and puts Kasabian on the table. Jan sits down at the far end of the sofa, as far from Koralin as he can.

"Fuck you, you Kraut shit."

I set Candy in a chair by the desk.

"You all right, Kasabian?"

"No thanks to these pricks. That bitch stood there while that crazy-ass angel stabbed Kinski."

"Sit tight and keep quiet. This will be over with soon."

"Excuse me," says Koralin. "You have your friends. Please put the pistol down."

I look at Aki and then at her and set the gun on the table.

"We're going to do this slowly and carefully so there aren't any misunderstandings, all right?"

"Of course."

"Good. Koralin, stand up with your hands where I can see them. Come down to the end of the table with me. I'll take the *Druj* from my pocket and hand it to you."

I stand up while Koralin comes around, put my hand in my pocket, and take out the *Druj*. I exaggerate my arm and hand movements so she can see what I'm doing. When it's out, I show her the *Druj* and that I'm not holding anything else.

"Put out your hands."

She does and I set the *Druj* there. I step back as Koralin smiles and holds it up so Aki can see.

"We have it, darling. It's ours."

She turns to me, all motherly and full of aristocratic outrage.

"You're all dead. I'll call every golem in the city down on you. They'll each get one shallow bite. It will take days for you to die."

Koralin really wants Drifters by her side, so they come to her. The ones I brought in from the hall and lobby stashed around the edges of the room earlier are drawn to her and the *Druj*. When she sees them she laughs with delight. She's amused just long enough for me to grab the na'at and whip the end of it into her chest like a dagger. There's no time to aim well, but I do all right.

The end slips between her ribs and into her heart. Another flick and the na'at retracts. Koralin falls to the floor grunting like an animal in shock and pain. Her milk-pale skin crawls with patches of red. Her lips fade from deep blue to bright crimson as she draws her first choked and agonized breath since birth.

"Did you know that the cure for a zombie bite is a Savant's blood? I learned that when Johnny Thunders gave me some of his. I used some to help out Brigitte and I put the rest on the na'at. Johnny must have been right because it looks to me like you're breathing again. How does it feel to be alive after all these years? Just another pathetic mortal lowlife. Weird, I bet. Don't worry. You won't feel it for long."

I pick up the *Druj* from where she dropped it, pull Candy from the sofa, and hand her Kasabian.

The Drifters crowd around Koralin. They move in slowly, a little uncertain of who or what she is. She was one of them a moment ago, but she must be starting to smell human. I wonder what her body temperature has to be before they know she's food.

"If you want to go, you can go," I tell Jan.

He stands there.

"I can't leave her to this."

"I'm giving you a break because of Eleanor."

"Please."

"No."

He grabs the athame from the table and throws it. He's good, too. He's handled a knife before.

I duck it, but Candy is looking at Koralin, so she doesn't see it coming. The knife hits her arm and goes in to the hilt. She drops Kasabian and I flick out the na'at, hitting Jan in the chest. It knocks him back onto the sofa and in a few seconds he's staring through watery eyes filled with the shock and deep-down horror of being alive. A moment later he starts to breathe. As his lungs begin filling with air he reaches for my gun, but his body is still in shock and he's too clumsy to reach it. I pick it up and put it in his hand. I help him steady it under his chin so he'll get it right when he pulls the trigger. The sound of a gun going off inside hurts my ears and the back of Jan's head explodes out in a red spray. The Drifters not heading for Koralin make a beeline for the gore. I take the gun back and put it in my jacket.

I tuck Kasabian under my arm, put my arm around Candy, and help her to the door.

"What about the boy?" she asks.

"He wants to be part of the family. Let him."

We're out in the hall when the screaming starts. I close the door and smash the grandfather clock to pieces, sealing the room. I grab Candy and Kasabian and step through a shadow and back to the old apartment.

I can see Brigitte through the bedroom door. She's propped up on pillows and her eyes are open.

Allegra is coming toward us.

"I'm sorry to always show up with walking wounded. But we don't have anywhere else to go anymore," I tell her.

Allegra takes Candy, lays her out on the sofa, and goes for first-aid supplies.

"You know you are always welcome. Family is difficult, but having none is worse."

Kasabian is still under my arm.

"Oh Christ. Put me back with the zombies, Strawberry Shortcake."

I go back to the bedroom. Brigitte sits up and puts out her hand. I take it, but only to make her feel better. She's still too weak to explain that the man she thinks she's looking at is gone.

There's a blast in the street. Then shouting. I look out the window and see a couple of girls and a young guy running from a pack of Lacunas. They have guns and are shooting. They're getting some pretty good hits, but it's not going to do them any good. They have to slow down when they aim.

In a minute or two they'll be out of bullets and the Lacunas will have gained on them enough that it will be over.

I turn to Brigitte.

"I'll be back in a minute."

I climb the stairs to the roof. When I get there I can still hear gunfire, but it's less frequent. They know they're running low on ammo.

From the edge of the roof I can see the whole city. It's a patchwork of light and dead blacked-out areas and the whole thing has turned orange and bleached yellow from dozens of fires.

The shooters are out of bullets and the Lacunas close in.

Koralin must have known something extra about how the *Druj* works. I could make the Drifters nearby do what I want, but there's no way I can control a whole city. She acted like she could. Maybe I should have asked her about that before letting the Drifters have her.

Even if I could control them all, would that save the day? Lucifer said not to rely on any one weapon. That I might not even be able to keep this one. Maybe that's the point. The fatal flaw that will reveal itself at exactly the worst moment. When would that be? When I sneak Downtown and use the *Druj* to hunt Mason? Now, when I try to get the Drifters to march back to their caves?

When I was still in the arena, I stole a knife to kill another fighter I didn't like. I tried stabbing him in the tunnel leading to the fighting floor, but the knife's weight was odd and the blade wasn't sharp enough. I found out later that it was a throwing knife, completely wrong for hand-to-hand fighting. It only had power when you threw it. To use it, you couldn't keep it.

I take the *Druj* out of my pocket and throw it off the roof. It turns over and over in the air like a coin tossed on a bet. It takes forever to hit the ground.

The Lacunas have caught up with the shooters. They're on them. I can hear them screaming.

The *Druj* hits the pavement and shatters into a million pieces.

The Lacunas freeze. For a moment they're horrible dummies in a Hellion spook house. Then quietly, like wind on a roof, they fall apart. They're dust before they hit the ground. The shooters, both girls and the boy, get up. They stagger, grab each other, and look around. When they see what's happened, they run away as fast as they can. The same thing is happening farther down the street. Drifters are falling apart everywhere. In the distance, civilians are single dots running from packs of other dots. Then the pack disappears and the lone dot stops running.

The fires still burn. Half the city is still blacked out. Sirens scream and helicopters cut up the sky. I go back downstairs.

WHEN IT'S LIGHT out, I take Kasabian back to Max Overdrive to see what condition the place is in.

Downstairs is trashed. It doesn't look like Drifters made it inside, but in the great tradition of all L.A. apocalypses, looters did. The windows and doors are smashed. The cartoons, action movies, and porn sections are pretty much cleared out. The cash registers are gone, too.

Upstairs, the lock on the door is broken, but the place is pretty much intact. There's a big circle of dried blood on the bed.

"That's where that crazy bitch got Kinski. I don't know what happened to his body. Sorry, man. I know you two were tight."

"Not really."

I wad up the sheets, take them and the bed downstairs, and leave them by the curb with the broken glass and burned-out cars. I can't remember the city ever being this quiet. Like a funeral on Christmas morning. I don't see any single people go by. Everyone huddles together in twos and threes and more. Walking wounded. Piles of dust mark the places where Drifters fell. Garbage trucks and commandeered pickups lined with plastic sheets cruise Hollywood Boulevard shoveling up human remains.

I go back upstairs and sit on the bed frame. I don't know what to do. An angel should have some idea of where to go from here. Stark would do something. Something stupid, but something. If I could keep him from drinking, he wouldn't be bad to have around sometimes. But he's gone.

"Are there any cigarettes?" asks Kasabian.

I look around, but can't find any. I go back downstairs and find a half-smoked butt on the counter. I take it upstairs, light it with Mason's lighter, and hold it out for Kasabian. He takes a couple of puffs.

"You don't want any?"

"No."

"You're different, man. Not like depressed different. I've seen that. That bite fucked you all up."

"I'm fine. I'm just not smoking or drinking. I'm better."

"A lot of laughs, too. You usually would have made some stupid joke by now instead of sitting there like you just got electroshock."

"It could have been ten."

"What's that mean?"

"It's a Hellion joke. When God threw them from Heaven, they fell for nine days, so when everything goes to shit you say . . ."

". . . It could have been ten. Nice. Now you're doing some demon's stand-up act. You're going to be a riot clean and sober."

"I wonder if anywhere still has food."

"And beer. You might be Sister Mary Dry County, but some of us are still people and need booze."

"I'll see what I can do."

I pull the door closed and go out through the front.

The boulevard is a ghost town. What a shock. There are patches of blood and a smoldering garage around the corner, but the worst seems to be over. I pass a dozen gutted stores, including some markets, but I can't make myself go in. I'm hungry and not above stealing, but I don't want to trip over any half-eaten bodies inside.

If I was a religious man (and no, knowing there's a Heaven and Hell, God and devil and angels doesn't help being religious one little bit), I might take what I see as a sign. There's a line outside Donut Universe. The windows are shattered and some of the booths have been trashed, but they have power and they're pouring coffee for a long line of shell-shocked civilians. Coffee would be nice, but if I get in line someone might try to talk to me. I keep walking.

"Hey!"

Someone is yelling, but it doesn't sound scared, so I don't turn around. There's a hand on my arm. I turn, ready to punch or shoot.

It's Janet, the donut girl. She's pale and her hair is spiked and messy and her eyes are dark, like she hasn't slept since Groundhog Day.

"You're alive," she says.

"So are you. How was the Chinese food?"

"The chow mein was greasy, but the mu shu pork was good. Here," she says, and puts a bag in my hand.

"We're out of fritters, so it's just an assortment of what we have left. We haven't made any new ones, so they're a little stale. But the coffee is hot."

"I think you just saved my life, Janet."

"We're even, then."

"It's really good to see you."

"You, too."

She kisses me on the cheek and runs back into Donut Universe. People in line glare at me, wondering why I rate special treatment.

I saved your lives, assholes. Let me have a fucking donut.

CANDY IS SITTING on the bed frame when I get back.

"Hi."

"Hi yourself. Want a bear claw?"

"No thanks."

"I guess you and Kasabian have met."

"Yeah. We talked about movies and gossiped about you last night."

I put the bags on Kasabian's table and sit down next to Candy.

"I'm sorry about the doc."

It takes her a while to say anything. She's trying hard not to cry.

"Yeah. You know about him, right?"

"That he's my father? Yeah. I heard."

"I'm sorry. I wanted to tell you, but he wouldn't let me. He wanted to do it when the time was right and it could just be you two for a while and you could talk or fight or whatever it is fathers and sons do."

"I think I'll miss him."

"Yeah. Me, too."

She leans against me. I put my arm around her because the angel knows I'm supposed to at a moment like this.

"I missed you, too," she says. "I know you thought that doc and I were lovers, but it wasn't like that. We were each fucked up in different ways and took care of each other, but doc never forgot what happened to the women he loved and what happened to the kids they had. He just didn't have it in him anymore. You're the only thing of his that survived."

"He kept you alive, too."

"Yeah, he did."

We're quiet for a minute, then she moves away and looks at me hard.

"You're not you anymore, are you?"

"No. I'm not."

"Are you in there somewhere?"

"If you mean Stark, I don't think so. Stark was a drunk and a fool and he's dead. Fuck him."

"Who are you now?"

"No one. Nothing. I don't know if I'm the end of something or the beginning. Let's pretend it's the beginning. You can name me, like a baby."

She looks at her hands and takes a breath.

"Take the cure. Your friends wouldn't want you like this. I don't want you like this."

"Stark is dead. He's gone. Maybe you should do the same. Go away and don't come back."

She loses it and starts bawling.

"I don't want Stark to be gone. Doc is gone and I don't want you to be gone, too."

"He's dead. You don't get a vote on dead."

"I'm sorry. I'm so sorry."

I get up.

"You should go now."

She stands, but doesn't move.

"I know you're not Stark anymore and none of this means anything to you, but can you please just hold me for a minute before I go?"

This is why angels find it so easy to kill you people.

"All right."

Candy grabs me hard like she's fallen overboard and is holding on to the side of a boat to keep from drowning.

"I'm sorry. I'm so sorry."

She must have had the knife in her hand the whole time.

Like me, Candy is a killer, so she gets me in the heart with the first thrust.

As I black out all I can think is, *Oh hell. This again.*

I PUT THE bowling bag on the bar at Bamboo House of Dolls and unzip it.

"Carlos, meet Alfredo Garcia."

"Fuck you, man. You said you weren't going to say that."

"It was a long walk. I forgot."

"I'm Kasabian. Are you the Carlos who makes the tamales?"

Carlos eyeballs Kasabian like someone seeing his first pickled punk at a sideshow.

"Yeah. That's me."

"They're awesome. They're what keep me from smothering this asshole with a pillow when he's asleep."

Normally I wouldn't inflict Kasabian on a civilian, but Carlos hasn't ever been a regular civilian. And what's a talking head when a few days ago you had dead men in here trying to eat your customers?

"Stark's told me about you, too."

"Yeah? What's he said?"

"Well," says Carlos, looking Kasabian over, "I thought you'd be taller."

"Very funny, beer jockey. Do you have any actual booze back there or is it just Hawaiian Punch and seashells?"

"I think we can find some booze. What are you drinking?"

"Beer. The more expensive the better. Put it on his account."

Kasabian turns to me.

"Put my bucket under me. I haven't been out in six months and I'm not planning on drinking responsibly. You're the designated driver."

I hope Carlos doesn't mind us being here. For the time being, he's pretty much my Plan A for not starving to death. Plan B, C, and D, too. Max Overdrive is dead and I don't know if it'll ever be back. I don't want to think about how many thousands of dollars fixing the place up and restocking the shelves will be. It's not like we have a dime. The insurance company canceled us after the explosion back in January. The Vigil is gone. And what are the chances that Lucifer will keep paying me a stipend after he goes home to Kansas? I'm too well known to knock over liquor stores and too ugly to be a rent boy. What's minimum wage these days? Maybe Carlos will hire me to clean up after closing.

It's good to see Bamboo House full of drunken monsters and crazy civilians. Maybe Brigitte was right after all. Maybe a little danger will bring in the crowds. The place still doesn't need a velvet rope, but I don't see business slacking off for a while. People need a drink when they survive an apocalypse. Speaking of which.

I look for Carlos to order a shot of Jack and there's already one at my elbow. Who says he's not psychic?

"How's that hole in your chest doing?" comes a voice from behind me.

"I have a nice new scar. I don't know how much of Johnny's blood you put on the knife, but it left a mark on my heart. I might need a doctor."

"We'll stock up on lollipops," says Candy.

She and Allegra squeeze in next to me at the crowded bar.

I say, "Next time you decide to stab someone to cure them from a horrible disease, try using a smaller knife."

"I could have given you the potion in a needle like I gave Brigitte, but no, you had to be a baby about it."

"You shouldn't stab babies either. I'm not even a doctor and I know that."

"We only stab the ugly ones," says Allegra.

Allegra and Candy have been stuck together like Chang and Eng since the night I came back from the Jackal's Backbone. With Kinski gone, we need a new hoodoo doc who can help Lurkers, take bullets out of chests without cracking them open, and juggle those hunks of God's broken glass.

"How's boot camp?"

Allegra does an exaggerated sigh.

"Harder than art school, but more fun than stopping kids from shoplifting *Faces of Death* at the store."

"She picks up on doc's magic healing gear fast," says Candy. "I never had the head for it, but she zeros right in."

"Eugène's books help with the obscure stuff. Did you know that when necromancers and Houngans are allergic to Mandrake root, their balls can swell up to the size of cantaloupes?"

"I never wanted to know that. Soon you'll be doctor to the stars and monsters. Dr. Kildare with two *l*'s."

"Florence Frightingale," says Allegra.

Candy smiles.

"I told her that one."

Allegra says, "We're going to head back to the clinic. Candy is going to show me fun things to do with leeches."

"It's always a party with you two."

It's good to see Allegra excited. And Candy with something to occupy her mind.

I hold up my drink.

"To Doc Kinski."

We clink glasses and drink.

"And Doc Allegra."

We drink again.

Candy nods at the door.

"We have to go."

"Don't let the leeches push you around."

They go out, talking and laughing. I've never seen two people more excited about golden beetles and fermented goat's blood.

"Be patient."

It's Vidocq.

"Patience isn't my best quality."

"She's not running from you. She and Kinski might not have been lovers, but she still loved him. It will take her some time to get over his loss."

"Yeah. Him dying right then was inconvenient for a lot of us."

Vidocq pats me on the shoulder. The French are like that.

"Don't drink too much."

"When I can spell out your name in shot glasses, I'll stop."

"I'll have to get a shorter name."

"I'll have to forget how to spell it."

Maybe I'm looking at this all wrong. Maybe I should be like Allegra and get a new job. The store closing might be opportunity knocking. I should go across town and see if the skinheads are back in business. I heard somewhere that a lot of skinheads support themselves by dealing meth. I wonder how much cash they keep around? It's not like they can call the cops if someone stops by and takes all their money. How many other gangs and crooks are there in L.A.? Is there a Forbes 500 list of the ones with the most cash? I might be on the verge of a new career.

I see a familiar face heading my way. She'd be hard to miss in a room twenty times this size.

"Hello you. You've been kind of scarce the last few days."

Brigitte nods, takes the glass from my hand, and finishes my drink.

"Yes, I needed some time alone to do what you Americans love most. Process my thoughts. Becoming a revenant wasn't something I'd planned for this trip."

"But you didn't. We stopped it in time."

"But I felt it. I felt the infection burning through me. I felt myself dying, but not truly dying."

"I don't know how many times I've been stabbed and shot. It's part of my job description. Taking a chance on getting bitten has to be part of yours."

"Of course it is. But there's the other thing."

"And what's that?"

She lifts a finger and Carlos brings us a couple of new drinks. She blows him a kiss.

"The way you left the Geistwalds, it upset some people, but I thought it was apt. If I'd been there, I would have helped."

"I know."

"But there's the other thing."

"So I hear."

"Your friend Candy was knifed. Your father is dead. Simon is dead. Lucifer himself almost died."

"Johnny is gone."

"Who was he?"

"Someone I only knew for a little while. A good guy. He had a sweet tooth."

"*Light Bringer* was canceled, of course. I heard that even the Golden Vigil has disbanded."

I sip the Jack and nod.

"It looks that way. I went by their warehouse to pull out Wells's spine, but he was gone and the place was empty. There wasn't a screw, a nail, or an oil stain on the floor."

"That's the kind of thing I mean by the other thing."

She pushes her way in closer so that we're side by side and leans against me.

"You're a lovely man. Do you know that?"

"I can hear a 'but' the size of the *Titanic* bearing down on me."

"People get hurt around you. They die. And worse."

"I'm a professional shit magnet. I know."

"You scare me to death, which, on the one hand, makes you more attractive, but you wear death like that long black coat of yours. I think if things had just been a little different, if we'd met at a different moment, I wouldn't feel quite so overwhelmed."

"If you're keeping score, don't forget Alice. I got her killed, too."

"Don't talk like that."

We drink without talking for a minute. She feels good against my side.

"So, where are you headed from here?"

"I'm staying with Gigi Gaston. Maybe you met her at the Geistwald party. She worked at the studio and has taken over since Simon is gone."

"Hooking up with the studio head is a smart move for an actress."

"And for my other work, too. Gigi is one of the ones I meant by 'my people' when I called for someone to take the bodies of the revenants from behind the bar."

"That work is over, you know. The Drifters are gone. They all died when the *Druj* broke."

"Are you absolutely sure?"

"Yeah. But worrying about it is a good excuse to go off with Gigi. If I was you, it's what I'd say."

"If you scared me just ten percent less."

"No. You're doing the right thing. Things are going to get strange again soon and I'm afraid I'm going to end up in the middle of it. If Gigi can take care of you, you should go with her."

She pushes away and looks at me, her forehead furrowing.

"You don't hate me? You don't think I'm a coward for deserting you?"

"Never. You were always the smart one."

She takes my head in her hands and kisses me hard.

"Take care of yourself."

"You, too. Go be a movie star. It'll be fun to see you fifty feet tall."

"Just for you."

She starts away and I yell after her.

"You know, you never told me your real name."

She smiles.

"I know. We'll just have to find each other down the road sometime and I'll tell you then."

And she's gone.

"Wow. Going out with you is a real boost to the ego," says Kasabian. "Shot down twice in one night. Even I'm doing better than that with these kinky Goth chicks."

"Drink up, Alfredo. I hope no one starts keeping their dirty socks in your bag."

I get up and start away from the bar.

"Where are you going?"

"To the men's room. You remember those?"

"Funny. When you get back you want to take me outside for a smoke?"

"Why not?"

I get the usual funny looks of recognition and curiosity in the men's room. It's not just civilians. Lurkers are just as likely to stare.

"If any of you want an autograph right this second, I'm going to have to do it in piss."

That usually breaks up the viewing party.

Marshal Julie is waiting for me when I come out of the men's room.

"Don't worry, officer. I washed my hands."

She nods and looks me over.

"You cost me my job, you know."

"Talk to Aelita about that. Or Wells. Besides, I thought

you worked for Homeland Security. Just 'cause the Vigil is gone baby gone, why does that affect you?"

"When the Vigil died, Washington panicked and burned our whole operation out here. They cut everyone loose."

"And now you're roaming the countryside like a Ronin. If you're looking for money or sympathy, I'm fresh out of both."

"That's not why I'm here. I don't want us to be enemies."

"I can't play bridge, so don't ask me to be your fourth."

"I'm opening my own investigations agency. My father was a PI, so I have experience. If it pans out, I thought that maybe I can throw you work sometimes."

I listen to her heart and watch her eyes. She means it. Her soul pulses steadily in her chest, a shimmering silver. A good color. Not everyone's is that clear.

"Why not? I'm not doing anything else. But no hits. And I'm not doing any divorce stuff. No peeping in people's windows. But if you have something specific that you think I can do, why not?"

"Okay, then."

She turns and looks around the bar.

"I'd heard all about this place. Some of the other marshals sneaked in here. Some Sub Rosa girls I knew at school. I never really believed them when they said that Lurkers and humans could hang out together like this."

"You ought to see it on bingo night."

"You didn't really think it was going to be that easy, did you?"

"What?"

"You were going to stroll in here with the *Druj* and put me over your knee like a bad boy? That's funny."

Marshal Julie's mouth is moving, but it's Mason's voice coming out. Her eyes are dead and vacant.

"Yes, it's me. Sorry I can't be there in person. This is the best my little homemade key can do for now."

Then a Nahual beast man steps up.

"Trust me. I'm working on new and better keys all the time. And with Lucifer taking a powder, it makes my work that much easier."

A civilian in a T-shirt with a software company logo on it crowds in.

"I hear you fed a whole family to golems the other night. Good for you. We were always more alike than you and Alice wanted to admit."

The girl in the leather jacket that Spencer Church tried to bite the other night opens her mouth.

"I wish I'd been there to watch you feed Mommy and the boy to the zeds. How long did it take to eat them?"

I grab the girl.

"*Druj* or not, I'm going to kill you. Hard."

Marshal Julie again.

"You know where I am. I'll leave a light on for you."

They walk away, some to the restroom, some back to the bar, like nothing happened.

"Don't worry. I wouldn't ask you to do something boring and normal," says the marshal.

She smiles at me. I stare into her eyes, looking for Mason. She stops smiling.

"What's wrong?"

"Nothing. I've just had too much to drink. I'm going outside."

"Give me your number before you go."

I tell her and head back to the bar.

"I'll call you if something comes through."

"Do that. Good luck with the agency."

I go to the bar to get Kasabian, but when he sees me he shakes his head and turns his eyes back to the Lamia chatting him up. I leave him to his succubus and go outside.

I bum a cigarette from a couple of young drunk Valley guys with asymmetrical haircuts and fake IDs in their pockets.

"Are you the guy?" one of them asks.

"Which guy is that?"

"The Sandman guy. You're skinny and you've got all those scars."

"So did the neighbor's kid back home. He had an eating disorder and kept falling off his bike."

The Valley boy bursts out laughing, the excited nervous laugh of a kid not sure if he's having a good time or not. The other boy grabs him and whispers something.

"Can we see your knife?"

"We heard it's really big."

That cracks them both up.

"Shouldn't you youngsters be home and in bed? Isn't it a school night?"

The one who gave me the cigarette says, "The school burned down. We're doing classes online."

"I hope it wasn't one of you bad boys who burned it."

"I wish. We'd be heroes."

Neither of the boys notices the small group gathering behind them. Sneaking up silently on civilians is what they do best.

The tallest one, lean and ghostly pale, leans over to one of the boys.

"Excuse me."

The kid starts and smacks into his friend.

"We'd like a word with Mr. Stark."

The one with the cigarettes laughs and says, "But he was going to show us his big knife."

The pale man brings his face down level with the boys. The whites of his eyes flash blood red, and then darken to black. The boys head back inside the bar.

"Don't bite either of them, okay? They're just a little drunk. And I don't even want to have to think about hunting another one of your young ones."

"We appreciate that," says the head vampire. "And we appreciate you handling the recent unpleasantness so quickly. As I'm sure you can imagine, zombies aren't much use to us and we're grateful to have them gone. We, the Dark Eternal, hope that you'll accept this with our admiration and gratitude."

He hands me a brushed aluminum Halliburton attaché case. Spies and billionaires carry these cases in Hollywood thrillers with expensive stars and crap scripts. I pop the latches and look inside.

The case is filled with neatly bundled stacks of hundred-dollar bills.

"We also hope that in the future you'll remember who helped you in a time of need."

"Trust me, I will."

"We also hope that you'll use some of the cash to reopen Max Overdrive. Clarice here likes spaghetti westerns and Ed is a Bollywood fan. Me, I like old Universal horror."

"How do you feel about the *Wolfman*?"

"Hate the bitchy little whiner."

"Good answer. You just got a free rental."

He high-fives Ed.

"Have a nice night," says the head vampire, and the whole group sweeps away into the night, something else vampires are good at.

I DUMP KASABIAN back in our room over Max Overdrive around 5 A.M. I didn't even bother putting him back in his bowling bag on the way home. Anyone wandering the streets at that hour deserves to see a severed head singing "Good Vibrations." He falls asleep the moment I put him down. I've never seen him drunk before. I didn't even know he could get drunk.

I go into the bathroom and throw some water on my face. Toss my coat on the bed frame and stash my weapons under the towels in the bathroom cupboard behind the door.

Kasabian has an MP3 player with speakers in his bachelor pad in the closet. I put them on the bed frame with the bottle of Jack Daniel's that Carlos gave me and a pack of cigarettes someone left on the bar. I pile all of it on the attaché case and step through the shadow and into the Room.

I set the case against the wall. No one's going to steal it there. I take the Jack, cigarettes, and music and go to the Thirteenth Door. The Door of Nothing. I haven't been through it since the night I sent the Kissi drifting out into space and left Mason in Hell.

The battered door still has the distinctive vinegar Kissi reek, but it's quiet. There's no scratching coming through from the other side. The Thirteenth Door used to scare me more than anywhere else in the universe. More than Downtown ever did. Now it's just one more old door with dead bodies on the other side. I open it and go inside.

The holes I tore in the fabric of the Kissi realm are still there. Stars and the flat ovals of galaxies hang overhead. The insect husks of long-dead Kissi crunch under my boots. I spark Mason's lighter and the place lights up. It takes me about an hour to find the ruins of the mansion Mason built here. A dusty reclining chair lies in the rubble on its side. I turn it right side up and sit down. The bottle of Jack goes on one side of the chair and the MP3 player on the other. I light a cigarette and sit in the dark and quiet for a while.

I still feel bad about Johnny and how he probably disappeared when the other Drifters ashed out. And about owing him a bag of jelly beans. I hope he understands how things got a little out of hand that night. At least Fiona didn't shoot me when I told her that I left Johnny underground with Muninn.

I feel bad about Kinski, too. And mad as hell. Couldn't he have said what he had to say? No. More dad bullshit. He had to control the moment and do it his way. There's not going to be a moment now, is there, old man? But thanks for keeping me alive all those times. If I run into you in Heaven or Hell or wherever I end up, I'll buy the first round. After I kick your ass for letting Aelita kill you.

I crack open the bottle of Jack and have a drink to him.

Like most nights, I wonder where Alice is and if she knows or cares what's going on down here. Parking in the afterlife must have gotten really shitty after a million new souls shot up there the other night. She must have noticed that. Maybe one of the Drifters who isn't too pissed at me for ripping out his or her spine will tell Alice it was me who set them free.

Right. And maybe Mason has an ice-cream truck and is handing out Popsicles in Hell.

I wonder if Lucifer made it back to Heaven and if his old man let him in?

Things are going to get bad. I can feel it. The parts of the angel that stuck around after Candy cured me can feel Heaven and Hell twitching, like rabid dogs just starting to foam at the mouth.

I don't want to be the new Lucifer, but I really want to kill Mason, and if I have to wear red underwear and carry a pitchfork to do it, I will.

I wonder if Aelita will come Downtown or if I'm going to have to backdoor my way into Heaven to kill her?

I manifest the burning Gladius and it lights up the Kissi realm for a million miles. What a dump. It looks like someone built the Matterhorn Ride out of fly eggs and shit.

Stars wink overhead. Did they change when I switched on the sword?

I get out another cigarette, light it off the Gladius, and let the world go dark.

I flick ashes into Mason's failed kingdom.

I've talked shit my whole life and, except for Alice and

Vidocq, pretty much done everything on my own. Luck and hoodoo pulled me through, but that's not going to work this time. Not if Downtown catches fire and Mason or Aelita bring the heat up to Heaven. I can't bluff and bullshit my way through that. I need backup. But I might have killed off the only things in the universe crazy enough to go head-to-head with the armies of Hell and Heaven.

Or maybe not. A lot of Kissi went spinning out into space when I ripped this place open. Kissi are almost angels, so floating around in the dark shouldn't hurt them. They're probably just shy. Or they found someplace better to feed. I'm not going out after them. They'll come to me eventually. I've got the deal of the century. And even semi-angels want revenge. Everything alive wants revenge.

I hit the MP3 player. Skull Valley Sheep Kill echoes off the walls, doing a burning cover of "Johnny Thunders."

I let the bass rumble in my chest like a second heart.

I smoke the cigarette and then another.

I have a drink.

I listen to the music.

I sit in the dark and I wait.

If you enjoyed
SANDMAN SLIM and KILL THE DEAD,
don't miss the next adventure, coming soon!

ALOHA FROM HELL
A Sandman Slim novel
by Richard Kadrey
October 2011

Coming back from Hell was just the beginning.

"TELL ME," SAYS the Frenchman. "How long has it been since you last killed anything?"

He's fucking with me. He knows the answer, but he wants to make me say it. Father Vidocq taking confession.

"I don't know. What time is it?"

"That long then?"

I shrug.

Vidocq and I are in a very dark room in a very large house full of very fashionable furniture and we're stealing something very valuable. I have no idea what and pretty much don't care. It's just nice to be hanging out and doing some crimes with the old man. Crimes where no one ends up zombie meat, shot or annoyingly decapitated.

"It's been a while," I say. "Six. Eight weeks. Somewhere around there."

I slipped us into the house through a shadow. Vidocq is working on the wall safe. He's good with safes. He's had over a hundred years of practice.

"So, no crusades? No great wrongs that need to be righted?"

I reach into my pocket for a cigarette then remember there might be smoke alarms.

"Nothing worth killing for. I'm no cop. The Sub Rosa has their own Mod Squad to deal with the small stuff."

I like watching Vidocq work over a safe. He has hands like a surgeon. Nimble. Precise. He could thread a needle while being shot out of a cannon.

"*Incroyable*. Perhaps you're reaching something of a rapprochement with your angelic half and it's having a moderating effect on your disposition."

Right. I'm part angel. Half if you want to get picky about it. It's great. A halo and five bucks will get you a cup of coffee in LA.

"Maybe. The angel screams at me sometimes, mostly at night when I'm tired and he can ambush me with one of his Give-Peace-A-Chance no-smoking veggie bacon sermons. But he isn't trying to run the show singlehanded anymore. We reached a kind of MAD pact the other day."

Vidocq looks at me.

"MAD?"

"Mutually Assured Destruction. I told him that if he ever tried to push me out of my brain and turn me into a clean living choirboy again I'd have to do something, you know, unreasonable."

"Such as?"

"I told him I'd get hammered and go through the Room of Thirteen Doors to the Pearly Gates. Then I'd find the Archangel Gabriel and thunderbolt kick him in the cojones in front of all the other angels."

"Whereupon the other angels would draw their swords and kill you."

"Exactly. Mutually Assured Destruction."

"That sounds much more like the old you."

"Thanks."

Technically, I'm what you call a nephilim. Half human, half angel. And I'm the only one. The others are all dead. Suicides mostly. Some people call my type freaks.

If you're one of Heaven's lap dogs you'll probably call me "Abomination." I say call me either of those things to my face and you'll get to see what your lungs look like as throw pillows.

The angel half of me got shaken loose a while back when a High Plains Drifter—that's zombie to you—bit a chunk out of my hand. The human half of me almost died and the angel half thought that was its chance to take over. It was for a while, but then I got my strength back and I locked the angel upstairs in the attic like Joan Crawford in *Whatever Happened to Baby Jane*. It still bangs on the door and shouts, but I've learned to ignore it most of the time. Some of the time. It depends on the day.

Vidocq goes back to work on the safe. Over his clothes, he's wearing a tailored gray gabardine greatcoat. Looks like his girlfriend Allegra's been dressing him again. He looks like the doorman at a speakeasy in the Kremlin. The greatcoat tinkles gently when he moves, like he's smuggling wind chimes. The sound of the hundred or so little potion bottles he has sewn into the coat's lining. I have my guns, my knife and na'at. Vidocq has his potions.

"What exactly are we stealing?" I ask.

"A golden brooch or device in the shape of a scarab. It's quite ancient. There is a clockwork mechanism inside. Perhaps it's God's pocket watch."

"He doesn't need a watch. He needs a compass so he can find his own ass."

There's a click and the front of the safe swings open.

Vidocq moves his hands in a graceful TV spokesmodel arc in front of the safe.

"A voila."

"You are the man, Van Damme."

He squints at me.

"Jean-Claude Van Damme is Belgian, not French."

"There's a difference?"

"Fuck you."

I like how Vidocq pronounces "fuck" "fock."

He whispers, "C'est quoi, ça?"

"Anything wrong?"

"No. It's very interesting. The owner of this safe is a very paranoid man. The inside is etched with spells and runes."

"Can you still get the swag?"

He flashes a small LED light around the inside of the safe.

"I don't see anything in here that should stop us. They mostly seem to be containment spells. He must have been afraid of this shiny scarab from walking away."

He reaches into the safe and pulls out a polished ebony box the size of a cigar box and pushes up the lid. A beautiful gold scarab lies on blood red silk. He hands me the box and begins packing his tools. I slip it into my coat pocket.

I say, "I have to admit, it doesn't feel bad, but it feels a little weird not raising a hand in anger this long. I can pretty much just talk humans and Lurkers out of doing stupid shit to each other these days."

"See?" he says from the floor. "By embracing your angelic half the mere force of your personality is enough to keep the peace."

"I think killing all zombies in the world in one night helps."

"Yes, that could be a factor."

"And Lucifer and the Vigil aren't around paying me to be hitman rent boy bitch."

Vidocq scrolls his gear into a leather tool roll and stands up.

I ask him, "Are we cool?"

He smiles and says, "As the North Star on Christmas Eve. But we aren't quite done."

He takes two potion bottles from inside his coat and pours the contents on the floor where we were standing and on the safe door, trying to shampoo away any magic or forensic dandruff that might lead back to us. When he tosses the contents of a third bottle into the safe I hear the scratching.

"You heard?" he asks.

"Get out of the way, Eugene."

He doesn't. Vidocq has a scientific mind. Instead of getting out of the way, he looks inside.

It wouldn't be my fault if the back of his stupid French skull blew out like a five-dollar retread, but I pull Vidocq out of the way just before the demon cannonballs out of the safe and hits the far wall.

The demon's carapace gleams like blue-black gun steel. The big bug doesn't have eyes, just two sets of jaws at an angle to each other and two huge hooked front claws. The moment it hits the wall it starts tunneling through it. That's what this particular type of demon does. It's a digger. A greed demon. It'll protect anything it thinks it owns. Like the contents of a safe. It's why the safe had containment spells on the interior. To keep the demon inside. Smart. Your basic bad guys—us for instance—will maybe test for eaters, but who's going to worry about a brainless digger until it's excavating the Panama Canal through your intestines?

Vidocq bumps against the desk when I pull him to his feet. The digger freezes and turns. It's blind but it has great hearing. I can slow my heart and breathing, but in a few seconds it's going to zero in on Vidocq. I step back from him, leaving him exposed to the digger. He turns and looks at me with wide horrified eyes.

Sorry, man. This is how it has to be.

The digger turns. It has Vidocq's heartbeat. It hooks its two huge digging claws into the wall and uses them to slingshot forward. A metallic blur, four glittering jaws and arm-size hooks going right for the old man's chest. He doesn't look at it. He never takes his eyes off of me.

As the digger's body blurs across the desk, I whip the na'at out. Twist the grip out from the body into a hair-thin serrated whipsaw.

The digger hits the na'at like a meteor with teeth. I twist the na'at's cutting edge into its body and the bug splits in two lengthwise. The halves come apart and smash into the wall on either side of Vidocq, imbedding themselves deep into the wood and plaster.

Vidocq swivels his head, checking out the giant insect shanks that flank him.

I say, "What do you know? I do remember how to kill things. Good news for our side."

"Fuck you, boy."

An alarm goes when a naked fat man kicks open the office door. I'm going to roll the dice and guess he's the homeowner. He points an exquisitely made over-and-under shotgun at us. It might even be a Tullio Fabbri. A hundred and seventy five grand worth of etched steel with a carved walnut stock and accurate as a cruise missile. I'm almost tempted to ask him, but his pupils are dilated and I smell the excitement in his sweat because he thinks he's finally going to get to use that Fort Knox popgun on actual human beings.

Through the angel's senses I hear the infinitesimal scrape of metal over lubricated metal as the fat man applies pressure to the shotgun's trigger. I grab Vidocq in a bear hug and jump through the window just as the gun goes off.

Davy Crockett here isn't Sub Rosa, but he must know some because he has an anti-magic cloak over his house and the grounds outside. What that means is no one's supposed to be able to throw any hoodoo or hexes around here. Whoever built the cloak probably pegged him for a mark right off. I figure they got him to pay a bonus to build it big enough to cover the whole estate, the perfect way to turn a cloak into something as reliable as a marshmallow condom. Anti-magic shields are powerful things when you do them right, and part of that's knowing they can only be so big. Blow them up too much and the skin stretches thin. Keep blowing and they can pop right out of existence. That's what Davy the Rube paid for one hundred-thousand-dollar soap bubble.

The cloak is stretched so thin I can throw all kinds of hoodoo in here. Like when we climbed the fence onto the grounds I could take us into the house through the Room of Thirteen Doors. But I can't get us off the grounds that way. Of course, I could have used some hoodoo to wrap Davy Crocket's shotgun around his neck like a mink stole and swung him around like a carousel pony while I shot the shit out of his office, but I didn't do any of that. Someone else might think that would earn them karma points down the line, but I know better. Karma is just loaded dice on a crooked table. Celestial pricks with wings and halos make the rules and the house always wins. Always.

So VIDOCQ AND I are falling. Tinkling glass falls with us like razor-blade snowflakes.

When you're jumping two floors with a civilian whose broken bones won't heal overnight like your own, you need to remember a couple of things. One, cushion the fall as much as you can and two, be prepared to use your body as an air bag. That means controlling the fall enough so the other, usually extremely startled, person lands on top of you. Does it hurt? Go outside, get a friend to drop a garbage can full of bacon fat on your chest and see.

Trying to control a fall is no tea party when you're holding on to someone who's thrashing around like a tasered octopus. But it's not impossible. The trick is to grab them just under the ribs and squeeze so they can't breathe. Then you let go just as you hit the ground so they breathe out hard when they hit. It helps absorb the shock, though it still hurts. Especially if you're the one on the bottom.

There's a tree below Davy's window. I aim for it, rolling us into the branches, hoping it'll slow our fall a little. It does. Coming down into the hedges helps too. We still have some momentum to burn off so I keep rolling and we end up on the lawn which Davy was kind enough to lay out with fresh soft sod in the last few days. Thanks, man. I'll send you a honey-baked ham for Christmas.

I pull Vidocq to his feet and we run for the wall like a couple of spooked raccoons. I look back over my shoulder and Davy is standing in the broken window with the shotgun at his shoulder. Wishful thinking. We're too far away for him to hit anything but the air.

Don't sweat it, Davy. Vidocq and I aren't going to touch your safe or wreck your office again. But I might have to come back some night for that Tullio Fabbri, and you can try to shoot me with something else. I am in severe need of something like that. It's so quiet and peaceful out here I'm getting bored with breathing. Maybe we'll get lucky and the world will go to Hell again. Fingers crossed.

I PARKED THE stolen Lexus half a block away. Vidocq is limping. He stops and opens his coat like a flasher. There are dozens of pockets sewn into the lining. Each holds a different potion. Batman has his utility belt. Vidocq has his coat. I have guns and a knife. None of us will be on the cover of GQ.

Satisfied Vidocq's little glass vials aren't broken and leaking about a hundred hexes into his underwear we head for the car. The old man is limping, but when I put a hand on his arm to help him, he shrugs it off. Another grateful customer. I have a knack for pissing people off, especially my friends.

He still won't talk to me, but at least when we get to the Lexus he lets me help him into the car. I start to close the door, but he blocks it with his hand.

"Who is that?" he asks.

I turn and see a man a few yards away. He's standing in the shadow of a big shade tree on someone's lawn. He doesn't move when I look at him. I reach behind my back and pull a Smith and Wesson .460, making sure he sees it. He doesn't flinch. I put the gun back and start toward him. Now he moves. He comes right at me.

"Is this Disney Land?" I say. "Are you Mickey Mouse? I always wanted to shake hands with giant vermin."

Not a peep. Maybe he's a Daffy Duck fan.

There's something wrong with his face. I can't make out any ears and there's a deep slit where his nose should be, like he's healed up from third-degree burns.

Must be a tough bastard to go through that and still walk.

We both stop about six feet apart, having a Sergio Leone stare down.

"I don't know if you're looking for directions or a date, but we're fresh out of both. Take a walk and stare at someone else."

He's fast for a guy who looks like he just escaped from a deep fat fryer. He lunges and grabs my arms over the biceps. He's strong for a cripple, but nothing I can't handle.

Then my arms are burning. Literally. My coat sleeves smoke and burst into flames where he's holding me. I have heavy Kevlar inserts in the sleeves, but in just a couple of seconds the heat is almost through and down to my skin.

I step back and bring up my forearms in an outward circle from underneath and hit his arms hard. Standard self-defense stuff every high-school kid knows. It doesn't work. It's like hitting Jell-O. And now my forearms are burning. Wrestling this guy is like is like waltzing with lava. I try to form hoodoo in my mind to knock Smokey The Asshole across the street or at least make him let go, but the pain makes it hard to think straight.

I bark some Hellion I learned back when I was fighting in the arena. If you do the hex right it's like a gar-bage-can-size gut punch that hits in a blaze of purple light and bores like an oil-rig drill through just about anyone or anything. I get it just right. The purple explosion, the whirlpool of power. Smokey's mid-action collapses in on itself. And goes through and out his back, dragging a long strip of lava-flesh with it like burning taffy. The prick doesn't even seem to notice.

The guy isn't a burn victim. His face churns like thick

liquid as we wrestle. Stupid. I should have known this asshole wasn't human.

The heat is down to my skin, cooking my arms. Being hard to kill means a lot of things. I have a high pain-threshold, but it's not infinite. Not when something a volcano shit out is trying to give you an Indian burn. Being hard to kill also means that you don't go down fast so whatever's cutting you, shooting you or burning you alive is something you get to experience for a good long time.

Being hard to kill isn't the worst thing that can happen to you, but it sure as shit isn't the best, and right now it isn't even fun.

Something clear and hard spins past my shoulder and hits Smokey in the face. He jerks his head away like I have bad breath. But he doesn't let go. Another vial flies past. And another. Smokey lets go this time. Vidocq is behind me, limping over and tossing potions like a pitching machine.

Smokey backs away, his arms pulled in close to his body. Something's hurt him. Good. He starts to shake like someone stuck a vibrator in a bowl of cherry Jell-O. I step back and grab my gun, but before I can use it Smokey melts like the Wicked Witch of the West, leaving a circle of scorched black earth on the green lawn.

Vidocq grabs my shoulder and pulls me back to the car. He bunny hops on his good leg into the passenger side and I slide into the driver's seat, jam the black blade I carried back from Hell into the ignition and we peel out.

"What the hell kind of burglar alarm was that? Why can't rich people have Rottweilers like everyone else?"

"I don't think that was an alarm. That was a demon."

I glance at him. My arms are throbbing now and between each throb they still feel like they're burning. I smell something, but I don't know if it's the coat or me.

"I've never seen a demon like that before."

"Neither have I, but the potion that hurt the creature was a rare type of poison. A toxin formulated to affect only demons."

I drive at a moderate speed. I pause at Stop signs and obey every light.

'Think it was after us?"

Vidocq shrugs.

"Possibly. But who knew we'd be here tonight? And why would someone attack you now? You've been a good boy for weeks."

I roll down the windows to let out the smell. I'm stinking up the Lexus, but who cares? I hate these luxury golf carts. Gaudy status symbols with as much personality as an Elmer's-glue-on-white-bread sandwich.

I say, "Maybe someone was settling an old score. Hell, maybe it was after you."

Vidocq laughs. "Who would send a demon for me?"

"I don't know. The few thousand people you've robbed over the last two hundred years?"

"It's more like a hundred and fifty. Don't try to make me sound old."

"'Course sending a demon for something like that sounds like overkill. Especially something rare enough that neither of us recognizes it."

"I'll look into it tomorrow when I'm certain I'll be able to feel my right leg again."

"Whiner. Your girlfriend is the best hoodoo doctor in town. She'll give you an ice pack and conjure you some kangaroo legs. Then you can do your own second-story work."

Vidocq pats me on the shoulder.

"There. There," like he's patting a five year old with a skinned knee. "I would have thought you'd be happy. You got to have a fight. Draw a little blood. Isn't that what you've wanted?"

I think it over.

"I suppose. And you killed it, not me, so my not-slaughtering-things record is still intact."

"Unlike your arms."

"A little Bactine and they'll be fine by the morning."

"Judging by the look of them they'll hurt in the meantime. Take this. It will help you sleep."

He reaches into his coat and hands me a potion.

"No thanks. Dr. Jack Daniels is coming by tonight. He's got all the medicine I need."

He slips the vial into my pocket.

"Take it anyway. He might be late."

"Yes mom."

"And don't forget to brush your teeth and say your prayers."

"Fuck you, mom."